America Under Attack

An Alternative History of World War Two

To Allison
Enjoy the Adventures!
Jeff Kildow
28 May 2011

America Under Attack

An Alternative History of World War Two

By

Jeff Kildow

Intermedia Publishing Group

America Under Attack
Published by:
Intermedia Publishing Group, Inc.
P.O. Box 2825
Peoria, Arizona 85380
www.intermedia pub.com

ISBN 978-1-935529-93-4

DEDICATION

This book is dedicated to my loving and patient wife, Janell, and to the memory of my mother Shirley, the most avid reader I've ever known.

ACKNOWLEDGMENTS

My thanks go out to my former Lockheed Martin colleague and fellow writer, Julie Dodd, for her early encouragement to take this project from concept to reality.

I would like to express my appreciation to Marty Coniglio, meteorologist at Denver's 9NEWS for his invaluable insights into weather forecasting in the 1940s, and the tip that lead to a wonderful plot idea.

My warmest regards go to Lisa Jester, Director of the Millville Army Air Field Museum, and Dona Vertolli, Museum Board member, for spending a full day with me on my research trip to New Jersey. My view of Millville AAF was broadened and deepened as a result of their efforts. Through them, I was introduced to Bill Rich, WWII fighter pilot and gunnery instructor at Millville, and Bill Hogan, a B-24 tail gunner and POW. It was a privilege to meet these gentlemen, and an honor to share their stories; my novel and my life is richer for the experience.

My thanks to Bob Francis, Town Historian, Millville Historical Society, for the opportunity to learn about civilian life in Millville during the war years.

I appreciate the time spent by Pastor Ken Kelly of Foothills Bible Church reviewing sections of my novel for Christian soundness, and for his cheerful encouragement.

Hearty thanks to my long time friend Don Shipman, and my sister, DJ Smith for thoughtful reviews of drafts and kind criticisms.

TO THE READER

The genre of alternative history is relatively new and often results in quizzical looks when I mention it. The essence of the genre is that an author asks himself "what if?" thus and so did or didn't happen in history, and the story flows from there.

For this novel, I have assumed that Germany developed long range, heavy bombers along with their adversaries Great Britain and America. The consequences of such development are the core of the story.

I attempted to restrict new weapons in the story to the technology available in the 1940s (not easy, when you "know" a better way to do it!). As an example, airborne RADARs in that era were restricted to about ten miles in range, which is frustratingly short for an author. I also took advantage of existing, but undeveloped technologies, the best example of which is air-to-air refueling, which was experimented with by the Germans in the late '30s and early '40s. It never gained the necessary backing from unimaginative generals, and so never came to fruition. Two-way trans-oceanic flight was just within the technology of the times, and with a gentle nudge by the author, happens in the story.

In some cases, events occur earlier in the story than they did in real life, in order to make the story work. The sad state of disarray of the defense of America's eastern seaboard is fact; we can thank God it was never tested.

1936

Chapter 1

13 June 1936

Templehof Airport, Berlin, Germany

1030 Hours

Air Show

Straight down; the gray-white runway rushing up at him. Heart pounding, stomach clenching, and bile in the throat. The deep roar of the engine now a banshee's scream; the ground hurtling up at him. Time slowed.

Stick back. Careful. Watch altitude. Wings level.

The seat cushion pinched his leg as the G's built.

Full throttle. Airspeed 350. Heat bumps from the runway. Level now, hold it, hold it; altitude 200 feet.

Spectators flashed by on the left, then the nose came up. More G's.

Fifteen hundred feet, knife edge turn to the right. There!

Joel Knight took measured breaths, to slow down his heart. He grinned; this Curtiss P-36 Hawk fighter was a sweetheart. He completed the 180 degree turn.

Around now, roll to the left, runway in sight. Nose down, airspeed building.

"This has to be perfect," he said out loud through gritted teeth, his gut a hard knot, eyes intensely focused, his left leg all but dancing with adrenalin, the control stick a live thing in his hand.

Airspeed – 170; good. Level wings.

He hurtled toward the grandstands from the opposite direction.

Careful; the aircraft was so low the propeller tips were clearing the runway by inches. Unseen by him, little tornados of dust blew back from the wings.

*Right wing **down*** – a great cascade of sparks arced into the air from the steel rod on the wing tip. Unheard by him, a ragged wave of gasps raced through the crowd.

*Wings level. Left wing **down***, a second shower of sparks. End of the spectators.

Nose up, 45 degrees; hold it. Aloud again: "Now, four point roll: one, good; two; not as good; three, yes; four, right where it needed to be. And done." He blew out his breath.

He climbed to 1500 feet, making a broad, gentle left turn, parallel to the runway a mile away, slowing now, his portion of the air show over. His heart rate began to slow; he blew out several more breaths, relaxing the tension. He prepared to land.

"Ladies and gentlemen, kindly applaud U.S. Army First Lieutenant Joel Knight, in his prototype Curtiss P-36 Hawk pursuit ship," the announcer droned, first in German, then French and English. Joel taxied past the spectators, zigzagging the tail, canopy back, a small silk American flag snapping in the prop's blast, the engine's lopping idle punctuating each wag of the tail. He waved a gloved hand, and smiled, showing his teeth. The aircraft's polished aluminum skin was a stark contrast to the dull greens and grays of the German, English and French aircraft parked nearby.

As he stopped, he saw Major Sandoval, and he wasn't smiling.

Uh, oh, Joel thought, *he sure doesn't look happy.*

The older man's jaw was clenched, his arms crossed on his chest. Joel shut down the aircraft, and turned it over to the waiting crewmen.

"Joel, are you out of your mind? What are you thinking? That wing drop pass was way too fast – are you trying crash in front of the whole world?" Major Sandoval demanded, waving his arms. "A great impression that would make! We're trying to sell these airplanes, not crack 'em up! What have I told you about bold pilots?" His neck veins were bulging.

"Sorry, sir," Joel tried to look contrite, "'there are bold pilots, and there are old pilots, but there are no old, bold pilots.' But it came off pretty well, didn't it? I mean, the air was bumpy, and the speed smoothed it out, and –" his voice trailed off at the continued scowl. He chanced an engaging smile, "How did the crowd like it?"

The major looked at him, frowning. "Joel, you are incorrigible. I've never seen a pilot execute a maneuver so precisely. Yes, you bloody fool, the crowd loved it. And so did the Germans, it seems. There's a German Captain looking for you."

He shook his head, visibly less angry, cajoling; "For God's sake, Joel, please be more careful; I don't want to write a condolence letter to your mother. Seriously, now, your margin of error is just too small at that speed; the sparks fly just as high at 130. Don't make me ground you." The threat was not an idle one, Joel knew. Then, there was a slight smile; Joel was forgiven. Again.

Minutes later, twenty-five-year old Joel Knight strolled toward the American hospitality tent, still wearing his leather flight cap, his goggles jauntily shoved on top, his brown leather jacket unzipped, but not all the way.

What a perfect assignment, he thought happily; *Curtiss provides the airplanes and all the support, hoping to sell the aircraft to overseas customers. The Army provides me, to show them off! I get all the fun and none of the responsibilities!*

The more airplanes Curtiss sold, he knew, the less each would cost the Army, so everybody would win. Secondly, it showed American technology to friend and potential foes alike. And, it put men like Joel in the unique position of being able to observe and assess foreign aircraft.

He had the barman pour him a glass of ice water, and turned, bumping into a German officer. "Excuse me, Hauptman," Joel said, in poor classroom German.

"You are pardoned, Oberleutnant," the man said haughtily. His eyes were a passionless thin blue, his nose sharp and aristocratic. "Let us speak English, as my English is far superior to your German." The dialect was clearly British, but still had the harsh overtones of his native language. He clicked the heels of his impeccably polished black boots, and bowed ever so slightly. "I am Hauptman [Captain] Freiherr [Baron] Gerhard von un zu Schroeder, Luftwaffe. May I join you?"

"Of course, sir," Joel replied, turning toward the barman, "give Hauptman Schroeder whatever he would like."

The German drank deeply from a foaming mug of beer, and eyed Joel's drink. "What is this you are drinking?"

"Sir, it's ice water; very refreshing."

"You are off duty, are you not? Why not enjoy a stein of beer or glass of wine?" Schroeder said expansively.

"Sir, I drink no alcohol." Joel replied.

"What?" The astonished German said, "No beer? No wine?"

"No, sir, nothing."

"Have you tasted German beer? It is wonderful! Some of the best is made by monks!" Schroeder said.

"No offense, Hauptman, I have tasted beer, and I don't like it; I think it tastes terrible."

"I am amazed!" Schroeder said, looking astonished; "I scarcely remember when I first tasted beer– I must have been seven or eight. Why, I've had beer nearly every day since then; it is part of my diet, like bread or cheese. How can anyone not like it? I've never heard of such a thing. So, you don't drink it only because you don't like it?"

"That, and because of religious conviction." Joel said quietly

"So, Oberleutnant, what religion forbids beer?" the German looked puzzled.

It was time to cut this off, Joel decided. "I'm sure you didn't come find me to discuss beer, Hauptman. What may I do for you?"

The man cocked his head, looking at him strangely. Joel noted the embroidered silver wings, surrounded by a garland wreath on the right breast of the German's blue-gray uniform; he, too, was a pilot.

"I am impressed with your airplane's performance, Oberleutnant." Schroeder said, changing the subject. "Would you like to test your prototype Hawk against one of my prototype Messerschmitts?"

Joel's mind leapt; *to fly against the newest German plane! That's something I just can't pass up. Now, I'll have to get the Major's permission. Probably the Colonel's, too. No doubt about it, though, the Air Corps would love to know what the new German ship is capable of.*

"Hauptman Schroeder, I would love nothing more." Joel replied, leaning toward him, his hands open. "Let me get my Major's approval."

Joel found the Major enjoying a German brat; after listening to Joel, he agreed that the opportunity to fly against the new Messerschmitt was too good to pass up.

"You could sand bag him, and find out what his ship can do."

The look on Joel's face gave away his horror at the thought of deliberately losing. Sandoval smiled; "Go ask this Schroeder when and where he wants to do this, then check with Sergeant Greene about the condition of your ship. I'll try to clear it with the Colonel. It may have to go higher, you know," he warned.

Joel went to the maintenance area, and found Sergeant Greene loudly berating a Private working under the engine cowling on the gleaming P-36.

"What's wrong, Sergeant?"

"Sir, this knucklehead broke off a back row sparkplug, and we can't get it out. There's a special extractor tool in Belgium, but Curtiss can't get it up here until tomorrow afternoon."

"What about the backup ship?" They always had two aircraft available for shows like this one, in case of last minute problems.

The Sergeant grimaced. "Lieutenant Cook left for England while you were still flying, sir. Remember? He's flying number two at London this weekend."

Without a plane, how am I going to take on this cocky German? Joel thought.

An important part of being a "demonstration pilot" was assessing the German Luftwaffe.

*What if—? Yeah, this is nuts! What if the German would lend me one of his **own** planes? What a crazy idea!* The more he thought about it, the more he was convinced it was worth a try.

Major Sandoval confirmed that number two was already in England. As soon as his plane was repaired, it too would be flown across the Channel, as backup to number two. Sandoval agreed Joel should try to talk Schroeder into letting him fly one of the Messerschmitts, but expressed doubts.

"Not even you can convince the Germans to let you fly that ship, Knight – he'll never let you get close to one of those birds, let alone fly one." he predicted.

Joel returned to the hospitality tent where von Schroeder was sipping a second beer.

"Well, sir, I guess we'll never know how badly I would have beaten you! And I was really looking forward to it. But, my ship is grounded." He quickly outlined the maintenance problem on the P-36.

"Yah," Schroder agreed; "it is increasingly difficult to find competent fitters."

"Yes, it's a real shame; I was looking forward to absolutely humiliating you, too!" He said it with a slight smile. It was a calculated risk, all but insulting the man to his face. *If this guy has the ego of most pursuit pilots –*

The nose went up. "You actually believe you could best me?" von Schroeder said incredulously. "You are serious?"

Joel looked him straight in the eye, the smile gone. "Hauptman, I could beat you flying a SPAD." He referred to the French biplane from the Great War. This was perilously close to an insult.

The German jumped as if he'd been prodded. "You insult me so? I am champion; do you know it? I am never beaten!"

Yeah, right! Joel was sure he was exaggerating. "Always a first time, Hauptman. You know what? It's really too bad we couldn't *both* fly Messerschmitts. It'd be even more fun to beat you flying one of your own ships." Joel laughed lightly, hands on his hips, the gauntlet thrown.

From the look on his face, Joel had opened an old wound. Apparently, von Schroeder expected to be catered to, and didn't like being challenged openly; the man had turned red in the face.

He slammed his hand on the table; "I can arrange this, Oberleutnant!" he said darkly. "You will learn what humiliation is!"

Chapter 2

15 June 1936

American Embassy, Berlin, Germany

1130 Hours

Ambassador Dodd

At first, Colonel Bigsby flatly said no; but with both Major Sandoval and Joel cajoling and explaining, he finally came around.

"OK, I'll permit it if the Germans agree, which I doubt. Don't say anything to them yet; I want to discuss this with the ambassador first."

Several phone calls later, they had the Ambassador's blessing, but with a stipulation: they had to come to Berlin and meet with him.

Joel's orders were changed; he was temporarily assigned to the U.S. Embassy in Berlin. He and Colonel Bigsby were driven to the Embassy.

Ambassador Dodd shook their hands, and invited them into his office. He gave their orders a perfunctory glance, and looked at them over steel rimmed glasses.

"Colonel Bigsby, Lieutenant Knight, thank you for dropping by to chat. As you are aware, the Germans are hell-bent on building their air forces to be equal to any in the world, and treaties be dammed. They've stopped pretending that they're defensive and are belligerently building both pursuit planes and bombers as quickly as they can. Part of why Army Chief of Staff, General Craig, sent you two here is so professional airmen could observe and assess the Germans.

"Let me re-emphasize: you are not spies. What you will do, however, is engage your German aviation counterparts, both military and civilian whenever and wherever you are able, watching what you see out in the open, to help our government paint an accurate picture of where Germany is today. This opportunity for the young Lieutenant here to fly a Messerschmitt is a Godsend."

Colonel Bigsby looked concerned, "Sir," he said, "you should know that neither of us are G2. We don't have intelligence training and don't know what information is valuable. Basically, we're both just aviators." G2 was the Army designation for the Intelligence Section.

"Precisely why you were chosen, Colonel. None of our intelligence men have an aviation background. Many are convinced that aviation will be a major player in any future war. We are quite uncertain where Chancellor Hitler's government is headed. Knowing their capabilities, based on your expert analysis of their aviation components, will help our government properly prepare, should, God forbid, another war ensue."

"Sir, you don't think we'll have to fight the Germans again, do you?" Joel blurted out.

The ambassador chuckled, shaking his head. "I surely hope not, Lieutenant; they would be a very formidable foe. At this point, one must take Chancellor Hitler's word as to his intentions, until such time as his actions confirm or contradict them. However, it is in the best interests of the U.S. to know as much as possible about what weapons they have and are developing."

He sounds like a college professor giving a lecture, Joel thought, not knowing that was exactly what the man had been before FDR appointed him Ambassador to Germany.

"Sir," Colonel Bigsby began hesitatingly, "isn't it a bit unusual for an ambassador to be involved in military matters? Are we to keep this conversation confidential?"

The ambassador smiled. "You are perceptive, Colonel! Indeed, you must both keep this conversation confidential. The Department of State in Washington would be not be pleased to know about this. However, the niceties of diplomacy get in the way of protecting the nation's best interest, betimes. This is, I believe, such a case."

Making a steeple of his hands, he went on "I was an observer during the Great War. What I saw still inhabits my dreams. I want to help you, and by extension, our nation, in preventing another such disaster."

He leaned toward them, "Therefore, let me caution you on two points: if the Germans decide you *are* spying, I will disavow any foreknowledge of your activities, and condemn you myself. You will be expelled and sent home immediately. Secondly, you must so conduct yourselves that even a suspicious man – and there are plenty of those here – would have no reason to fault you.

"I believe that you can interact normally with German aviation interests as fellow aviators without arousing undue attention. But it is up to you to be sure of that. You both come highly recommended; you, Colonel, for your insights into aviation command structure and tactics, and you Lieutenant, for both your aeronautical engineering degree and already broad flying experience. You comprise a formidable team. You are free to exchange details about Army aircraft, the P-36 Hawk in particular, to the limits of restricted information. You can be sure they are fully aware of whatever is in the press."

He sat back in the big leather chair, thinking. Presently, he said "It is amazing that you have persuaded our hosts to let you fly against this—what's his name? I disremember," he consulted his notes "—this Hauptman Schroeder. He is part fraud, part German Horatio Alger. One of my military staff, Master Sergeant Smith has written a quite detailed dossier on him. I shall turn you over to him shortly."

He leaned toward them again, his face very serious. "Colonel, at this point, we do not believe the Germans are aware that Lieutenant

Knight is an engineer; it seems doubtful they would allow him to fly the Messerschmitt if they did. Therefore, I recommend that this fact be left unmentioned. It would also be wise to prepare a quick way for him to depart the country should they discover that fact. Since he is attached to the Embassy, he has de facto diplomatic immunity, but I misdoubt that would greatly detour the Gestapo."

He turned to a concerned Joel Knight and said, "Lieutenant, by all means, learn everything you can about the Messerschmitt, but be most careful during and especially after the flight. Flatter them about the aircraft, no matter what you actually think; don't confront them. When you return, you will quietly depart for the States." He stood, the interview over. "Master Sergeant Smith is waiting for you."

The burly sergeant offered Colonel Bigsby the comfortable leather chair at the head of the conference room's table.

"Sirs, I am Master Sergeant Clarence J. Smith; please call me Charlie, everybody does. May I get you some coffee or other refreshments?" he asked courteously.

Their cups filled, and a silver carafe standing by for refills, he turned to the two officers.

"Gerhard von und zu Schroeder was born in western Germany, near the border of France around 1905 or so," Charlie began.

"His father inherited a small piece of property, about 150 acres, which once made a decent living for the family, mostly raising grapes and producing wine. By the time Gerhard's old man got it, though, the land was pretty much used up. Apparently, he didn't know much about cultivating grapes, 'cause the quality of the wine went down steadily, to where they were only producing vinegar, which doesn't yield much profit.

"When the Great War came Gerhard's old man – his name was Gustavus– used an old barony associated with the land to get a commission in the Kaiser's army. He didn't last long – got killed in one of the early battles, don't remember which one off the top of my head."

The sergeant scratched the short, gray hair behind his left ear. "That left Gus's wife, Gerhard's mother, in a tight place, 'cause he had several brothers and sisters. She bundled up the whole brood and headed for her brother's place in Heidelberg, but they never made it."

He shook his head. "An ammunition train exploded beside the train they were on. Everybody was killed but Gerhard. He was about ten at the time. He spent the war years in a state-run orphanage, where he mostly got three squares a day, and a bed along with his schooling. With the Armistice, and the awful inflation, the orphanage ran out of money. They just turned the poor kids out on the streets. He lived by his wits." The graying sergeant shook his head; despite his tough exterior, the man had a soft spot for kids.

"By his middle teens, he'd had several run-ins with the cops, which means he was a tough customer, because they mostly left kids alone. They tossed him in jail for a while, and then let him out –don't know why. That was when he ran into the Nazis." he said with a grimace.

"The National Socialist Party was a natural place for a thug like Gerhard," the Master Sergeant continued. "He was deeply bitter, and vengeful, just looking for someone to vent his hate upon. The Jews suited his purposes just fine, 'cause his role in life was to bully and manhandle any opposition to the party, Jews or otherwise.

"He was assigned to guard an airplane used for party officials. He was fascinated, and talked to the pilot, who had flown for the Kaiser. The guy gave him a ride. That hooked Schroeder on flying.

"With the pilot's help, Gerhard applied to a 'glider club.' The competition was brutally stiff but he showed exceptional aptitude, and learned quickly.

"He soloed in gliders, and built a reputation for careful flying. Twice, he placed second in time and distance contests. His instructors took note; when the first cadets were selected to clandestinely train in powered craft, his name was on the list."

"Sound's like you're reading a book," Joel commented, very impressed with the sergeant's thoroughness.

"Well, sir, I did write the Embassy biography for him, so I know his story pretty well."

"Please continue, Charlie," Bigsby invited, with a side look at Joel.

"Thank you, sir. He flew trainers and built time faster than anyone. When it came time for solos, he thought that he'd be first. Didn't happen. He was third, behind two aristocratic guys; he thought it was unfair, and was again bitter and resentful. It's a pattern with him."

The sergeant was really into his story, "Now, it was common practice then to let the advanced students tutor those behind them. His file says Gerhard treated them harshly, and set extremely high standards for them. In the end, though, nothing was said, because his students performed very well."

Joel was impressed, in spite of himself. "How'd you get his file?" he blurted out.

"No comment, sir!" The master sergeant said with a twinkle in his eye. Colonel Bigsby shook his head slightly. Joel took the rebuke; he shouldn't ask questions the sergeant couldn't answer.

"When the Luftwaffe began recruiting pilots," Master Sergeant Smith told them, "Gerhard was among the first. His first military airplane was the Heinkel HE-51; that's a real nice biplane. "Yes, I know it," Joel said. "It's a very pretty ship."

"Well, he loves it, and flies the heck out of it. When Chancellor Hitler announced the Luftwaffe to the world in 1935, Leutnant Gerhard von und zu Schroder was already an experienced pilot. He's fiercely proud of his uniform. He's still stung by the perception that others are better than him, and insisted on the title 'Baron'. The Luftwaffe, well, they were eager to show 'Aryan superiority' even by questionable lineage, so they let him. He was abandoned all those years ago, but the Luftwaffe gave him a home, and most important to him, a place that respects him for who he is and his abilities."

"He sounds ruthless, Charlie."Joel said.

"Sir, you'd better believe it. He's a diehard Nazi. He feels he has nowhere else to go; he'll do anything to stay. He has a real 'inferiority complex,' Lieutenant. I'm no psychologist, but I know that anybody that challenges him gets a Lulu of a reaction. Be careful of him, sir. He can get very violent."

"Yes, I've already encountered some of that," Joel replied dryly.

"What else can you tell us about this tendency to violence, Sergeant?" Colonel Bigsby asked.

"Colonel, this guy is a time bomb. I've heard, but haven't confirmed, that he actually killed some guys who mocked him at a rathskeller." Joel blanched, remembering how he had taunted him.

After Smith left, a somber Joel sat quietly thinking.

This Baron Gerhard von und zu Schroeder isn't at all what I expected. I'll have to be real careful, he decided. *To do otherwise—.*

Bigsby interrupted his thoughts. "Well, Lieutenant, you may have bitten off a bit more that you expected. Now, you have the dilemma of deciding whether you'll let him beat you, or fight him straight up, and suffer the consequences if you beat him."

"Sir, if I don't fight him hard, we won't learn much about the airplane. I'll just have to trust that you and his superiors will prevent him from going crazy when I beat him." Bigsby noted the confident statement was made without braggadocio.

Chapter 3

18 June 1936

Hannover, Germany

0800 Hours

Competition and Conclusion

The Embassy provided a driver and a spotlessly clean 1932 Nash formal sedan. Colonel Bigsby accompanied Joel, along with an official photographer. A graying Luftwaffe Oberst [Colonel] sporting a thin, Errol Flynn style mustache greeted them. His age and silver wings had him and Colonel Bigsby eyeing each other; could they have fought each other during the Great War?

Joel was so focused on the upcoming encounter that he scarcely was aware of the formalities. At last, they headed for the flight line.

Carefully, aided by an English speaking German crewman, Joel walked around the trim pursuit ship, and performed a careful preflight check, over protests from von Schroeder. The Messerschmitt surprised him; close up, it seemed smaller than his P-36; the wing span was certainly less. It seemed square and very Teutonic compared to the sleekness of his Hawk. Finally satisfied, he turned, climbed up the left wing, and sat in the cockpit.

The cockpit is cramped for someone of my height, Joel thought, *and I really don't like the way the canopy hinges on the right.* It was full of strange angles, and small, flat panes of Plexiglas. *Apparently, the Germans don't like the distortion of curved Plexiglas. This ship has radio*, he noted. He'd been told that not all German pursuits were so equipped. He was mentally cataloging everything.

A German instructor pilot began briefing him in serviceable English on the controls and instruments. The layout was entirely different from anything he'd flown, but after a few minutes seemed logical enough. He'd boned up on metric to English conversions, and the instruments made sense to him, he was gratified to note.

I like the throttle and engine controls, but not the positions of the landing gear and flap controls, he thought, continuing to memorize his comments for later commitment to paper. He shifted his weight from side to side – *If I maneuver violently, I'll be banging my shoulders on the cockpit edges. The seatback is too low for my height.*

They spent the entire morning familiarizing Joel with the aircraft's characteristics and controls. Finally the instructor approved Joel starting the engine. It had a bumpy idle, its inverted V12 water cooled engine sounding completely different than the 14 cylinder air cooled radial engine in his P-36.

It was another half hour before the German released him to do some slow taxiing. The ship was more stable than the center hinged landing gear made it appear, and the brakes had a solid feel.

I'd rather have a tail wheel than that fixed skid, he thought. Taxiing complete, he returned for clearance to fly around the pattern.

He felt every eye on him as he turned into the wind on the grass runway, and advanced the throttle. Per the instructor, he let the tail fly off on its own, and then just nudged the stick backward. In seconds, he was airborne. He reached in the wrong place at first for the lever to retract the wheels. But it took only a few moments before he began to feel comfortable. Soon, he was turning, rolling, doing stalls, until he had something of the measure of the craft, at least on a superficial level.

The $64 dollar question, Joel thought grimly, *is can I beat this guy with only thirty minutes in his own ship!*

Inevitably, the moment of truth arrived, and Joel was facing "The Baron," as he had come to think of the German.

"Now," von Schroeder said very much in command, "at my radio command, we will come at each other from opposite ends of the field, yes? Level, at 1000 meters, passing on the left, like the Autobahn, yes? When we pass, the fight is on. It requires ten seconds on the other man's tail for a 'kill,' agreed? This we will do four times." He held up the fingers of his hand.

"Yes, that sounds OK." Joel said.

Von Schroeder turned, and walked toward the other ME-109. On its tail was painted a bright red slash with a gold baronial seal; Schroeder was flying his personal airplane!

1017 Hours

They took off, von Schroeder leading the way. When von Schroeder radioed his readiness, Joel banked away, and went to the far end of the airfield.

Joel turned heading back toward von Schroeder's airplane – it was hard to see, it was so small. As von Schroeder flashed past him, Joel slammed the throttle full forward, and pulled the stick back into his stomach.

He zoomed upward several thousand feet, and holding the stick, began to go over onto his back. Straining his head to see out of the top of the cockpit, he saw that, inexplicably, von Schroeder had turned left, stayed level, and was way below him!

"I've got you!" Joel shouted gleefully, and dove toward the other plane.

Von Schroeder didn't see him; Joel roared down behind him, and flashed past, shouting over the radio, "Guns! Guns!" Round one was his!

Again, they flew to opposite ends of the field. At von Schroeder's command, they started toward each other. Among the men watching them were von Schroeder's staffel [squadron] mates and Joel's small entourage.

The two airplanes flashed past, and as Joel expected, von Schroeder turned left and climbed with him; both were going nearly straight up only about 100 feet apart, canopy to canopy. When von Schroeder saw him, Joel chopped his throttle – von Schroeder climbed as Joel's airplane slowed. He snapped in behind the German's tail.

"Round two! Gotcha!" Joel shouted over the radio.

Von Schroeder was shouting too, but in frustration and anger. He'd seen his men watching him; he had to win at least once!

As they were flying to the starting position, the radio announced; "Return to the field at once; there is a thunderstorm about to cross the field."

Von Schroeder banked obediently toward the airfield, and Joel joined him. They landed, and taxied to where ground crewmen quickly tied down the aircraft. Von Schroeder stood aloof and said nothing as they waited for the storm to pass.

1230 Hours

Fight Concluded

The storm passed, and the German Colonel informed them the contest could resume. The airplanes had been refueled.

Joel again carefully checked his airplane. Von Schroeder was clearly exasperated at the American's excess care.

Don't pop a gasket, Baron, Joel thought. The two men mounted their aircraft, and started engines.

For the third contest, they again began at the extreme ends of the field. Joel had been thinking.

He's broken left every time – I bet he'll to do it again.

Von Schroeder's Me-109 shot past. Joel turned up and rolled to his right. *There he is!* Von Schroeder had repeated his left turn, and was climbing. They flashed past each other, Joel now turning as hard as he dared to his left, still climbing. Von Schroeder turned to his right, taking him away from Joel. Rolling into a right turn, Joel tried to get behind his opponent. Von Schroeder would have none of it, and turned more tightly to his right than Joel could.

They began to joust, with Joel trying to gain the position on the German's tail, and the German dodging away. The way to resolve this, Joel knew, would be to slow his aircraft, and turn more tightly, inside the other plane's path. With so little experience in this plane, Joel didn't dare risk slowing too much, which could cause a stall and spin into the ground.

Von Schroeder nosed down a bit, turning to his left. In seconds, with Joel starting to catch up, he turned right.

Wait! He's repeating himself; he feints twice one way and then turns the other.

Instinctively, Joel slowed slightly, and began a left roll. Just as he thought, von Schroeder was mechanically turning back to his left, to evade his attacker. Instead, he flew all but in front of his opponent, and Joel had won again!

The German snapped, "We will go one last time," his voice brittle. They returned to the starting positions.

Joel knew he'd be smart to let the German win once, but he shoved the thought aside. He had decided to see if the haughty von Schroeder would continue his left break habit; he deliberately slowed down as von Schroeder roared past him.

Sure enough, there he is, Joel thought. He let the German see him, then slammed the throttle forward, and banked very hard to his right.

Von Schroeder dove after him. Joel raced toward the ground, turned to his right, and skimmed along the open countryside fifty feet above the not-yet-ripe wheat. A glance over his shoulder proved that von Schroeder was in hot pursuit. He let the German gain on him, and then made a very tight, air show style low altitude right turn, his wingtip parting the green wheat stalks. He hoped von Schroeder would be surprised; he was. Joel went straight up and rolled to his left. Von Schroeder had turned wider than Joel, and was slightly below him, giving the American the advantage, which he took savagely. Now, he was on the Baron's tail.

They climbed, twisting and turning, back in the direction of the airfield. Joel predicted most of von Schroeder's moves, and countered them.

He's still trying the twice-one-direction fake moves! Finally as they crossed the field itself, Joel went for the kill; "Guns, guns, guns!" he shouted over the radio.

The German Colonel's voice was angry; they were ordered to land at once. *Schroeder is in hot water now, for sure!* Joel thought, laughing, *The Baron's zero for four!*

As they climbed from their airplanes, Joel saw that von Schroeder was sweaty, red-faced, and very angry, clinching his fists.

"Curse you!" he shouted at Joel. "You shamed me in front on my men! I demand satisfaction!" He threw a flying glove at Joel's feet.

He wants a duel! Is this guy nuts?

Joel forgot the ambassador's advice in his excitement.

"You are no pursuit pilot, Baron!" he said with sarcasm, "you're pathetic; you fly mechanically, like a poor student. I predicted every move you made! Perhaps you are better suited to transports or bombers!" There could hardly be a greater insult to a pursuit pilot!

Von Schroeder's face was black with rage, "I will kill you! I will kill you if I have to follow you to America or to Hell!" He shouted and then snapped his mouth shut as his Oberst [Colonel] stamped in front of him.

Joel moved away in alarm. Von Schroeder stood at stiff attention as he got a stern dressing-down from the beet-red Oberst. Joel understood only parts of it; the Oberst was talking way too fast, his arms flying. The meaning was clear enough, though.

Abruptly, the Oberst turned to him, and said through clenched teeth, "You are dismissed, Oberleutnant. No longer are you welcome here."

Colonel Bigsby raised his eyebrows in an "I told you so" gesture, and walked with him toward the waiting car.

On the way to the Embassy, Joel felt a little smug knowing he was the first American to fly the ME-109. What a report he would have for the Air Corps Technical Division! But deep inside was a profound disquiet over what von Schroeder had said.

Chapter 4

24 June 1936

American Embassy, Berlin, Germany

0930 Hours

Departure

The next morning, a somber Colonel Bigsby interrupted Joel as he was writing his report.

"Lieutenant, I have news," he said. Joel stood and waited expectantly.

Colonel Bigsby said seriously, "you will be declared *persona non grata* if you are not out of the country within twenty-four hours. Pack your bags, son. There's a British Airways DC-3 leaving Templehof just after noon today. You will be on it."

"What does this mean, sir?" Joel asked him.

"It means a permanent blot on your service record if you are still here tomorrow. It could mean an international incident if the Gestapo arrest you and forcibly put you on an airplane. Be in the lobby ready to depart by 1100 hours," the Colonel said forcefully.

"Yes, sir. Did they discover I'm an engineer, sir?"

"No, Lieutenant," he answered "you really embarrassed the Luftwaffe, and the Baron, and they are reacting to it the strongest way they know."

At fifteen minutes to 11:00, Joel was packed and ready. Several embassy personnel in the lobby were listening intently to a German radio broadcast.

"What's happening?" he asked.

"A German light bomber crashed at the Berlin airport, but nobody was killed; a Lieutenant General Walther Wever and his aide were on board."

"Wever – is that the Wever who's Chief of Staff of the Luftwaffe?" Joel asked.

"Yeah, that's him; he's called the 'Billy Mitchell' of the Luftwaffe," the embassy staffer said, "He's their biggest proponent of heavy, long range bombers."

"It would have been a huge loss for the Germans if he'd been killed," Joel said.

1941

Chapter 5

19 August 1941

First Air Force, 135th AAF Base Unit

Millville Army Air Field

Officers Club

0815 Hours

Spanish Situation

"Well, well, isn't this interesting?" said Major Henry as he ate his eggs.

"What's that, Jimmy?" Joel asked.

Henry rattled the newspaper, "The *New York Times* says that the Germans have sent large numbers of quote 'administrative advisors' unquote into Spain, and not just to Madrid. Herr Dr. Goebbels says they have come at 'Generalissimo Franco's express request to aid in the mutual development of modern society structures as part of continued great friendship with Germany.' Reuters says that they're all young, fit men, but are not soldiers."

"Yeah, and Donald Duck is a pig!" said Joel. "May I see that?"

A glance at the article confirmed what Henry said. Joel thought *the Germans have co-opted Spain in such a way that they might be able to maintain the façade of neutrality.*

"Say, I'll bet the Brits are plenty upset," the Major said thoughtfully. "Now, their Gibraltar garrison's at risk for invasion from the inland side *and* the Med; that'd be tough to defend."

"No doubt about that," Joel said, "but I wonder what else they have up their sleeve? Is this a 'friendly invasion,' if there is such a thing? Think about it; if the Iberian Peninsula is Hitler's new playground, he could threaten shipping going into the Channel or the Med."

"Yeah, if they wanted to be openly hostile," the Major said thoughtfully, "but the Nazis could also use Spain as a trans-shipment agency and bring in strategic materials using Spain's so-called neutrality."

"Say, that 'd be whole new bucket of worms, alright."Joel said. "I think I'll see what G-2 has to say. May I borrow your paper?"

Headquarters Building, Room 214 G-2

Joel found the men in intelligence well aware of the situation described in the *Times*.

"It's a lot worse than this article lets on, Major," one told him. "From what we know, the Germans have put their people into nearly every major bureau in the Spanish government, at all levels. For all practical purposes, Spain is now a German vassal."

"So, Franco makes the 'decisions,' but the Nazis control how or if they are carried out, is that it?"

"Yes, sir, that's it. We haven't heard how the Spanish military is taking it. If I had to guess, I'd say that the Spanish Air Force will greet them with open arms, and welcome every Messerschmitt and Heinkel the Germans will give 'em."

"What about the Spanish Army?" Joel asked.

"That's an unknown, Major," said a studious looking Captain as he peered through his rimless glasses. "I doubt they'll be anxious to let the Nazis take control, but the Germans have them in a tight place. Most of their hardware, tanks, artillery, even rifles, are German; all the Nazis would have to do is cut off the supply of parts, and the Spanish Army would grind to a halt."

Joel said, "Could the Nazis could use Spain's neutrality to get strategic materials?"

The captain blew out his breath. "Wow. Hadn't thought of that, sir. That could open up South America and the Caribbean as sources of rubber, oil, and bauxite." He made some scribbled notes on a pad already filled with them.

"How's FDR taking all this?"

"Sir, we heard he hit the roof and has been burning up the transatlantic phone lines with Churchill."

"I'll just bet," Joel said.

Chapter 6

20 August 1941

1600 Pennsylvania Avenue

Washington, D.C., The White House

1000 Hours

Oval Office

Franklin Roosevelt leaned into the telephone, gripping it hard.

"Winston, I have confirmed what you told us. It is outrageous! Congress is debating whether to declare war against Spain. The newspapers are clamoring for it. As much as I agree with that sentiment, and I do, I assure you, on the face of it, there is precious little legal reason we have for doing so. They have finessed us! The Spanish ambassador is all smiles and unctuousness. He says their status is unchanged, they are, as he put it, 'unalterably neutral,' which is pure unadulterated rubbish."

Churchill growled back, "Our feelings are mutual, Franklin. Parliament are prepared to direct the government to declare war as soon as cause is found, but just as with congress, we have no legally justifiable rationale as yet. We are watching them as hawks; the least violation of the Neutrality Act will bring our wrath down upon their heads. In the meanwhile, there is little we can do but watch." He sighed heavily.

Roosevelt said, "Reuter's in Lisbon says that a huge new oil refinery is being built on the Spanish coast not far from Seville—."

"Yes," interrupted the Prime Minister, "we have men there. It is next to the port town of Punta Umbria, on the peninsula in the river Odiel. They apparently had planned this for some time, as the ground was prepared a year ago, and the docks are nearly complete. My concern is from where they will obtain the feed stocks for the refinery. Using neutral hulls, they could bring oil from the Middle East or even Venezuela or Brazil. It is too soon to calculate the refinery's capacity, but in terms of sheer physical size, it's at least as large as the Romanian facilities at Ploesti."

"Even should they use the output only for themselves, it would still deprive the Allies of that much oil," Roosevelt said.

"I believe that we shall soon see that the capacity is far beyond what Spain itself can consume; that can only mean that they intend to supply the Nazis." He pronounced it "Nasties." "How they do so may be one of the reasons we both are searching for, Franklin."

"Perhaps. My suspicion is that they will transport it over land, perhaps via rail through France. Proving what they are up to may be very difficult, absent the capability to overfly their territory. Without such clarity, neither of our legislative bodies will entertain declarations, Winston. I propose that we form a joint, clandestine effort to emplace people in the proper situations, either within the refinery staff or perhaps within the rail system to gain us the knowledge we lack in this regard. Perhaps General Donovan can suggest the appropriate personnel on our side."

"I quite agree, sir. Our SAS have already begun; kindly advise me of your arrangements so the two groups can coordinate and not tread upon each other."

Roosevelt said, "I shall, of course. Now, I must prepare a 'fireside chat' and attempt to reassure our nervous populous, and especially the newspapers, that for now, our hands are tied. This may be far easier said than done, I fear."

"Indeed," Churchill replied dryly, "I must myself attempt to temporarily dampen the fires whilst searching for the fatal chink in the Bosch armor. We must speak often, Franklin, for our mutual benefit. Good morning."

Chapter 7

Sunday, 7 December 1941

Bachelor Officers Quarters

Millville Army Air Field

1130 Hours

Shock

Joel sat in the Day Room, reading a *Colliers Magazine*, when an excited young Lieutenant suddenly burst through the door.

"The Japs bombed Pearl Harbor! They sank the fleet! Guys, we're at war!"

"What! Say, are you crazy? Why would the Japs attack Pearl Harbor?" someone responded.

"Yeah, well, turn on the radio, you'll see," the Lieutenant was adamant.

The beat up Stewart Warner console radio was turned on. When the tubes warmed up, it burst into voice, "—and reports from the Hawaii Territory are that the Air Corps has also been struck hard. All of the pursuit planes at Hickman Field Army Air Field – I believe that's right – at Hickman Field near Honolulu City in the Hawaiian Island chain, in the South Pacific – all those aeroplanes have been destroyed or damaged to some degree. To repeat our earlier bulletin, a massive force of Japanese airplanes in at least two waves has bombed and sunk all the Navy ships at berth at Pearl Harbor, in the U.S. Territory of Hawaii. First reports are that half a dozen capitol ships are sunk, and human losses are in the many hundreds.

"This was taking place as representatives of the Empire of Japan and our government met in serious talks to *forestall* war. I don't understand. I'm at a loss for words, ladies and gentlemen. I am shocked. We have been attacked by surprise, without warning, and without declaration of war. How can that be? Civilized nations don't attack one another without provocation or declaration of war. Further bulletins will be forthcoming, I am sure. Stay tuned to this network for the latest information."

Joel felt a sick feeling at the pit of his stomach. A dread sense of foreboding came over him; the young Lieutenant was right; America was at war.

1942

Chapter 8

24 February 1942

Gotha Waggonfabrik, Gotha, Germany

1540 Hours

Projekt Rheinwasser

Obertstleutnant [Lieutenant Colonel] Freiherr [Baron] von und zu Schroeder sat in the director's office at Gotha Waggonfabrik (GWF), reviewing GO-447 flying wing design concepts for the secret Rhinewasser project. He, the Director, the Chief Engineer, and the Chief Engineer's assistant had just finished an awkward, silent lunch. He watched as the Director made a quiet telephone call before the meeting restarted.

"Now then, what have we here?" von Schroeder asked, holding a drawing. Von Schroeder was a decorated pilot, an accomplished leader, even a card-carrying member of the National Socialist Party, but he was no aircraft engineer. He knew he was way out of his element with these highly educated men, but this was his responsibility as head of the project. To make matters worse, his adjutant, who *was* an engineer, was sick in hospital. Von Schroeder was on his own.

GWF's Chief Engineer glanced at the drawing, "This shows how rockets attach to the aircraft to aid take offs with heavy fuel and bomb loads, Herr Schroeder. Eight are attached in groups of two, using this structure," he pointed to a sturdy looking structure, "the aircraft can go aloft with nearly twice the normal useful load." It seemed to von Schroeder that the man was talking down to him.

Von Schroeder studied the drawing carefully, "So does *this* give us the range we require?"

The Chief Engineer answered reluctantly, "Ah, no, Oberst. Even with the rockets, we are still approximately 2,400 Km [1,500 miles] short."

Von Schroeder sat back in the chair and rubbed his eyes. It had been a long and frustrating meeting. Unconsciously, he loosened his necktie; his notoriously short temper was being sorely tried. By sheer strength of will he kept his voice even, his words measured. *I will not shout,* he told himself.

"Are you telling me then, Herr Projekt Engineer, once again, that this modification will not allow these aircraft to fly to America and back?

"You have described to me external fuel tanks – not adequate; an elevated runway – not sufficient; landing gears which drop off after takeoff – not adequate yet again; minimal crew with no defensive weapons – helpful, but not sufficient. Have I left anything out?" he demanded, the sarcasm increasing as he spoke.

 "What shall I tell General Wever, I ask you? Should he cancel this critical mission because your engineers are not up to the task? Shall he cancel your production contract as well?"

Despite his resolve, his voice rose as he looked at the Director and he slapped the table loudly.

"Shall he? All we want is an aircraft to fly to America and back. Is this really so difficult? The American Lindberg did it in 1927. Are we Germans so backward that more than fifteen years later we cannot duplicate as a nation what he did as an individual?"

That Lindberg had only flown one way never occurred to him; he was also unaware that he was showing a profoundly superficial understanding of the difficult problem.

Von Schroeder's point had hit home; all of the men seemed suddenly pale. Men had been shot for less, he knew, and so did they, obviously enough.

Chapter 9

24 February 1942

Gotha Waggonfabrik, Gotha, Germany

1400 Hours

New Player

"Of course not, you fool!"

The resonantly low voice startled all four men. Turning, von Schroeder saw a short, twisted figure, leaning heavily on a thick cane. The man's tweed jacket stretched across his distorted body like a too-small slipcover on an overstuffed couch. A slide rule case hung from his left hip like a knight's sword. A cold intelligence was behind the thick round glasses.

"Why are you so dense? Do you not see? How can you not see? It is the *combination* of modifications that will permit success. That, and the ability to receive fuel in the air."

Heinz Berthold did not suffer fools gladly, and his voice was heavy with sarcasm, like a teacher dealing with particularly slow students.

"And a new addition to the wing tips!" he grinned at them in a twisted fashion.

Von Schroeder reacted as if he were the most sinister man in Germany. "Who is this – creature?"

Berthold saw von Schroeder's lips curl in disgust as he involuntarily shrunk away. He could almost predict what the man was thinking: *Cripples should be hidden from sight or shipped to the camps; they are a disgrace to the "Master Race."*

The Director regained his composure quickly.

"This is Herr Doctor Heinz Berthold, Herr Schroeder. He holds doctorate degrees in aeronautics and physics and is responsible in very large part for the success of the Gotha GO-447. It was he who took the Horton brothers' original flying wing design and made it practical."

"You are a cripple," von Schroeder blurted, as if it were a death sentence.

"Yes. And I see you have been blessed with the gift of discovering the obvious." Berthold's cold eyes fixed him like a butterfly pinned to a display.

"Fools like you always want to destroy that which doesn't appear perfect. Do you want my help or not? You will utterly fail without it, of course."

He stamped his cane loudly for emphasis, and crossed his arms in defiance, balancing against a chair. His balding head, oversized for his shrunken torso, and his pale white skin gave the appearance of something nearly dead, which often was more offensive to people than his crippled legs, he knew.

Von Schroeder appeared shocked; *I doubt anyone has spoken to him like that since he was young,* Berthold thought with secret amusement.

The man leapt to his feet, "I should have you shot!"

"What would that gain you, you idiot? Sit down. You would only fail to carry out your own orders and be shot yourself."

My patience is wearing thin with this fool.

Von Schroeder was speechless.

The chief engineer interrupted, anxious to defuse the situation.

"What do you mean, Herr Doctor Berthold? What wing tip change? And combine the modifications how?"

The Berthold shifted his icy blue eyes to the Chief Engineer.

"Horst, Horst, even you must surely see that none of the changes *alone* can provide the range required. But if we carefully combine them, there will be sufficient range, and a small surplus of fuel for emergency situations."

Berthold's tone was conciliatory, for he thought of this man as a colleague.

His added smugly, "And, the wind tunnel confirms that adding a vertical plate to the ends of the wing produces additional lift, but no additional drag. Well, very little more," he corrected himself. "And it could yield a 20 percent increase in lift."

Von Schroeder appeared to be intrigued, but then surprised Berthold by asking an entirely different question.

"How would you take fuel in the air? And how would that help?"

Patiently, Berthold said, "Oberst, since 1939 there have been extensive experiments with fueling aircraft in flight. GWF has participated from the beginning. We now have a means by which we can efficiently transfer fuel from one aircraft to another without spilling a drop." *A small exaggeration, but suitable for this discussion*, he decided.

The officer seemed to regain his composure, "So? Again I ask, how does that help this mission? I suppose you must fly these aerial fueling stations to mid-Atlantic and somehow meet up with aircraft on the return? Do you know how difficult that would be?"

Berthold regarded him as if he was a dimwitted child, his patience at an end.

"Of course I know that. And you suppose wrongly."

The sarcasm fairly dripped from the statement. He cocked his head, gauging von Schroeder's reaction to what he was about to say.

"Do you know this? An aircraft can carry far more fuel in flight that it is able to takeoff with? Do you understand what that means?"

"Taking fuel while in the air could mean—a much longer range for the aircraft?" von Schroeder replied, after a moment, as he if were wondering if he was walking into a trap.

Berthold smiled that sinister smile again.

"Indeed! Perhaps you are not so dull after all. Here is my thinking: we takeoff with a full bomb load, and half full internal fuel tanks. Four large external fuel tanks which can be dropped later would hang from the wings. Here, look at these drawings my draftsman prepared."

He moved awkwardly to the table, his cane thumping as he walked, and spread out the large sheets of paper. He leaned over the drawings and pointed.

"I have added other changes, as you will see. The complex iron carrier brackets for the rockets are far too heavy. They can be made much lighter."

He glanced at the Chief Engineer's assistant, who looked chagrined.

"The aircraft can be modified to accept more of the rocket's stress. The new rocket carrier will disengage by itself by means of a simple, light weight, mechanism. The landing gear drop-off feature requires a bit more work, but it will save considerable weight; I estimate more than 700Kg. That's 250 more gallons of fuel." He continued describing the changes he had made.

Berthold stood and added, "One more thing can be done to maximize the range: use only two of the four engines." He crossed his arms and waited for their reaction, smiling inwardly.

Chapter 10

24 February 1942

GWF, Gotha, Germany

1410 Hours

Revelation

There was a brief, stunned silence, and then all four of his listeners objected at once. Berthold held up his hands, motioning them to be quiet. He knew they'd respond this way.

"Yes, yes, despite your objections, gentlemen, I assure you that this aircraft *can* be flown on just two engines, just if the crew will follow a prescribed discipline."

All four men were listening intently. *Now I've got them!*

"The discipline is this: after a certain amount of fuel has been used, and the aircraft is at the proper altitude, the outboard engine on each side is shut down, its propeller feathered. The aircraft slows, but sufficient power is available from the remaining engines to maintain an airspeed of approximately 350 kilometers per hour [217 MPH]. The fuel usage is half compared to normal cruising at higher speeds and using all four engines. This makes for a long mission, approximately thirty hours, perhaps a bit more. The crews can be trained to do each other's jobs and take turns sleeping for short periods and cope adequately."

"Does this still require the elevated runway?" von Schroeder asked with apparent trepidation as he made notes.

A pertinent question. He said with little sarcasm, "Yes, it does, Herr Oberst. Calculations indicate that the aircraft could *just* take off using rockets alone on a flat runway, but the margin for error is too small. You have seen the depictions of the runway site, yes?"

Von Schroeder nodded. The concept for the runway started at the top of a bluff, then descended down a slope to level out below.

Berthold said, "By elevating the starting end fifty to seventy-five meters or so, gravity provides forty or fifty kilometers per hour additional speed, assuring that the aircraft will become airborne."

Standing for any length of time was painful, so Berthold sat on the arm of a chair and continued.

"The mission scenario is this: the elevated runway assists the engines in accelerating the aircraft. Then the rockets are fired, in pairs. The aircraft lifts off, and the rockets and their bracket drop off. The landing gear is jettisoned at about seventy-five meters altitude or so. Fuel from the interior tanks of the aircraft is consumed as it climbs in the direction of the target, and its rendezvous with the aerial tanker."

Berthold looked carefully to be sure the Colonel was following him; he seemed to be, so he continued.

"The flying tanker then fills the bomber's fuel tanks, including the empty external tanks. The bomber will now weigh more than it did at takeoff!"

To Berthold's satisfaction, his audience showed amazement and even disbelief.

He went on.

"As the aircraft continues, the fuel in the four external fuel tanks is consumed first, and then those tanks are dropped, further reducing weight and drag. When cruise altitude is achieved – that exact height has not been determined yet – the outboard engines are shut down, and the propellers feathered. From there on, it is a task for the crew of proper navigation and monitoring of the aircraft systems until approximately 200 kilometers from the target."

The look on his face is amusing, Berthold thought, looking at von Schroeder.

"At that point, the engines are restarted, and the bombs dropped. The aircraft reverse their course. Once out of range of American fighter planes, they climb to cruise altitude. The engines are shut down once more, and the journey home continued. The engines are restarted for safe landing. The aircraft land on grass; reinforcement to their undersides protects them from significant damage. With minimal refurbishment, they will be ready for subsequent missions."

He stopped, then added, "Of course, the new model will not require such heroics."

Oberst von Schroeder was stunned, confused, and in spite of himself, impressed. This brilliant little misshapen man had not only resolved the range and fuel problems, he had completely planned the entire mission.

Cripples are inferior. How did he do that? he thought.

Despite himself, initial disgust had turned to grudging admiration. Trying to resolve his internal dilemma, he latched on to Berthold's last statement.

"What new model?"

The Director shot a wicked glance at his resident genius.

Speaking carefully, he said, "There is a proposed GO-447 successor, Herr Oberst, which will be larger, and more capable of transatlantic missions. We have not yet received approval from Reichsluftart Ministerium [RLM]."

This was forbidden territory, outside his purview, and so he asked as if disinterested.

"Does this aircraft exist?"

Now the look from the Director was white hot.

"Yes, Oberst, a single experimental example. This is a tightly held State Secret; rather I should say, is *supposed* to be tightly held. I may not tell you more without proper authorization. I trust you understand."

"Of course, Herr Director." von Schroeder said smoothly; he would follow up on *this* as soon as he returned to Berlin. He turned to Berthold, to put the man on the spot.

"Tell me, Herr Doctor, what are the chances of success of Projekt Rheinwasser with this aircraft?" he said, tapping the drawings.

Berthold replied immediately, "My opinion is about 60 percent, six chances out of ten, for a single mission."

The quick response surprised him. "Why not a second?" von Schroeder asked, spreading his hands.

Berthold sneered, "Because Americans are not stupid, Herr Oberst. We may, *just may*, be able to attack them once with unarmed aircraft, but only if we maintain complete secrecy. A second attempt would be a bloodbath; the Americans will be well prepared for a second attack, if I do not misread their national mindset."

Von Schroeder's thoughts showed in a woebegone expression.

Berthold said conciliatorily, "Don't worry, my dear Oberst. Surviving aircraft will have plenty of English and Russian targets to choose from, to say nothing of ships in the North Atlantic."

Von Schroeder was silent, considering his next move. The others knew that his next response would be crucial. They all held their breath.

Von Schroeder said, "So, if these modifications should be approved, how quickly can they be made? How soon can you provide at least sixty aircraft?"

This was more to the Director's liking.

"These are not minor changes, Oberst," he said seriously, starting the negotiation.

"I think six months for that many aircraft. Working twenty-four hours of the day, of course. Then there is the training of crewmen. You are acquainted with the difficulties we have in obtaining materials. I trust you can provide the necessary priorities?"

Von Schroeder nodded at him; *if General Wever approves, we'll have be no problem with funds or priorities.*

The Director seemed to read his thoughts, "Good. Out of my control, of course, is building the fueling aircraft. Junkers Aircraft is whom you should discuss that with."

He looked at his calendar and glanced at his Chief Engineer, who nodded.

"Yes, I will agree to modify sixty aircraft by the end of August if you provide them within ten days. The price would be—"

Chapter 11

25 February 1942

Berlin, Germany

Office of the Chief of the Luftwaffe, General Walther Wever

0945 Hours

Approval

Oberstleutnant Freiherr Gerhard von und zu Schroeder stamped smartly, gave the Nazi salute and shouted, "Heil Hitler!" He carried a large leather drawing folder in his left hand.

Wever gave a delusory wave, "Be seated, Oberst."

"So, then." Wever snubbed out a cigarette. "What of our friends at the Gotha Werkes? Can Projekt Rheinwasser be successful with their design?"

I am doubtful about the success of this proposal, and even less sure what it would accomplish. Like any good soldier, I will follow my orders, which are clear: if von Schroeder can obtain aircraft to do the job, I must do everything possible to help him. The only benefit is getting von Schroeder and his rabid anti-American schemes out of my hair for a while. And, if by some miracle he succeeds, it will be a major propaganda victory, and in the process, a very useful new tool will be developed: an aerial tanker. General Galland of Fighter command is very interested in that. Wever made a note to discuss it with him.

"Yes, Herr General," von Schroeder answered eagerly, like an anxious schoolboy.

He thinks of me as his mentor, as if his father, Wever thought.

"They have developed remarkable modifications to the GO-447 flying wing, which make Projekt Rheinwasser possible. The missions could last thirty hours, which would strain the crew, but the aircraft itself is quite capable of the task." He looked pleased with himself.

He hesitated, and then continued, "There is the most unusual man there, Herr General, who has contrived a number of quite innovative ideas. He has the most audacious plan for the mission—."

Wever chuckled knowingly, "So you met Herr Doctor Berthold, did you? You must admit he is a most remarkable man, is he not?" His eyes sparkled at von Schroeder's discomfort. "Did he intimidate you, Gerhard?"

"Yes, sir, he did," von Schroeder admitted.

"I don't doubt it," Wever said, "that man could intimidate Satan himself. Even the Führer is in awe of him."

"He is brilliant, but he is a cripple, a dwarf—"

"Oberst, Germany could use many more such cripples," Wever said seriously. "Now, I have only yet twenty-five minutes until my next appointment. What has Berthold proposed?"

When von Schroeder finished, Berthold's drawings were scattered across the General's desk. Wever sat chain smoking another cigarette, deep in thought.

"Unlike most proposals, this one has a reasonable chance for at least technical success. There are other missions these aircraft could be used for as well. Take this material to Major Goddard, at Technical Division – you know him, yes? Good. Have him and his merry band of gnomes look this over. If they agree, we go forward."

He snubbed out the cigarette and eyed von Schroeder sharply. "What price did you agree on?"

Von Schroeder showed him the contract, "These figures are tentative, of course, sir, pending your approval."

Wever was impressed, "No, you have done well, Gerhard; the schedule is impressive as well. If they live up to this, you have a mission. What about the tanking aircraft?"

The Oberst was quick to reply, Wever noted, "Herr General, Junkers is test flying a modified JU-290." The JU-290 was a big, four engine cargo transport with a ramp which could be lowered in flight. "They have transferred water simulating fuel, but their design is unrefined. The reel for the transfer hose jams, it often doesn't seal properly, and the entire apparatus is clumsy to control. I wish Doctor Berthold could help them—"

Wever knew about the progress at Junkers; the question was a test of von Schroeder's honesty; he was pleased the man hadn't lied. He said, "I agree. I will arrange for the good Doctor to 'consult' with Junkers."

He removed a typed order from his ornate desk, and signed it with a flourish. "Here is your authorization, Oberst von Schroeder, in advance of Technical Division's approval. You will advise me on your progress monthly, or more often should there be good success or bad news. You are dismissed."

Von Schroeder saluted, collected his drawings and left. Wever saw a huge smile break out on his face as the man closed his office door.

Von Schroeder shook his fist in triumph. *Now! Now those verdammit Americans will feel my wrath! Projekt Rheinwasser is real!*

Chapter 12

14 August 1942

Millville Army Air Field

Millville, New Jersey

0800 Hours

Packard

Major Joel Knight rapped his knuckles lightly on the door jam. Lieutenant Colonel Randolph, Deputy Base Commander, looked up. "What's up, Joel?"

"Sir, a question," Joel said. "I've got a chance to replace that wheezing old '35 Plymouth of mine with a pretty nice '41 Packard Model 110 coupe. I wanted your opinion as to the propriety of it, my being just a lowly major and all!"

"Packard, huh? Well, you're probably OK! Now, you're not going to show up my Betty's Buick are you?" The Colonel shook a finger at him, jokingly. "If you do, she'll be hounding me for a newer car! Then you'll really be in trouble!" Mrs. Colonel Randolph whisked about the base and town in a beautiful buttercup yellow 1940 Buick convertible sedan; it was a grand automobile, and she watched jealously for any that would show it up. "No, I don't see a problem, Joel. After all, the old man drives a Cadillac limousine."

The "old man" was Lieutenant Colonel Tarleton Watkins, the base commander. He was driven about in an elegant 1940 Cadillac Model 160 sedan, officially painted in Army olive drab.

Joel saw his boss was pleased. Colonel Watkins had been visibly irritated when some younger pilots showed up with expensive, show-off cars. It was an unwritten law: lower ranking officers didn't drive cars more ostentatious than their seniors; it just wasn't fitting.

"So, tell me about this Packard!" Randolph said, sitting back in his chair and lighting his pipe.

Pleased, Joel filled him in. "My old Plymouth needs an engine overhaul, and it isn't worth it. I think with the decent tires it has on it, I could probably sell it for $50 or $75. The Packard's only $800. It's two-toned," he told his boss, "a grey top over a medium blue body. It has a blue and white stripped broadcloth interior with jump seats in the back. It even has a radio," he enthused. "And only 4,000 miles! The tires are perfect!" New tires in the Packard's size were impossible to obtain due to the strict rubber rationing.

"Why's he selling?" the Colonel asked him, blowing a fragrant cloud into the air.

"Well, I hate to take advantage of another fellow's misfortune, sir, but a doctor in Vineland is going blind, poor guy, and has to sell. I heard about it from a friend in the squadron who knows him from church."

"Too bad for him, but the car sounds good," mused Randolph; "now, go buy it and get out of my hair before I put you to work on these reports, many of which are yours anyway!"

"I'm leaving! I'm leaving!" laughed Joel. "See you Monday morning, sir!"

The next morning, a friend drove him to Vineland, and he purchased the car. It had a bright red "C" gas rationing sticker on the windshield; they were reserved strictly for physicians. Joel carefully removed it, and returned it to its owner.

He'd get his own sticker, a green "B" designating its use for official purposes. He knew that he could get gas on base, too, as long he was doing official errands.

1943

Chapter 13

3 February 1943

Gotha Waggonfabrik, Gotha, Germany

1000 Hours

Future Plans

Generalleutnant Walther Wever sat with his deputy Oberstleutnant [Lieutenant Colonel] Karl Berger, and his senior aide, reviewing plans. A magnificent wood model of the new six-engine Gotha GO-460 flying wing sat on the desk.

Berger said, "This, sir, is the force structure we propose, which constitutes the initial Geschwader [group] of four Gruppes [wings] of six Staffels [squadrons] each. A normal compliment would be twelve of the Gotha's for each staffel, or a force of 248 aircraft, plus a Geschwader Stab [staff] aircraft for each, for a grand total of 252 aircraft. We have also included a training squadron comprising an additional ten aircraft, which could be pressed into duty, should the need arise. Finally, there is a 200 man maintenance and logistics group. The basing concept would be similar to the typical twin engine bomber bases, but with larger hangers, taxi ways, and runways. My team will recommend possible locations for the base soon. When the RLM approves the funding, we are prepared for four more groups as fast as Gotha can build them. The total force would be approximately 1000 aircraft. The proposed designation is Schwergeschwader (SG) [heavy bomber]."

"That designation is satisfactory. To include the GO-447 in the same Kampfgschwader [medium bomber] (KG) designation with the HE-111s and JU-88s never made sense to me. I'm glad to see a fitting designation for a truly heavy bomber. Now, where does Gotha propose to build the production plant?" Wever asked, snubbing his cigarette. The initial aircraft had been built in an old, cramped WWI vintage building, which was far too vulnerable to Allied bombing for Wever's liking.

With some excitement in his voice, Berger said, "Sir, we have an innovative answer for that – we propose a site on the Western side of the Pyrenees, in central Spain. There are several rail lines from both France and Spain. The local workforce is not terribly skilled, but they are very willing to work, and eager to learn. We shouldn't have the normal labor problems."

Wever knew he was referring to the unreliable slave labor used at many German aircraft plants.

"And, there is good access to the plant site from the new Spanish aluminum plant. They are willing to supply us with adequate petrol as well, although the price may be steep."

"Indeed? That location would make it difficult for the Allied bombers to reach us even when they discover us! This is good. Is the geography such that we can build long runways?" Wever was impressed with his aide's cleverness; building a plant in Spain hadn't occurred to him.

That the plan violated Spain's territorial sovereignty, as well as her position of neutrality never passed either man's mind. Neither did the near impossibility of building 1000 complex aircraft.

"Yes, sir," the aide continued, "and because the GO-460 is basically an upgrade of the GO-447, it will quickly go into production. At first, it will be manufactured conventionally. But by approximately sixty to seventy units into production, there will be a major change."

General Wever lifted his eyebrow; Berger knew that meant the man didn't understand.

"Dr. Berthold has worked another of his wonders, sir. He has modified the design so that it will be manufactured remotely in major parts – he calls them sub-assemblies – then assembled in

Spain. With Minister Speer's approval, he has already directed that production of the components the GO-447 and GO-460 have in common to begin."

"The factory buildings for Spain will be pre-fabricated in Germany, and shipped in pieces by rail to the location. Assembly should require approximately thirty days. When the buildings are completed, we will move both completed sub assemblies and tooling to manufacture them from Gotha here in Germany, to Spain by train."

He stopped and consulted his documents.

"Sir, according to Dr. Berthold's schedule, there should be a first flight by early June, with sixty or more completed aircraft by the end of this coming September."

"That is an ambitious schedule," General Wever observed.

"Yes, sir, it is," Oberstleutnant Berger said, "but Dr. Berthold has obtained a very high level of priority for this project from no less than Minister Speer; we will have equipment, materiel, and manpower in abundance, it appears."

General Wever shook his head in happy disbelief, "This is unexpected, but most welcome; well done, Berger."

Thirty minutes later, Wever was very pleased as the men left his office. He'd sign the necessary orders at once. *The magnificent new Gothas will be a force for the Allies to contend with. I wonder how long we can maintain the secrecy of their manufacturing facility.*

Chapter 14

5 April 1943

Berlin, Germany

Monday Evening

2030 Hours

Conspirator's Plot

He had been a conspirator for six months; he'd lost fifteen pounds with the worrying and fear. The constant pain in his stomach was surely an ulcer. He'd become so paranoid even his own wife wasn't above suspicion.

If the SS get the slightest whiff of this, I'll be arrested, tortured, killed, and my wife and family with me, he thought despondently.

SS Führer Heinrich Himmler's Gestapo were always sniffing the air, like hungry, predatory wolves, searching out the smallest plot, the ill-advised disloyal statement, any gesture of contempt. Even the thought of falling into their hands made the sweat break out on his forehead again.

Oberstleutnant [Lieutenant Colonel] Claus Schenk, Count von Stauffenberg, was an aristocrat, born into a prominent family in southern Germany. He had reached prominence in the eyes of the German high command as a result of bold decisions he made in the North Africa campaign. He'd been nearly killed by a land mine, losing an eye and his right hand. A handsome, virile man, he had been peripherally involved in an earlier plot involving high ranking generals, but became disenchanted with their hesitation and inaction. As he suspected, the plot came to nothing.

Joining this conspiracy had been an incredibly difficult decision. As the grandson of a Napoleonic War hero, he'd been raised and educated at the finest military schools where above all, the honor of the officer corps had been stressed. He had to defend his country against the Nazis, and especially Hitler, his outrage at their brutal actions coming from deep within his soul. But in doing so, he had to violate the oath he'd taken to support Hitler. It had taken months for him to resolve the deep moral dilemma; he must be loyal first and always to Germany. He had to try to bring Hitler and the Nazis down.

Carefully, he began to explore whether there were others, perhaps outside the military, who felt as he did. With Hitler gone, a more reasonable administration could seek peace. That an assassination might set off a civil war seemed a risk worth taking.

The seven men had spent long months feeling each other out, careful to reveal as little as possible until at last they came to trust each other. The event that pushed them over the edge, from talk to action, was that fool Hitler's invasion of Russia! Then, his refusal to fall back at the approach of winter.

Can't the man read history? Even mighty Napoleon came to a bloody, humiliating end in the Russian snows; what makes the "little corporal" think he'll do any better? "General Winter conquers all" was the Russian slogan, and not without much truth.

One of the conspirators, Dr. Heinz Ottoman, was an octogenarian widower.

"Come," he told them, "let's use my parlor; we can play at bridge as a camouflage. That way, if we meet every week, there is evidence in the score sheets of our innocent games!" So they began to gather, and discuss how Hitler could be removed. And they actually played bridge.

Hiding behind the ruse of the card game, they began to analyze the problem. "I don't see how we could poison him," said their thoughtful farmer, Johann Schmitt, "he has an official taster; that's a poor fellow, to say nothing of the SS watching every stir of a spoon."

"No, that won't do," said Vernor Stroebel, former Bürgermeister [mayor] of a nearby small town. "And, it would be equally difficult to shoot him – to use a pistol, one would have to be nearly at his side."

"And the SS would swallow you up before the gun was out of your pocket!" interrupted Schmitt, clinching his fist to demonstrate.

"True. To use a rife would be almost as bad, I think," interjected von Stauffenberg.

"Those long range shooters? What are they called? Ah! Heckenschüte [snipers]! What about one of those rifles?" asked Warren Housner, who had been forced out of retirement to work as a pharmacist.

"These are impossible to obtain, and their ammunition is special. We would reveal ourselves just trying to get them. Not a workable idea," von Stauffenberg summarized.

They thought in silence and continued the game.

"Well, then what about some sort of a bomb? Couldn't we do that?" said Schmitt. He played his card.

"If we did build a bomb, how would it be placed?" said Stroebel.

"This is something that I could do," von Stauffenberg said quietly. "I have been assigned as General Hoepner's aide, the cold hearted Nazi pig. Because of him, I have been in the same room with Hitler on several occasions. What sort of bomb?"

The discussion went far afield that night, with no conclusion. They agreed to consider it, and continue the next time.

Two weeks later

"Let's use one of the captured British bombs – the timers are silent, not like a ticking clock," said Bürgermeister Stroebel, looking at the cards in his hand. A number of British-made time bombs, using acid triggers, had been taken from captured partisans.

"Two problems with that," said a man who had been mostly silent to this point, "they are very hard to obtain, and they are unreliable; we need to be sure the fuse will work."

"You know this how—?" Stroebel asked.

"I am a policeman, do you forget? They have warned us about these devices, the SS, and told us to leave them alone – even some SS ordnance disposal men have died, trying to disarm them. No, we need something from the Army." He played his card, took the trick, and looked at von Stauffenberg.

"No. Not military explosives – they are watched far too carefully. What we need is some sort of, say, mining explosives, something like that," von Stauffenberg said.

"Because of my farms, I have some good Swedish dynamite," Schmitt offered quietly, "how much do we need?"

"Better too much than too little –six sticks."

"So then, a dynamite bomb. We need detonators as well – can you get those?" Schmitt nodded silently.

At their next meeting, the discussion continued.

"What would we use as a timer?" asked Housner. "We dare not use a clock; the noise would give it away."

"I know an old clockmaker, who is sympathetic to our cause; perhaps he could make us a timer from a Swiss watch, or so; they run quietly, and we could wrap it in cotton to muffle what sound it does make," the policeman said.

"How would we make it into a timer?" asked the Bürgermeister.

"I think – perhaps the clock maker could attach electrical contacts to the hour and minute hands, then set it to, say, ten minutes to noon. When the contacts touch, an electrical spark goes to a detonator and so goes the bomb."

"So. And how would one set this clever timer going? I can't reach into my briefcase and set a watch!" von Stauffenberg said, miming with his hand a clumsy man setting a watch. There were chuckles.

"I have a thought," Dr. Ottoman, whose passion was wood working, told them. "Look at this." He turned over a score sheet and quickly sketched a wooden box that would hold the watch, and then drew a simple lever which would press against the stem of the watch. "You see, a short, stiff wire attached to the lever, and going up inside the briefcase can be pulled, starting the watch. The action would be as if you were reaching inside for a paper." A murmur of agreement greeted the idea.

"Destroy that score sheet," von Stauffenberg said.

Within two weeks, the initially reluctant clockmaker had fashioned an old watch to work as a timer. Several tests using a flashlight bulb as a substitute for the detonator convinced them the idea would work.

At their next card game, their wood worker proudly showed them his handiwork "Look at this!" He had changed the wooden box to a simple piece of white pine a centimeter and a half thick; on each end were three groves to hold the dynamite sticks and detonators.

"Here in the center, just so, the watch fits, the lever pivots on this brass rod, and the trigger wire goes out through the top. The batteries fit into this cavity, and the wires route along the notch, here."

He continued, "A flat cardboard panel, covered with grey felt, matching the inside of the briefcase covers it." He set the panel and pine slab in place. "The trigger wire is hidden in the lining of the briefcase; a slit in the seam permits access. Anyone looking inside the briefcase would see exactly what they expect – the bottom of the case," he finished.

Von Stauffenberg carefully performed some more tests, again using the flashlight bulb, convincing them again that the device would work. "This will do nicely," he said nodding. The doctor beamed.

"Should we really use all six sticks of dynamite?" asked the mayor.

"Let's be sure we get the job done," von Stauffenberg insisted firmly "God help us if we only wound him." They nodded in grim agreement.

Their weapon prepared, they now had to seek out the time and place to best use it. Several weeks passed.

"We have our opportunity," Oberst von Stauffenberg, newly promoted to Colonel, told them. "There is to be a conference in the Russian woods – what foolishness! – where Hitler will meet and 'confer' with his generals. General Hoepner will attend, and I am to brief the Führer myself, on recruitment and training issues. Well, my friends, I shall do my best. I have arranged for a telephone call to take me from the meeting, at which time I'll set the timer," he said. "If we don't see each other again, God be with you all." They all murmured solemn goodbyes.

Chapter 15

29 March 1943

London, England

1700 Hours

Göring's Demise

"This is the BBC. The Prime Minister's office at Number 10 Downing Street have informed us that the Reichminister of the Third Reich and Chief of the Luftwaffe Herman Wilhiem Göring has been killed in the crash of a light aircraft. The location and the precise circumstances of the crash have not been announced. Neither was there any indication as to whether the crash may have been the result of combat with Allied aircraft.

"It has been widely assumed that the Reichminister was to have been the successor to Chancellor Hitler in the event of the latter's demise; it is not clear to whom that honor will now fall. In addition, speculation is rife as to who might follow him as head of the German Luftwaffe, but no announcement has been made as of the time of this broadcast.

"In further news on the European front,—"

Chapter 16

7 April 1943

Millville Army Air Field

Millville, New Jersey

Base Theater, Building 68

0730 Hours

Commander's Call

There was a low buzz of conversation as the officers waited for the meeting to begin.

Base commander Lieutenant Colonel Tarleton H. Watkins called his officers together regularly to pass down the latest news from the Army Chief of Staff, and to discuss the problems or achievements of their units.

The door at the rear opened with deliberate noise, and First Sergeant Blaisdel shouted "Atten-shun!" The men sprang to their feet at attention, almost by reflex, conversations ended mid-word. The Colonel strode to the front, looked at his men for a moment, then commanded, "At ease. Be seated, gentlemen."

Taking his place behind a wooden lectern, he began to systematically address each of the items on the list that First Sergeant Blaisdel had prepared. Most of the information was old hat, things they had all heard through the grapevine days before.

"It's possible that General Ernst Udet may take over Göring's place; that's not good news for the Allies because he has a pretty fair understanding of modern air tactics, unlike fat Herbert. The bomber commander, General Weaver, is pushing for a major expansion; Intel is that he'll probably get it. He's got the Brits plenty worried."

Listening with half an ear, Major Joel Knight was mentally reviewing a duty roster issue he needed to resolve.

"Finally, gentlemen, as you know, the Third Bond Drive is officially underway, and we're going to do another round of 'penny' bond drives at the local schools."

"Penny bonds" was how Watkins characterized the bonds bought with the pennies, nickels, and dimes contributed by school kids. Generally, not a lot of money was raised this way, but it served two useful purposes: it gave the kids a sense of participation in the war effort, and it was good publicity for the Army to be out among the citizens. The comment was greeted with some groans and muttered comments, which the Colonel silenced with a single glance over the top of his reading glasses.

"This time, we'll do it differently – instead of your senior non-coms, I want each squadron commander and his deputy to take a school. As it turns out, the number of elementary and junior high schools nearby neatly matches the number of commanders and deputies, so nobody gets left out! First Sergeant Blaisdel has the assignments. We've already announced this to the newspapers, so you're on the hook. And unless you're on your deathbed, nobody is skipping out on this! We've got War Department movies for each of you to show – they run about ten minutes, and then you'll convince the kiddies that the war will grind to a halt without every one of their pennies."

After he answered a few questions, the sergeant again called the room to attention, and the Colonel departed.

"Sirs, if you will kindly come forward with your deputies, I'll give you your school assignment."

"Blaisdel, I see your grubby mitts all over this!" a squadron commander growled.

"Why, sir, whatever *do* you mean?" Blaisdel responded with such feigned innocence and fluttering eyelashes that they all laughed.

Joel shuffled forward and received his "assignment": Alexander Hamilton Junior High, in Stanton Township. He knew the town; it was five or six miles from the base, on the winding rural roads in this part of New Jersey. He had the address, directions from the base, and the principle's name and phone number. His assigned date was a week from Wednesday, which he knew conflicted with his monthly currency flight. *Well, that won't be the first time that had to be changed.*

When he returned to his office, he called the principle of Alexander Hamilton Junior High School. Mr. Theodore Kneebone seemed a kindly man, though his slightly quavering voice betrayed his age even over the phone.

"I would be delighted to have a squadron commander address my students, Major Knight," he said. They agreed on the time, and Joel made a note in his daily schedule, making sure to tell his sergeant. Joel discussed his idea of offering a prize for the best class participation, and the older man agreed enthusiastically.

Chapter 17

12 April 1943

Alexander Hamilton Junior High School

Stanton Township, New Jersey

0730 Hours

Bond Drive

Joel left early in the freshly washed and waxed Packard, partly because he wasn't completely sure of the way, but truthfully, because he hated being late anywhere. That was one of the things they pounded into you at the Academy. Besides, it was a good excuse to drive his "new" car. He had chosen his freshly cleaned dress uniform, with green blouse and "pink" trousers. He carefully aligned his ribbons on the left breast of the blouse, and put a shiny pair of wings above them. His service cap, of course, had that calculated, crumpled look resulting from wearing radio headphones; no Army pilot worth his salt would think of wearing anything else!

He was nearly to the Stanton Township city limits when he heard a siren; a motorcycle cop. Dutifully, Joel pulled over, expecting to see the motorcycle go around him. *Now what*, he wondered.

The cop was middle-aged, and not smiling.

"Where's your gas ration sticker, Bud?" he demanded.

Joel glanced at the windshield; yes, the little sign was still there. He pulled it off, and handed it to the officer.

"Official Government Business, officer," he said smiling.

The cop seemed to suddenly realize Joel was in uniform, "Oh, sorry, sir. I didn't see your sign. Where are you headed?"

"I'm giving a speech at Alexander Hamilton Junior High, if I can find it," Joel said.

"Just follow me, Major," the cop said, smiling now, "I'll escort you."

Off they went, the siren on the motorcycle wailing.

Oh, great; they'll either think it's an emergency, or that somebody important is coming, he groused .

The cop got him to the school ten minutes early, and he pulled into the parking lot. The cop waved, and motored off. The school was one of those imposing stone structures built in the early 1900s, whose very look conveyed seriousness. These days, though, it had an old-fashioned sense of weariness about it.

He couldn't help noticing that there were few cars in the parking lot, and those that were there were older, inexpensive models. There was even a Model T sedan. There were kids playing on the athletic field – *it must be recess*, he thought. They stopped their games and stared at the Packard.

They must think I'm a big shot or something, with that police escort, Joel thought.

Inside, Mr. Kneebone greeted him warmly. He was in his late seventies, with a white ring of hair around the back of his head. He was slightly stooped over, making his five foot, six inch height seem shorter. His gray eyes were clear, and full of intelligence.

Joel noticed that his tweedy suit was years out of date, giving him a slightly rumpled look, and his wide, bright tie *might* have been in style in the 1920s. A lot of older men like him had been called out of retirement to take the place of draftees. Kneebone introduced him to the ladies of the office staff. While they spoke, Joel heard a bell ring, ending recess, he decided. He showed Mr. Kneebone the film can and asked about a projector, and someone to run it. Kneebone quickly dispatched a student to bring the school projectionist to the auditorium.

"Well, it's time, I'm afraid. This way, if you please, Major," the principal said, looking at the oak schoolhouse clock. They walked down the hallway which glowed with old polished wood on the floors and lower walls.

As Joel and the principle walked onto the wooden stage, he saw students being led into the big room by their teachers. Many were middle-aged ladies, who hurried their charges along with self-important authority. Here and there, though, Joel saw younger women.

In the two years I've been in New Jersey, seems like all I see are peroxide blondes or brunettes. No red heads, he thought idly. *And I can't stand the peroxide blondes – they always look so phony; aren't there any natural blondes around here?*

As the classes came in, he abruptly noticed one young woman who clearly *was* a natural blonde – even standing on stage, he could see her strikingly blue eyes; her complexion was clear and white. Where the older women looked somewhat frumpy, she was wearing a crisp, starched white blouse and a stylish blue wool skirt.

For an instant, she looked right at him and smiled, showing perfect, white teeth. Joel felt an electric shock. Time seemed to stop, then she looked away. Joel realized he'd been holding his breath.

*Well, now! I've gotta find out who **she** is!* he said to himself, surprised at his own reaction.

The 300 youngsters seemed to be glad for the time away from their studies, but some appeared to be interested in what Joel might have to say.

Mr. Kneebone clapped his hands loudly, twice, "Quiet, please!" The murmur of voices and scuffling feet quickly faded away.

"Children, today we have a speaker from Millville Army Air Field, who is going to show us a brief movie, then speak to us all about the new Third Bond drive. He is a pilot and squadron commander there. Please welcome U.S. Army Air Forces Major Joel Knight."

The applause was polite. After thanking them, Joel gave a brief introduction to the film, and asked for it to be run. It differed little from most War Department films – it was both uninspired and unimaginative. Thankfully, it was also mercifully short. The kids were restless, especially toward the end, and he knew he'd have his hands full convincing them to contribute. He hoped the little prize he'd cooked up would help.

"OK, thank you for your attention, boys and girls," he began. "This Third Bond Drive will be a lot like the other ones, but this time, there will be a special prize. We'll talk about that later. First, I'd like to answer any questions you have."

There was a short silence, and then one of the younger boys raised his hand. Joel pointed at him, "Yes, sir, what would you like to know?"

"You don't talk like us, Major; where're you from?" The distinctive New Jersey accent pervaded even the simple question.

"Well sir, I was born and raised out West, in Colorado." Now he had their attention; in this era, few had been outside their own state, and none had ever been west of the Mississippi.

"Were you a cowboy?" the same youngster asked, somewhat in awe.

Joel chuckled; "Well, sir, I was raised on a ranch, but my dad never thought I was much good at wrangling cows!"

Joel knew that cowboys and the West fascinated most of the kids and they all followed the adventures of their favorite cowboy in the movies or on the radio. Even the older, more "sophisticated" kids were listening now.

"So, where's your ranch, and what's your brand?" asked a serious looking boy, testing him.

"It's my dad's ranch, son. It's about twenty miles from the small town of Calhan, north-east of Colorado Springs. Our brand is a capital K with a knight's lance on the end of the upright on the K, setting on a rocker; we call it the Rocking K."

"Do you have a horse?" a girl asked eagerly.

"Oh, yes. Or I should say, I used to. I'm afraid he died. Raised him from a colt. He was a nice little paint."

"What was his name?" shouted another boy.

Joel looked down at the floor and laughed a little. "Well, sir, you're going to laugh at this. I mean, I didn't think about a good name like Trigger, or Tony, or Silver. When my dad gave him to me, I was about ten, and at the time, well, I was really fascinated with a neighbor's old steam car."

"Oh, no, you didn't name him Stanley!" a boy shouted.

Shaking his head, Joel admitted it. "Yes, sir, I named him Stanley!" The room erupted with laughter. "Stanley, the horse!"

1010 Hours

The Prize

Standing along the wall, Susan Johansseson listened carefully to the handsome Army officer. He was slender, tall and had a quiet sense of self-confidence about him. His hair was short, and looked like it might have been blonde before it changed to the light brown she saw.

He has a special way with the kids, she thought. *He's respectfully answered every question, even called the kids "sir" or "ma'am." It's plain that he likes kids and they are responding to him unusually well. His sense of humor is self-deprecating; what a refreshing change from the egotistical pilots I've met before. How interesting; a man who isn't one-dimensional. And he's not a kid,* she thought, *remembering the twenty-year-old pilots she'd met.*

The questions from the kids quickly covered what sorts of cowboy activities he'd done.

"I have 'rodeoed' some," he told another girl. "I tried bucking broncos, and got tossed right off, I'll tell you! In the kid classes, I did pretty well in steer wrestling; truth be told though, they were really calves! I was always a pretty good rider, so I tried barrel racing – do you know what barrel racing is?" The number of "no's" told him he'd need to explain, which he did.

"Did you win?" another child asked.

"No, I got beat, and would you believe, I got beat by the girls! Boy, they can really ride!" That brought another bout of laughter, especially from the girls.

"What airplanes do you fly?" asked another boy.

"Thanks for that question, sir! Our unit trains new pilots how to shoot targets on the ground and in the air. Right now, we mostly fly P-40 Warhawks, like the Flying Tigers in China. We're beginning to get the new Republic P-47 Thunderbolt."

"Is it hard to fly a plane?" asked a shy looking girl near the front.

Joel leaned toward her conspiratorially, his hand beside his mouth, "Nah, it's really easy! But don't tell anybody, 'cause they'll stop paying me so much to do it!" he winked at her. The students laughed.

"When did you learn to fly?" asked a bright-eyed boy.

"Well, sir, you might be surprised to know that I learned to fly when I was just a youngster, not a lot older than you. A neighbor was a pilot during the Great War. He bought a brand new war surplus JN-4D Jenny airplane in a crate. Cost him all of $500, and he got an extra engine to boot! Do you all know what a Jenny is?" Most of the kids nodded.

"He offered to take me up, and I loved it. I asked him to teach me to fly. I soloed two weeks after my sixteenth birthday."

"Did the Army make you learn to fly again?"

"Yes, they did! My civilian experience meant nothing to them, although it gave me an advantage over my classmates. I soloed at Randolph Field, in Texas. And it was just as exciting as when I did it at home."

The easy banter went on for several minutes.

Finally, Mr. Kneebone stepped forward and held up his hand "Now, children, that's enough questions for the Major. Let's have him tell us about the prize he mentioned earlier."

1022 Hours

Kids and Joel

Joel grinned at the audience, his hands on his hips. "How many have ever flown in an airplane?" he asked. In the whole auditorium, only two hands went up. Anticipation filled the room.

"How many would like to fly in an *Army* airplane?" Virtually every hand shot into the air.

"I thought so! Now, here's the story. I talked my Colonel into letting me borrow his airplane; it's a brand new Beechcraft C-45 Expediter – that's a beautiful twin engine light transport with two tails like a B-25, which can carry about six people. Each teacher and her class will compete to see who can raise the most money by a week from Friday. But! It has to be coins, and it has to be your own money – no fair asking Mom or Dad!" He shook his finger at them, smiling.

"To make it fair, we'll limit each student to a maximum of fifty cents each. And, as a tie breaker, we'll also do a scrap drive. We'll take iron, steel, aluminum, rubber, newspapers, rags, all the normal things. The homeroom teacher whose class raises the most money *and* the most scrap by weight by the end of the school day a week from this Friday, will win a thirty minute ride in the C-45 for herself and a boy and a girl of her choice.

"The *Millville Daily Republican* newspaper will be there to take your picture, and so will the *Millville Army Air Field* newspaper! We'll fly over each child's house, and then over the schoolyard so you can all watch! What do you think?"

There was instant bedlam as excited students shouted their approval. Mr. Kneebone beamed; he had assured Joel that they'd raise more cash this time than last, even if it was coins, and it would clearly be a morale booster for the student body. The scrap drive was something he had suggested to Joel at the last minute – not all these kids or their parents had even a couple of quarters to throw around, but everybody had scrap to contribute.

Susan Johansseson followed all of this with careful attention, smiling at the reactions of the children. She was impressed with a pilot who wasn't so full of himself, and who interacted with kids so well. He spoke to them, not down at them.

What a clever approach. The kids are all so enthusiastic about flying. He handles children so well. And what an interesting background! Wouldn't it be fascinating, she thought, *to hear more about Hawaii? He was there before Pearl Harbor, it must have been beautiful. I think my class will work a little extra hard at this contest.*

Chapter 18

26 April 1943

Alexander Hamilton Junior High School

Stanton Township, New Jersey

1000 Hours

Bond Drive Competition

In two weeks, the kids collected an amazing amount of money and scrap; most of the money was pennies. A teacher carefully looked through them, just in case someone might have slipped in a valuable coin, intentionally or otherwise. After all the previous scrap drives, it was amazing that there were still worn out tires, old pots and pans, several antique cast iron flat irons, and lots of flattened tin cans. One kid even found a rusty old car fender to drag in; it must have been buried in a field, it had so much mud on it. He looked disappointed when Mr. Kneebone made him knock off the mud, "We're collecting steel, Tommy, not mud!"

The township provided a portable scale, and the local scrap collector was drafted as the official weigher. The whole school gathered around to watch. A reporter from the *Stanton Township Weekly Gazette* snapped some photographs for next week's edition.

The old scrap collector had a pencil stub stuck behind his hairy ear which he snatched down to record each object's weight on a thick, yellow tablet. Each class had a separate page. A murmur went through the crowd of kids when an old cast iron stationary engine block was lifted onto the scale, accompanied by a mighty grunt from the old man. It was by far the heaviest object– it weighed almost 100 pounds! The kids looked back and forth among themselves – who snuck this in? The old man finished weighing, and gave the sheets to Mr. Kneebone for totaling. The principal in turn handed the sheets to prim Miss Farley, the old maid math teacher, who was visibly pleased to be recognized.

Minutes passed, the kids murmuring among themselves, and at last Miss Farley finished her task, adjusted her thick eyeglasses, and handed the sheets back to Mr. Kneebone. He looked at them, making little noises as he saw the totals.

"Well, well, boys and girls, we have a winner! Do you want to know which class it is?" The children roared "Yes!" back at him. He beamed, and cleared his throat.

"All together, we have collected $111.07 in cash to buy War Bonds, and it's amazing, but we have collected more than 1,200 pounds of scrap!"

"Who's the winner?" someone yelled.

Mr. Kneebone was chagrined at having to be reminded; "The winner, at $17.13 and 233 pounds, is – Miss Johansseson's class!" The cheers from her class drowned out the groans of the other classes.

Mr. Kneebone called Joel that same day, "Major Knight, I am pleased to tell you that we had wonderful success with our Scrap drive – the children collected 1207 pounds of scrap, and more than one hundred dollars in cash. The winning class was Miss Johansseson's. I will contact you again as soon as she has chosen the students to fly with you."

The following Tuesday, he called again to tell Joel that they had chosen two youngsters, and all they needed from him was to know when he could make arrangements for the airplane.

Chapter 19

8 May 1943

Millville Army Air Field

0815 Hours

Reward Flight and Consequences

The Saturday morning dawned bright and clear, a perfect May day. The winners were to meet him at Millville Air Field's main gate at 0830, and he would escort them to the flight line. Mr. Kneebone again told him the winning teacher's name, and that of the two children accompanying her, but her name didn't register. Passes had been arranged for all, so there should be no problems getting on base.

Joel had explained, "You'll need to dress warmly, it's cold at high altitude. You don't have to dress up formally like you would to fly in a civilian airliner; this will be casual. Bring binoculars, and cameras too, if you wish."

Joel decided to drive the squadron's staff car, a 1941 Plymouth sedan, to pick them up. *I might need the room, if the teacher is one of the more portly ladies.*

There was a small parking area just outside the main gate, where visitors and vendors could park to obtain their credentials. They were to meet him there. The entrance was guarded by a small hut in the center of the road, splitting the incoming and outgoing traffic. A heavy steel gate was rolled back on each side, ready to be moved into place at a moment's notice.

He drove through the outgoing side, and turned left to park. As he did, he saw two civilian cars, and a somewhat battered Model A Ford pickup truck. *Looks like they're waiting for me!*

As he parked, he saw a tall, slender woman standing by one of the cars; her blonde hair spilled out below a colorful scarf, her features hidden behind dark sun glasses. She was wearing very fashionable dark blue slacks and a puffy-shouldered cream colored blouse. On her arm was a folded, light blue jacket. As he got out of the staff car, the doors to the other car and the pickup opened; both children also had jackets.

Walking up to the young woman, he was pleasantly surprised to realize she was the blonde he'd seen at the school. He tried to cover his surprise by offering his hand, "Good morning! I'm Major Joel Knight."

She removed her sunglasses with her left hand and shook his hand firmly, looking straight at him – her eyes were an incredible blue, full of intelligence.

Even her eyebrows are blond; she's a real blond, he thought distractedly, but with delight.

"I'm Susan Johansseson, the sixth grade teacher whose class won the free airplane ride." she said evenly, her head slightly cocked. "I'm so pleased to meet you, Major." Her smile was warm and welcoming.

"My pleasure, so nice to meet you," Joel responded, feeling like he should have said something far more witty or profound; strangely, his mouth had gone dry. *Gad, what am I, sixteen again? Man, she's beautiful!*

"Miss Johansseson, would you please introduce me to these young people?" he said, turning to the youngsters, to hide his sudden nervousness.

"Only if you promise to call me Sue" she smiled, flashing perfect white teeth.

"Of course, Sue! And whom have we here?"

"This is Miss Beryl Whitmore. She's here today because she gathered more scrap than anyone else in the class. She also has the highest grades in the entire sixth grade." The girl beamed at him, proud that her teacher was recognizing her, and reached out her hand.

"I'm happy to meet you, sir." she said politely. Turning, she indicated the older woman standing at her side. "Mother, please meet Major Knight. Major Knight, this is my mother, Mrs. Whitmore." The girl was a younger version of her mother, both of them pretty with intelligent eyes, curly dark hair, and clear complexions. Joel shook her mother's hand, noting the look of concern in her eyes as she smiled at him. She turned to an elderly gentleman standing behind her. "This is Mr. Carlyle, our neighbor, who drove us here. We don't own an automobile."

"Pleased to meet you, sir; thank you for your kindness," Joel shook his hand.

The old fellow put his pipe back in his mouth, and nodded.

The young man stepped up; "Sir, I'm Elmer McDonnell, Jr., and this is my father, Mr. Elmer McDonnell, Sr."

"Hello, young man." Joel smiled, shaking his offered hand. "Nice to meet you, sir," he said to the big man in bib overalls. McDonnell, Sr., was in his early forties, and looked the Scot he was: big, ham fisted, ruddy faced. Joel wondered, *How can a man this large fit inside the tiny confines of a Model A Ford pickup?*

"How safe is this aeroplane ye propose to take my son flying in?" Senior asked bluntly, with a brogue.

Joel liked a direct man.

"It's as safe as they make them, sir." he replied firmly. "I've flown it, and it's like a Cadillac with wings. The Army and Navy have bought hundreds of them, and so have the British and the Canadians," he continued. "There are two good engines for safety, it's all metal, and it's as modern as science can make it."

The sturdy man looked unconvinced. "How often do they crash, sonny?" he queried.

"Only once," Joel deadpanned, hoping his risk of humor would pay off. The big Scot looked at him silently, then broke into guffaws, slapping his leg. His son and the others joined him in laughter.

Joel turned to the girl's mother. "Have you any concerns, Mrs. Whitmore?"

"Oh, why, yes; yes, I suppose I do," she said, wringing her hands, her voice a little high pitched. "Do you keep it fixed up, and put enough gas in it? I mean—" she trailed off, embarrassed.

"Oh, yes ma'am," Joel said gently. "We take real good care of this airplane – it's Colonel Watkins', who flies down to Washington, D.C. He'd be very unhappy if it wasn't kept in tip-top shape. And please understand this, too, Ma'am – I've flown over 2,500 hours in the Army, and you don't get to fly that many hours without paying real close attention to the airplane you fly. This is a good, sturdy, reliable airplane."

She still looked a bit unconvinced.

"Ma'am, I would fly my own mother in this airplane, it's that safe." She smiled at that, more at ease now.

He looked at his watch. "Now, we need to go, so we can depart on time. The four of us will meet you back here at about 11:30, and we'll all go have lunch at the Officer's Club, my treat. Is that agreeable?" The parents reluctantly nodded, and went to their vehicles. Joel escorted Susan to the front seat of the Plymouth, and held the door for her.

Oh, nice perfume! he though as she moved past him and sat on the seat. He then held the door for the girl. Junior let himself in the back seat on the other side. Reaching over the seat, he handed them a paper name badge and a safety pin.

"Please pin these to your shirt or blouse, and leave them there until we leave the base, OK?" The children agreed. He handed one to the young woman beside him "You'll need one too, Sue." She smiled and pinned it to her blouse. It was centered and absolutely level on the first try.

How do women do that? Joel wondered to himself.

He drove to the gate and the waiting guard. The young MP snapped to attention, and saluted sharply.

"Thank you, Private. These people are with me, and I vouch for them."

"Thank you, sir." the man replied, and waved them through the gate. Behind them, Mrs. Whitmore looked wistfully after her daughter. McDonnell's Model A truck clattered off toward home; there was work to do.

They drove through the base, watching troops marching and busy work details. Soon they drove onto the flight line. The boy was craning his head every which way, looking at the parked airplanes.

"Those are P-40 Tomahawks," he announced authoritatively, "and two P-47 Thunderbolts!"

"Wow, look at those neat guns."

The girl seemed intimidated by the size and harsh reality of the war planes. Susan – Sue, he noted, was taking it all in with little visible reaction.

The C-45 was polished aluminum, with Colonel Watkins' name in blue over the door. Joel turned to the children, "Please stay with me, and don't touch anything."

A Technical Sergeant in green fatigues walked around the nose of the airplane, wiping his hands on a rag. He saluted and greeted Joel with, "Good morning, Major Knight! Are these our lucky winners?"

"Indeed, they are, Mike." He turned to Sue and introduced her.

"Sue, this is Technical Sergeant Mike Rogers. He's the crew chief for this airplane. That means he's responsible for making sure the Colonel's plane is always in great shape. Mike, please meet Miss Johansseson."

"Hello, Ma'am. How are you?" he asked, nodding his head. She returned his greeting and offered her hand. Mike held his hands out to the side.

"Ma'am, I've got hydraulic fluid on my hands – please forgive me if I don't shake your hand. It's nasty stuff to get out of clothes." Her eyes widened a bit, and she thanked him for his courtesy. Joel turned to the youngsters.

"Mike, this is Miss Beryl Whitmore and Mr. Elmer McDonnell, Jr., our student winners. Better watch 'em! They're smarter than the two of us put together!" Mike chuckled, and nodded hello.

Joel turned to the three. "Now, even though Mike has done his usual outstanding job getting this ship ready for us to fly, I'm going to do what we call a 'walk around' inspection, and I'd like you to follow me."

Starting at the left wing root next to the fuselage, he slowly walked counterclockwise around the aircraft, touching, looking, explaining what he was inspecting, and what he was looking for.

Susan thought, *He doesn't speak down to the children, and answers even their silly questions. He's being so careful. It was nice that he treated that enlisted man so respectfully.*

As they finished the last check on the left hand wing flap, having walked completely around the airplane, they were met by another Sergeant, the base photographer. He lined them up and took pictures with his big Speed Graphic camera. He checked when they were to return, and promised to meet them for more photos. He mentioned that the photographer from the *Millville Daily Republican* newspaper would be there as well.

Joel turned to his three passengers.

"Miss Johansseson, I'd like you to enter first, and go all the way up to the cockpit, and sit in the right seat. Miss Whitmore, please take the front seat on the right, behind your teacher, and Mr. McDonnell, the seat across from her."

Joel could tell that Susan was surprised at how nice the interior was; she looked all around, touching the seats. The light brown leather chairs had starched white napkins across their headrests. In the center of the cabin was a small table, folded against the left wall. Each window had starched curtains and the floor was carpeted. They all climbed up the sloping floor, and took their seats. The boy gawked at the instrument panel. "Wow! Look at all the clocks!" Beryl quickly informed him that only one was a clock.

Joel had closed and locked the cabin door, and heard the exchange as he entered the cockpit. "Actually, Beryl, there *are* two clocks, one for the pilot, the other for the copilot." He pointed them out to her.

He sat in the left seat, and carefully explained each instrument and control, and its purpose, answering their questions. Then, he showed them how to fasten their seat belts, something none of them had ever done before.

"Is everyone ready?" he asked. "Now, here's what we'll do. I'll start engine number one first – that's the one on the left wing. When it's running smoothly, I'll start number two, on the right side. Once they are both running smoothly, we'll taxi out to the end of the runway. There, I'll test the engines – we call it a 'run up'– to make sure they're OK. It'll be pretty loud, and the plane will shake – but, that's all right. Then, we'll move out onto the runway. When the tower says it's OK, the motors will get real loud and we'll start rolling down the runway. In a few seconds, the tail will take off, and the plane will be level. We'll accelerate really fast then, and when we're going fast enough – about eighty-five miles an hour, we'll take off."

He saw the eyes of both children widen at the thought of going so fast.

"During our climb, you'll want to look out the windows. I'll circle around the base so you can see it, then we'll go over toward Stanton Township. Elmer, your dad told me where your farm is, and we'll go there first. Then, we'll fly over Beryl's house, and finally, over the school. Before we come back, I'll take us out over the ocean so you can see what that looks like from the air. Any questions?" There were none.

The tail-wagging taxi made both children laugh; Joel explained that it was the only way he could see over the raised nose. They still thought it was funny. The run-up was uneventful, and Joel taxied onto the runway. The tower flashed a green light at them, and Joel moved the throttles forward.

Both kids got very wide-eyed at the noise, though Joel couldn't see them. Beryl gripped the armrest of her seat as if it was the only thing that could save her. Elmer had a smile a mile wide on his freckled face. The silver airplane lifted off smoothly, and climbed into the morning sky, with teacher and children alike totally enthralled.

They had taken off into the wind, toward the northwest, over farmland below.

Chapter 20
8 May 1943
Off the Northwest Corner of Runway 190
Near Millville Army Air Field
0815 Hours
Renaldo Giovanni

Renaldo Giovanni had farmed this land on the northwest end of the runway for nearly forty-five years, like his father and grandfather before him. He raised a few pigs and cows, but made a pretty good living from his nut orchards and excellent vegetables. When the War Department came to him, they had attempted to buy his best orchards to build their silly airport on. He shrewdly had redirected them to the part of his property they eventually bought.

That ground is the poorest on the farm, he thought triumphantly, *and they still paid me top dollar, the fools.*

Not everything went his way, though, as one of the runways did encroach on some of his trees. They paid him extra to remove the trees for something they called an "overrun," and told him he was never to make use of the land for any purpose.

Even though they paid his asking price, the demand to stay off of what he considered his own land rankled. Almost immediately, he had begun dumping the waste from the orchards, fields, and the butchering house into a small dry stream bed a couple of hundred yards off the end of the runway. Twice, he'd received stern letters from the Colonel on the base. Even a visit from the base Provost Marshall left him unimpressed.

This very morning, before sunup, he'd chugged out to the improvised dump on his green Oliver tractor with a trailer load of rotting vegetables and the offal from the six pigs he'd butchered. Even before he got back to the barn, the birds discovered it. Sea gulls, ever vigilant for just this sort of rotting foodstuff were there first. Only slightly later, the vultures arrived, along with a pair of golden eagles.

Chapter 21

8 May 1943

North East Approach to Millville Army Air Field

1017 Hours

And Then Birds

It had been a delight. The flight over the McDonnell farm was fun, the boy whooping when he recognized his mother, shouting as he saw familiar landmarks. He was very excited, all but jumping out of his seat. His father waved back from the seat of his tractor.

Joel missed Beryl's house the first time, but that only brought out more neighbors to watch. The second pass was right over her street at 200 feet; he tipped the right wing down so she could see better, and she all but frantically waved at her mother and friends below. The crowd below waved as wildly back at them. Wagging the wings, Joel turned toward the school.

Many of the students and their parents were waiting on the school's athletic field. Joel saw them at a distance, and flew over first with the left wing down, then a second time with the right wing down. Many waved handkerchiefs at them. A final pass with Joel wagging the wings in salute, and they turned back toward the base.

"We have plenty of fuel and there's time, so let's fly over to the shore," Joel said. He began a gentle climb to about 8,000 feet.

"It's a lot cooler up high, so you'll all want your jackets," he reminded them.

Elmer was searching the scene below with a battered pair of binoculars, while Beryl snapped pictures with her mother's Kodak Brownie camera, carefully winding it between pictures.

In fifteen minutes, they crossed the shoreline, and watched the mesmerizing lines of white surf marching onto the sand.

Through it all, Susan continued watching Joel almost as much as the scenery.

He is very good at this, always looking at the instruments and watching for other airplanes, she decided, *that's very reassuring. He's so confident in the way he handles the airplane. You'd hardly know you were in an airplane, except for the noise. I'm so lucky my very first plane ride was with him.*

Reluctantly, Joel said, "Well, I'm afraid it's time for us to head back." Susan put her hand on his right arm and thanked him. He smiled broadly, then radioed for approach instructions. He was directed to land to the southeast on the same runway they'd taken off from. Both the children and their teacher watched very closely as he slowed the aircraft, then lowered the flaps and landing gear. They looked out the left side as the Army base passed by on the downwind leg of the approach, and then he banked left into the short cross wind leg.

Just as they turned onto final approach, a great mass of birds rushed up from Giovanni's illegal dump. Whether it was the planes' shadow, or the noise of the engines that startled them, the birds leapt off the ground by the hundreds.

1019 Hours

Impact

Joel saw the first bird a split second before it hit the left engine, then there were many. Bang! Bang, bang! The airplane shook with their impacts. A large, dark bird caromed into the left windshield, shattering both panels, splattering blood and feathers. He felt a hard impact on his face, and sharp pains on his left cheek and nose, and almost immediately, blood running down. A split second later, a second large bird hit the windshield in nearly the same place, and Joel was splattered again with broken Plexiglas, blood, feathers and entrails. Behind him, the girl screamed, and Susan said, "Oh, my!" The boy let out a decidedly adult expletive.

Joel's hands were full. He couldn't see out of his left eye. The left engine had nearly stopped and backfired as yet another bird slammed into it. The airplane slewed wildly to the left. The girl screamed again.

Joel's hands flew around the controls, as he slammed the right engine to full power, pulled the feathering control for the left propeller, and corrected for the dead engine. He yanked on the landing gear handle, retracting the wheels, and pulled up the flaps. A glance at the instrument panel: *no fire lights, thank God.*

He yelled into the mic, "Army 6761, bird strike, bird strike! Going around!" The aircraft begin to slowly climb as the remaining engine roared frantically.

"Army 6761, are you declaring an emergency?" the tower queried.

"Roger, 6761 is declaring emergency. We had a bad bird strike. Number one engine is dead; the windshield is shattered and partly blocked. We're going to do a 180 and land down wind."

The tower acknowledged.

"Call out the emergency vehicles, including ambulance," Joel ordered.

Students flying nearby were directed to climb away from the airfield to give the wounded C-45 a wide berth. The silver aircraft slowly climbed to a thousand feet while Joel gingerly checked to make sure they could safely turn. Then, he turned them gently to the right, keeping the dead engine on the outside of the turn. The prop on it was still slowly rotating; apparently, it hadn't fully feathered; that increased the drag a lot. It took all of the rudder he could use to keep the plane straight.

Joel felt Susan's hand firmly on his arm, breaking his concentration; she was handing him a hanky.

"Put this on your nose," she told him. He did.

Joel glanced over his shoulder at Beryl, who was white-faced and beginning to cry. When she saw his bloody face, her eyes widened even more in fear.

"Are we going to crash?" she asked in a small voice he could barely hear.

Joel winked at her with his good right eye.

"Nope; what do you see there on the right wing?"

"The other motor," she said weakly.

"That's right, sweetheart, that big, beautiful engine is going to get us home just fine!" She looked a little relieved, and wiped away her tears.

"Now, listen, all of you," Joel shouted over the roaring engine; "when we land, there is a chance, just a chance, that the left landing gear might collapse. If it does, we'll tip over to that side and slide on the wingtip. That's OK, we can handle that. As soon as we come to a stop – *wait 'till we stop!* I want you, Elmer, to run down the aisle and open the door – make sure there's no fire, then run as fast as you can away from the plane. If there is a fire, yell at us, and come back up here, and we'll get out the cockpit windows. Understand?" The boy nodded vigorously.

"Beryl, you be right behind him. Susan, help either of them if they need it. Everybody understand? Tighten your seatbelts as I showed you."

They nodded numbly and did as he said. The aircraft finished its turn, and they were facing down the runway they'd just flown over.

"6761, on final; get those fire trucks out there!"

Susan was frightened, but still marveled at his calm, his professionalism.

Even in this strange emergency, he knows exactly what to do! He doesn't seem frightened at all. What marvelous self-control. Oh, God, please watch over us.

Joel was sweating, knuckles white on the control wheel, and praying hard himself, for the first time in a long time. The wind through the broken windshield was frigidly cold.

Oh Lord, please don't let me hurt these innocent little kids; please help me get this thing safe on the ground!

Gritting his teeth, he forced himself to fly the airplane and stay ahead of it, blinking away the blood in his left eye. Susan's handkerchief was shoved unceremoniously up his left nostril; it still bled. He could feel the heat of his blood down his shirt front. What windshield was left on his side was mostly obscured by all the blood and the cracks in the Plexiglas. The very cold breeze blowing on his face through the jagged holes was making his right eye water. To see the runway clearly, he awkwardly skidded the airplane to look out the windshield on Susan's side. Behind him, Beryl audibly gasped. He lowered the landing gear again, and noted with relief the two green bars on the instrument panel: both down and locked. He kept the power up on the engine as he lowered the flaps, then slowly retarded the throttle and they began sinking toward the runway.

"Hold on tight!" he shouted.

He counted *one, two, three*, as they crossed the runway threshold, and then pulled the power back some more. He was going to do a wheel landing rather than a three point landing, to maintain control as long as possible. Some sage had opined that if you have to crash, the smartest thing to do is to fly the airplane as far into the crash as possible. Joel planned to do exactly that.

The tires squawked lightly as they touched down, one of the best landings he'd ever done in this plane. He held the tail up as long as possible, and then it sank when they were too slow. Gently, he tried the brakes, unsure if the ones on the left side would work – if it didn't, they'd swerve to the right. They held, and he began braking hard, the brakes squealing, the tires smoking. He eased up just as they stopped, to prevent a nose over.

"*Now*, Elmer!" he shouted, as he shut down the engine. The kid was out of his seat in a flash, and raced down the short aisle. In seconds, he'd opened the door.

"No fire!" he shouted over his shoulder in a high pitched voice, then disappeared. Beryl didn't need a second invitation; she was right behind him. Susan was a bit slower, but still moved very quickly, glancing back at him in concern. Joel slammed off the master caution switch, turning off all aircraft power, and dived after her.

1021 Hours

On the Ground

Joel didn't notice the two newspaper men snapping photos as he stepped out of the airplane, unaware that his face and jacket were covered with blood and worse. He saw Susan and the children huddled on the side of the runway, crying.

Thank you, Lord! I've gotta see what happened.

He headed toward the nose of the airplane. Tendrils of stinking, acrid smoke were rising out of the left engine, the scorched feathers of some unidentifiable bird still burning on the hot cylinders. Several push rod covers were bent, spark plug wires were torn loose, and oil was dripping everywhere, smoking as it hit the hot exhaust manifold. Several pieces of the cast iron cylinder fins were broken off, and the cowling was heavily dented in several places. One prop blade had clearly taken a hit too. When he looked at the windshield, his knees went weak.

"Dear God! Did we hit an entire flock?"

Not only were both panes of the Plexiglas windshield on the left side shattered, but the aluminum nose cone was dented in. Most of the front of the airplane was covered with drying blood, feathers, and entrails.

An ambulance attendant pulled on his arm, "Probably seagulls, sir, or maybe a golden eagle. There's been a pair hanging out at that dump at the end of the runway. Please sit on this gurney and tip your head back."

Hesitating to look at the aircraft again, Joel saw that even the leading edge of the left wing was dented. Bloody feathers were sticking out of a very bent pitot tube.

All around him, the firemen were inspecting the aircraft, looking for fires or fuel leaks, but he was oblivious.

"Sir, you've been injured. Please let me take a look at your face." The ambulance attendant was insistent this time.

For the first time, Joel was suddenly aware of the sharp pains in his face and the blood still running down.

"Yeah, you better do that," he said, feeling light headed. He sat heavily on the gurney, and then lay down. His world was swirling.

As he was rolled toward the waiting ambulance, Colonel Watkins drove up.

"Dear God, man! What happened? Are you OK, Major?" His face was contorted with concern.

Joel wretched away from the pain of the medic cleaning his wounds.

"Sir, – birds – that – dump – old man Giovanni – bent your ship, sir." He was losing consciousness; he'd lost a lot of blood.

The medic forced his face back to where he could work on it. He pulled out the hanky and stuffed cotton up Joel's nostril; it hurt badly. Blood gushed out, and the medic swabbed it with cotton sponges.

"Don't worry about the airplane, Major! Are your passengers all right? Did anyone else get hurt?"

"Don't think – not hurt—" the last words were mumbled.

"Yes, you are, Major! We're heading to the Dispensary, *now*. Please excuse us, Colonel, but this man needs a doctor."

"By all means! God speed, Major!" Lieutenant Colonel Watkins exclaimed, moving out of the medic's way. Distantly, Joel felt the gurney being loaded into the ambulance; he passed out as the ambulance driver put the car in gear.

Chapter 22

8 May 1943

Millville Army Air Field

Base Dispensary, Building 71

1102 Hours

Diagnosis

The doctor, a gray-haired Lieutenant Colonel, finished bandaging the stitches he'd just put in place.

"You're going to have quite a shiner, Major, maybe two! That maxilla bone in your left cheek is at least cracked, probably broken, and so is your nose." He touched his own face just under his eye to show what he meant.

"The nose I've already fixed, while you were out. Not much I can do about the maxilla bone; you're fortunate that it isn't depressed; it'll just have to heal. We had to give you a blood transfusion, you'd lost so much. Don't be surprised if your face swells up a lot and you have trouble seeing out of your left eye. You've got ten stitches where I opened up that wound. They should come out in ten days or so. There will be a scar. I also put several stitches in that cut on your shoulder. You'll have bruising from the impact of the birds and from what I've been doing. The lacerations across your forehead look a lot worse than they really are; you might get a hairline scar from them, they're minor."

He continued working and said,

"You have lots of small cuts on the rest of your face; I pulled out several little pieces of Plexiglas. It's possible there may be more. The remaining cuts are just lacerations, which may or may not leave a scar. I'm going to keep you overnight for observation. If we decide you're going to be OK tomorrow, we'll change the dressings on the wounds and send you on your way. I do want you to see the ophthalmologist; you may have a scratch on your left cornea. We'll have to keep a close eye on all of it for infection, since I found feather parts inside your cheek. I used a lot of iodine on your face, so you'll see that too."

"Now." He stepped back and looked sternly at Joel over his glasses.

"Keep that bandage over your nose. And do not remove the packing. Take some APCs for the pain; if it's not enough, tell the orderly and I'll fix you up with something. By the way, you're grounded until we're sure your eye isn't involved, and the wounds have begun to heal; I'd guess at least two weeks. I'll notify your boss."

"Thanks, doctor." It sounded flat and harsh. "No, I mean that – didn't mean to sound sarcastic, sir!"

"No offense taken, Major. Now get some rest. And don't worry, the incident report can wait 'till tomorrow, do you hear me?"

"Yes, sir," Joel responded. An attendant took him to a room where he slept for twelve hours.

Late the next morning when he looked in the mirror, Joel realized the doctor hadn't been kidding. Besides two black eyes, the entire area around his left eye, in fact, most of the left side of his face, was bruised a rich purple-blue. Even with all the bandages, it was obvious his entire face was swollen. Where it wasn't bruised, it was a sickly yellow from all the iodine. There were scratches all over his face, like he'd been attacked by an angry cat. The eye was badly bloodshot, and more than half closed.

"Ya shoulda seen the other guy!" he cracked to his image. It hurt to smile.

He was shocked when the orderly told him a beautiful blonde woman had come to check on him, and had prayed over him as he slept. *It had to have been Susan, but how did she ever get into an Army hospital?*

To his great relief, the ophthalmologist told him, "Major, there is a small scratch on your cornea, but it isn't serious." The man put some stinging drops in his eye and said, "You'll have to wear a patch over the eye for about a week or ten days."

A final check up by the doctor on duty got him released. With several new bandages covering most of the left side of his face, and pain pills in hand, Joel had the driver take him to the squadron area. He couldn't avoid the incident report any longer.

He was just completing it in long hand to be typed later, when his sergeant knocked at his door.

"Sir, Colonel Watkins sends his regards, and requests that you join him and the base JAG officer at Colonel Watkins' office at 1300 hours this afternoon, if you're feeling up to it. Colonel Randolph will be there as well. Shall I tell him you'll be there?"

When the Base Commander "requests" something of a major, the major doesn't have many options.

"Of course, Bill. Get me a driver, will you? I'm not up to driving yet." He didn't mention that the medication had made him woozy.

He put the draft report in a folder, and prepared to leave.

Chapter 23

9 May 1943

Office of the Commander

Millville Army Air Field, Millville, New Jersey

1300 Hours

Promotion

He walked into Colonel Watkins' office, and reported; all three men waiting for him stood and moved toward him.

"How are you feeling, son?" inquired Lieutenant Colonel Watkins with a concerned look on his face.

"Well, sir, like I just went ten rounds with Jack Dempsey and a wildcat! And lost to 'em both!" Joel replied. Watkins laughed.

"That's quite the dramatic eye patch, Joel," said Lieutenant Colonel Randolph, his boss. "Is that why the flight surgeon grounded you? Is your eye going to be OK?"

"That's not why he grounded me, sir. My eye's going to be fine. He grounded me because of possible infection where the bird split my cheek; he's afraid it could go into the eye. Cheekbone's pretty sore where it's broken, too; he said it could really be painful at altitude, so I have to pass on that for a while. I've got a small scratch on the cornea of my eye, which will heal quickly, according to the doctor."

Watkins said, "Good. Glad to know the injuries aren't permanent. Have a seat, Major. The first thing is to introduce you to Lieutenant Colonel Marion Green, from the JAG corps."

The two shook hands. He was a solid man with brown eyes, and short reddish-brown hair. The Judge Advocate General was the Army's legal branch.

Colonel Watkins said, "The reason we're here is to get your version of what happened. This is not a punitive hearing; we

103

believe Mr. Giovanni is probably the responsible party here, but we have to get your statement first."

Carefully, Joel recounted the trip and the accident, referring frequently to his hand written report. Colonel Green made notes as he spoke. The questioning went on for more than an hour.

"Major," Colonel Randolph said, following Colonel Watkins' nod, "we think you performed admirably in recovering your aircraft from a very serious bird strike, and safely getting your civilian passengers back on the ground. We are considering a citation. Say, have you seen today's paper?"

When Joel shook his head, Randolph held up the *Millville Daily Republican*.

The headline read:

Army Hero Saves Teacher, Children
Flight Was Bond Drive Prize
Birds Strike Plane; Local Farmer Implicated

Below the headline was a photograph of a bloodied and battered Joel. A second photo showed Susan with an arm around both kids. A third showed the smashed nose of the C-45. Quickly, Joel scanned the article – they had it essentially right and even named Giovanni as the farmer on whose land the illegal dump was located.

"Where do we go from here, sir?" Joel asked Colonel Green.

"Mr. Giovanni has been formally warned on several occasions," the Army lawyer said seriously, looking at his documents; "I am recommending charges against him and will attempt to recover damages."

"And I will approve those charges," Colonel Watkins said firmly.

"Sirs, with all due respect, what needs to be done is to get rid of that—" he hesitated, suppressing a rare expletive. "Get that darn dump buried before it kills somebody!" Joel burst out.

"Already underway, Major." Colonel Watkins said, "An Army bulldozer is covering it, and is taking down some of the trees encroaching on the flight path as well."

"I'm real glad to know that. What about your airplane, sir?" Joel asked him. He had to turn his head from side to side to look at the men as they spoke; the eye patch was a major inconvenience.

"We don't have a full damage assessment yet, Major, but my guess is at least $10,000 worth. If it requires a new engine and prop, that could double. Mr. Giovanni may not make a profit this year. One other thing, Joel," he glanced at Randolph.

"Colonel Randolph has received orders to Europe, to join the 8th Air Force. He is to leave in about six weeks. As soon as you are able, we want you to begin to take over for him. Here is a little something you'll need to do the job," he held out a small blue box.

"Congratulations," all three officers said.

The box held a shiny pair of silver oak leaves; Joel had just been promoted to Lieutenant Colonel.

"You're now the junior Lieutenant Colonel at Millville, Joel!"

"There's one more thing, *Colonel* Knight," Colonel Watkins said smiling. "In spite of what this command does, we've never been able to convince Air Corps headquarters that we ought to have our own G2 detachment. Now, while I continue to work on that, I've arranged for you to be 'invited' to a newly established weekly intelligence briefing at the Pentagon for 'Non-Combat Units'." He said the phrase with distaste.

"Your first briefing will be at 0800 this coming Tuesday. You are authorized as my representative to obtain a copy of the briefing materials and to ask questions on my behalf."

He looked at Colonel Randolph, "Has transport been arranged?"

"Yes sir. He can either fly down to Washington on the courier the night before, or take one of the base flight aircraft, which ever works out best." He stopped and looked at Joel,

"Oh, that's right, you can't fly yourself. Well, we'll make sure you get on the courier."

"Uh, sir," Joel said, "I shouldn't fly at all, according to the doctor. How about if this intrepid aviator just takes the train?"

Chapter 24

11 May 1943

Bachelor Officers Quarters, Millville Army Air Field, Millville, New Jersey

1930 Hours

Letters

Joel sat writing a letter to Susan. His face wasn't as swollen as it had been, but it often throbbed, especially when he was sitting quietly, like right now.

My Dear Miss Johansseson;

I'm writing to apologize for the terrible scare you and the children had this past Saturday. I sincerely hope that the unfortunate incident won't scare either of the children away from flying again, or for that matter, you either!

I feel especially badly that I ruined your nice handkerchief, and will replace it as soon as possible. Would you prefer silk or linen?

By way of expressing my apologies, and since I never delivered on my promise of lunch, I would like to invite you to be my guest for dinner at the Appleton House dining room in Millville, at a date and time of your choosing.

I have spoken to the parents of both children, and everyone seems to have recovered from the shock. Those are two very brave kids! You have taught them well.

The base Judge Advocate General lawyer who is involved in this case has assured me that the farmer who operated the dump from which the birds flew up will be charged with damaging government property, and ignoring a lawful order, among other charges.

My injuries are healing quickly. My temporary eye patch makes me look like Terry and the Pirates! I have been told that I should be reinstated to flying status by the end of next week, or the week following. I'll have a rakish scar on my cheek to always remember our flight together!

By the way, thank you so much for coming by the hospital to see me; I regret I was unable to suitably receive you!

I'm looking forward to our dinner. Please give my best to Mr. Kneebone and your fellow teachers.

Sincerely,

Joel Knight, Lieutenant Colonel

US Army Air Services

He added his office phone number, and the one in his quarters as well.

Three days later, he received a reply in the mail.

Dear Lieutenant Colonel Knight;

I was very pleased to hear that you are recovering from the injuries you suffered. The children and I prayed for you. I was very much afraid at the time that you were more severely injured. Thank God you were not! You looked so horribly battered that night at the hospital.

I, too, have spoken with the children. Elmer is treating it as the grand adventure of his young life, and has all the boys hanging on his every word whenever he talks about it! He thought it great fun, and brags how he'll become a famous pilot himself, someday.

Beryl, as girls will be, has been quite introspective about it. She realized we all could have died, which is a pretty big thing for an eleven-year-old to deal with. I found her crying in the girl's room one day, and was able to comfort her. The personal note you sent her was a great encouragement and has given her some bragging rights with the girls! Thank you for that.

As to your kind invitation, which I appreciate, would you consider having my friend Mildred and her friend Charles join us? They are both teachers, she at Alexander Hamilton and he at Millville Senior High. We could all pool our ration coupons for dinner and the gas to get there if that would be *acceptable for you.*

Please let me know.

Sincerely;

Susan Johansseson

She included the phone number at the boarding house where she lived, but not that of the school, Joel noted.

Joel spent only a moment considering Susan's offer.

Well, if it takes a double date the first time, I'm all for it, he thought, smiling to himself.

He called her at the boarding house, and arranged a date and time. Joel called the restaurant and got reservations. They decided that Joel would meet the others at Susan's boarding house, and they would all go to the Appleton House Hotels' dining room in his car.

Chapter 25

Saturday, 15 May 1943

Stanton Township, New Jersey

2017 Hours

Dinner for Four

The evening was warm and clear when Joel drove up to the elegant old boarding house in Stanton Township. He was admitted to the parlor by the matronly housekeeper, who eyed him suspiciously, despite his sharply creased dress uniform. She viewed his bandages with obvious suspicion. Susan introduced him to her friends.

"Mildred Rossini, please meet Lieutenant Colonel Joel Knight. Joel, this is my dear friend Mildred, of whom I spoke."

Joel shook the young woman's hand. She was about 5'2", slender, with dark brown eyes and black hair. Her dimples were charming, and her eyes were bright; Joel guessed she was about twenty-two.

"Oh, please call me Millie; everyone does," her voice was high pitched, giggly, almost childlike.

She turned to the man standing beside her; "Joel, I'd like you to meet my boyfriend, Charles Angleton. He's from Vermont."

The men shook hands. He was a solid looking man, with sandy hair and thick glasses. His smile was warm.

This guy is definitely not a "Chuck," Joel decided, *he's a "Charles" if I ever saw one.*

Charles cocked his head, and looked at Joel's bandages and bruises. "Lose a fight?" he laughed.

"And how! But I'm afraid the eagles lost the round," Joel responded with a grin, "to say nothing of about a dozen gulls."

"Yep, read about that, and of course, Sue told us, too." His distinctive Vermont accent contrasted with Millie's.

"How is your eye, Joel?" Susan asked with concern, touching his cheek. He'd found a white silk eye patch to wear, which he thought looked rather natty.

"To tell the truth," he said, "it still stings like anything and waters a lot, but the doctor says it's doing fine. I can stop wearing this silly patch soon, I hope."

"I think it looks very distinguished," Mildred told him reassuringly, nodding in agreement with herself.

Glancing at his watch, Joel told them "We'd better move along; don't want to be late!" They walked out to the Packard.

"Oh, it's very pretty, Joel," Susan smiled.

"Packard! Army must pay well!" said Charles, chuckling.

"Hardly, Charles. I recently bought it second hand. There's room for two in the back, just lower the jump seats," he instructed.

Charles walked around the car, looking it over. "Two colors. Fog lights. Nice. No fender skirts? Take 'em off?" he asked.

"No," Joel replied, "the only accessories are fog lights, a radio, heater, and refrigerated air."

"Refrigerated air? Cools you while you drive? Heard of it, never seen it. We try it?"

"Sure," Joel said.

This guy talks like a machine gun – in bursts, Joel thought with amusement.

Susan sat in front with him, while the other couple shared the smaller but comfortable rear seats. The talk was mostly about the Packard; none of them had ridden in one before.

"Quiet, smooth," summed up Charles. "Love that cool air."

Mildred rubbed her hands on the broadcloth seat. "This feels like an expensive couch," she said approvingly.

Joel kept a furtive eye on the gas gauge; he still hadn't learned to judge how far the Packard's six cylinder engine would take him on four gallons of gas.

Looks pretty good so far, he decided; *hope that refrigerated air machinery doesn't take too much gas.*

There weren't many folks dining that night, so the foursome had the restaurant mostly to themselves. The menu was limited.

"No beef is available at all; rationing, y'know." said the small woman waiting on them.

"You will all have to use your ration cards, and I have to see 'em up front. The soldier will pay the full price, of course. Now. We got some nice local pork roast, and a good selection of fish."

She handed them hand written menus.

"We got us fresh coffee today, and a peach cobbler just out of the oven." She eyed Joel's bandaged, battered face with no comment.

Joel had eagerly anticipated the meal; he'd developed a taste for seafood since joining the Army, and assignment to the East Coast allowed him to indulge it.

"Now, speaking for myself, I think the swordfish looks good, and lobster would make a great compliment, don't you think?"

Mildred demurred, saying, "I haven't had pork roast in the longest time; it sounds yummy! That's what I'm having." Nodding her head again, she put down her menu, the decision made. Then, she spotted the dish of hard rolls.

"Oh, look! Is that real butter? I haven't had butter in just ages; oh, do pass it to me, Joel."

He passed her the small jars of homemade jam too. *She sounds more and more like a high school girl*, thought Joel; he had to suppress the image of her wearing saddle shoes and a pleated skirt.

"Yummy pork. Hmmm," Charles looked at her, and shook his head, bemused.

"I think fish. Cod. Can't beat it," Charles was succinct.

"Oh, I believe I'll have clams and oysters as an appetizer, with the fillet of flounder; is that all right?" Susan asked Joel.

"Sure," he said, "just save room for desert; I hear they have mighty good chocolate cake with ice cream here, and that cobbler sounds good, too."

This is going just fine.

The meals came with mounds of the wonderful fresh vegetables New Jersey is famous for, along with steaming baked potatoes. They all had ordered coffee; finding fresh coffee was a treat. The meat portions were adequate, if not generous.

"So, Joel. You Christian?" Charles asked between bites.

Joel was surprised, wary.

"Well, yes, I am. I was saved as a kid back home, when I was about twelve. How about you?"

"Hmm," Charles said, swallowing a mouthful of the cod. "Me too. Since '36."

"Where do you attend services, Joel?" Mildred asked him brightly.

"Millie, I haven't much since I was assigned to Millville. I was raised Assemblies of God, but none around here," he answered, knowing the excuse was flat. "To be honest, I haven't attended regularly since West Point, where it was mandatory." *Where is this going?* he thought.

Charles eyed him for a moment.

"Baptists call that 'backsliding.' Consider your profession, Joel. Dangerous, even in peacetime. With the war on—," he snapped his fingers, "Europe in the blink of an eye, right in the thick of it. Best get things right with God." He winked to lighten the moment a bit.

"Ouch!" Joel said. "That hits close to home." He knew in his heart Charles was right.

"Susan, I've never asked you where you attend; where do you go?" Mildred asked, interrupting the men, for which blessing Joel was thankful.

Susan said, "I was raised Lutheran, but like Joel, I haven't been able to find anywhere to go around here. Or at least anywhere that I liked. I tried the Lutheran Church in Millville, but it was – well, you know, kind of stuffy, and no young people. So, it's been a long time for me, too. Where do you attend? Do you two go together?"

"Yep. Stanton Township First Baptist," Charles answered for her.

"Oh, say, you must come and go with us, Susan! You too, Joel. It's a real friendly church. Why, we could go have a bite to eat afterward, if you liked. Oh, do come!" Mildred gushed.

"Sounds like food is becoming the basis of this friendship," laughed Joel. "But that's a good idea; would you like to go, Susan?" *Strike while the iron's hot,* he thought.

She was taken off guard a bit, Joel realized, and he was almost ready to let her off the hook, and then she said, "Why, yes. That would be very nice. What time are services?"

Mildred took a printed bulletin from her purse, and showed them.

"May I pick you up, Susan?" Joel asked. *Please say yes, please say yes!*

"Certainly," Susan smiled, "I'd like that."

Joel smiled internally, as he took another bite of the broiled lobster, which was really quite good. He'd hoped for the opportunity to see her again.

This is perfect, he thought.

"So, you worried about the draft, Charles?" Joel asked as the plates were cleared away, aware it was an awkward question.

"No. Rheumatic fever. Bad eyes. Bad heart," he said in his staccato fashion, tapping his chest.

"Been 4F since '41. Can't do a thing about it. Want to do more than teach. Applied to Martin Aircraft, over in Baltimore. Maybe I can build 'em if not fly 'em."

Chapter 26

16 May 1943

Bachelor Officer Quarters, Millville Army Air Field, Millville, New Jersey

0001 Hours

Contemplation

Joel lay in his bed, staring without seeing at the ceiling in the darkness. Around him, the temporary wooden building creaked and popped as it cooled. His tiny room still smelled like sawdust and fresh paint. He could hear some of the floor's more lusty snorers through the thin plywood walls. Privacy was a relative thing in this barracks even if it was a BOQ [Bachelor Officers Quarters].

Over and over in his mind, he considered what Charles had said, and how inadequate his reply was. Since the Point, he probably hadn't been in any church more than a dozen times. He'd been raised better than that. Christ had been alive for him once. What had happened?

When he answered himself honestly, he had to admit that he had left Christ, not the other way around. He'd just gotten too busy doing – things. He was building an exciting career in the Army, doing what he truly loved. He had been to exotic places around the world. He worked with men he respected and who respected him. He got to fly the most advanced airplanes in the world, and flying was his life. Now, he'd even found a woman he could fall in love with. Yet, here in the quiet darkness, he knew that all of that wasn't enough.

He remembered his dad's rough hand on his shoulder. He'd been about twelve, and had been caught committing some minor infraction – he couldn't remember what now.

"You apologize, now," his dad had said, "and when you're finished, you go get on your knees and pray for forgiveness.

That's an advantage we Christians have, son; we can always go to the Father and ask forgiveness. You must always keep your accounts with the Lord short ones."

His accounts were far from short now. How long had it been since he'd followed his dad's advice? Five years? Seven? Ten? He couldn't remember.

He knew what he should do, but just couldn't bring himself to confess. He'd piled up too much in all those years. Even that fact shamed him. Eventually, he fell into a fitful sleep, the issue unresolved.

Chapter 27

16 May 1943

Village of Tomsk, Occupied Russia

1132 Hours

Forest Village

Adolf Hitler was canny and more than a little paranoid, and with good reason. He had already survived several assassination attempts by the skin of his teeth and he fully intended to make it as difficult as possible for anyone making future attempts. As a result, he very seldom traveled anywhere exactly as initially planned, and rarely arrived at the announced time. Although careful preparations had been made for him to fly to Russia in his specially equipped Focke Wulf FW-200 four engine airliner, at the last minute, he took his armored train, improbably named *Amerika*. He was driven the last mile in an armored truck and arrived with little initial fanfare.

Tomsk, Western Russia

The small village was home to the impressive country dacha of a wealthy Russian Commissar, one of Stalin's cronies. German troops had captured the small village easily and the unoccupied building was undamaged. Expertly made of heavy timbers, the exterior was made to look like a larger, grander version of a humble peasant's log house. Inside, it was the height of luxury, as might befit a Commissar, or the Führer. Red and black flags with Swastikas and Hitler's personal banner had been quickly hung in the entry way. In the big dining room they would use for the conference, a huge, heavy oak banquet table was pressed into service. The room's lighting was augmented by fixtures borrowed from a field marshal's mobile command center. A trusted cook prepared Hitler's vegetarian lunch.

Outside, fifty yards away, a mobile telephone switching center was set up. Miles of copper wire were strung to connect to a bank of phones for the important visitors. The Adolf Hitler Liebstandarte [life guard], the hand-picked, fanatical and superbly trained protective troops for the dictator had set up a strong defensive perimeter all around the village.

With the pomp and genuflecting that always accompanied him, Adolf Hitler swept into the dacha. Looking at the impressive interior, he nodded to the general acting as host.

"These decadent Bolsheviks seem to know how to live well! Pity they won't be enjoying this any longer!" Everyone in the entourage chuckled on cue. "Now, then. Let us promptly get down to business," he directed.

Hitler sat himself at the left front of the heavy table, his ever present bottle of mineral water at hand. In front was a movie screen and a large paper tablet on an easel. A second easel held covered aerial photographs. Around him were senior generals and field marshals. As each man gave his presentation, he moved to the rear, and those waiting moved to the next seat closer.

Von Stauffenberg had moved forward, and was two seats from the Führer when a young courier stepped to his side. "My apologies, Oberst; an urgent telephone call from Berlin." he whispered.

"Thank you," von Stauffenberg said softly, his heart beginning to thump. He placed his folder back in the briefcase. Quickly, he pulled the wire to start the timer, snapped the briefcase closed, and taking his leather folder, rose to walk out of the building. "Please excuse me, General Hoepner," he whispered to the man sitting beside him, on Hitler's right. "My aide is calling with the new information I mentioned." The man waved dismissively, not taking his eyes off the speaker.

It was among the most difficult things he had ever done, walking steadily, but not too quickly toward the telephone center. His heart was hammering. Knowing the conversation would be monitored, he had arranged to be given legitimate, new information.

"Good morning, Herr Oberst," his young sergeant greeted him; "I have finished compiling the new recruitment figures by district, sir. I trust that I am not too late in getting them to you?"

"Not at all, Horst!" von Stauffenberg replied evenly, trying to hide his excitement, "I am to speak to the Führer in the next half hour; I commend you, you are just in time. Wait just a moment as I get my pen." He took out an ornate fountain pen, and opened the leather-bound tablet. Handling the two with one hand was difficult, but it was a skill he was quickly learning. He cradled the phone with his shoulder.

Nearby, inside the telephone truck, the SS man monitoring them was already bored. He made some entries in his log sheet, and switched to another conversation.

Von Stauffenberg made the noncom go through the numbers slowly, repeat them, and then he read them back, making a show of careful preparation.

"One does not speak to the Führer often, and I must be absolutely correct," he reminded the young man. He had almost forgotten the bomb as they meticulously went over the information.

Chapter 28

16 May 1943

Village of Tomsk, Occupied Russia

1217 Hours

Explosion and Attack

The explosion was huge, loud, sudden, and savage, like a vicious slap. The ground beneath him heaved. Von Stauffenberg was thrown down roughly, a bloody gash on his right cheek, his leg collapsing under him. He was as startled as everyone else – this was a far greater explosion than he had expected!

"Dear God! The Führer! Quickly, get medics!" he shouted, his voice one of many. He was amazed at his own presence of mind. All around, chunks of log, wooden shingles, and bits of stone pounded down out of the sky like a demented rain.

He raised himself on one elbow, and saw a towering cloud of smoke billowing up over the far end of the building. His ears were ringing as he saw more than heard the building begin to fall in on its self.

To his amazement, there were more explosions; it took his addled brain long seconds to understand that they were under attack! From the woods came a murderous rain of mortar rounds, machine gun fire, and even hand grenades! The Russian army had somehow found the camp! How had they gotten through the ring of Liebstandarte sentries?

Like a bad dream, von Stauffenberg saw several men struck down, then the crack Liebstandarte troops guarding the Führer began to rally. At first ragged, their answering fire quickly became focused and disciplined.

An SS major leapt up to direct the solder's fire. A fusillade from a heavy Russian machine gun cut him down. His shouted commands died in his throat, and his empty helmet rolled a few feet and stopped. An SS sergeant took his place and the counter attack continued.

With a thunderclap, another mortar round went off only a few dozen yards away, and von Stauffenberg was hit with a glancing blow by a ricocheting piece of shrapnel. His head hit the ground, and all went black.

He awoke slowly, in a fog, not knowing where he was. He started to lift himself, and was stabbed so sharply with pain in his upper chest and left arm that he cried out.

"Not so fast, Oberst!" a male voice said gently, a hand pushing against his left shoulder. "You are incapacitated. Kindly lie back down and allow me to examine you."

Blinking his eye, von Stauffenberg saw a white coated man, a stethoscope around his neck. The "ceiling" above him moved in ripples; it took a moment to realize he was in a tent.

"Where am I? What has happened?" he began. Then memories flooded back.

"Rest easy Herr Oberst; you were wounded in the attack on the Führer, and have been unconscious. You have deep wounds, on your face, right leg, and side. I believe the leg may be broken as well, so kindly lie still."

"The Führer! Is he—?"

"We don't know," the doctor said quietly, "they have flown him back to Berlin."

"What about General Hoepner and the others?"

The doctor regarded him sadly; "He is dead, Oberst, along with almost everyone in the building. You narrowly avoided death yourself."

He lay back and let the man look at his wounds. His head was spinning and the pain was screaming inside him. He knew how to control pain; this wasn't his first encounter.

All around him, white coated men hurried to tend to other figures, some of whom were moaning. Outside, he heard a sharp burst of gunfire, then silence.

"Didn't we drive the Russians off?" he asked anxiously.

"Yes, yes, don't worry. It was a bloody fight," the doctor replied, suturing a deep cut with strong hands. "We captured several of them, the bastards. What you just heard was their firing squad."

"It was terrible! Did the building collapse?"

"Yes," the doctor said. "A direct mortar hit, maybe several. What was left burned to the ground." He interrupted himself to give his patient another shot. "This will ease your pain, even let you sleep."

Von Stauffenberg started to object, and then thought better of it. He'd gained little from his refusal of pain deadeners in Africa. He'd take what they had to offer here in Russia.

The doctor continued, "There were many, many deaths; you are one of the few lucky ones near the building. Now, I'll have my assistant splint that leg; it is broken. The Luftwaffe is flying home wounded senior officers; you will leave within the hour. When you get to the Fatherland, that leg will have to be properly set. You will survive again, Herr Oberst; I have seen men with much worse wounds do so. There are others here also needing my attention, so I must leave you. I wish you God speed in your recovery. Heil Hitler!" He left the tent.

Von Stauffenberg lie thinking about what had happened.

*The Russians attacked **us**! What a literal Godsend! I cannot believe it! It hid my bomb! They thought it was part of the attack. With any luck, the Führer will die, if he isn't dead already, and the Russians will get the blame!* A slight smile crossed his lips, then the drug took effect, and he slept.

Chapter 29

20 May 1943

Office of the Minister of Propaganda, Berlin, Germany

1037 Hours

Germany in Shock

Radio Berlin had been playing mournful, funereal music all morning long. Everyone knew a solemn announcement was coming. The nation had been stunned at Göring's death; what could have happened now? Not least among the very interested listeners were the members of the conspiracy. They had begun to carefully add senior military men. A plan for quickly seizing control of both the civilian government and the military was in place, waiting.

Dr. Joseph Goebbels worked furiously; *this announcement must be handled very carefully. I must convince not just the German people that the Führer was only wounded, and will soon recover, but the Allies as well.* He knew there were teams of listeners in Great Britain who monitored and analyzed everything broadcast from the Fatherland. Should he be less than convincing, there were even Germans ready to overthrow the Nazi government, if Himmler was to be believed. For himself, he doubted the Führer would survive his horrible wounds. The whole side of his head was caved in, the chief doctor had told him confidentially. A great piece of the oak table had been flung into him.

If he survives, he will be a vegetable, a pitiful relic of his powerful former self; better he should die! At least it would be a warrior's death. This way, to waste away, slowly... this is no way for a Teutonic warrior to die.

For himself, he fully planned to be a big part of whatever government came out of this disaster. He was acutely aware his own neck was on the line.

The announcer said importantly, "Citizens of the Third Reich, the Minister of Propaganda, Dr. Joseph Goebbels."

Goebbels' distinctive voice rang out:

"People of Germany! Today we have learned that the cowardly Bolsheviks have feebly attempted to strike a deadly blow against Germany and our beloved Führer. While he was meeting with our indomitable generals and field marshals, in a remote section of occupied Russia, they attacked unexpectedly, secretly, and with great force, like the cowards they are.

"The Führer's own legendary Adolph Hitler Liebstandarte Guard bravely fought the cowards, at great loss: not a single Russian survived. Despite the valiant efforts of our dedicated medical men, several German general officers have given their lives in defense of our glorious Reich. They will be immortalized at formal state funerals, as befits selfless leaders willing die for the Führer!

"Our beloved Führer lies wounded, grievously so, in hospital at an undisclosed location. He is being attended, the clock around by the very finest medical experts in the Reich. His wounds, though serious, are not fatal – do not fear, my stalwart Germans! Our great leader will soon rise and lead us again. He will yet again inspire us.

"The undaunted military chiefs of the Third Reich have already closed ranks around our fallen leader, to stand steadfastly in his stead for the short time until he once more arises to take his rightful place in history, to continue and finish our march toward undoubted, certain victory!

"Our fury toward the Communists is unabated and irresistible. Already, massive forces are moving on the Russian capital. Revenge will be ours! Moscow will fall in days at most. The madman Stalin will be hung in a public square like a dog, his henchmen along with him; I promise you this!

"Our soldiers will be ever valiant, we shall not falter, we shall triumph in our mighty Führer's name! Heil Hitler!"

London, Number 10 Downing Street

Five days later

"So tell me Raleigh, just how is the so-called German man on the street taking Dr. Goebbels' remarkable speech?" Churchill asked his intelligence aide, as he knocked the ash from his ever present cigar.

"Prime Minister, it would appear that most are highly skeptical, but of course, not publically. They have long since learned to read between the lines, so to speak; it seems the general expectation is that he – Hitler – is either dead or will soon be so. There is some indication that ordinary Germans are hopeful this may lead to an early end to the war."

"I fear their hopes shall again be dashed," Churchill growled almost to himself.

Raleigh shuffled some papers in his hands.

"Within the German government, it rather seems chaos is the order of the day, to mix a metaphor. Civil service are continuing to go through the motions, with a wary eye toward whomever may take the reins. The German military are, to be blunt, paralyzed. It would appear that to a man, the OKW leadership are hesitating to make decisions that Hitler might oppose should he suddenly regain consciousness. No less so, we believe, is the SS leadership gripped by the fear of acting contrary to 'Der Führer's' wishes."

Chapter 30

22 May 1943

Union Lake Park, Millville, New Jersey

1145 Hours

Picnic

It wasn't New Jersey hot yet, in late May, as Joel and Susan walked from the Packard and found a shady spot under a huge, old, maple tree.

"This is a nice place," Susan said, looking around.

"Ah, yes, a spreading tree, 'A loaf of bread, a jug of wine and thou—'" Joel quoted.

"Well, not quite," Susan said, laughing. "It's more like a couple of pieces of fried chicken, cold Cokes, and each other."

"As long as we have the last one, I'll take it," Joel smiled at her. She seemed to like the comment.

They sat on a blanket and admired the view; Union Lake stretched out into the distance. The light breeze rippled the water agreeably, and the occasional water fowl dove after elusive fish. The peaceful scene belied the violence an ocean away; for now, the two of them were happy just to be away from the constant barrage of war news.

"Are they still tender?" Susan asked, lightly touching the bright pink scars on Joel's face.

I love her touch, Joel thought.

"No, they're mostly healed. The surgery scar still hurts, where he dug out the feathers, but it was pretty deep. Thank God I didn't get infected there. Did I tell you I found another little piece of Plexiglas shaving yesterday?"

"Ouch, that must have hurt," she said, wrinkling her nose.

"So tell me about your family, Joel. How long have they been in Colorado?" Susan asked as she snuggled up next to him.

"Well," Joel began, putting his arm around her, "my great-granddad, Obadiah Knight, came out west from Ohio in 1870. They homesteaded in the Calhan area northeast of Colorado Springs. Had some rough years, but once the railroad came, they were able to get cattle to market easier.

"My dad, Jubal, was born on the ranch in 1885. He married my mom Ilene in 1907. My brother, Samuel, was born the next year. I came along in 1911, and my baby sister Edna was born in 1915. She and I were both born in Colorado Springs."

"Obadiah, Jubal, Samuel, Joel – your family likes Bible names," Susan observed.

He shrugged, "Been sort of a family tradition. My uncles and boy cousins all have Bible names, too. Sort of getting to be a challenge to find one that hasn't been used already."

"No repeats, then?"

"Nope. I'm the only-est Joel Knight there is, Ma'am." Joel deadpanned with an exaggerated western movie twang.

She elbowed him playfully in the ribs, and began to unpack the picnic basket.

Obertstleutnant [Lieutenant Colonel] Freiherr [Baron] von und zu Schroeder sat at his stark, military desk, reading the report somberly. Not even at his level had the German military been fully informed about Hitler's true condition, or how the beheaded government was going to survive. There had been assurances that the Luftwaffe hierarchy was still in place and functioning, including a message to all Bomber Command officers from Generalmajor Wever.

Von Schroeder could read between the lines as well as any German.

They wouldn't be putting out this nonsense if Hitler was alive and well; he must have died! Deep in his mind, the fear that the Allies would use this turmoil to strike a mortal blow churned despite the propaganda. He believed without reservation that Germany would prevail in the vast struggle; she had to. He clenched his fist.

To lose again – it is unthinkable. Morose thoughts of the dark times after the Great War only added to his depression.

If only they would permit me to strike America, he thought, *the Americans are cowards; they will cower and sue for peace as soon as we kill a few of them on their own homeland. I can do it. I know I can. I must convince Generalmajor Wever. He must permit it.*

He reached for the bottle of English whiskey in the bottom drawer, oblivious to the irony that what he was drinking had been distilled by an enemy, and poured himself a tall glassful.

More focused, a goal in mind, he began to write what he would say to Generalmajor Wever, how he would convince him to support the concept of a trans-Atlantic attack. Surely he would see the advantages of an America reeling from an attack on her own countryside. As he wrote, the thoughts became clearer; yes, he could convince Wever, he was sure of it. His confidence returning, he began to flesh out the presentation.

Susan and Joel were laughing and enjoying their lunch and conversation, when an ominous, deep rumble of thunder interrupted them. Across the lake to the west was a big, fast-building thunder cloud, and it was headed right for them. Even as they watched, lightening snapped to the ground.

"OK, time for us to pack up and move," Joel said starting to do just that.

"Why?" Susan asked reluctantly. "This nice tree will keep us dry."

Joel shook his head, "This tree is a lot taller than the others around here; that makes it a prime target for that lightening."

As he spoke, another crash of thunder resounded across the water; the storm was moving onto the lake.

In minutes, the picnic gear was in the trunk of the Packard, and as they clambered inside, the rain began to rattle against the windows. A brilliant flash and a deafening thunderclap startled them both.

"Oh! Oh, look," Susan said, her eyes wide, "it hit the tree, just like you said."

A huge, smoking branch slammed to the ground not far from where they had been sitting.

"That's twice now that you've saved my life, Mr. Knight!" she said with a touch of awe.

"Ah, shucks, Ma'am, twarn't nothin'," Joel twanged.

"Yes, it was, and it deserves a reward," Susan said softly, and reached over to kiss him.

They both were startled at the electric shock when they kissed.

"I think we better try that again," Joel smiled. It was several minutes before they realized the storm had intensified.

"Joel, this dirt will turn into mud quickly; we'd better get out of here and back on some pavement."

"You're right." He started the engine and they slipped a bit on the already muddy surface.

"Just in time," he said as they bumped back onto the paved road back to Millville.

Chapter 31

24 May 1943

Amalgamated Radio Network Broadcast Studios, New York City

1900 Hours

Chaos Reported

"This is your announcer speaking. I am Henderson Caldwell, the host of *Answers and Questions*, the radio program which explores 'What's behind the news with those in the know.' Today's guest is Mr. William L. Shirer, the well known author of *Berlin Diary*, and long time CBS Radio Network correspondent. Welcome to the program, Mr. Shirer."

"Thank you, my pleasure to be here," Shirer said politely.

"Let's jump right into it, if we may, Mr. Shirer; is Germany undergoing civil war?"

Shirer said, "The short answer is no, not in the conventional sense. It is possible that the situation could evolve into civil war, but at this time, no, it has not risen to that level."

"Upon what do you base that statement, sir?"

"I have – shall we call them correspondents? – in Germany with whom I remain in contact. I trust you will forgive me if I identify neither their names nor the cities in which they reside, for obvious reasons. These correspondents inform me that the violence has been constrained mostly to the larger cities, and mostly between the SS forces and the Whermacht – the German army, with occasional exceptions. The smaller towns appear to have been unaffected so far. "

"What do you predict the outcome to be?"

Shirer chuckled, "I am surely no prophet, Mr. Caldwell, neither am I the son of a prophet. My guess, and it's only that, a guess, is that the SS will be divided into its two parts. Those parts are the police arm of the Nazi party, and the elite military units. I believe that the police arm will wither away, most likely by force, and the military units will be absorbed into the German Army."

"Who will take Adolph Hitler's place, do you believe?"

"That's a very difficult question. Hitler's heir apparent was Göring, of course. Following Göring's death, there was silence on Hitler's part as to whom he would impart his blessing. Heinrich Himmler made some strong moves to take over, but has been thwarted in his efforts, for the most part, by the assassinations of nearly all of his highest ranking people."

"That is amazing, sir! We have not heard about these assassinations; are you sure of these facts?"

"As sure as I am of any other."

"Is the Nazi party dead then, as some have said?"

"No. It has been beheaded, and is being dismantled, but there are still powerful forces, both civilian and military in Germany who are still slaves to Hitler worship. If I may say so, the Anti-Nazi forces have shrewdly used the chaos around them to continue that dismantling process. And it has been far from bloodless. May I be just a bit philosophical here?"

"Of course."

"There is something about the German psyche that craves strong leadership. This has been true for hundreds of years. With Hitler out of the picture – and my correspondents tell me that he will never again be an actor on the German stage, there is a power vacuum. The old saying that 'nature abhors a vacuum' is never truer than in politics, especially so in German politics. Now, this next part, I must put strong caveats upon, for if it is true, it would be unprecedented in German history."

"You have our rapt attention, Mr. Shirer, I assure you," the announcer said.

"What I am hearing –none of the factions within Germany trust each other – it's closer to loathing, but at the same time they are very much aware that they cannot exist as a country without cooperating. The outcome of the war hangs in the balance. The result of this conundrum may – I emphasize, *may*, we are certainly not sure – result in some sort of shared governance. Perhaps they will take turns at the Chancellorship or rule as co-equals in some manner. As I said earlier, always in the past, going back many hundreds of years, it has been a single, powerful man at the top. This may be changing."

"What forces or factions are involved here; surely the Army, what other factions?"

"The Army, of course – the Army within Germany has been a government within the government since the first Kaiser; nothing happens there without the Army's approval. The Germans being who they are, another faction will likely be a civilian police entity, perhaps the Gestapo. Almost certainly not the SS. The last aspect, and the one of which I am least sure, would be some representation of the civilian or production portion of the population. Whether this will take place, or whether it will be stable enough to last is very much up in the air."

"Another difficult question, if I may?" the announcer said.

"Of course."

"Do Germans, the ordinary Germans, believe that they can win the war? Surely, they must see the inevitability of an Allied victory."

"Nothing is inevitable, Mr. Caldwell, least of all an Allied victory. The Germans are a very resourceful, determined race, a formidable foe. To answer your question, however, the German man on the street has had significant doubts about the outcome of this war since even before I left Germany in 1941. That pessimism runs much deeper and higher today, especially among professional military officers. I have no doubt that our Allied leaders will do all they can to exploit it."

Chapter 32

23 May 1943

Delsea's Diner, Millville, New Jersey

And Then Dinner

Joel wiped his mouth. "Now, that's good fried chicken."

"Yes, it's quite good, isn't it? Even if we did just have fried chicken on our picnic," Susan answered. "And the mashed potatoes are delicious, too."

They were enjoying a traditional Sunday dinner at a diner in Millville. Joel had picked her up at the boarding house and they had gone to Millie's church together that morning. He had to admit he'd enjoyed it, and it wasn't just because he'd had a beautiful woman by his side; it'd been a long, long time.

"So, what'd you think of that sermon this morning, Sue?"

The pastor at Millie's church had announced he was beginning a new sermon series on the New Testament book of Philemon; Joel couldn't believe there was enough material in that short one-chapter book to support one sermon, to say nothing of several, and he had said so. To his surprise, the first sermon was interesting, and actually had some pretty profound insights.

"I was amazed he could bring so much out of so little. I mean, there just isn't much there in Philemon, is there?" she said.

He shook his head, his mouth full of biscuit.

"Was the service a lot different than what you were used to?" Joel then asked. "I've never been to a Lutheran service."

"Well, yes, it was." she said. "I'm used to a lot more formal service order, and our pastor always wears a vestment. I must say, though, that everyone was so friendly. Why, there must've been a half-dozen people who said hello before we even got to our seats. And, say, there was scarcely any Bible-thumping at all!"

She dimples beautifully when she smiles, Joel thought.

"Yeah," Joel said, "maybe these Baptists aren't so bad after all."

She laughed and Joel thought her voice sounded like bells.

Joel, Joel! he told himself. *She can get to you so easily.*

They lingered over pie and coffee.

"Have you thought about what Charles said?" she asked, her voice gentle.

Joel felt his gut tighten. "Yes, to be honest, I've thought about it a lot," he replied.

"Have you done anything about it?" Her voice was soft.

Conviction poured over him, and he put his head down, saying nothing.

There were a few seconds of awkward silence, then she said, "Joel, I simply must get home. I've papers to grade, and more than a dozen essays; oh, how I hate those! You can't imagine how poorly eleven-year-olds think, to say nothing of spell. And the hand writing, especially the boys—. I have to get ready for final exams, too." She shook her head ruefully.

He walked her to the boarding house door, holding her hand. "So, shall we go see that new cowboy movie next Saturday?"

"Yes, lets," she said, squeezing his hand.

He walked back to the Packard with a spring in his step.

The Next Saturday

The movie was disappointing; it was just another "B" Western with "stars" no one had heard of. They sat alone at the same little diner. This time the dessert was bread pudding, with fresh raisins and pecans. The coffee was good this week, too.

Joel put his chin on his fist, "OK, I just have to ask: how'd a nice Wisconsin girl like you end up teaching school in Stanton Township, New Jersey, of all places?"

She gracefully wiped her mouth. "I was tricked, you might say," and laughed at his raised eyebrows.

"No, not really. I'd finished college, and wanted to do some graduate work at Georgetown University, but I had this little money problem."

She laughed in a self-deprecating way.

"I saw an ad in a Philadelphia paper for a Junior High teacher in a 'nearby township.' By the time I discovered how 'nearby' it actually was, I was committed. It's not so bad, actually. I like the other teachers, and the pay isn't all that great, but being so far from the city, I've managed to save a lot of it. I should be able to start classes next fall. We'll see."

"Masters degree, huh? That's unusual."

"For a girl, you mean?"

"Ah, uh, no, for anybody; you don't see very many in either sex."

It wasn't the smoothest recovery from a gaff, but she let him off. Grateful, he tried a follow-up, "So what will your masters degree be in? Education?"

"Oh, no, silly. I'm going to pursue my masters in Psychology."

Joel nearly choked on his coffee. "Psychology? Really? Why would you want to do that?"

He stroked his chin and tilted his head, and in a terrible German accent said, "I haf dis vision of der egg-headed Viennese professors mit goatees, nodding sagely and saying profound things like 'Ach, so!'"

He squinted one eye, as if holding a monocle in place. "That's a psychologist, not a beautiful blonde!"

She laughed, her head back, her fine, slender neck accenting her flawless complexion.

"Why? Because I'm very good at it, fly boy! Besides, that's what I got my undergraduate degree in."

"Really? Now that's something! So you know all about Jung and Freud and those guys?"

"Well, yes, but I think they over-emphasize the influence of mothers or mother figures on boys, and all but ignore girls and women."

"You want to study women and girls, then?"

"No, not particularly." She leaned forward enthusiastically, "What I want to do is study Predictive Behavioral Psychology, because I'm more interested in analyzing behavior patterns in people in general, to observe how they respond under stress. What makes them react as they do, and whether or not their actions can be predicted. If they can, it could be very useful in say, law enforcement, to know whether your local gangster will do this or that when you put the squeeze on him." She held up her finger like a gun and squinted along it.

"Or," she looked at him levelly, "perhaps if you understand what makes him tick, you could predict what a general might do when he's forced to make a decision on the battle field."

"Wow!" Joel said. "That makes driving an airplane for a living seem a little on the mundane side." *Now, this young lady has some depth to her,* he decided.

Chapter 33

31 May 1943

The White House, The Oval Office

0913 Hours

Phone Call

"Mr. President, Prime Minister Churchill is on the transatlantic telephone, sir."

Franklin Roosevelt wheeled himself to the telephone, and picked up. He glanced at the desk clock set to London time.

"Good afternoon, Winston. Have you some good news for me for a change?" His tone was light, even though he was sure the call wouldn't be.

"Good morning to you, Franklin," Churchill growled. "No, I sorely regret that the news is not so good this day. Our spies have informed us that the German government are not as close to collapse as we had dared hope. We may have missed a most opportune moment, to my regret. It appears that they have responded rather promptly, and are in process of putting some sort of 'troika' into place. As yet we are unaware of whom the members would be, but we suspect that they will be military."

"Such arrangements as that are seldom stable for long," Roosevelt commented. "What about Hitler? Is he dead, or are we all to suffer his miserable existence still longer?"

"It is most difficult to ascertain much reliable information regarding him, Franklin. Our best estimate is that the paper-hanging reprobate remains in a comatose state, neither alive nor dead. It appears they have him at the so-called Wolf's Lair. That however, is not the subject of my call. I must inform you about Uncle Joe; have you heard?" He referred to Joseph Stalin, the Russian dictator.

"I can't say that I have. What has happened?" A cold sense of foreboding came over Roosevelt as he waited for Churchill's reply.

"Well," Churchill said, his voice a bit tinny through the transatlantic connection, "the Germans have again moved against Moscow with considerable force, and this time have moved far enough east to have begun shelling and bombing directly into Red Square. The Kremlin itself has suffered considerable damage. Actual invasion of the city could take place at any time. Uncle Joe and his cohorts bravely leapt aboard an east-bound express train toward Kazan, leaving the defense of the city to those few military and civilians still there." Sarcasm dripped from the last sentence.

"It seems that whilst they were en route those Dammed bat bombers found his train and gave him a rather bad time of it. The train was derailed and wrecked. The old man was injured – rather badly – and is terrified for his life. Most concerning, rumors have it that he may be receptive to offers of a separate peace."

Roosevelt was staggered. "Dear God in Heaven! We can't allow that! If Stalin should capitulate, the forces on the eastern front would fall upon our invasion armies in no time. How can we prevent this catastrophe from occurring? Will we have to delay the invasion?"

"I do not know, Franklin," Churchill said heavily, "we have no official contact with the Soviet government whatsoever. One supposes they will set up a government-in-exile in Kazan, possibly, or perhaps as far east as Chelyabinsk. With the reach of those bat bombers, not even Novosibirsk is entirely safe. Now let us agree that we will both attempt strongly to reach the Soviet government and squelch this dastardly cowardice. Until we resolve this, we must stop sending materiel; it would be used against us, surely. We must suspend all convoys to Russia at once."

Roosevelt quickly agreed, "And we must immediately turn back convoys already under way, and divert them to the UK, do you agree?" He made notes on his personalized stationary, in a fluid hand.

"Yes, an excellent point; diversion signals must be sent straight away. Time, as always, is of the essence."

"I shall notify the Navy immediately. I must confer with my generals and admirals immediately, Winston, if you will forgive me. We must decide about the invasion."

"Yes, yes, and I with mine. I shall call again soon, with better news, I hope. God protect us all. Goodbye."

"Goodbye to you, Winston. May God be merciful to us, indeed."

Chapter 34

1 June 1943

Lieutenant Colonel Knight's Office

Millville Army Air Field, Millville, New Jersey

0915 Hours

Headaches

Taking over Colonel Randolph's job wasn't as easy as he'd thought.

He took his deputy with him, Joel thought, shaking his head ruefully; *so now I've got to find one of my own.*

He had been studying a list of candidates, and had narrowed it down to two. As he thought about the men, the decision made itself when he applied the ultimate test: *who can really take over for me without compromising the mission?*

He'd made Bill Madsen his First Sergeant when he assumed Randolph's job, a move that was already paying off. The guy was amazing. Like just now, for example, when Joel had asked him to have the winner come to his office, the First Shirt calmly told him the man was waiting in the outer office.

How'd he do that? Joel wondered, not for the first time.

Captain Derek Chapman sat across from him, all but expressionless, his hands in his lap.

"Let me save you the anxiety, Chappie," Joel said, using his call sign. "If you want the job, I'd sure like you to be my deputy."

Chappie was all smiles, "You bet I would sir! When can I start?"

"You just did," Joel deadpanned. He picked up his phone and dialed Bill. "He's accepted, Bill. Get the paperwork to me right away – You do? Already? OK, I'll sign it when we finish here."

"I swear, sometimes I think that man can read my thoughts," Joel said, shaking his head. "Now, you'll get your first chance to run this outfit on Tuesday when I go down to Washington for my almost-every-week intelligence briefing. I'll get your clearance raised so we can talk about what's really going on down there in Foggy Bottom."

Chapter 35

3 June 1943

The Oval Office

1037 Hours

More News

Franklin Delano Roosevelt picked up the telephone receiver with a tug of trepidation; what would Churchill have to tell him this day?

"Franklin, old friend, good morning. We have a few bits more of information regards the situation in Berlin. The troika, so-called, has been at least defined, if not yet populated. It seems that the first of the three posts will reflect the military, with the Abwehr representing itself, the Luftwaffe and the Kreigsmarine. As you well know, the German military is all but a nation within the nation, and many of the professional military class have chafed under the leadership of the 'little Corporal.' They will have a very strong voice. We don't as yet know whom they shall name. We've heard of some bitter struggles as they decide.

"The civilian production sector will almost surely be headed by Albert Speer. There is no joy for us in that instance. He is all too capable, and apparently ambitious in the bargain. We had expected that the third leg of this unrighteous stool would be the SS. Now, with Himmler under at least house arrest, there is a fair likelihood that 'Gestapo' Müller will be in charge of whatever they decide to call it." He paused to catch his breath.

"Is this unholy trinity unopposed, Winston? I cannot conceive that these men could be allowed to simply step up and take over." FDR said.

"Not at all, not at all, Franklin. There has been a veritable bloodbath all round, next thing to civil war. Only the firm hand of the Gestapo and the presence of the military have prevented the situation from slipping over the edge."

"Hmmm. That can only be of benefit to our cause," FDR said. "But is it only internecine warfare? We have heard rumors of a fair number of assassinations of party leaders at all levels."

The Prime Minister growled, "Yes, we've heard the same. There's simply too much killing to attribute to internecine warfare. Himmler's SS lost well over a hundred of his highest ranking men, probably more. His power base, I should say, has been all but eradicated. Adds a good deal of credence to the rumor that 'Gestapo' Müller is taking the job. Additionally, it has come to our ear that a goodly number of these assassinations were planned prior to Hitler's injury. It appears likely that there is an opposition group at work, but sadly, we know no details."

"Now, Franklin," Churchill continued, "I will counsel against taking heart in this news, despite its surface appearance. Let us not forget that both Speer and Müller are capable and pragmatic; I misdoubt that the military man, whomever he may turn out to be, will be any less. This may mean many fewer amateur decisions such as we have learned to love with 'Der' Führer."

Chapter 36
27 May 1943
Berlin, Germany
1106 Hours
Peeling a Bad Onion

General Heinrich Müller, the newly promoted Director of State Security, sat at his desk, and pondered the turn of events that had placed him in this new position. It had been only twenty days since the Führer was injured, mortally, Müller was sure. The other two members of the "Dreifach" [triple] trying to hold the Third Reich together looked to him to review security measures, especially communications.

Müller had started his career as a minor police official in Bavaria many years before, and had developed himself into the nation's foremost counterintelligence specialist. He was an expert on Soviet espionage as well. As he re-read the reports of the attack in Russia, he became more and more convinced that either the Russians had infiltrated the German communications system, or they had broken the "invincible" Enigma coding machines. There was no question, the Russians had known exactly where the Führer was to be and when.

A serious, intelligent man who was unimpressed with himself, he wore the trappings of power with a sense of unease, still thinking of himself as a "simple country policeman." The more he pondered the issue, the more he was convinced that a Soviet spy inside the German communications network was unlikely to the point of impossibility. All of the men (and a few women) were carefully investigated, carefully watched, reliable Germans of long ancestry.

No, he thought to himself, *this is not likely at all. That leaves—*. He ran his hand through his thinning brown hair, then leaned forward and lifted his telephone, "Horst, please find Major Fleischer and have him come here immediately." He sat back and thought some more.

Fifteen minutes later, Fleischer reported. He was a little red-faced from the exertion of running to the General's office.

He is far too fat for a soldier, thought Müller.

"So, Fleischer, explain to me the encrypting machine 'Enigma.' You know of it, yes?"

"Jawohl, General, what would you like to know?"

"What I want to know, Major, is how it works."

"This is a very high State Secret, General—"

"I need to know this. Explain it." His voice was controlled, but menacing.

"Yes, sir. The machine is used to convert ordinary language into nonsense—"

"I know that. What I want to know is *how* it does this." his voice now impatient.

The Major was sweating visibly. "Oh. Well, sir, it is somewhat complicated. You see, there is a slightly different version of the machine for the Army, Kreigsmarine, and the Luftwaffe. And an even simpler version is used for weather reports.

"For example, the Army machine consists of four wheels on an axle, each of which can be connected to the other by rotating one or all of them. They all have twenty-six positions, one for each letter in the alphabet. For the other services, there can be as few as three or as many as thirteen wheels. A keyboard selects the first letter of the message, and the first wheel is set to that letter. The remaining wheels are then rotated either clockwise or anti-clockwise according to a daily key. Based on their new locations, an electric current can be passed from a depressed key to first one wheel then another, from front to back, then finally back to the front. When the current reaches the front, it illuminates a new letter, which is the first letter of the encrypted message.

"The message is typed in a letter at a time, and the corresponding coded letter illuminates, and is written down. When the entire message has been written, the encrypted version can then be sent by Morse code over a teletype or radio. The machine on the receiving end is set to the same wheel positions as the sender. The receiving operator puts the coded message into the machine letter by letter, and the keys illuminate showing the proper letter of the plain language message." The man tilted his head, to see whether Müller understood.

Müller considered the description. "So, if I properly understand, in order to decipher a message coded by one of these machines, one would have to have the machine itself, have knowledge of how many wheels it consists, and access to the daily 'key,' as you called it. This is correct?"

"Yes, sir. Without all of that, the message remains garbled nonsense."

"What is the likelihood that the Russians could have a machine?"

The man looked startled at the question. "Oh, sir, the machines are very closely guarded. It is impossible—"

"I didn't ask for the *political* answer, Major. I want your professional opinion as a trained intelligence officer: how likely is it that they could have obtained one of our machines?"

The portly man flushed at the rebuke. "Mathematically speaking, sir, I would put the likelihood at 0.5; a fifty-fifty chance. They have had several opportunities. In each case, we have been convinced that the machine was destroyed, but—," he hesitated, "the possibility remains, I must admit, that they might have obtained one intact, or perhaps more likely, assembled one from parts of several."

"How about the key? How is it distributed and how do they know when to use what version?" Müller asked him.

"Herr General, it is taken always by courier, by hand, by a trusted man escorted by armed soldiers. Only a senior officer may receive it. In the case of the Kreigsmarine, it is the ship's captain who receives it and places it in the ship's safe before sailing. Or, a coded signal is sent, directing him to a page in a book of settings. We have had no known cases of the loss of a book of keys. A separate book lists the pages and the dates they are to be used. Without both the key and the date book, any message sent could not be decoded. The receiver simply could not receive any message and decode it. It is very safe, General."

"Yes, that is what the Führer believed, too," Müller said dryly, "I am not so sure."

❖ ❖ ❖

Müller was silent a long moment, leaving the young Major to squirm uneasily, wondering if he had said something wrong.

"So. Who prepares the book of keys and the date book?"

"Herr General, that is the Signals and Intelligence Group. They are very tightly controlled in the security sense. Generally, no one from the outside can even enter their building. New keys and date books are distributed quarterly, occasionally more frequently."

"So, every ninety days, or so, a new key book and date book. How often are the machines themselves changed?"

The young Major looked shocked. "Machines, sir? They haven't been changed since I first was part of intelligence, to the best of my knowledge. There is no need, for the system cannot be broken."

Müller made notes on his desk pad. *No significant changes in the machine since 1939 or so. What hubris to assume no one could unravel our mystery,* he thought.

Chapter 37

7 June 1943

The Pentagon, Washington, D.C.

Navy Briefing Room

0645 Hours

Pentagon Morning Brief

Bartholomew Stuart, Admiral, U.S. Navy, swept importantly into the room, scowling behind his bushy, white eyebrows. He observed the men at attention for a moment, and took his place. "Be seated. Please begin."

Joel carefully reminded himself of the man's reputation for brusqueness to the point of rudeness, and his unwillingness to suffer fools gladly.

"Good morning, Admiral; I am Lieutenant Commander John Bell Higgins. I will be briefing this morning."

"Higgins? Where is Fisher? And why three names?"

"Sir, I regret to inform you that Captain Fisher was taken to Bethesda Naval Hospital this morning around 0300 with acute appendicitis. The operation was successful, and his prognosis is positive. He should be back on limited duty in five or six weeks. I was asked to brief in his absence. I use my middle name, sir, to distinguish myself from Captain John Thomas Higgins, a distinguished officer who is also assigned to this unit and who should bear no responsibility for my gaffs."

"Well said. Give my best to Captain Fisher. Continue."

"Thank you, sir. In the Pacific Theater—," Higgins spent forty-five minutes covering the war in the Pacific. He was interrupted several times by pointed questions and comments, all of which indicated to Joel the quick intelligence of the men in the room.

"Turning to the war in Europe, —" Higgins said, and continued, discussing progress on the Continent.

"Our English friends have provided some interesting information regarding the outcome of a competition the Luftwaffe held for heavy bombers. They—"

Admiral Stuart interrupted him; "Why is the Navy interested in Luftwaffe bombers?"

"Sir, I believe that this is of direct interest to the Navy. Would you prefer I go directly to the threat, or provide background first?"

"Background first, but make it snappy." The man scowled at the interruption of the flow of the meeting.

"Yes, sir! The Luftwaffe requested design submitals for a new, heavy, long range bomber eighteen months ago; there were six industry responders, of which three were chosen to build prototype aircraft. They were Heinkel, with a modified HE-177, Messerschmitt with a version of their ME-264, and Gotha with their GO-447."

"Never heard of Gotha. Who are they?"

"Sir, Gotha Waggonfabrik [GFW] built huge, multi-engine biplane bombers during the Great War. They bombed London on several occasions. During the '30s, they researched all-wing aircraft, and proposed a so-called flying wing for the competition. The Horten brothers, who work for Gotha, are among the foremost designers of flying wing type aircraft in the world."

He nodded to the projectionist; "Here is a photograph of one of Heinkle's HE-177s; it's a very complex ship, four-motored despite the appearance – two engines in each nacelle. They have had a number of in-flight fires and crashes due to the engine arrangement. Following the latest crash, a British source reported that the project had been cancelled. We have no independent confirmation of that.

"Next, here is the Messerschmitt ME-264. It's a more conventional four-engine ship, but also extremely complex, difficult and expensive to manufacture. Its performance—"

"Didn't the Air Corps hit that plant recently?"

"Yes, sir, they sure did, ten days ago. Not only did they knock out the production facilities, but with a follow-up raid, they destroyed the tooling and more importantly, the tooling drawings."

"Tooling? What's that?"

"Sir, it is the forms, made of wood, plaster or concrete, on which the aluminum skin panels or internal supports for the aircraft are made. Some are used with hammers, but most require large presses. The point is that tooling requires very skilled workers; without tooling, no aircraft parts can be made. Work will be halted until the drawings are replaced and new tooling is made; our estimate is at least six to nine months, minimum. "

"Hmm. Very good! So two of the three are out of business; what about the third?"

Again, Higgins nodded to the projectionist. "Sir, I apologize, we have very poor photos of the Gotha aircraft, but some of General Donovan's men have secured better ones, which we ought to see tomorrow or the next day."

"Donovan!" the Admiral snorted, jerking in his chair, "That son of a—." He stopped himself; Donovan, Army "General" Donovan, had been hand-picked by Roosevelt to run a separate intelligence gathering group, and promoted from colonel. Because he was working outside normal military channels and had direct access to the President, the man was uniformly despised by senior officers in both services, despite having been awarded the Medal of Honor in the Great War. Controlling his temper, he motioned to Higgins.

"Why a flying wing?"

"Admiral, if you would like, there is an expert here, an Army Air Service Lieutenant Colonel Knight, who could brief you on the technical details." Joel had been sent to Washington to brief both Army and Navy senior officers about the new threat.

Joel saw that the Admiral wasn't too pleased to be briefed by an Army man; inter-service rivalry was no mere concept here.

Scowling, he said "Very well. I don't know why a Navy man couldn't brief this."

"Good morning, Admiral! I am Lieutenant Colonel Joel T. Knight," Joel said as he stepped behind the wooden lectern. "A Navy man isn't standing here, sir, because knowledge of flying wing aeronautics is pretty limited, and I was about the only fellow on the East coast available on short notice."

"What is your background, young man?" the Admiral demanded. "Say, are you related to the late Rear Admiral Josiah Knight?"

"Yes, sir, he was my uncle."

"Why didn't you join the Navy, Colonel? With such a distinguished relative, you could have gotten into Annapolis easily."

"Actually, sir, I applied to Annapolis and West Point at the same time. The Navy just took longer to show interest; I was already a Plebe at the Point! As to my qualifications, I graduated from West Point in 1932, with one of the first Bachelor's degrees in aeronautics. My class and I built a scale model flying wing which we flew as our senior class project."

"Again, I'll ask; why a wing?" Stuart pressed.

"Sir, an all wing aircraft offers several advantages, not the least of which is less aircraft weight for a comparable size. Aerodynamically, a flying wing is far more efficient that a conventional airplane, because of the much smaller wetted area—"

"Define 'wetted area.'"

Joel thought for a moment. "Admiral, to use a Navy analogy, the wetted area on a ship is the hull below the water line. All that surface area creates drag which must be overcome by the engines. That's why battleships have such graceful hull lines; it minimizes the wetted area, and smoothes the flow of water past the hull. In comparison, the entire exterior surface of an airplane is affected by the air it moves through, so it all is considered wetted. By not having a fuselage, a flying wing may have as little as half or even less wetted area than a similar, conventional, airplane."

"So why aren't we building them?" the admiral asked bluntly.

"With respect, sir, we are working on such designs; the Northrop Aircraft company in California has built and flown a couple of small prototypes, and a much larger plane is on the drawing boards. That's classified. I have consulted with them on several occasions. Unfortunately, the control of flying wings is a lot more difficult than anyone here appreciated. Apparently, the Germans have mastered the control problems ahead of us."

"You said these flying wings are more 'aerodynamically efficient' – what does that mean in the practical world?" Stuart demanded with an impatient wave of his hand.

"Sir, that means that a given airplane could carry the same payload of bombs or torpedoes a much greater distance, or, to state the opposite, the more efficient aircraft could carry a far heavier bomb load the same distance."

"Good brief, Colonel." Stuart said, cutting him short; "Now Commander Higgins, how does this threaten the Navy?"

Higgins said, "Thank you, Colonel; please stand by for any questions the Admiral might have. Sir, one of the missions for these airplanes is interdiction of convoys and fleets. The much greater range of the Gotha flying wing could put many more ships at risk."

"Ha!" the Admiral snorted. "We've seen what success the Army has had trying to bomb ships underway; why should the Germans be any better at it?"

"Sir, the answers to that question require that all personnel not cleared for TOP SECRET leave the room."

"Make it so."

With a scuffling of feet and shuffling of papers, several men moved out of the room. The Admiral looked around.

"Very well, Commander, you may continue."

"Thank you, sir. There are two highly secret German projects we just learned about, both of which have serious potential impacts to the Navy."

"Go on."

"The first is referred to as a Relative Motion Bombsight, or RMB. They have developed a method to account for a ship's motion relative to an airplane, using a small, tightly focused RADAR on the aircraft – it increased the probability of a hit by more than three times in the first experimental version. We have several independent reports of this device, all accompanied with similar information on accuracy. The Brits—"; he nodded to the projectionist; "sent us this movie taken from a Royal Navy submarine."

The black and white movie was somewhat grainy, and overlaid with the reticule marks from the sub's periscope. A small cargo ship was suddenly struck repeatedly by a number of bombs, first on the stern, then repeatedly forward along the length of the ship. By the end of the short movie, the ship was rolling over, sinking. The camera jerked upward, to show a German JU-88 twin engine bomber banking away.

"We believe the ship was controlled remotely by radio waves. This same technique has been observed on two other occasions; one of them involving a ship maneuvering in a classic zigzag pattern."

The briefer cleared his voice. "There have been unconfirmed reports that this RMB device has been fitted to the Gotha. Given its long range, sir, we believe that even convoys in the North Atlantic could be at risk."

The Admiral had slunk down a bit in his seat; "What other encouraging news do you have?"

"Admiral, the Germans have also developed a new gun-like weapon for aircraft. No photos are available, and we don't know its designation. It is comprised of a fairly large diameter tube of thin-wall steel, and an insubstantial-looking receiver mechanism. The rounds it fires are actually small rockets. They are about 60mm in diameter [2 ½ inches]. The shells propel themselves out of the barrels and continue to increase in velocity until the propellant burns out. They use no separate casing, and cause no recoil. The result is accurate rounds at very high velocities for long distances, compared to gunpowder projectiles. The huge size of the shells means that nearly any hit on an aircraft would be extremely damaging. At this time, we have no information as to the shell types – high explosive, incendiary, shrapnel – but we assume they will have the same variety as conventional shells soon if they don't already."

He continued, "Most lightly armored or unarmored ships like merchantmen would also be at severe risk."

"Is this weapon still in development, or—?"

"Sir, a large number have been seen, being fitted on numerous airframes. My educated guess is that the weapon is in advanced testing or initial stages of production. To my knowledge, it has not yet been encountered in combat. God help us when it is."

Chapter 38

31 May 1943

Signals and Intelligence Group Headquarters, Berlin, Germany

1319 Hours

Exposing the Rotten Core

Tenaciously, Müller minutely evaluated the process by which his government encrypted messages. Within days, he had narrowed his search for possible leaks to a short list, at the top of which was the key and date books, and the print shop.

The young SS Hauptstrumfuhrer [SS Captain] responsible for overseeing the process haughtily assured him that there was no opportunity for the documents to be stolen or copied.

"Always, they are under the supervision of an SS officer or unteroffizer [sergeant]," he told Müller as they watched books being prepared for shipment.

"You print them here in this building, yes?" he asked him.

The Hauptstrumfuhrer hesitated, "Yes, General. Most of them."

"Most of them? Where are the others printed?"

"At the Eisenbach Brothers Publishers a few blocks from here, Herr General. They do a great deal of work for the Reich."

"Are they supervised by the SS as well?"

"Sir, there is often an officer present during—"

"Often? How many do you print?"

"Between 800 and 1,000 copies, sir."

Müller was incredulous. "You are telling me that 1,000 copies of these incredibly important, secret books are printed and distributed every ninety days, is that it?"

"Oh, no sir. We often don't distribute them all, as some units are withdrawn or ships sunk—"

Müller's eyes narrowed dangerously, "What is done with those not distributed, Hauptstrumfuhrer?"

"General, they are gathered together and burned, I believe, sir."

"You believe? Do you not know? How are they accounted for?" he asked with steel in his voice.

The Hauptstrumfuhrer had a fine mist of sweat on his upper lip, and his eyes were looking from side to side, as if seeking help. "Um, sir, we count the bundles, record the number in the Daily Log, then bag them for disposal in the furnace."

"Individually. How do you account for them *individually?*" Müller demanded icily.

"The Log Book records each unit or ship receiving a pair of books, and—"

"Do not waste my time, Hauptstrumfuhrer; do you serialize each book so it can be traced?"

He answered in a small voice, "No, sir."

There was a frigid silence as Müller considered the answer. "Let me understand this; you print 1,000 copies of the most secret books in the Reich, yet you have no way of telling if one or two, or a dozen copies were to vanish? Is this so? And many of them are printed in a civilian building with 'occasional' supervision?" The icy voice had turned glacial.

The young man pulled himself to attention, "I assure you, Herr General, that I perform my duties precisely as they are prescribed."

"No doubt you do, Hauptstrumfuhrer," Müller said dryly. "Nonetheless, we shall speak to your superior at once."

With the increasingly terrified Hauptstrumfuhrer in tow, Müller made his way to the chief's office. SS Standartenfuhrer [SS Colonel] Heinz Koller was a tall, thin, graying man in his early fifties. He affected a poor imitation of Hitler's mustache, and wore thick, rimless glasses over pale blue eyes.

"What is it you require, Herr General? I am a busy man," he demanded haughtily.

"Not busy enough, from what I have seen, Koller," snapped Müller. Koller's eyes opened wide; no one ever spoke to an SS Colonel that way! Just in time, he remembered Müller's new position and bit back the acerbic reply on his tongue.

"Your man tells me you neither serialize nor track the key and date books for Enigma and that they are in part published at a civilian printer without full-time SS supervision. Is this so?"

A chill ran down the Standartenfuhrer's back. He was being interrogated as if he was a mere private, and by a man who could have him summarily shot.

"It is essentially so, Herr General, but never have we suffered a loss."

"Truly?" said Müller sarcastically. "How do you know this? I have strong suspicions that such a loss directly contributed to the Führer's injuries. Can you demonstrate otherwise? Or should I call for the Sicherheitsdienst [SS Security Service]?"

Now the Standartenfuhrer was really afraid; if Hitler's wounds were traced to a leak in his command, he was a dead man. Quickly he said, "Come, let us pay a visit to the publisher, Herr General, and let you see for yourself." He hated the quaver in his voice. It was more bravado on his part than any expectation that a visit would put Müller's mind at ease. At least, he hoped, it would give him some time to think of some way to extract himself.

Half an hour later, the three men were standing in the press room of Eisenbach Brothers Publishers, shouting over the roar of huge presses printing propaganda posters. Müller watched the machines for a moment, then shouted into the Standartenfuhrer's ear.

"The key and date books are small, the size of a book. These are the size of newspapers. Where do you print the books I am interested in?" His tone of voice made clear his increasing impatience.

To his amazement, the SS Colonel leaned over and apparently asked the same question of the civilian employee running the press.

Has this man never been here before? Müller wondered. *This is appalling.*

The pressman wiped his hands on a dirty apron, and signaled that they should follow. The press was smaller, though scarcely quieter. A bored looking young SS Gefreiter [Private] spotted them, leapt to his feet and stood at rigid attention.

"This is the supervision you provide, Herr Standartenfuhrer? A boy soldier? Does he even know the importance of what it is he is watching over?"

A few feet away, another man operated the smaller press oblivious to them. He had obviously been severely injured; his left eye was covered by a large patch, his face damaged horrifically. Some movement caught his eye. He turned to his right and saw three men, two of them in SS uniforms, looking at him and talking. In an instant, he bolted away toward a doorway. Their escort stopped the press.

Müller instinctively knew the runner was the source of the leaks.

"You," he pointed at the pressman, "call the guards at once." He turned to the men with him. "Where does that doorway lead?"

The Colonel didn't know, but the Hauptstrumfuhrer spoke up, "Sir, it's an auxiliary room, where the men change their clothes, take cigarette breaks, and eat their lunches. There is a toilet room attached, but no other exit."

"What's in there? Tables and chairs? What else?"

"There are wooden lockers, for their street clothes and jackets, and personal belongings."

The pressman returned from the telephone, as the roar of the big presses in the other room stopped.

"What is that man's name?" Müller demanded.

"He is called Schmitt. I do not know his Christian name, Herr General."

Müller went and stood to one side of the door as several armed guards rushed into the room. He waved them to stand back.

"Schmitt! Listen to me. You cannot escape, there is no other exit. Give yourself up, and it will go easier on you," he shouted.

They heard a muffled voice from the room, and then a heavy shot rang out.

"Sir!" one of the guards said, "That's a Russian Markov! I know it well!" A moment later, a second shot echoed off the concrete walls. No one moved.

"Schmitt is a veteran, wounded in Russia, Herr General. He may have brought such a pistol home with him as a souvenir," suggested the pressman.

"We shall see," Müller said, not taking his eyes off the door. "Shut off the lights in this room."

There was a shuffle of feet, and they were plunged into semi-darkness.

"You there, lie on the floor and look under the door. What do you see?"

A teenaged guard nimbly lay down and peered under the door. "There is someone on the floor, Herr General. I cannot see his face. There is blood…"

"There was someone else in this room. Who?" Müller said.

The pressman looked around at the gathering crowd of print shop workers, "I have not seen George Herbst in some time. He is in there perhaps?"

"Schmitt! Schmitt! Answer me!" Müller demanded. There was silence. "Herbst, are you there?" Nothing.

"We must see what has occurred. We will treat it as a military assault, yes?" he said to the officer leading the guards. The man nodded, and signaled his men.

Moments later, the door was smashed down, and the armed men rushed in.

"There are two dead men here, Herr General," someone shouted.

"Poor George, he must have tried to stop him," the pressman lamented.

"And got himself killed in the bargain," Müller looked at the body of the eye-patched pressman, who had shot himself. The pistol was a Russian Markov.

"He's wearing his Army Identity Disk," Müller said as he lifted it off the body. "It looks authentic enough." He rubbed the metal disc between his fingers. "It feels as it should." Russian imitations often had an oily feel.

He turned and spoke to the late arriving Sicherheitsdienst Hauptman.

"Take this body to the Gestapo morgue, and have them examine it. I want to learn of every tiny detail, even every piece of lint from his trousers, and his clothes in that locker as well. Check the authenticity of this Identity Disk. Call me when you are finished," he said, handing him a card. The man started to protest, and stopped when the Standartenfuhrer shook his head.

Chapter 39

10 June 1943

Millville Army Air Field, Millville, New Jersey

1710 Hours

Millie and Charles

Joel had been calling Susan a couple of times a week since their movie. Neither could get away on most week nights, so a few minutes on the phone helped make up for it. And a few minutes it was, as Susan's landlady strictly enforced the five minute rule on use of the only phone in the boarding house.

"Oh, Joel! The best news!" she told him enthusiastically, "Millie and Charles are engaged. They're to be married next May."

"Well, we saw that coming, didn't we? They way they looked at each other like moon-struck cows, or something. But good for them, I'm happy for them."

She laughed. "The sad part is that he did get hired by that Martin airplane plant in Baltimore. He's to start there Monday. Millie, poor thing, won't get to see him except for when he can take a train here."

"It's too bad they'll be apart so much, but they'll be able to save up enough in the meantime to get a nice apartment, maybe even a house, so it'll be worth it, don't you think?"

"Oh, probably, in the long run, but it will be hard while they go through it. I—"

"Time," said the landlady in a no-nonsense voice.

"Sorry, Joel, I must go. Bye 'till next time." She hung up, leaving Joel feeling like he'd walked into a wall he didn't see.

Chapter 40

11 June 1943

Berlin, Germany

General Heinrich Müller's Office

0800 Hours

Fraud Exposed

Standartenfuhrer Heinz Koller himself brought the autopsy results to Müller's office. To Müller's secret amusement, the man was still afraid.

"We spent the night searching his flat, Herr General. Hidden behind the walls were several of the current key and date books. He must have smuggled them out of the printing plant," he explained unnecessarily.

"We found also a book and documents written in Russian. The documents are being translated now. The Identity Disk belonged to the real Hans Schmitt, who was killed in Russia. This man, this imposter, somehow got it and took on his identity. As for the body, it is positively that of a Russian: he has stainless steel dental work instead of proper gold."

Müller sat stone faced and silent for a moment, looking at the terrified man.

"You have done well, Standartenfuhrer, in a very short time. My report will reflect your devotion to duty."

The relief that flooded the man's face was palpable.

It is always good to have an SS Colonel in your debt, Müller thought to himself wryly.

"Please provide me a complete report on this entire incident at your earliest convenience, Herr Standartenfuhrer. I must report to my superiors, and I will have need of your expert opinions, and the details of how this imposter was foisted on you."

Now a look of gratitude swept across the SS man's face. Müller had set the hook deeply.

Chapter 41

24 June 1943

Gotha Werkes, Gotha, Germany

1000 Hours

Proof of the Pudding

Oberst Freiherr Gerhard von und zu Schroeder walked down the fight line, inspecting the modified aircraft.

They have worked wonders, he thought to himself. *Here are forty-four aircraft nearly ready for me, and it is only late June. Remarkable!*

He heard engines starting and turned around. They had prepared one for him to test fly. He was anxious to see what it would be like, whether this big tailless airplane could fly as well as Dr. Berthold promised.

Two Hours Later

Von Schroeder made the last landing, and it wasn't bad. He'd flared just a bit high, but was easily able to recover and landed smoothly. He turned to the Gotha test pilot beside him.

"This airplane is surprisingly nimble for such a large craft, and it has a better feel on the controls than either the ME-264 or the HE-177. It is even quite stable. I believe you have a success here."

Chapter 42

Saturday, 26 June 1943

Lieutenant Colonel Joel Knight's Office

Millville Army Air Field, Millville, New Jersey

10:45 Hours

Black Widow

"Colonel! There's a plane coming in on fire!" Joel jumped up from his desk and grabbed his hat. "Let's go, Bill," he told the excited First Sergeant.

The staff car skidded to a stop near the base of the tower. Joel jumped out and ran up the stairs, powerful binoculars in his hand. The stricken plane was evident by the long, black trail of smoke boiling off the right hand engine. Hollywood might have depicted the troubled plane wandering and skidding all over the sky, but this aircraft was headed straight toward them with solid, determined precision. Joel strained to determine what it was, focused the binoculars, and was surprised to see one of the new twin-boom Northrop P-61 Black Widow nightfighters.

They're not even in production yet! Amazing to see one this far away from the Air Corps desert test center in California!

As he watched, the base fire trucks and rescue vehicles raced toward the flight line, sirens screaming. The pilot clearly had his hands full; as Joel watched, there was a bright flash, and portions of the cowling around the right engine blew off, sailing through the air. The smoke changed to gray, evidence the fire was running out of fuel. The big four-bladed prop slowed and stopped, feathered. The aircraft smoothly turned to its right, lowered its landing gear and flaps, and began flaring to land. It touched down firmly, just beyond the start of the runway, and bounced. Parts scattered as the pilot firmly applied the brakes, smoking the tires. The emergency vehicles raced after it, dodging the parts on the runway. The left hand propeller stopped before the aircraft did.

The roll out was straight, and as the big aircraft lurched to a halt, the crew bounded out and raced away while the smoking engine captured everyone's eyes. Joel nodded approvingly as the fire crew quickly sprayed the smoking engine. Still, the aircraft was severely damaged, with portions of the cowling missing, others twisted, the right engine clearly drooping on its mounts. The right tail boom was oil covered and dripping.

An ambulance crew was checking out the obviously shaken crew as Joel walked up. To his surprise, the only officer was a Marine Corps Captain. The young man, perhaps twenty-two or twenty-three, straightened and presented a tolerable salute.

"Sorry about my abrupt arrival, sir!" he said. "The number two engine started running rough, and I guess it must have blown a jug. Gosh, what a mess! I'm Mark Best," he said belatedly.

Joel returned his salute and introduced himself.

"I've got to ask, Captain, what's a Marine doing flying an Army airplane?"

The Marine grinned boyishly, "The Corps wanted one of these new birds to evaluate, so I got chosen to bring one back to Pawtuxent, sir. This one is actually a YP-61, one of fifteen pre-production models. Of course, the Marines don't call it that: it's now a F2T."

Pawtuxent Naval Air Station, in nearby Maryland, was the base where both the Navy and Marine Corps put new aircraft through their paces before accepting them into the fleet.

"OK, now who is this gentleman?" Joel queried, turning to the obvious civilian.

"I'm Oliver Pearson, the Northrop test pilot assigned to this exercise." Nodding toward Mark, he said, "This young man is a pretty good stick, Colonel. I'm not sure I could have gotten this beast back on the ground in one piece myself." They shook hands.

"And the sergeant?"

He's Army; a lot of variety in this crew, Joel thought.

"Sir, Tech Sergeant Richard Arthur; I'm the crew chief. At least 'till we turn it over to the Corps." He saluted, and Joel returned it. He was about thirty, and had a serious mien about him.

"At ease, Sergeant. What do you think went wrong?" Joel asked.

"Can't say for sure until I get a close look at it, sir, but that was as bad an engine failure as I've ever seen."

"I agree." Joel said. He liked that the sergeant didn't jump to conclusions about what caused the problem. Too many post-incident problem evaluations were led astray by somebody deciding in advance what the cause was, and only looking at evidence that supported that conclusion.

Pearson stepped forward. "Your troops have the fire out, Colonel. I stowed a tow bar in the rear; if you'll get us a stout tug, we can clear your active."

"Good idea," Joel countered, and turned to his sergeant. "Bill, have base ops send a tug over, and take this broken bird over to hanger 321, where we keep the base flight B-25; it ought to fit inside."

"Already on the way, sir."

Turning back to the crewmen, Joel said, "If everybody is OK, I can offer you a ride to Base Ops. Captain, you'll want to call Pawtuxent; they're probably worrying about you!"

"I'll need to call Hawthorne and give them the lowdown, too, Colonel," said Pearson. Hawthorne, California was the home of Northrop Aircraft, where the P-61 was about to begin production.

"Sir, if you don't mind, I'd like to follow my ship to the hanger, and start looking it over," said Sergeant Arthur.

"Excellent; I'll have my senior maintenance NCO send some folks over to help you. Don't forget to check in with your unit," said the Colonel.

Chapter 43
Monday, 28 June 1943
Lieutenant Colonel Joel Knight's Office
Millville Army Air Field, Millville, New Jersey
1122 Hours
Sabotage

Bill stuck his head into Joel's office; "Lieutenant Brody and Master Sergeant Hillborne, sir."

Brody was the Second Lieutenant assigned to oversee the P-61 incident. Hillborne was the senior maintenance NCO on base, and an old Army veteran with decades of experience working through the vagaries of new and varied aircraft as the Army added them to the inventory. He was a no-nonsense man, not easily intimidated, with a keen insight into all things mechanical. Joel was anxious to hear what he had to say.

The two men reported, and were seated.

"What have you found, Lieutenant? What caused that beautiful new airplane to nearly self- destruct?"

"Sir, we suspect sabotage." The young man said, looking as if he feared the worst for bringing such unwelcome news.

"What? Fill me in, Master Sergeant." The boyish lieutenant looked slighted.

"Sir," said the man in his gruff voice, "when we looked at the engine, we saw that the cylinders were coming loose from the engine case. Didn't make sense. Those Pratt and Whitney R-2800s are good, reliable airplane motors. The best ever built, in my opinion. *Never*, ever, seen one fail like this." He shook his head as emphasis. "I had the troops pull the remaining cylinders. Three were loose, and several others showed signs of movement on the case. Took us a while, but we narrowed it down to this." He held out a handful of heavy nuts.

"What are these, Hillborne?"

"Colonel, those hold down the cylinders, on studs coming out of the engine case. Sir, you'll notice that they are distorted, and cracked. When enough of them split, the piston forced the cylinder up, or tilted it to one side. Then, it probably only took a few seconds for the piston and cylinder to bind, and destroy the engine."

"Where does the sabotage come in?" Joel asked sharply. He had a sense of what would ensue if it was true – the FBI, the Army's Inspector General's office, and who knows who else, all over the base, interfering with their mission.

"Sir, look inside the nuts," offered the Lieutenant. Joel took a nut that was cracked and peered inside it; the nut had been sawed internally.

"Are they all like this?" he asked in astonishment.

"Every one we looked at," replied Hillborne grimly; "and that's really sneaky, sir, because you can't see it when the nuts are installed. And, they probably wouldn't fail right away, because it could take hours for the saw cut to turn into a crack that would break the nut."

"Dear Lord, that's diabolical! There are hundreds of R-2800s flying on all sorts of Army aircraft! All of our P-47's have them."

"Yes, sir, and even more on Navy and Marine airplanes, to say nothing of civilian airliners," countered Hillborne. "And hundreds on the ships we've sent to the Brits and the Russians."

"Did you inspect the other engine?"

Hillborne looked even more grim, his voice now a menacing growl; "Yes, sir, we tore it down too. Virtually every nut had been tampered with. That plane was a flying death trap; either or both of those engines could have failed anytime; it's a wonder it didn't happen on takeoff."

Joel made up his mind quickly.

"OK, Lieutenant, listen up. You will immediately secure the hanger where that airplane is – nobody goes in or out unless I say so. Log everybody that goes in or out. Put a guard on it around the clock. Hillborne, make sure none of your guys take any souvenirs, just drop everything, even tools, and leave them where they are. Have each one write down what they found, without collaboration, and get it to me right away. You are dismissed; I've got to go see the Colonel."

He spoke to his sergeant; "Bill, call Colonel Watkins' office and tell them I must see him as soon as possible – we found sabotage on that P-61. And call Colonel Randolph too."

Consequences

On the way to Colonel Watkins' office, Joel mulled over how he'd bring this unwelcome news to the base commander.

The Colonel's adjutant showed him in immediately.

"Colonel, what the hell's this about sabotage on that P-61? Are you sure?" the Colonel demanded, as he stood.

Joel saluted and said "Sir, I'm sorry to say we're very sure. Sergeant Hillborne brought me these engine cylinder nuts from the number two engine; they have been sabotaged – sawed internally before they were installed. Even worse, sir, when they pulled down the other engine, they found the same thing."

The officer inspected the heavy steel nuts Joel had handed him. A pilot since the Great War, he had seen many broken parts over the years as part of post-crash analyses. He put on his reading glasses and examined all of them closely, then took a small magnifying glass from his desk drawer. He was silent for a moment, thinking about the procedure he now had to put into motion.

He looked up at the waiting Lieutenant Colonel.

"Joel, we'll have to bring in the FBI on this right away. That airplane and the hanger it's in is now a crime scene! I want you to secure everything and stop all work immediately."

"Already done, sir," Joel told him, glad to have correctly anticipated the Colonel's wishes.

"I believe that we'll have to notify Army IG's office too, sir," Joel said.

"Yes, of course; you are right; take care of that will you? I'll call the FBI. I want any conferences on this matter to be held in my conference room, with Jerry in attendance." Captain Jerry McDonald was Colonel Watkins' adjutant.

White was frowning, deep in thought. "Did that Northrop pilot leave for California yet?"

"Yes, sir, yesterday afternoon on the west bound C-47 shuttle. The Marine Captain, Mark Best, took the train to Pawtuxent this morning."

"Well, looks like this mess is ours to clean up, Colonel!"

Chapter 44

Tuesday, 29 June 1943

Lieutenant Colonel Joel Knight's Office

Millville Army Air Field, Millville, New Jersey

0730 Hours

FBI

Two FBI agents were at Joel's office first thing the next morning.

They look like Hollywood central casting sent them over, Joel thought with amusement. *Look at 'em: clean shaven, rugged jawed, perfect blue suits over impossibly white shirts, conservative neckties, perfectly shined shoes. Where are the Tommy guns and swelling music?*

"Lieutenant Colonel Knight?"

"Yes." Joel answered simply, suddenly remembering that all FBI agents were lawyers first.

The unsmiling man flashed a badge and ID in a leather wallet, as his counterpart did the same.

"I'm Agent Barnet; he's Agent Rangely. Tell us about this sabotage. Now." he demanded roughly.

Joel bit back his resentment at being ordered around in his own office. "Let's take this slow and easy, gentlemen – we're on the same side, after all. First, though, let me offer you both some coffee; no reason we can't be civilized about this."

The first agent reddened a bit at the gentle rebuke, and nodded. "Yes, thank you. Some coffee would be fine."

Joel asked Bill to bring them coffee, and invited the men to seat themselves. Bill, always on top of the situation, had already made the coffee. Joel nodded at him, wordlessly thanking him as he left the room.

Stirring his coffee, Joel related the events surrounding the emergency landing of the P-61 the day before.

"When the senior maintenance NCO brought me these," he laid the split nuts on the desk, along with a magnifier; "Colonel Watkins notified the FBI immediately. They are clearly sabotaged."

The second agent looked at several of the nuts. "Where is the aircraft now? Has any more work been done on it? Did you keep all the parts?"

Joel noted that he didn't ask where on the airplane the nuts came from.

"We secured the airplane immediately; it's in a hangar, which we also secured. All work was stopped as soon as the sabotaged parts were found. I had each mechanic separately write down what they found." He pushed several sheets of paper toward them.

"I personally went over both engine logs," he said, sliding the documents toward them. "They are both brand new. Northrop installed them fresh from the Pratt & Whitney factory. The plane has less than forty hours on it."

The agents passed a knowing look between them.

"We've seen this before," said Barnet. "Counting this airplane, we now know of thirty-one engines with tampered cylinder nuts."

Joel leaned forward, frowning in surprise; "Thirty-one? Has anybody been hurt? Who's doing this?"

"We can't give you details, Lieutenant Colonel Knight, but there have been several crashes and deaths. We're afraid that some affected aircraft have gone to Europe. You can expect a mandatory inspection notice for all your aircraft with Pratt & Whitney R-2800 engines by the end of the day. I believe the correct term is 'Emergency Time Compliance Technical Order' [ETCTO]. That will ground all of those aircraft until inspection proves them safe. You are to impound all aircraft that do not pass inspection for these tampered nuts, and contact us immediately." He handed Joel a business card. "That means any time of day."

"As to your last question, we will have a suspect in custody shortly. We cannot say more. Now, we need to inspect the aircraft. We will, of course, confiscate the engines and all their parts as evidence."

Joel took them to the hanger in the 1941 Plymouth staff car. The guards were still on duty, and let them in at Joel's orders.

The two FBI Agents looked around for a few moments, and then turned to Joel. "We'll send a truck to pick up the engines. Could you provide us an office with a telephone, Colonel?"

"Certainly; you can use this one," Joel indicated a nearby doorway.

Agent Rangely told him, "We'll need to interview the mechanics who worked on this aircraft and the tower personnel on duty as well. Please arrange for the tower log to be copied – we have to keep the original."

He thought a moment; "Please let the mechanics know that they aren't suspects – they're more like witnesses to a car wreck; we need their stories."

"We'll also need to interview the crew, of course. Please make them available."

"Sorry, Agent, I can't do that. This bird is a transient, and the crew has dispersed. Here's contact info for them, though." The agent looked chagrined, but took the paper Joel handed him.

As Joel left, they began to photograph everything in sight.

The Spartan office in the hanger was quickly equipped with a table and several chairs. Shortly afterward, the parade of men being interviewed began.

At the end of the day, Joel received a call from Sergeant Hillborne.

"Sir, they've interviewed all six mechanics, Lieutenant Brody, the tower guys, and myself. They asked me to stand by with a couple of men to help load the engines. The main gate just called and the truck is on its way. We should be wrapped up in a couple of hours at the most."

"What about the IG team?" Joel asked him.

"Sir, they finished and left about 1500 this afternoon; my guess is that they didn't want anything to do with an FBI investigation."

"Can't blame them. OK, Sergeant, please make sure Colonel Randolph is kept informed about all this as well."

"Will do, sir," he replied.

"And Hill? That ETCTO arrived; all our P-47s are grounded as of now."

Hillborne sighed, "Right, sir. I've got guys waiting to start on it. We'll work through the night. I'll have a report for you at Stand Up in the morning."

Joel knew that the man would work through the night; he was the definition of dedication.

In the hanger, the engine-less P-61 sat in the corner, nose high, still dripping oil, looking forlorn and abandoned.

Chapter 45

1 July 1943

Berlin, Germany

1515 Hours

Compromise Explained

General Heinrich Müller collected his thoughts and carefully prepared himself; this would be the most important presentation he would ever make. Albert Speer and Field Marshall Fedor von Bock held the real reins of power in Germany; he was the wobbly third leg in an uneasy Dreifach [triple]; none fully trusted the other two, yet the arrangement was holding together, however shakily. Müller suspected that it would last only until one of them gathered enough power to overthrow the other two.

Von Bock, as always, was blunt, even rude to those who he considered his inferiors. He looked at Müller through his small, round glasses with pitiless, pale blue eyes.

"Do not waste our time with pretty speeches, General; tell us what you must, and go."

Müller put on his best expressionless face, "Sir, I regret to inform you that the Enigma system has been compromised, in every aspect of its use. Our enemies are reading dispatches of every kind within hours of when they are sent. I most urgently urge you to instantly direct changes of the most fundamental sort."

"How can this be? Enigma is unbreakable!" von Bock roared, coming to his feet.

"Not so, Fedor," Albert Speer told him calmly, as he leaned back in his chair. "Any machine one man can devise can be understood by another. We know the British and Americans have been working on this for years; apparently, they have succeeded."

Field Marshall von Bock went to the heart of it; "If they can read our dispatches, we are exposed in every move we make. What can we do?"

"Sir," Müller said deferentially, "we have a few days' supply of 'one-time-pads' for nearly all units and facilities currently using Enigma. These can be used temporarily until a new or modified Enigma can be fielded."

Speer shook his head, "Developing a new coding device could take months, even years. One-time-pads should not be used for more than a few days; they are too clumsy and subject to physical interception. We must devise a substitute quickly. We could use the Geheimscheiber for the most important messages, but most smaller units do not have the equipment." Geheimscheiber meant "secret writing"; it was a system that encoded a message using a perforated paper tape that fed the coded message directly into a radio transmitter. The problem was that it was easily broken.

Müller was again deferential, "If I may, Herr Speer? One of my men has devised a modification to the Enigma machines that could possibly be fielded quickly."

"What would that be, Herr General," Speer said somewhat suspiciously. Every hair-brained idea some farmer or shop keeper thought up seemed to come to his desk, with only one idea in thousands worthy of consideration.

Mentally crossing his fingers, Müller said, "This man, an engineer, has proposed replacing the wheels within the Enigma machine with six rotating hexagonal rods." He moved his hands up and down, showing that the rods would be mounted vertically.

"Each rod would contain 100 alphabet characters in random order on each face; no two faces are the same. By inserting the rods to different depths into the machine, and rotating them, the number of combinations is all but incalculable. Best of all, sirs, he has built a manually operated model which performs well."

"Is it complex, this design? How difficult would this be to manufacture?" Speer pressed, already mentally searching for a facility that could take on such an important and high priority project.

Müller spread his hands, "Herr Speer, with respect, I am only a policeman, not an engineer. My man assures me that making the new parts is not difficult."

"While we investigate this, could we not double – encrypt our messages using one-time pads?" asked von Bock.

"Yes, sir, that would work. The complication is, of course, that we would use up our stock of pads twice as quickly. If I may suggest, Gestapo couriers would be ideally suited to both protect and distribute the new pads as they are created."

Müller smiled internally; he had been able to involve each man in a way that he saw it was to his own advantage, and now they were in agreement.

Within days, a small manufacturing firm nestled near the Alps was working around the clock producing the parts.

Chapter 46

9 July 1943

German Base near Santiago de Compestela, Spain

1013 Hours

Getting Started in Spain

Oberst Freiherr Gerhard von und zu Schroeder strode back and forth along the top of the bluff, watching bulldozers pushing dirt over the edge. He was anxiously looking quickly at the operators, then at the work, his hands jerking up as if to direct them, then holding back.

A few yards away, a Construction Battalion Major with a deeply tanned face and wearing a dusty work uniform watched him.

"May I explain anything to you, Herr Oberst?" Von Schroeder's head snapped around, he had been unaware he wasn't alone.

Von Schroeder said. "I am concerned that they do not fall over the edge, Herr Major, and that they will not have enough – um – material to fill in under the runway."

"May I assure you, sir, that these men are accomplished builders? Most have worked for me for many years. We have built roads through the Alps, we even did the improvements on the road leading to the Führer's Wolf's Lair. We have constructed runways throughout the Reich, and in Africa. They most certainly know how to operate at the edge of a precipice. And I myself have calculated the amount of fill we will require; there is more than enough to allow the 10 in 100 slope you require." The man exuded confidence, and the decorations on his chest testified to his expertise.

This is a relief, he thought. "Will you be able to pave on such a slope, Major?"

"Sir, I assure you, this will not be a problem. The only unresolved issue at this point is where best to direct the flow of rain water so that it doesn't undermine the lower runway. I am proposing catch basins, but my terrain specialists have not yet finished evaluating other possibilities."

"Ah," von Schroeder replied. *I don't really understand what he means, but I must not let him know.* "And the level upper runway will be sufficient to land the aircraft initially, and to park them until we depart, I trust?"

"Herr Oberst, I have recommended a larger parking area, because I believe that an insufficient area was allowed for maneuvering such large aircraft. This will not affect the completion date. The rockiness of the terrain is a bit greater than expected, but nothing we can't easily cope with. This project will be ready within the time limits you have specified."

The tightness in his stomach began to ease as von Schroeder returned to his quarters. *This seems to be going well.*

The same major came to him a few days later, "Oberst, I have good news! The Spanish government has decided that this is to be a new air base for them after we have launched our mission. They will build a second runway, and in place of our railroad tank cars, they intend to install modern fuel tank farms."

The "Spanish government" had been not so gently prodded in that direction, von Schroeder knew.

"This is indeed good news, Herr Major! First they sell us the fuel we need from their new refinery, so it is no longer necessary to transport it from the Fatherland, and now that they are building this launching area into a military base, our use of it will be disguised!"

"Speaking of disguises, sir, here is the plan to hide the sloped runway."

He unrolled a drawing, and pointed. "After you depart, we will randomly perforate the sloping surface with thousands of holes, and plant fast growing shrubs, such as grow naturally on the hillsides nearby. Within a short time, the sloped runway will become indistinguishable from the surrounding area. We will scatter dirt, rocks and plants over the lower runway, so," he pointed on the drawing, "which will disguise it. Within two months, at the most, no improvements save those of the Spanish will be visible." He looked pleased with himself. Von Schroder happily slapped him on the back and congratulated him.

Von Schroeder's Temporary Headquarters

The same day

His adjutant entered, and waited quietly for von Schroeder to finish. When he looked up, he said, "Herr Oberst, three more of the modified aircraft have arrived. They are in the same excellent condition as the others, I'm pleased to tell you. The Director at Gotha sent a telegram announcing that the remaining seven aircraft are to arrive by next Monday. If that is so, we will have the full complement of sixty aircraft a week ahead of schedule."

Von Schroeder sat back in his chair and smiled uncharacteristically.

"Dieter, this is such good news. Things seemed to have gone so well of late, I almost wonder what we have forgotten." *This is truly good news; we are actually just ahead of schedule.*

"In that regard, sir, I have the most current status of our efforts; do you wish to review it with me?" the young Major asked him earnestly.

Von Schroeder nodded.

I must remember that this young man is an engineer, and always laces his information with numbers; it's his nature.

"Foremost is training. Of the 350 assigned flight crew –we have trained an additional fifty men, in case of injury or illness – 92 percent have successfully completed proficiency training for their primary function; in addition, over 80 percent have now been trained to take over for another man in case of emergency; that's a large improvement over last time.

"All the pilots assigned as primary pilots have performed at least three mate/de-mate connections with the aerial tankers. Many have done six or more. What amazes me is that we have had so few problems. After all, most bomber pilots are not at all used to flying close formation, which is what refueling requires, after all."

Von Schroeder asked, "How have Herr Doctor Berthold's changes to the Junkers design worked out?"

As promised, Generalmajor Wever had sent the genius to visit the Junkers factory the next week after von Schroeder's worrisome comments about their design for the refueling mechanism.

Major Dieter Osterman smiled wryly at his boss, "Well, sir, with his usual aplomb and grace, our Doctor Berthold set them straight. In truth, they were very close to the final design; he lengthened the refueling hose several meters, it was far too short, causing the two aircraft to be too close together, which made them bounce around quite a bit. The controls for the little fins that maneuver the end of the hose were too sensitive. With a more deliberate way to move it, the hose operators have an easier time of it. He also had Gotha move the receiving pipes closer to the aircraft centerline, which makes it easier for the bomber pilot to see his own position relative to the hose. The latching mechanism has been refined; it rarely disconnects on its own now, and leaks seem to be a thing of the past.

"The navigators and their backups have progressed well in their refresher courses as well." He hesitated a moment, "To touch on a delicate subject, sir, I feel pressed to remind you that if you intend on commanding this mission, by your own order, you really must take the refueling training yourself."

"Ah, 'hoist on my own petard,' as the British would say," the Oberst replied. "But you are correct, Dieter; will you schedule me for tomorrow, and tell me where to be and when?"

"Of course, sir," he made a note. "Late this afternoon, a train arrived with the last of our armaments, especially the missing incendiaries. The damaged external fuel tanks have been replaced. Except for a few very minor items, all we lack in materiel for the mission is the fresh food, which we'll load just before departure."

Von Schroeder allowed himself a deep sigh of satisfaction after the man left.

This is really beginning to come together; we are actually going do this.

Chapter 47

10 July 1943

The Oval Office, The White House, Washington, D.C.

1113 Hours

Transatlantic Telephone

"Franklin, my wizards at Benchley Park say we have been unable to decode German messages of any kind for more than a month; it appears the Jerrys have done a serious switch on us. Have your lads seen any success?"

"No, Winston, and I am most concerned about it. Our losses on the Atlantic have begun to climb again."

"Yes, yes, we know. Air raids have again begun to slip in with distressing regularity over Great Britain as well. Even Liverpool was hit hard by Gothas. Our RADARs have the Devil's own hard time seeing them. As you may know, *HMS Redoubt* was rather badly handled two days ago when she went to rescue a convoy from one of the German pocket battleships. The convoy diverted to the south-east, and almost immediately came under heavy attack from Gothas, with grievous losses. It would almost seem that we are blind and they are not."

"I assure you, Winston, that every effort is being made on this side of the Atlantic to break this impasse.

"We are embarking on another attempt to capture a German weather ship, as we did in 1940; perhaps we can again obtain a new code machine intact. SAS are planning some raids. Until one of these efforts succeeds, our losses may continue to mount."

Chapter 48
22 September 1943
German Base near Santiago de Compestela, Spain
0910 Hours
Doctor's Orders

The doctor sat back on his stool, observing the weary-looking officer in front of him.

"Herr Oberst, Generalmajor Wever was right to send you to see me, despite your protests. You are physically exhausted, and in no condition to lead this mission. Fortunately, there is yet time to remedy the situation. This is what you will do – this is an order, as if by Generalmajor Wever himself; yes?"

"Jawohl, Herr Doctor," von Schroeder said with resignation.

"Very well." The man raised his head as if he were about to make a proclamation.

"These pills are for sleeping; you will take one and only one each night before retiring, for the next ten days. You will retire at 2100 hours, no exception, and no alcohol after mid-afternoon." The man's index finger was pointed at his chest. "Your batman will awaken you at 0600 hours for your toilet and breakfast. Then and only then are you to resume your duties. Do you understand?"

"Jawohl, Herr Doctor." He relaxed a bit; *this wasn't as bad as I'd feared – they might have taken the mission away from me.*

The doctor smiled at him, "Do not despair, my dear Oberst. You have delegated well and the entire organization is full of enthusiasm. Morale is excellent. I asked your adjutant about preparedness; he tells me the crews are ready, and are just polishing their techniques. You have done your duty well. Follow my directions, and you will be fit to complete the mission, to the glory of Germany."

Being a good German, he obeyed the doctor's orders to the letter, of course. To his surprise, the sleeping pills and regular hours of sleep did wonders for his sense of well being. The bags disappeared from under his eyes, and he actually felt good again. He was less snappish with his men. Even so, a deep sense of anxiousness was building. This was worse than any of the missions he'd flown in Spain: it was bigger, so much more was at stake, and this time, he was responsible.

He flew the necessary training flights to learn how to refuel from the big, lumbering Junkers. He smiled as he thought of the instructor, a twenty-two- year old Oberleutnant. The poor fellow had been openly nervous about correcting his Colonel's technique. Von Schroeder had done all he could to put the man at ease, explaining that he'd flown with all sorts of instructors in the past ten years, and he would do his best to follow the younger man's instructions.

Even with his many hours of experience flying formation in fighters, he admitted to the young Oberleutnant that it was intimidating getting the Gotha so close to another airplane. He was also surprised how much the wake from the Junkers affected his bomber. It was controllable, but required more attention than he'd expected.

The other thing that caught him a bit off guard was the change in the way the bomber flew as it took on the heavy fuel load. Again, it wasn't terribly difficult to adjust for, it was just that he hadn't expected to have to do so. His young instructor was excellent, and taught him well once von Schroeder overcame his initial reluctance.

"Here you are, Herr Oberst, you have passed your training, in accordance with the standards set by a very strict commanding officer." Von Schroeder laughed, and slapped him on the back good naturedly; that strict commanding officer was himself, of course.

Chapter 49

Thursday, 30 September 1943

Atlantic Ocean, 350 Miles East of New York

0430 Hours, New York Time

Aboard U-156

Kapitan Werner Hartenstein was irritated. He always followed orders, of course, like any good German, but this got his goat. Here he was in command of a mighty Type IXC, one of the most fearsome weapons the Kriegsmarine had, a submarine with nearly a 100,000 tons of sunk Allied shipping to her credit, and he was playing nurse maid to a – Luftwaffe weather observer!

When Feldwebel [Senior NCO] Arnold Klein-Schmitt had first come aboard, he had hardly impressed the Kapitan; he was tall, skinny, bespectacled and sickly looking.

This is a Teutonic warrior? Werner Hartenstein had thought. *Even with the insignia of a Luftwaffe Feldwebel. I wonder, did he really earn the rank?* He eyed the four pips on the young man's collar with suspicion; there was only one man aboard with equivalent rank, and he was years older.

Then, Klein-Schmitt got seasick every time they surfaced; it amused him to think of it. But to the man's credit, Hartenstein never heard him complain. Hartenstein remembered the young man coming to his cabin the day after they got underway.

In the Kapitan's Quarters

"I can tell you now of my mission, Herr Kapitan, if you please."

Klein-Schmitt's brown eyes seemed watery, weak; his thick glasses made them seem overly large. He had adopted the casual uniform of the seamen aboard, Hartenstein noted, with the four pips sewed on his sleeve.

"Yes, do so." Hartenstein would not countenance impertinence by an underling.

"Just so. Sir, I have been ordered to have you transport me on this ship to a position approximately eighty kilometers [fifty miles] east of the city of New York."

It shouldn't have, but it rankled Hartenstein that Klein-Schmitt called his submarine a ship; *doesn't everybody know a submarine is a **boat**?* he thought.

"It will be necessary for you to allow me at least thirty minutes on the surface with the ship at rest for me to make my observations, sir. I understand that is a long time for you—"

"A long time?" Hartenstein was incredulous. "A long time? This is an eternity! So close to the American coast? They are not asleep, you know, Klein-Schmitt."

He ticked off on his fingers. "They have destroyers, patrol boats, aircraft large and small, dirigibles, and submarines of their own, to say nothing of the merchantmen with their lookouts and the occasional civilian day-sailor. No. It is a death sentence. I will not permit it." He folded his arms, the argument over.

Klein-Schmitt regarded him expressionlessly, then said respectfully, "Sir, they said you might be reluctant. Admiral Canaris instructed me to give you this in the event you hesitated to do as I ask."

"Canaris? You spoke personally to Admiral Canaris? He instructed you?" Hartenstein narrowed his eyes dangerously.

The Kapitan took the offered envelope; he saw the Admiral's seal, and his own name handwritten on the front. He opened it and read the enclosed letter, then read it again. He cleared his throat.

"It would seem that I am to be at your disposal, Feldwebel." His face contorted under the awkwardness of the situation. He was humiliated to be ordered by an enlisted man. Or was he?

"I promise to disturb your routine as little as necessary, Herr Kapitan," Klein-Schmitt said calmly, but without any sign of humility or subjugation.

"Why would they want a weather observer—?"

"I am not merely an observer, Kapitan; I am a meteorologist, trained at Berlin University. I was not permitted to tell you beforehand, but you must now know this: there is to be a Luftwaffe attack on the city of New York. I am to evaluate the weather conditions as the attack force proceeds across the Atlantic; my observations will drive the final decision to have the attack continue or to have the aircraft return to their takeoff location."

Hartenstein was shocked to hear that such a daring attack was underway.

Well, a comeuppance for the arrogant Americans, he thought. *Perhaps it will draw some of the attention away from us.*

Now he understood why he had not been informed beforehand. He regarded the spare young man standing so seriously in front of him. There was steel behind the watery brown eyes, to say nothing of very high level direction, Hartenstein realized. He bowed to the inevitable.

"So. On what day and at what time will you require me to place my boat at such risk, Herr '*Feldwebel*'?" The emphasis on the rank made it obvious he didn't believe it was real.

Klein-Schmitt ignored the hint to tell more.

"If the sea state permits, Herr Kapitan, the time of thirty minutes before sunrise would for me be best. If we are fortunate, I will be able to make my measurements when the chances of being seen are minimal. The day will be 2nd October."

"But thirty minutes; why so long? We are at very great risk on the surface and not making way. Do you understand we could be attacked, sunk? You could be killed along with us?" He was all but pleading, Hartenstein realized.

Klein-Schmitt seemed unperturbed, "I must inflate and launch a balloon, which I will carefully watch for several minutes; it will tell me of wind speeds and direction. I must also measure temperatures, atmospheric pressures, and even humidity. Most importantly, I must study the cloud formations and types of clouds; they will reveal what possible storms are behind them."

Hartenstein was unconvinced, and it must have shown on his face, he realized.

"I am not a fool, Kapitan; I am fully aware my life is at risk like yours and your crew. I will be completely at your command should we be discovered. I have practiced quick reentry into the ship. My observation tools can be abandoned instantly should you order the ship to submerge."

Two days later, fifty miles off New York City

The sea is unusually calm this morning, especially for this time of year, Hartenstein thought as he completed his periscope survey. *Good for us. Good for Klein-Schmitt as well, I hope.*

He detected no shipping that threatened them; far to their north, a fairly large convoy was forming up, from the look of all the smoke, but nothing nearby. He saw no aircraft.

Reluctantly, he gave the order, "Take him to the surface; gunners and lookouts prepare to go topside."

Klein-Schmitt was there with his paraphernalia, he saw.

Let's see how he gets it all up through the hatch, Hartenstein thought with amusement.

The boat surfaced, and began to roll in the swells. Klein-Schmitt clambered up the ladder as if he'd been doing it for years. Hartenstein followed his men, and took his place on the sail's weather deck. Klein-Schmitt already had partially inflated the balloon, and soon launched it. As calm as it was, the slight breeze had a real bite; winter on the North Atlantic was not far away.

Hartenstein had to remind the lookouts to watch for aircraft and ships, not the soaring balloon. He didn't like the way the balloon caught the light of the not-yet risen sun. When it had climbed quickly to the south-east, and was lost from sight, Hartenstein breathed a small sigh of relief.

He watched, fascinated in spite of himself as Klein-Schmitt made notes and swiftly deployed strange looking gear from his wooden box and cloth shoulder bag.

"Ten minutes," intoned the seaman tracking how long they were on the surface.

Now, Klein-Schmitt had some sort of whirly-gig spinning in the light breeze. As it twirled, he was spinning a strange device around in vertical circles at the end of a chain. He stopped, wrote some notes, and threw something else over the side at the end of a line.

Is he measuring sea temperatures too? Hartenstein wondered. *What could that possibly tell him about the weather?*

"Twenty minutes."

Hartenstein recognized the weather vane as Klein-Schmitt set it up; he could also see that it was showing a slightly different wind direction than what the balloon had taken.

A voice at the open hatch announced, "Kapitan, sonar reports screws about twelve kilometers [eight miles] to our south-west, making about eighteen knots. He estimates that it is an American destroyer. The ship will pass within a 1000 yards of us if they do not turn."

"How much longer, Klein-Schmitt?" Hartenstein demanded urgently.

This was what I've feared; getting caught on the surface.

"I am finished, Herr Kapitan. I will descend into the ship in forty-five seconds." His hands were flying, replacing his instruments in the case. He leapt to his feet and scrambled down the ladder with several seconds to spare.

"Dive. Dive. Lookouts below deck."

Less than a minute after the destroyer had been reported, U-156 slipped silently and undetected beneath the Atlantic.

"My pardon, Herr Kapitan," Klein-Schmitt said. "We must now proceed at high speed on this heading for approximately one hour. If there are no ships in the vicinity, we must again surface long enough to send a radio message." He handed Hartenstein a card.

Hartenstein raised an eyebrow, and said sarcastically, "Am I to run at flank speed for an hour, Herr 'Feldwebel'? That will exhaust our batteries."

"No, sir, that will not be necessary. I need us to be approximately twenty-five kilometers [fifteen miles] from our last location before I radio my measurements and recommendations. Use whatever speed will accomplish that. I shall be at the table in the Officers Mess doing my calculations; kindly inform me when we have reached our destination."

Hartenstein opened his mouth to reply, and then snapped it closed again.

This man does not act at all like a Feldwebel; more likely, he is SS or so, he thought; *I'd better do just as he says. At least we won't have to expose ourselves on the surface again. I hope.*

Klein-Schmitt had covered the cramped table with graphs and charts, several of which Hartenstein recognized as the coastal area near New York City. He had filled several pages of tablet paper with symbols and mathematical calculations. A slide rule lay nearby, next to an open book of obscure tables.

Hartenstein cleared his throat, "Herr Klein-Schmitt, we have reached a point approximately twenty-five kilometers from where you took your observations. The boat is at rest, awaiting your instructions." The sarcasm was slight, and Klein-Schmitt either ignored it, or didn't recognize it.

"Ah, excellent, Kapitan. I am just complete. I need now to see your radio man; I shall temporarily make a change to your ship's radio."

"Boat," Hartenstein absently corrected, "what changes to my radio?"

"Just this, Herr Kapitan," the man held up a small metal device. "This crystal is adjusted to a secret frequency only used by the aircraft we discussed before. When I am finished, this will be thrown into the sea, and no one will discuss it, yes?"

The submarine's crew had taken a wary view of this strange Luftwaffe man; when word of a secret radio transmission spread through throughout the boat – there are no secrets on a submarine – the distrust began to edge toward fear.

U-156 hovered silently just below the surface as her Kapitan carefully surveyed the sea's surface and the sky. The sonar man had already given his "all clear."

"Raise the radio mast." A hydraulic hiss signaled compliance with the command.

On the deck below, as the boat's radio man watched critically, Klein-Schmitt sat at the radio with a headset on, seemingly very much at home. He keyed the telegraph key in a manner which indicated more than passing familiarity.

In moments, he sat back in the chair, and spoke into the microphone, reading from the papers he'd brought with him. Twice, he repeated himself, in careful, precise language. Finally, he sat back, and acknowledged the radio man's presence.

"I shall be finished in a moment, then you may have your set back," he said. He turned, and skillfully removed the crystal he had installed moments before, and re-inserted the standard Kreigsmarine crystal in its place.

"I think you will find everything in order," he said as he rose, and climbed the ladder to the command deck.

"My duties are complete, Kapitan." He handed Hartenstein the crystal. "That must be disposed of overboard, sir. The ship is again yours to perform your own duties as they have been prescribed. I shall be as inconspicuous as possible for the remainder of our voyage."

Chapter 50

1 October 1943

German Base Near Santiago de Compestela, Spain

1700 Hours

Takeoff

The day had come, inevitably, finally, and von Schroeder sat anxiously through the weather and target briefings with his crews. The ride to the aircraft was quiet, with none of the usual joking among the men. The fitters who had prepared the big bombers were somber, too. The "good byes" and "good luck" wishes were subdued.

Von Schroeder thought about the previous day, when Generalmajor Wever had called him.

"I wish you God speed and good luck, Gerhard. You and your men will perform well, I am sure of this. Bear this in mind, whether it goes perfectly or is a disaster, the first mission for any aircraft is seldom a good predictor of what is to come. Learn all you can, and attempt to view it all dispassionately. We must be prepared to improve upon what we have done."

The words echoed in his mind; *is this encouragement, or shall I take warning?*

His crew was busy, serious, and very professional as they prepared for the long flight ahead. He wouldn't tell them, but he was already proud of them.

Von Schroeder sat in the left seat of the lead aircraft, mentally reviewing and rehearsing for the hundredth time. His handwritten notes were dog-eared and smudged from heavy use during practices. One more glance at the engine gauges, all safely in the green, and he took up the microphone.

"Rheinwasser aircraft, prepare for takeoff." He forced his voice to be low, confident; he hoped it sounded more confident to the men than it did to him.

He released the brakes, and with a gentle lurch, his big Gotha began to roll. Steering with the brakes, he followed the truck with red flags as it guided them to the runway. On both sides of him on the parking ramps, he could see the other aircraft, propellers turning, ready to follow him. He felt their eyes.

They taxied to the run-up area only a few hundred meters from the start of the sloping runway. A bright red "commit line" had been painted across the concrete; once an aircraft crossed that line, it was committed to going down the incline. Only the most extraordinary actions could prevent an aircraft from taking off or running off the end of the runway once it accelerated down the slope.

Von Schroeder's heart was racing, and his hands were sweating inside his gloves; this was no ordinary take off. He carefully performed the engine run-ups.

"Are we ready?" he asked his flight engineer over the intercom.

"Jawohl, Herr Colonel," the man said crisply

He keyed the mic, "Rheinwasser One, ready to roll."

The control tower responded immediately, "Rheinwasser One, and Rheinwasser Flight, cleared for takeoff."

He took a deep breath, and advanced the throttles.

They accelerated very quickly, in spite of the airplane's incredible weight. The sinking feeling as they lunged down the sloping runway still seemed strange. The co-pilot read off their speed as they hurtled toward a second red line: rocket ignition.

"Rockets *now,*" he announced, and von Schroeder flipped the switch. Instantly, they were pushed back in their seats; the roar of the rockets was louder than the engines.

"Takeoff speed," the co-pilot announced. Von Schroeder smoothly eased the big bomber off the runway. There was the familiar bump as the first pair of rockets dropped off and the second ignited. He swallowed hard, anxious for the takeoff to be over. His heart was racing, and cold sweat ran down his sides. He had already looked at the air speed gauge several times; a stall would be death to them all.

"One hundred meters."

He pulled the landing gear release, and silently breathed a sigh of relief when both sides dropped off properly. The last pair of rockets was almost finished as they crossed the coastline. The roar abruptly stopped, and he pushed down the nose a bit, so their climb wasn't so steep. He felt the airframe vibrate as the rocket assembly dropped away. They had survived the takeoff.

As the co-pilot announced "One thousand meters," he leveled the aircraft, and finished retracting the flaps. He turned them on a gentle left bank, and watched the aircraft following them lift off.

Twenty-five minutes later…

Refueling was going very smoothly, as if it were an ordinary training exercise. Within another twenty minutes, by his watch, all sixty bombers would be refueled, and the mission would truly begin. He was almost afraid to think that it was all going so well. Generalmajor Wever's words again played through the recorder in his mind. He was prepared to abort this mission if everything wasn't perfection.

Finally, the last aircraft detached from the tanker fueling it. The tanker turned toward Spain. The formation was in excellent condition.

"Navigator, give me the heading for New York City," he said a bit theatrically. Projekt Rheinwasser was finally underway.

Aboard Rheinwasser One

The radio operator turned to von Schroeder with a look of satisfaction. "I have just received the transmission from the submarine, Herr Oberst. We will encounter a cold front approximately two hours prior to landfall, with some turbulence and possible rain. After that, smooth sailing on to New York."

"Ah," von Schroder responded, "this is good. You will contact the others with the low power set and inform them." Von Schroeder said to his co-pilot who was flying, "Now I shall take some rest. You will awaken me when you have flown for six hours."

He turned, and made his way to the bunk, slipped off his shoes, and laid down. He immediately sat up again; the doctor had warned him to take a pill. He found the vial, and swallowed the medicine. In moments, he was asleep.

Chapter 51

Friday, 1 October 1943

Base Operations, Millville Army Air Field, New Jersey

0730 Hours

Flight Preps

Lieutenant Colonel Joel Knight walked into base ops and went to the weather desk. "Good morning, sergeant! What're you weather-guessers saying about tomorrow morning?" he said cheerfully.

The young sergeant forced a laugh, "Where are you going, sir?" he asked.

"Over to the coast, then up north toward the Twin Lights – I'll be flying an AT-6. I plan to leave early."

The sergeant consulted his charts.

"Sir, if you leave early, before 0700, you should be in good shape. There's a storm moving through tonight, but in the morning, it will be just high, thin clouds moving out to sea. Along the coast you should have filtered to bright sunlight once the light overcast burns off, probably before 0800. Then the cloud cover, such as it is, will be 15,000 to 20,000 feet, and moving out to sea. Surface temperatures will be around forty-eight degrees. Winds should be out of the north – northwest at zero to ten knots. I assume you'll be flying fairly low, sir?"

"Yes," Joel replied, "below 5,000 feet most of the time, and down on the deck for the photographs."

"You shouldn't have any problems, Colonel. Remember the Navy has their sub chasing blimps moving out to sea around that time, flying out of Lakehurst. There is often other traffic out of Lakehurst, too; F6Fs, PBYs, and the like. Be sure and check in with their controller if you get closer than five or six miles. The morning hours should be just fine. I'll caution you, though, sir, that late afternoon looks a bit unsettled – looks like there's a small cold front moving down from the Buffalo area. We might get some light wind and maybe a couple of little showers, but it won't last long. Probably after 1600, I'd say."

"Oh, we'll be back long before that," Joel said. He finished his notes, thanked the man, and stepped next door to the scheduling desk, to reserve an airplane.

A Tech Sergeant looked up, and greeted him, "Good morning, Colonel Knight! Do you need a bird?"

"I sure do, sergeant!" he replied, "I need a 'T-6 early tomorrow morning."

Like most Army Air Forces bases, Millville kept several aircraft on hand for miscellaneous duties, from flight officers logging their required monthly hours, to training and courier missions, and other errands. Along with other aircraft, Millville had a pair of new North American AT-6 trainers. Powered by a 450 horsepower Pratt and Whitney R-1340 radial engine, the aircraft transitioned new pilots from smaller trainers into a more sophisticated, powerful, and much larger airplane. Most pilots had fond memories of the gentle, easy flying bird, and even active fighter pilots were known to check out a 'T-6 for a spin around the field.

Joel hadn't flown his minimum number of hours in the past month yet, so he had decided to combine a necessary flight with a personal desire to see some historic lighthouses.

The Tech Sergeant checked the glass status board showing the serial number of every aircraft assigned to the base, its status, location, and availability. Grease pencil entries kept the status current.

"Looks like they're both available, sir – which would you like?"

"How about 163?" Joel replied. He was familiar with both airplanes, and knew that tail number 163 was the newest, with less than 100 hours on it.

"It's reserved for you, sir. What time will you depart?"

"I've planned on a 0700 departure, Frank – can you have it ready for me?"

"Sure thing, Colonel Knight, shouldn't be a problem." He wrote Joel's name on the board with a grease pencil.

One more thing, thought Joel as he drove to the maintenance hanger. Inside, he stopped a young mechanic in the hallway, and asked for Master Sergeant Hillborne.

"Sir, I think you'll find him out in the hanger, working on that 'hanger queen' Jug that's giving us such fits."

Nodding, Joel headed toward the maintenance area.

Figures, he thought; *Hillborne would much rather be out there on the floor actually working on those birds than sitting in his office doing paper work.* The thought was in admiration, rather than criticism – Hillborne had a reputation as a hands-on guy who could fix a problem on almost any airplane.

Sure enough, there was the senior maintenance NCO on the base, with his head deep inside the space behind the engine of a big P-47 fighter. It had earned the nickname Jug because it looked like a milk bottle. Military courtesy was a bit relaxed in designated work areas like the hanger, so the young private who spotted him didn't call for attention. Instead, he tugged on the burly sergeant's sleeve, and nodded toward Joel. Master Sergeant Hillborne slipped down off the work stand, wiping his hands as he walked over to greet his boss.

"Good morning, sir! How can I help you?"

Joel returned his grin – the two had a good, collegial relationship of mutual respect.

"Sorry to interrupt all that hard work on the monthly report, Master Sergeant Hillborne!" he said dryly with an arched eyebrow.

"Sir, the boys had a problem with the supercharger intercooler and relief valve relays, so I was just lending them a hand."

"Is that why none of them had to wipe *their* hands? No bad cylinder nuts on this one, I hope?" Joel smiled.

Laughing, Hillborne shook his head, "Honest, sir! I was just helping out! And no, this mess doesn't have that as an excuse; we haven't found any sabotaged engines on base." He nodded his head toward the aircraft, "I still think it's a short in the wire harness; we'll see."

"Good. Just get that report on my desk Monday morning!" he finished with mock seriousness. "Now, what I really came to ask you about is whether you have Ledbetter scheduled for work tomorrow. If you can spare him, I'd like to borrow him for a couple of hours early in the day."

"Sure, sir, I don't see why not. I've got plenty of people, and all we've got to do this weekend is a couple of 100 hour inspections, and finish trouble shooting that flying mess." He indicated the airplane behind him. "What's up, sir?"

"I've gotta get my hours in, and if you remember, I promised my kid sister I'd get some photographs of the lighthouses along the coast for her; thought I'd kill two birds with one stone. And just to make it a package, your boy Ledbetter is writing an article on local lighthouses for the base paper."

Hillborne nodded, "Yeah, that should work for everybody. Who'd ever think a girl in Colorado would be so enamored with lighthouses?" he mused.

"Not me, that's for sure, but I did promise her."

"By the way, sir, that requisition you sent in for the P-61 parts has been approved! All of it! You must be living right. They're gonna send us engines, props, cowling, even motor mounts. And they're all the latest stuff, too. That Widow' is going back into the air. I would've never believed it."

"Hey, that's good news. Be sure and let me know when the parts get here. Now, this jug—." Changing the subject, they began discussing the problem-prone P-47.

Sergeant John Ledbetter was supervising a couple of privates changing a fuel filter in a P-47 as Joel walked up. "Morning, Colonel Knight!" he said smiling.

"Hi, John; Hillborne says I can take you flying with me tomorrow morning, if you're up to it. I thought we might take in some lighthouses." Joel told him.

"Hey, that'd be swell, sir! That would help me on the article I'm writing for the base newspaper on lighthouses, you know?" They'd flown together several times previously, to the young man's obvious enjoyment.

"Yes, I remember. I thought we'd go north up the coast and shoot some of the lighthouses along the way, especially the old Twin Lights up north of Fort Monmouth. The weather guys tell me we should have pretty good light – filtered sunlight and high overcast, then clearing."

"Say, that sounds like we ought to get some swell pictures, Colonel. I've never had a chance to see the Twin Lights yet. What time do you want me at the flightline, sir?"

Joel briefed him on the planned departure time, and which aircraft they'd be flying.

Joel's choice of Ledbetter was no accident. The buck sergeant had been a professional photographer before being drafted. With mind numbing "Army logic," they'd made him an aircraft mechanic, of course. He acted as Millville AAF's unofficial social photographer, and it wasn't unusual for Sergeant Hillborne to be asked for his services. He was in great demand for promotion parties, and birthday parties for the base kids. He had a real knack in the darkroom, too, with the ability to bring out interesting details, and judiciously omit them, as he did when he "fixed" pictures of the commanding colonel's wife that revealed unflattering wrinkles.

Chapter 52

1 October 1943

Office of the Ministry of Production, Berlin

Albert Speer's Office

0858 Hours

Alliance of Opposites

Albert Speer's secretary barely hid the contempt on her face as she admitted the crippled visitor. "Herr Minister Speer, may I present Herr Doctor Heinz Berthold?" She all but spit the words.

Berthold ignored her. He was determined to make a good impression on this man, one of the few senior Nazis with any sense, in his opinion. He mentally reminded himself to follow conventional courtesies, no matter how silly they seemed.

The tall, handsome man was oblivious to his deformities, or at least that was how he acted as he strode across the room to shake Berthold's hand. His tailored gray wool suit contrasted sharply with the uniformed officers Berthold was used to dealing with.

"How kind of you to come, Dr. Berthold. I have been anxious to meet you, and to congratulate you on the amazing advances you have made with the Gotha project – what is it called? Oh, yes, Projeckt Rheinwasser. They are underway as we speak, you know."

Berthold didn't know, but didn't let on. "Yes, this is good, Herr Minister. I wish them every success."

Speer regarded him for a moment, then said, "This mission is at best a diversion, of course. If we are fortunate, it may result in a few dozen fighter aircraft held back by the Americans for self-defense. There are far more important steps we should be taking with our aviation assets."

Berthold was immediately encouraged; Speer seemed to have a practical understanding of his country's precarious position. They walked into Speer's palatial office, Berthold's cane creaking.

"I could not agree more, Herr Minister. For example, I would point out that we are manufacturing and supporting far too many different aircraft types. In my opinion, we would do best to concentrate our efforts on a few good ones, and not only discontinue production of the others, but immediately scrap many of the old ones."

Speer's eyebrows went up in surprise and pleasure, from the smile now on his face.

I think he likes my idea.

"It would seem, my good doctor, that we are in complete agreement. This has been one of my most vexatious concerns. What types would you discard?" He motioned toward a comfortable leather chair, next to a table laden with pastries and a coffee service.

Berthold limped to the chair, sat heavily, helped himself to a pastry, and poured them both coffee.

"I have considered this at length, Herr Minister. Some aircraft that we have in quantity are all but totally useless to us: the Junkers JU-87 Stuka being a prime example. Without total command of the air, it serves only as target practice for enemy fighters. And we seem seldom to have total command of the air," he observed dryly.

"I agree. That aircraft is high on my list as well. Would you address me as Albert, please? And may I call you Heinz? If we are to work closely together, formalities will get in the way, don't you think?"

Berthold blinked in surprise, *this is going far better than I had hoped.*

"Very well, Albert," Berthold said, an uncommon smile on his face, "another candidate I propose to eliminate is the

Messerschmitt ME-110; they are such poor 'fighters' that they themselves require an escort! Ridiculous! We might use a few as target tugs to train pilots to shoot. In addition, my view is that only a few of the similar ME-210s are useful either, except for the night fighter variants. The ME-410s, now, especially those with water injection or nitrous oxide, do well as photo-intelligence vehicles, or for other special purposes."

He hesitated for a moment, judging his companion. He spoke solicitously.

"May I be especially bold? Not to pick excessively on Messerschmitts, but many older ME-109s barely hold their own against even older Allied types. And they require far too much maintenance. We ought, I believe, to relegate a few of the best of them to training, and replace the remainders with new production aircraft, such as the Focke Wulf FW-190D, or the Tank TA-152, or the TA-153, as fast as we are able. Furthermore," he said, thinking, *now I shall push the boundaries.* "I think production of the ME-109 should cease at once."

"Herr Messerschmitt might take exception to that, Heinz." Speer said blandly, as he sat back in his chair; his expression unsearchable.

In spite of himself, Berthold burst out, "Perhaps Herr Messerschmitt should be reminded that he is *permitted* to manufacture aircraft, and also to earn a profit, only at the pleasure of the state. He is a greedy fool. And do you know this?"

Berthold leaned forward, pointing his finger, "Our 'patriotic' Willy Messerschmitt earns more than two times as much profit from each of his obsolete ME-109s as he does from a Me-262 jet. Of course he wants to keep building them! He should be ordered to build what we say, or have the State take control of his facilities, as we did with Junkers." Berthold mentally held his breath, wondering, *what have I done now? How will he take this?*

Speer smiled thinly; his voice was cold; "It would seem you understand the situation precisely, my dear Heinz," he said.

"Messerschmitt's facilities should be dedicated to production of the ME-262 only, and its successors," Berthold said flatly. "Excess capacity should be put to use building sections of the Gothas, as well as the advanced FW-190Ds."

Speer nodded agreement as he made precise notes with an expensive English fountain pen, "I suspect that direction would rankle Herr Messerschmitt as well, but your idea is sound. I will direct that it happens.

"Tell me about this building of aircraft in sections one place and assembling them at another."

"This is not my original idea, Herr Speer, but rather the American industrialist Henry Kaiser. He builds his 'Liberty' cargo ships – do you know them? – in sections or parts manufactured at different locations. This concept would allow us to build portions of the Gotha in smaller facilities, and only bring them together to assemble the whole aircraft. It scatters our factories, and should greatly complicate our enemy's attempts to destroy them."

"Remarkable. How do you assure the parts built in separate locations will fit?"

Berthold tapped his right index finger into his left palm. "They must all work from identical drawings, Herr Speer. Not so simple as it sounds, but it can be done."

"You will please provide a paper describing this to my office at once; if it is approved, we shall put it into force immediately. We may be able to use the technique to advantage on other projects as well."

Changing the subject, Speer said, "Now then, Heinz, how would you suggest we take advantage of the aircraft we no longer need?"

Berthold spread his hands, internally grateful that Speer hadn't risen in defense of the nation's most prolific aircraft builder. Despite himself, his emotions drove him.

"We have been stupid! Our approach to aircraft recovery and reuse of materials has been haphazard, at best, Albert. What a waste! We fail even to make good use of the enemy aircraft that fall on our soil. We are wasting the very materials that are in shortest supply!"

He smacked his hand for emphasis. "If that effort were to be properly organized, in combination with the new flow of raw materials through Spain, I believe that we could substantially increase the production rates of those types we continue to build. Let me show you the plan to correct this."

Speer raised his eyebrows in surprise.

Apparently, he did not expect such preparations, Berthold thought smugly. *The man who has a plan, no matter how poor, is always ahead of he who has none*, he told himself.

The two men bent over the document for more than an hour. In the end, Speer had agreed with nearly all of Berthold's recommendations, to his gratification.

"What new aircraft do you recommend? There are so many being offered, and we dare not choose the wrong ones," Speer asked him a little more warmly than earlier, as they refreshed their coffee cups.

Berthold knew this was a test, "Messerschmitt's ME-610, which is based on their design study P1101-28 – do you know it? – is already moving toward production. It will be faster, and more maneuverable than the ME-262, and because of far better engines – it will use the new Hirth HeS 011 Turbojet – will be less susceptible to the enemy during takeoffs and landings. I believe this will be an excellent aircraft for us; we can use early ME-262s as trainers. I recommend continued production of the ME-262 until it proves itself, however."

He consulted his notes, "Now, there has been a proposal from the firm Blohm und Voss – do you know them?"

Speer nodded, "Yes, they build those remarkable, huge flying boats."

"Yes, good. They have proposed an impressively powerful ground attack aircraft designated BV-271. It appears strange, but the flying prototype has shown it will be formidable."

He removed a folded drawing from his large leather folder. "As you can see, its design comprises a long, slab-like straight wing with a massive radial engine in the center and one on each wing tip. The pilot sits here, at the rear of the tailless, center fuselage; dual rudders are on the end of each wingtip nacelle. It easily carries heavy loads of bombs and rockets, as well as a nice selection of machine guns, and cannons. It is also fast enough to defend itself against Allied Mustang P-51s and Spitfires, although less maneuverable. Our new rocket guns are also a possibility. It is, if I may say, a step up from the American Lightening P-38 concept. With external fuel tanks, it could take the fight to English soil. It lacks only the approval from this office; the Luftwaffe is begging for it. So is the Abwehr; experiments with captured enemy tanks show that this aircraft is a strong deterrent against armor. I recommend immediate, priority production."

Speer nodded again, "I received an urgent request from the Luftwaffe only this morning concerning this aircraft, so yes, I concur," and made further notes in his expensive leather folder.

Berthold pressed on; *so long as he listens so, I must tell him my opinion.*

"The firm Dornier is exploring a clever modification to their impressive push-pull DO-335 Pfeil [Arrow] night fighter. They have begun installation of a jet engine in the tail, in place of the piston engine. Calculations indicate a substantial increase in performance, and yet the airplane could be flown economically on the front engine alone, saving the speed of the jet until it is needed. It would make our most deadly night fighter even more deadly."

"That is most intriguing, Heinz; how long until it could reach production, do you think?"

"With proper priorities, the prototype could be flying in about thirty days; full production in no more than four months from approval. As they have designed it, with my help, existing airframes could be converted, so in the end, all or as many as we wish, would have this superior performance, at a small fraction of the cost of a completely new aircraft." From his reaction, it seemed to Berthold that Speer liked that idea very much.

Berthold pulled out another drawing from his folder.

"Lastly, for a relatively small expense, the Arado AR-234 jet could be upgraded. A new bubble canopy, so, greatly increases visibility for the pilot, and rids us of one of its great vulnerabilities, lack of rearward vision. Using the same improved engines as the ME-610, we gain almost thirty knots in speed, and a range increase of about 125 kilometers [75 miles], due to efficiencies."

Speer shook his head. "An elegant concept, but this I disapprove. Arado has proposed a four-engine variant, with two crew, that I prefer; it would also use the Hirth engines."

Berthold felt his ire rising, then pushed it aside with mighty mental effort.

Arado didn't show me all of their concepts. But, better to lose such a small battle, and win the larger ones, he told himself.

He shifted in his chair, and continued.

"A less glamorous aircraft that deserves our support is the Junkers JU-290 transport. We all love Iron Annie, the wonderful old JU-52, but it is sadly obsolete. The changes made to the JU-290 for von Schroeder's mission have shown us how versatile this aircraft is. They have a design for a transport/aerial tanker which deserves urgent, serious review, in my opinion. If we could refuel fighters in the air, they could take off with much heavier loads of ammunition or bombs, or they could escort the Gothas much deeper into English airspace. According to their proposal, they could refuel simultaneously four fighters."

"Impressive. But aren't they very vulnerable to enemy fighters?" Speer asked.

"They are – what's the American expression – ducks sitting? Yes, they are indefensible and would be shot down all but immediately if caught by Allied fighters. However, the added range and payloads they would make possible for our aircraft makes it worth the risk, I believe."

Berthold hesitated, wondering if this was the time, then decided to press ahead.

"Are you aware, Herr Speer – Albert – that the experiments combining jet kerosene with alcohol derived from waste are successful? A great advantage is the simplicity of making the alcohol from almost anything organic, in small facilities scattered about which are much harder targets for the enemy. To be fair, however, the fuel has a short useful life, only about three weeks. Using it would not only increase the available fuel for the jet propelled aircraft, it would free up feed stocks for gasoline."

Berthold left two hours later, smug in the knowledge he had significantly contributed to his nation's defense. Albert Speer had gained a powerful ally in reordering Germany's production of aircraft. It did not bode well for the Allies.

Two days later, Berthold received a call from Speer's office, "The Herr Minister invites you to attend a meeting with himself and General der Luftwaffe Adolf Galland. Will you attend?"

Berthold quickly agreed; the last thing he wanted was to somehow alienate this powerful man who had become his friend.

4 October 1943

Berlin, Albert Speer's Office

0145 Hours

Berthold was last to arrive, not purposefully late, but thanks to an attempted strafing attack by an American P-51. It galled him to the depth of his soul that this enemy could penetrate so deeply into Germany's heartland. He had watched with cold satisfaction as a sleek Ta-152 dispatched the intruder. He hoped it would set the tone for the meeting.

"Ah, there you are, Heinz! Please come in."

Albert Speer gestured to the man sitting in the chair as if introducing guests at a party, "General der Luftwaffe Adolf Galland, may I introduce Herr Doctor Heinz Berthold, of whom I have told you so much." Speer was always the gentleman.

The handsome man who stood to shake Berthold's hand was a genuine national hero. Where some SS thugs swaggered with their power and supposed invincibility, this man exuded confidence based solidly on practical experience. He was, after all, Berthold reminded himself, a multiple ace and a legitimate hero, not one of Goebbels' created phonies.

"My dear Doctor! How good to meet at last the man who has given me tools I can actually use. I am in your debt, sir." They shook hands.

"You are too kind, sir." Berthold always felt awkward in formal situations, especially around legitimate heroes. He decided to say little.

Speer led them to the same comfortable chairs Berthold had sat in only days before. Coffee awaited them, and from the silver bottle holders, some stronger fare as well.

"So, Herr Doctor, Albert tells me you have plans to take away my aeroplanes." The dark eyes snapped with humor and intelligence.

Berthold felt flustered; "Oh, no, General, not at all. Only the obsolete ones, and the ones which are more trouble to you than help. And only as we replace them. Do you not understand this?" He looked first to Galland, then to Speer.

Both men laughed. "My dear Heinz, of course we understand. The General was only having at bit of fun at your expense."

"This is true, Berthold," Galland said, serious now. "I think your ideas are exactly what we must do. Like all pilots with their favorite airplane, I fell in love with the lovely ME-109. It made me an ace, after all. But times change, and I am here to offer suggestions and to help coordinate the changes. It may be a case of too little, too late, but we must leap into this and make it work, yes? I am also very interested in your aerial refueling of the Gothas; do you think fighters could be refueled so as well?"

Berthold brightened.

I should have known such a man would grasp the significance of this at once, he told himself.

"Yes, of course General. One of my associates is drawing plans for kits to refit existing types as well as incorporating the capability into new airplanes as they are built."

"For existing aircraft, the process should take about ten days per aircraft at first, then perhaps as little as two days when we have learned the process. You would know better than I, of course, but I believe that training the pilots to perform aerial fueling could take longer than equipping their airplanes."

"This is very good. Do you propose to convert aircraft a staffel [squadron] at a time, then?"

"Yes, and if we are clever, Herr General, we ought to be able to reequip aircraft as they undergo heavy maintenance, and add in other upgrades as well."

The meeting broke up hours later. Speer had even brought in a professional planner, who laid out the first of the needed detailed steps for turning Berthold's ideas into reality.

Berthold left the office more hopeful than in months.

Perhaps, just perhaps, we can blunt the attacks of the Allies long enough to find a way out of this miserable war that isn't a repeat of the Treaty of Versailles.

Chapter 53

Saturday Morning, 2 October 1943

Millville Army Air Field, Millville, New Jersey

0430 Hours

Lighthouses, Interrupted

Joel woke up early, even for him, and grabbed a light breakfast at the Officer's Mess. By 0600, with the sun just coming up, he headed to the flightline, with a stop at the parachute shop for a seat pack 'chute for both of them. AT-6 tail number 43-00163 was sitting out in front of the maintenance hanger. Two mechanics were fueling it. Joel waited for them to finish, checked the fuel levels and verified that both fuel caps were on securely. Just then, Sergeant Ledbetter walked up, with two cameras slung over his shoulders

"Colonel Knight, the base photo shop only had high speed film, but for what we're shooting today, that shouldn't be any problem."

"No, I'm sure that'll be OK, John. Be sure to get the receipt to me, so I can reimburse you. Your parachute is on the seat. I'll get the pre-flight done."

The morning was beautiful, and Joel went about the preflight check whistling a big band tune.

A bright green flash from the handheld light in the tower cleared them to taxi onto the runway. In position, he keyed his mic, "Army 163, ready to go."

"Army 163, cleared for takeoff."

Joel clicked his mic twice in acknowledgement, and advanced the throttle. As always, he got a thrill feeling the aircraft come alive.

He retracted the landing gear and they climbed out, turning toward the Atlantic Ocean. In minutes, they crossed over the little village of Strathmere, and banked north to follow the shoreline.

"Our first target will be Absecon Lighthouse, just south of Atlantic City, then the Barnegat Lighthouse, to the north," he told the young photographer over the intercom. "I'll do a fly-by first so you can see how you like the light, and then you tell me where you want me, OK?"

"Sounds, swell, sir. If you slow us down when we get there, I'll open the canopy, and it'll be easier to take the pictures."

It only took minutes to fly up the coast to the Absecon Lighthouse. Making a couple of passes while the photographer judged the light, Joel swung back around at about 200 feet, lowered the flaps, and slowly flew past first on the ocean-facing side of the lighthouse, then its land side.

This is a fun way to fly, he decided.

Finishing, they flew ten miles to the scenic Barnegat lighthouse which Ledbetter captured on film as well. As they climbed back up to altitude turning north, they saw a pair of big, grey Navy blimps slowly moving out to sea. As clumsy as they seemed, they provided yeoman service to the country in spotting and tracking, even sinking German submarines, Joel knew. Easily avoiding the slow moving lighter-than-air craft, they continued north.

"What's next, sir?" asked Ledbetter over the intercom.

"That'd be the Twin Lights, John. Quite an interesting old building, with a light house tower on each end. Still use it, too! I think it was built in the late 1800s."

Within minutes, the distinctive building was visible. "Gee, sir! I've never seen anything like that!" exclaimed Ledbetter.

"Yeah, it's the only lighthouse like that in the world; at least that's what I'm telling my sister!"

The early morning light made the red brick building glow, and the faceted glass covering the lights contrasted sharply with the green grass around the building.

They flew past at 1,000 feet, with John clicking off as many shots as he could. Dropping down, and again lowering the flaps, Joel slowed them to make several passes. Ledbetter kept making little exclamations as he twisted in his seat to get just the right view.

After the last south-bound pass, Joel turned inland and began once again to climb, heading north.

"Now we'll go shoot the Sandy Hook Light, up in New York harbor," Joel told him.

Ledbetter looked slightly off to their left toward New York City, and shouted, "Hey, sir, look at that! A whole formation of B-17s flying down the Narrows! Hey, what's all that smoke over the city?"

Joel looked with astonishment at the spectacle.

Why, there must be fifty or sixty of them! Why didn't they tell me the Air Corps was flying a formation over the City?

Then, with a chill of fear, he realized that the airplanes were not B-17s.

"Dear God, protect us! Those are German! They've bombed the City!" he shouted.

Chapter 54

2 October 1943

Aboard US Army AT-6 43-00163, Near New York City

0710 Hours

Enemy Encounter

"God Almighty!" Ledbetter cried. "What are they? They look like giant bats!"

The aircraft began to turn eastward away from them, climbing, heading out to sea.

That distinctive V shape – they're the flying wings I briefed the admirals and generals about!

Instinctively, Joel slammed the throttle wide open, and the aircraft leapt higher. Without thinking, he was flying to intercept them, as if he was in a fighter. The enemy formation was climbing away from them.

We'll have a hard time catching them in this 'T-6.

"John," he shouted anxiously over the intercom, "if you have any telephoto lenses, take as many pictures as you can. I'm going to try to catch them."

Turning to the right as they climbed, they began to slowly overtake the enemy craft.

They're closing up the formation for protection, he thought. They were only about a quarter of a mile away.

They should be shooting us! And we're unarmed!

He leveled out, almost in formation with the lead aircraft.

*Swastikas! They **are** German!*

With a jolt of surprise, he spotted a distinctive bright red slash and baronial badge on the lead aircraft's upper wing.

"That's von Schroeder! Gerhard Schroeder, the ersatz baron! It's gotta be!" Joel burst out. They were the same marking he'd seen on von Schroeder's Me-109 back in 1936, he was sure of it! Joel was stunned; he'd never expected to see his old nemesis again, and certainly not over New York City!

"Get pictures of that one! The one with the red stripe!" he shouted at his passenger.

In the rear seat, the terrified Ledbetter was taking pictures as fast as his camera would allow. He ran out of film. Switching to his backup camera, he shot more pictures, including several of the plane with red markings. Somehow, he managed to keep his hands from shaking.

"I've used up all my film, sir."

"That's OK, they're too fast for us anyway, John. Now we've got to get those photographs back home ASAP." With bitter reluctance, Joel rolled away to the right, and began a diving, straight line, full throttle return to his home base. The engine tachometer was redlined, the airspeed still climbing, at nearly 180 MPH. He pushed the aircraft as hard as it would go.

"Close your canopy, John. It won't be so cold or loud."

He tuned the radio to113.6 MHz, "Millville Control, Army 163, emergency straight in approach requested!"

"Army 163, what is the nature of your emergency?" the reply was laconic.

"Millville Control, Army 163; this is Colonel Knight; inbound from Sandy Hook, ETA 20 minutes. The Germans bombed New York City, and I photographed their aircraft! Have a car meet us on the runway. Call Colonel Watkins and Colonel Randolph and tell them I have pictures! These pictures have to get to Washington immediately! Call Lakehurst; maybe the Navy can intercept those bastards!"

"What? The Germans bombed New York?" the control tower man replied. "How could they? Is this a drill?"

"This is no drill!" Joel shouted, unconsciously echoing the famous radio call from Pearl Harbor.

"I say again, this is Lieutenant Colonel Joel Knight, in AT-6 number 163; we flew right alongside them. New York City is on fire; they bombed it sure as Sunday! Now, clear me for a straight in approach ASAP!"

Chapter 55

2 October 1943

Main Runway

Millville Army Air Field, Millville, New Jersey

0811 Hours

Post Attack

The flight seemed to last forever, but in twenty-five minutes, they were in sight of the base. Joel flew straight onto the runway, not flying the normal pattern, took the first high speed turnoff, and stopped quickly beside the waiting staff car.

"Give me the cameras!" Joel shouted at the still pale buck sergeant. He jumped off the wing, shed his parachute, and raced to the waiting car.

He leapt into the Olive Drab 1941 Ford sedan and was stunned to realize that he was sitting beside Colonel Watkins, the base commander.

"Oh! I beg your pardon, sir!" he said in astonishment; "I thought this car was for me!" He reached for the door handle.

"It is, Colonel Knight." Turning to the driver, he instructed, "Take us to the photo lab, Building 102, immediately." The car lurched forward, and sped off.

Turning to Joel, Watkins said, "We heard about the attack right after you called in. We're all shocked! It's Pearl Harbor all over again!"

"That's sure what it feels like, sir!" Joel replied, shaking his head in disbelief.

"You were up there in a 'T-6? What did you see?"

"Sir, I was getting in my hours, and taking some lighthouse pictures with Sergeant Ledbetter. He spotted the Germans coming down the Narrows – thought they were B-17s at first. There must have been thirty or forty of them – maybe more, climbing out to the east. The whole city's on fire! I think they're that new Gotha design I briefed you on."

"What? What did they look like, son?" the older man asked, incredulous.

"Colonel, they were flying wings! No tails! And they were big, four engines, pushers, with buried engines. They were bigger than a B-17. There was a cylindrical section sticking out in the front for the crew, almost as if they had tacked on the forward fuselage of another plane. They were a strange color – a flat gray top and bottom, but the Swastikas were bright enough! Funny thing – they never shot at us! And they had to see us!"

"What! You weren't fired upon?" The older man seemed incredulous.

"No, sir, I don't even think they had guns! I didn't see any! We were a1000 yards from them – they should have shot us out of the sky! Oh, Dear God, how I wish I'd been in a Jug!" he said in anguish.

"Did any of them have battle damage – did you see any feathered props or smoke?"

"No, nothing I saw, sir. The photos will tell the tale – oh, darn! I should have brought Ledbetter! He does magic developing film!" he said regretfully.

"Don't worry, Colonel; I ordered that you both were to come to the photo lab. He'll be along presently."

"I know who the lead pilot was!" Joel burst out.

"What? How could you know that?" the Colonel said, his eyes hard.

Quickly, Joel gave him an overview of his encounter with then Hauptman Freiherr Gerhard von und zu Schroeder. "The red slash with the baronial badge was unmistakable, sir. Nobody else in the Luftwaffe uses it!"

The older man rubbed his chin thoughtfully. "He's a colonel now, you see. We'd lost track of him after all the excitement about Göring and Hitler. He must have finagled command of this strike, damn his eyes!"

"He really hates America, sir, and I'm partly responsible, I'm afraid."

"How's that?" an eyebrow went up.

"I humiliated him pretty badly in front of his squadron in 1936, sir. And not just once; four times. He wanted to dog fight, and I beat him and in a ME-109 to boot. The Gestapo wanted to arrest me; I got sent home after that. Honestly, sir, the man wanted me to fight a duel! He threatened to kill me several times."

"Yes, he's known to be short of temper and long on ego."

They rushed inside the photo lab.

The two were ushered into the big darkroom, and the film technicians took the cameras from Joel. Under a red safety light, the cameras were opened and the rolls of film began to go through the various chemical baths. They heard the light-shielded door open, and Sergeant Ledbetter joined them.

"What do you see, Corporal?" Ledbetter asked, very much in charge as he walked to the work bench.

"Not much, yet; we're still sorting out your lighthouses, Sarge," the lead technician said.

"Let me help," Ledbetter said as he put on protective rubber gloves.

"Have the G-2 officers arrived yet?" asked Colonel Watkins as he carefully watched the processing.

"Should be here any minute, Colonel." the photo lab boss told him.

Minutes later, the intelligence officers began to carefully examine the still wet photographs.

"Anybody recognize the planes?" asked Watkins; he glanced at Joel and shook his head slightly

"No, sir, that's new to me."

"Same here, sir; never seen anything like 'em." It was said in awe.

"Sirs?" a youthful voice said. "I think I know what they are."

"Who are you, soldier, and why do you think you can identify them if we can't?" said an intelligence officer testily.

"Sir, I'm Private First Class Henderson. Besides developing photographs, I build model planes for the Army, lots of them, for briefings and GOC aircraft ID training. It's my duty to model new aircraft from all over the world, including classified ones. Those photos show the Gotha GO-447 flying wing that won the Luftwaffe long range bomber competition."

The officers were stunned by his comments. The younger of the G-2 officers spoke first; "Sir, he's right; that's almost surely what they are."

"*Corporal,* you just earned yourself another stripe! Congratulations, young man, well done!" the Colonel said. He looked at Joel "That's a pretty solid confirmation, Colonel."

"Now," he said, turning to the senior intelligence officer, "get a dozen copies of the airplane shots, and take them, and the negatives, to the Pentagon ASAP. Send a fighter, get them there as quickly as possible. I've got some urgent phone calls to make."

Chapter 56

2 October 1943

Office of the Commandant

Brooklyn Naval Ship Yard, Brooklyn, New York

0710 Hours

Grim Assessment

Rear Admiral Monroe R. Kelly wore impeccable dress whites, as always, but his face was pale and drawn. He'd seen the explosions as he came into the facility, and had even gotten a glimpse of the bat-winged bombers. Several anti-aircraft guns on the north end of the Yard had still been hammering away at them.

He laid his hat on his desk and turned to his adjutant.

"How bad is it, Andy?" His voice was a little shaky.

The younger man was pale and shaken himself.

"Admiral, we're still getting reports, but here's what we know: *Missouri* took four or five hits, a couple of which were glancing blows. She's still solid on her hull supports, but she may have serious damage. We'll get a thorough report in an hour or so. Both baby flattops took nasty hits; *Ferguson's* foredeck was holed, and her below decks machinery and hanger bay are badly damaged. She's on fire. *Grover* took a direct hit on the bows. Damage isn't too bad from that, but she was knocked off her hull supports; it may have bent her hull when she hit the dry dock wall. Her island is knocked sideways, too; looks bad. None of the destroyers seem to have been hurt, but a couple of dry docks were breached. Real assessment will have to wait 'till we can drain them. A lot of the dockside machinery is busted up, and there are fires all over the yard." He handed his report to the Admiral.

"I can't believe it; I just can't believe that they could actually bomb us. Who else got hit, or was it just the Yard?"

The Lieutenant Commander shrugged, "We can't say for sure yet, sir, but the City was bombed, and from the smoke, probably that oil refinery in 'Jersey, too."

"Casualties: what is the casualty report?" he asked, dreading the answer.

"Sir, only a few, scattered reports so far, but it looks like a couple dozen dead, and a hundred or more injured."

"Well." Kelly was beginning to get his feet under himself as his mind coped with the disaster. "Get me the direct line to SecNav right away; I've got to report this."

Four Hours Later

"That's correct, sir." Kelly was making his third call of the day to the Secretary of the Navy. "*Missouri's* keel was partially broken about mid-ships; we think a direct hit. The ship's architect is still inspecting her, but thinks she's repairable. The fire's out on *Ferguson*; she took pretty serious damage below decks and we're waiting on details. I'm sorry to say we may have to write off *Grover*. Her hull is severely bent and twisted with a lot of sprung hull plates. Her island is un-useable and would have to be cut off and replaced. Worst of all, her engines were knocked off their mounts and are severely damaged. Repairs may cost more than she's worth at this stage, sir." Bringing this kind of news to your boss was never good for your career.

"No, sir. Our casualty reports are incomplete. Preliminarily, the numbers are 310 total, with about eighty confirmed deaths.

"Another issue, sir. The Germans dropped incendiaries, and many didn't go off. They must have timers, because new fires keep breaking out all over the Yard. I'm requesting any ordinance disposal men you can spare, sir."

Chapter 57
2 October 1943
Aboard Baron One
0943 Hours
Heading For Home

Von Schroeder realized his crew was avoiding him. He'd been irritable and nervous on the long trip to New York even though he'd taken the sleeping pills the doctor had insisted upon. The rest hadn't eased his nervousness. He nearly panicked during the bomb run, despite his efforts at self- control. To his delight, the new RMB Bombsight worked perfectly on still targets too.

He looked at the formation as they steadily climbed through the light overcast.

Nearly 3,500 meters [~11,500 feet] now, he thought, checking the altimeter. With no oxygen on the planes, he'd have to make sure they stayed low so no one would have a problem with the thin air.

His aircraft had a mirror over the cockpit, like a fighter. The smoke-smudged horizon had dropped out of sight; no vapor trails betrayed them – good. Soon every bomber would shut down its outboard engines to economize on fuel. Through the scattered clouds, the Atlantic had the look of blue-grey wrinkled silk. As far as he could see in every direction, its surface was unmarked by a ship's wake.

"We did it. I think we actually did it," he said in disbelief.

He shook himself. "Did we suffer any damage?"

"No, sir, I don't believe they even shot at us."

"Excellent! Contact the other aircraft and get any casualty reports. And remind them to watch their altitude."

At once, the radio operator turned on the low power radio transmitter, and sent the message to the other aircraft. The transmitter had a range of less than three miles; even a ship directly under them wouldn't be able to intercept the message.

Von Schroeder checked his watch again against the aircraft's chronometer.

It has been nearly two hours since we struck, and no American airplanes have attacked us. And it's too late now, we're too far at sea. Remarkable! he thought.

"What do you hear on the America radio stations?" he asked the radio man when he finished sending the damage report request.

His radio operator grinned. "They're in shock and confusion, sir! They can't believe that it was actually German aircraft. One announcer said that we came from aircraft carriers! Can you imagine it?" the young man laughed, relief strong in his voice.

"From what they are saying, sir, we set a lot of fires. The oil refinery on the west side of the river blew up. There've been no references to the aircraft factory or shipyard. If I may give my opinion, sir, it sounds like chaos!"

The man listened on his headset for a few moments, "More good news, sir. None of the aircraft suffered damage. One has a rough engine, which may have to be shut down, but not due to enemy action. Rheinwasser Yellow 2 reports that his radio man is ill."

Von Schroeder digested this for a moment; no one in their wildest dreams could have predicted such success! Surely they would send him again to punish the arrogant Americans, despite what that dwarf Berthold said. His promotion was all but assured!

He took a large, deep breath and let it out, a wide, rare smile on his face. "You will have medals! I promise it! What a magnificent crew!" He felt magnanimous.

"Tell our fellows congratulations on my behalf. They are to strictly follow the flight protocols; we will celebrate on the ground.

Oh, yes, we shall celebrate!" The radio man began sending the message.

"Now then," von Schroeder said with self satisfaction, "it's about time for me to send a little message."

The radio operator readied the powerful short wave transmitter. Only von Schroeder's airplane was so equipped. Von Schroeder savored his next words, a deliberate play on the words the Japanese had sent following their success at Pearl Harbor. He intentionally sent them in the clear, unencrypted: "Climb Mount Rushmore. Climb Mount Rushmore."

Chapter 58

Monday, 3 October 1943

Lieutenant Colonel Joel Knight's Office

Millville Army Air Field, Millville, New Jersey

0700 Hours

Aftermath

First Sergeant Bill Madsen brought in a stack of newspapers.

"Thanks, Bill. Let's have a look"

The New York Times headline screamed:

NAZIS HIT CITY, DAMAGE SEVERE
HOW? WHY?

The Philadelphia paper continued in kind:

NYC BOMBED!
"Impossible" Raid Kills Hundreds,
Burns Much of City
Army Stumped How

The Baltimore paper shouted:

SECOND PEARL HARBOR!
CAUGHT UNAWARE AGAIN!

The *Millville Daily Republican* was no different:

JERRYS BOMB NYC!
Secret "Bat Planes" Reach Across Atlantic,
Cause Much Death and Damage
Wide Fear of More Attacks

The editorial page in the *New York Times* carried a savage attack on the Roosevelt Administration and the War Department. Joel read it aloud:

For shame! Our government is again guilty of the most egregious dereliction of duty! The first duty of the government in Washington, according to the Constitution, is to Protect the People. FDR and his War Department have again failed to carry out this sacred duty, and for the second time in only twenty-two months, America has suffered severely at the hands of our enemies. There can be no excuses for this! Once again we were unprepared, and this time while actually conducting the war! Correction of this grave fault must be immediate, and the consequences severe, starting with the firing of the heads of the Army and Navy. Courts Martial must be convened at once. Impeachment of the President must be given serious consideration, for it is he who serves as Commander in Chief, and who must bear the ultimate responsibility. Congress, too, shares in this dubious attention, for they have repeatedly refused requests for funding and equipment for our Coastal Protection Services. They must make do with cast off aircraft, overage reservists and too few Navy vessels. We have heard a further outrage, as yet unconfirmed, that not a single shot was fired at the attackers! How can this be? This is truly criminal neglect of duty. Will we discover, as we did after Pearl Harbor, that the ammunition our fighting men needed was under lock and key, as if in peace time? Surely not everyone was caught off guard! Or, were we?

"Wow! Strong message to follow! This is gonna get really ugly before it's all squared away. I just hope that while they're busy hanging the guilty, they don't forget to give us what we need to defend against the next attack, 'cause you know if they can do it once, they can do it again. God have mercy on us all!" Joel lamented.

Chapter 59

Tuesday, 4 October 1943

Office of the Commander

Millville Army Air Field, Millville, New Jersey

0800 Hours

Washington Bound

Joel and Sergeant Ledbetter sat in Colonel Watkins' office, describing the attack one more time. The intelligence officers and Colonel Randolph queried them sharply.

Colonel Watkins' telephone rang. "Tarleton Watkins here," he answered. He listened for a moment, nodded, and hung up the instrument. He turned to the men.

"Gentlemen, we have been 'invited' to brief General Marshall and the Joint Chiefs tomorrow morning. They want to talk to both of you, as well as the rest of us. Let's see, there are seven of us. Can we all get in the B-25, Joel?"

"Sir, we could, but it'd a lot more comfortable in the C-47 and we'd get there almost as quickly."

"Make it so; we'll leave as soon as you are ready, Colonel."

An hour later, Joel sat in the big plane's cabin, while a teenaged Second Lieutenant flew them toward Washington, D.C. Joel shook his head; *the kid still has pimples, for crying out loud! But, he seems to know what he's doing.* Joel turned to his fellow officers.

"How did they do it? How did they fly all the way across the Atlantic, bomb New York, and fly back to Germany?" mused Colonel Randolph over the roar of the engines.

"Yeah," said an Intel guy, "we sure don't have anything that can fly that far, not even the new B-29. Worse yet, why didn't we know they were going to do this?"

"And just as bad, why weren't they seen? Why weren't they intercepted and shot down?" added Colonel Watkins. He turned to Joel. "Colonel, were there *any* other aircraft in the vicinity?"

"Only the Navy blimps I mentioned, sir; they were a lot lower, and headed south-east, so they probably wouldn't have seen the Germans. I've flown up there before on a Saturday, sir, and usually the Navy has some F6F Hellcats flying around, but we didn't see any that day."

"And you, Sergeant Ledbetter? Did you see any other aircraft?"

"Not a thing, sir. Of course, I was taking photos, but I don't recall seeing any other airplanes."

"They flew over Grumman's plant on Long Island – why didn't those guys attack them?"

"Because the Germans bombed them first; Grumman took a lot of damage, from what I heard," said an Intel man.

"Well, there will be hell to pay with the President; and the papers will crucify us. And Congress! They'll have a field day! The Army and Navy will look like incompetent fools again, just like Pearl Harbor. Maybe Coastal Defense will finally get some funding, as usual, after it's too late," Colonel Watkins lamented.

Chapter 60

10 October 1943

The White House, 1600 Pennsylvania Avenue, Washington, D.C.

1257 Hours

Deflecting Blame

The four men comprising the Joint Chiefs of Staff waited nervously outside the Oval Office. That they had been summoned all at once had an ominous feeling. Admiral William Leahy, the Chairman, fidgeted slightly; he was convinced that all their careers were over; at the very least, he was confident that his own surely was. None of them had ever given much credence to the cockamamie idea that Germany would actually attack America on her own soil, much less that an airborne attack was possible.

What can I say? he mused, *what can I possibly say that would excuse the fact that such a brazen attack could happen so soon after Pearl Harbor. The simple, bald truth is, we were caught with our breeches down, again.*

His thoughts were interrupted by the carefully neutral voice of a Presidential Aide; "The President will see you now, gentlemen."

They moved into the famous room, and the aide silently closed the door behind them.

"Have a seat, gentlemen," FDR said in a voice neither clear nor commanding.

Dear God, he looks awful, Leahy thought. The man was slumping uncharacteristically in his wheel chair, his face ashen, hair askew. The jocular attitude and confident grin were absent, and his eyes didn't have the normal snappy look to them.

Roosevelt composed himself, and sat a bit more upright.

"The press is saying, with surprising uniformity, that I should sack the lot of you," he said without preamble. "I suppose I could throw you all to the ravening wolves, but that would leave me with a most uncomfortable dilemma: how should I run this war, and whom should I choose to advise me in your absences? I have come to the inescapable conclusion that neither I nor the country can do without your services, notwithstanding what the gentlemen of the Forth Estate say. That conclusion having been reached rather quickly, I was then confronted with deciding by what means could I justify your staying on."

He stopped and pursed his lips, and tilted his head up toward them, a spark of determination shinning in his eyes.

"I have therefore decided that we shall commit a small untruth, the five of us, in the service of freedom. I will give a radio address to the nation this evening in which I shall exclaim that you were all directed – ordered – by me, over your strident protests, of course, to ignore coastal defense in all aspects so that the maximum efforts of the country could go toward supporting the war efforts in Europe and the Pacific. I will proclaim that you have been unfairly attacked by the press, that you were in fact only obeying your Commander in Chief."

The men seated in front of him looked shocked.

"Mr. President, you know that we can have no involvement in politics, but even we know that such a position this close to the election could severely hurt your chances for reelection," General "Hap" Arnold said earnestly.

"Oh, do not concern yourself on my account, Hap," FDR replied. "You all now have the very difficult job of putting into place the safeguards the American people thought were there all along. If you accomplish that, the uproar over this will be a tempest in a teapot. Mind you, the Germans will almost surely attack us again; at the very minimum, the very least," he smacked a fist on his hand, "we *must* have a credible defense force to oppose them. Even if we can't fend them off, even if we should take heavy losses in the process, the American people will gather behind us in the effort, but we must make a credible effort!"

The President looked each man in the eye, "I know you are convening small groups of mid-grade officers to advise you. Good. Take their wisdom and make it reality. I will do everything in my power to help you. But I warn you, collectively and individually: do not let inter-service rivalries impede this, or I will fire you, publicly, immediately, and without pensions. Do you understand me, gentlemen?"

Walter Winchell began his broadcast, "Hello, Mr. and Mrs. America, and all the ships at sea! Let's go to press. The President spoke to the nation this evening in an address carried by this network and its affiliates. In the aftermath of the dreadful attack on New York City, he proclaimed that the neglected condition of the defense of the nation's coastline was deliberate, was directed by him, and proclaimed the innocence of the Joint Chiefs of Staff. Mr. Roosevelt proclaimed that by so doing, men and materiel were provided to the war efforts in Europe and the Pacific that otherwise would have remained here at home. Most Republicans and not a few Democrats are proclaiming that the president's position is a ruse to protect the Joint Chiefs. There is also widespread concern that this action could badly affect the president's chances for reelection in the elections coming up in November. In other news—."

"Well," Joel chuckled humorlessly, "Drew Pearson has done it again." He handed Chappie the paper.

"Roosevelt's blatant attempt to protect the near-criminal acts, or should I say inaction, of the military's Joint Chiefs of Staff would be funny, except for the fact that it is so serious. The neglect of our nation's coastlines is criminal, and in violation of the Constitutional requirement that the government's first duty to its citizens is to protect them. We are in fact exposed to attacks on both our coasts, and no lies, bald-faced or otherwise, no matter how glib, can conceal the fact.

"The military is beginning to scramble to firmly close the barn door now that the horses have escaped. May God protect us if the Germans attack us again; we are still defenseless and unprotected. The shame of suffering such a humiliating attack will gradually fade with time, I suppose, but the deaths, the needless deaths suffered in New York City and environs, will hang like a millstone around Roosevelt's neck for all his life, and beyond. It is this reporter's opinion that unless Mr. Roosevelt cleans up this stinking mess, he will be handed a stinging, and well deserved defeat in November."

Chapter 61

Wednesday, 6 October 1943
Joint Chiefs of Staff Briefing Room
The Pentagon, Washington, D.C.
0700 Hours
Joint Chiefs

Joel suspected that the Joint Chiefs were angry and looking for scapegoats. Personally, he expected that the Chiefs would be fired, or worse. Congress was sure to come down on their heads. The President's radio talk defending them had only added fuel to the fire. The debacle of the post-Pearl Harbor congressional investigations was fresh; some were still on-going. More than a few newspapers echoed the *New York Times* editorial, and called for heads to roll.

To their credit, reprisals weren't the chief topic on the Joint Chief's agenda. Joel and Sergeant Ledbetter retold their stories, with frequent interruptions for questions. The photographs had been blown up to poster size. Both men rose to indicate various details.

"Lieutenant Colonel Knight, I understand that you believe you know who the lead pilot was. How is that possible?" asked Admiral Ernest King.

Joel cleared his throat, and proceeded to succinctly explain his encounters with von Schroeder in 1936.

"Were you assigned to Army G-2 then, Colonel?"

"No, sir; my boss, Colonel Ryan Bigsby and I, along with twenty-five others, were assigned to fly prototype Curtiss P-36 Hawks on a European demonstration tour that summer. G-2 briefed us before we left, and told us what to look for, but we were specifically ordered not to do any spying of any kind; just look at what was out in the open," he explained.

"Bigsby? Wasn't he on MacArthur's staff?"

"Yes," answered General Henry "Hap" Arnold quietly. "He was killed by the Japanese during the retreat from Manila."

"What do we know about this Baron von und zu Schroeder? If he was flying fighters in '36, how'd he end up leading bombers on a raid on New York?" the question was directed at the Intelligence officers.

"I may have had something to do with that, sir," Joel said quietly.

"How's that, Colonel?" The question was sharp; these men didn't suffer fools gladly, neither was self-aggrandizement tolerated under such serious circumstances.

"Well, sir, after I beat Schroeder four times in a dog fight—"

"Beat him? Four times? In a dog fight? What do you mean?" the incredulous general asked.

"Yes, sir. Four times. In 1936. Flying a prototype ME-109."

"You're the pup who did that? Now, that was a real piece of flying! And your flight report was amazing; first real Intel we got on the '109."

"Yes, sir; thank you sir. I told him that day, in the hearing of his Colonel, that he wasn't fit to fly fighters, that all he should fly was transports or bombers. Looks like the Jerrys took me up on that."

"We confirm that, sir. After Colonel Knight embarrassed him, von Schroeder was reassigned to bombers. He met Generalmajor Wever, then Luftwaffe Chief of Staff, and became one of his fair-haired boys. Von Schroeder really went after the 'Bomb America' campaign after Göring was killed. The last information available has him as a senior Oberst – that's full Colonel, sir – but he dropped out of sight several months ago."

"Mr. President, I have a preliminary version of the report you requested about jurisdictions and responsible authorities for coastal defense."

"Excellent. Give me the condensed version, if you would."

"Certainly, sir. I'm afraid it's not a pretty picture no matter how short the version."

"I didn't expect it would be. Please continue."

"Yes, sir. We did a quick examination of the states from Maine to the Florida Keys. The lack of uniformity boggles the mind; we found jurisdictions as small as 100 yards and as large as 300 miles. Responsible parties ranged from governors to local representatives of every branch of the armed services, including the Cavalry, to police departments, constabularies, sheriffs, magistrates, state guard units, militias and so on, down to individual private land owners. There is no common reporting mechanism or recipient of such reports. Reports, if they are generated at all, are mostly in the form of letters! One in Florida still required a letter to the king of Spain! More than half have no access to a telephone. Those few that are equipped with weapons have virtual antiques. All are intended to repel ships or landing parties, often pirates or Revolutionary War era English attacks. The more modern are of Spanish American War vintage. Nowhere did we find anti-aircraft defenses or modern means of even detecting an air raid. At the risk of sounding sarcastic, sir, I doubt we could successfully repel an invasion by a band of Vikings, let alone modern war planes."

Chapter 62

6 October 1943

The Vestibule of the Joint Chiefs of Staff Briefing Room

The Pentagon, Washington, D.C.

1030 Hours

New Assignment

Joel and Sergeant Ledbetter finished and were dismissed. As they left, an Army Major with the shoulder rope of a general's aide-de-camp approached them.

"Sir," he said to Joel, "the Chiefs want you available for a meeting tomorrow; I can arrange quarters, as well as transportation. Sergeant, you may return to your base with our thanks."

Joel sought out a phone to call Chappie.

❖ ❖ ❖

The next morning, in a fresh shirt, shined shoes and pressed uniform, Joel was picked up at the Washington Hotel and delivered by Army car to the Pentagon. An Army MP Staff Sergeant gave him an ID badge.

"Sir, please wait in this room, you will be escorted to your meeting."

Joel was thankful he didn't have to navigate the Pentagon's labyrinth of corridors by himself. He'd gotten lost in the huge building before. He found the coffee, and sat in a leather chair. About a dozen other officers were waiting, as he was, for their guide. He began to read a magazine.

"Lieutenant Colonel Knight?" Joel looked up to see a fuzzy-cheeked Second Lieutenant holding a clipboard. He couldn't have been over eighteen.

"That's me, Lieutenant," Joel told him.

"This way, sir," the young man said, and began to lead him through the halls.

"Where are we going?"

"Sir, I have been ordered to bring you to a specific room without conversation."

Well, that qualifies as strange, even for the Army, Joel thought.

The room was down the hall from where he and Ledbetter had briefed the Joint Chiefs the day before. He went to the Corporal sitting at the desk, and announced himself.

"Sir, please be seated. You'll be called in momentarily." The Corporal picked up a telephone. As Joel sat, he saw two other officers, a Marine Major he didn't know, and the Lieutenant Commander he'd met at the briefing for Admiral Stuart.

"Commander Higgins? Colonel Knight, sir. We met at the briefing to Admiral Stuart."

"Good morning. Joel, isn't it?" They shook hands. Before they could begin a conversation, the door opened, and an Army Captain stepped out.

"Sirs, would join us, please?"

They followed him through the door, and immediately stopped and came to attention. Sitting at the desk was a U.S. Army full Colonel. He was a bull of a man, ruddy-faced, with short salt and pepper hair, and broad shoulders. His uniform had six rows of ribbons; the insignia on his blouse was Infantry. One ribbon was a Silver Star, Joel noted, and that was surely a West Point ring.

"Stand at ease, gentlemen. Please take a seat. I am Colonel Thomas A. Regan, on General Marshall's staff. I have been charged by the Joint Chiefs with giving you a very important assignment. First, though, some introductions and brief bios so you all know with whom it is you are working.

"On my left is Lieutenant Commander John Bell Higgins, USN: Annapolis class of 1930, a history major; fleet pilot, squadron commander. Shot down over Guadalcanal, Silver Star and Purple Heart. Next, Lieutenant Colonel Joel T. Knight, USAAF: West Point class of 1932, Airman's Medal. An aeronautical engineer, and an expert on flying wings. First Allied military pilot to fly an ME-109. Extremely broad flying experience. Squadron commander. Finally, and not at all least, Major, Lieutenant Colonel-select, Beverly C. Tucker, USMC: Annapolis 1931, a combat engineer. Three amphibious landings in the Pacific, Bronze Star. Battalion commander. Expert on logistics and supply. Colonel Tucker, I expect you and Commander Higgins know each other, being at Annapolis at the same time." The two men nodded.

Solid, impressive men, Joel thought.

"Now, why you are here," the Colonel's visage was grim. Joel felt the tension in the room ratchet upward.

He looked at them sharply, "It's clear to everyone, in uniform and not, that the military has severely screwed up the coastal defense of this country. Everyone who wears the uniform is embarrassed that the Germans attacked us with such impunity, especially in the aftermath of Pearl Harbor. Not to understate it, gentlemen, despite what he said in his radio address, the President believes that this debacle occurred largely because of divisions between the services. He will tolerate no more inter-service rivalries: he has threatened to make us all one service, which would be a disaster for all us professional soldiers, to say nothing of not curing the problem. And don't fool yourselves; he absolutely means it.

"You three comprise one of four sub-committees charged with independently developing defense plans. You will ignore which service now has responsibility for what. You are to use your common sense and logic to determine who *should* have responsibility. You are also to recommend changes in weaponry, manning, location, and so on as you deem necessary. You will present your plan to the Chiefs in thirty days, along with the other teams. Your plan will recommend the best use of existing assets, no matter what service owns them, and how to effectively bring command of those assets under a single, unified commander.

"We were specifically directed by the President to bring in O-5s [Lieutenant Colonel] and below to accomplish this. He believes that as experienced, academy educated officers, you have enough hands-on experience, and that you probably haven't yet been 'fatally infected with the disease of service prejudice', blindly assuming your parent service is the only one capable of doing it." The sour look on the Colonel's face made it clear to Joel that he didn't agree.

He looked at them seriously. "I needn't tell you, gentlemen, that if you succeed, you will have done your country a great service, and will assure your ascension in rank. Fail, and you will have wasted a month of irreplaceable time, and perhaps, condemn your careers to obscurity."

The Colonel's stark briefing went on for another hour. They were to be supplied with an office suite, staff members, and clerical help. Their clearances were Top Secret, with access to almost everything available.

"If you think you can use it, ask for it," he told them bluntly. "You have priority over almost every other activity, so ask for what you need. We have detailed information on facilities, manpower, weaponry, including ships and aircraft, as well as radios and RADARs. Use it. Support is available around the clock, including a print shop. Commander Higgins, you have worked in the Pentagon for several months, so I'll expect you to provide your colleagues guidance on that score. Your task is code named Stalwart Guard Three; that will give you priority. Everything you produce will be labeled with that name, and will be classified Top Secret. Are there any questions?"

The three men, stunned with what they had been charged with, had nothing to say.

Chapter 63

6 October 1943

An Office, The Pentagon, Washington, D.C.

1115 Hours

Stalwart Guard Three

"The first thing is, who's in charge?" said Bev Tucker, the Marine, a puckish smile on his face. "It's one of you guys, 'cause I don't pin on for another ten days." He referred to date of rank, the long established way of deciding who out ranked who.

"OK, Joel, my date of rank is 9 October '42; what's yours?"

"Looks like I draw the short straw," Joel said. "Mine is 15 June '42."

Remembering the old dictum, *if you're in charge, take charge*, Joel said, "OK, let's get started. First, we need some coffee." The other two laughed.

"I like to work on a blackboard so it's easy to change. We'll need a secretary to copy everything. Ideas?"

John Higgins said, "There's a rating I know in the Graphic Arts Shop. He could use a tablet, draw what's on the board, and have it redone to make it presentable."

"Sounds good to me. Call him and I'll try to round up that coffee, and get us some office supplies," said Joel.

"Let me do the coffee, Colonel," said Tucker. "I know a Marine cook in the mess who can give us a full coffee service, and make sure we have food when we need it too."

"OK, but first, let's agree – no ranks; we've got way too much to do in a very short time to bother with that. Call me Joel, all right?"

"That suits me; call me John, no middle name necessary!"

"And call me Bev or BC, your choice."

Within an hour, a pair of large wooden framed blackboards on castors arrived, with several boxes of colored chalk. Coffee was brewing in a large pot, the Marine cook very practically noting that it would be quicker for them to make their own than to call for it every time the carafe got low. He had also thoughtfully provided a tray of sandwiches.

John extracted a promise that the rating would available the next day. Joel ordered easels with flip charts and thick pens, notebooks, pens and paper and every other supply he could think of. By late afternoon, desks were moved in, including one in the outer office. Phones were on hand, to be hooked up the next day. A pair of typewriters and two boxes of paper sat on one of three desks.

"I got a clerk," Joel said, "to run errands, make calls, and the like. The personnel office had been contacted by Colonel Regan's office, and there will be people on hand to support us around the clock."

"Joel, we need a way to lock up this office. That door lock wouldn't keep out a curious kid," said Bev.

"Excellent thought. And we'll need some safes, too, don't you think?"

"What about somebody to supervise the office staff; we won't have time for that," said Bev. Joel made notes on a borrowed steno pad.

"What else?"

Thirty minutes later the safes and locks had been ordered, an Army Chief Clerk assigned, and the sandwiches consumed; they adjourned to the suite's conference room.

"Joel, I think we need to record what we accomplish on a daily basis. For now, we could take turns writing it, but we'll need a stenographer soon. I'm thinking that if we do that from the beginning, by the end of the month, we'll have something that documents where we've been. It ought to make writing the report easier, too." said Bev.

"Good. We'll take turns; you're first! We ought to have it typed up daily, too, I'm thinking," Joel said.

"OK, boss!" Bev laughed.

Chapter 64

6 October 1943

An Office, The Pentagon, Washington, D.C.

1345 Hours

Concepts

"Well, let's do it," Joel said at the blackboard. "I'll write it down so we can get our arms around it; you guys jump in whenever, OK?"

He wrote

Challenges
-Raid Detection
-Target Protection
-Counter Attack

"Now as I see it, each of these breaks down further into two or three areas, like this:"

Challenges
-Raid Detection
     .. At sea (mid-Atlantic? Near shore by ship visual and RADAR)
     .. In the air (visual and RADAR?)
     ..Ground based observers (visual, sound; includes civilians GOC)
-Target Protection
     ..Camouflage
     ..Barrage balloons?
     ..Search lights
- Counter attack
     ..Antiaircraft guns
     ..Local fighters
     ..Regional fighters?

Both men spoke at once. Joel pointed to John, "You first."

"OK, let's add carriers for the mid-Atlantic. They're in short supply, but even a couple of 'jeep' carriers could put a real damper on the Germans. Carrier aircraft could detect and shoot down raiders."

"That's a very good idea," Joel said as he added it to the board.

Bev said, "Here's an addition for the detection category: ground based RADARs. They can see a lot farther than airborne ones. We could use them to direct fighters for intercepts."

"Good!" Joel said, and added that.

"At sea, you're assuming picket ships, is that it?" John asked.

"Yes, something like that, but I don't have any idea where they should go, or how many. The Atlantic is a darn big place, but that would be the first opportunity to see the bombers."

John said, "Picket ships are good in theory, but practically, it won't work. As you said Joel, the Atlantic is a big place. If we put patrol ships out there, they'll just draw German subs. That's especially true of the 'jeep' carriers, now that I think of it. They're pretty slow, and need a lot of escorts. Maybe patrol planes like PBYs or British Sunderland flying boats would work better."

Joel nodded, and updated the blackboard. *These are a couple of bright guys.*

"Closer to land, I'm thinking long range fighters, like P-51s, or maybe P-38s. Not sure how long the legs are on F6Fs, but I'd guess we need a range of about 1,000 miles for a mission. So whatever birds can fly a long ways and carry guns, we want 'em."

"We left out the middle," Bev pointed out. "We could use long range aircraft, like B-24s or the Navy's PB4Ys, maybe even some older B-17s, say, to help us spot them and direct fighters in. Catalina's have really long legs, if we could get some; 'course, they can't fly very high or fast. Can any of those big four engine numbers carry RADARs, too?"

Bev took on an especially thoughtful look, and Joel asked him about it.

"Well, it occurred to me that we've been assuming that the Germans would only hit us during daylight. I don't know of anything to keep them from hitting us at night, do you?"

John said, "Say, you're right, we didn't think about night raids. That's a harder problem, because we have virtually no night fighters. If we send day fighters up after them at night, about all we guarantee is that we kill off a lot of our own guys."

"I'm afraid you're right, "Joel said. "And if they do come at night, we lose most visual detection, especially by the civilians. I'm not convinced that spotlights do much good, when you get right down to it, even if we had enough of them. We've really got to get more RADARs."

Bev said, "That also suggests that we need to strongly enforce blackout regulations all up and down the seaboard, and probably even inland a good ways. Even since the New York raid, there hasn't been a lot of tightening up."

"Make good notes on these points, Bev, " said Joel.

They continued several hours, filling both blackboards, erasing and starting in again. A knock came at the door, and a skinny sailor entered with a cart. "Gunny said ya'll'd be needin' some supper, sirs," he said with a West Virginia twang.

The interruption made them all realize they were hungry, and how much time had passed. It was already dark outside. They adjourned to the suite's small foyer to eat.

Between bites, Bev nodded toward the door and said, "That's exactly what I meant about security, Joel. That kid just walked in on us. Who knows what he saw or who he'll tell?"

Another rap at the door, "Message for Colonel Knight from the Joint Chief's office, sir."

Joel slit open the sealed envelope with his pocket knife. His face took on a look of surprise.

"What do you know? Boys, they've already pulled the plug on us! Stalwart Guard Three is cancelled as of 1700 hours today. We're to provide a one page summary to the Joint Chief's, and vacate this office!"

John Higgins shook his head, "One page! Excuse my cynicism, but it doesn't surprise me that the Chiefs don't want direction from underlings like us."

"Yeah," said Bev, "it was short and not so sweet. Well, it's too bad they didn't let us finish; I think we had some good ideas, but there you go."

From the outer office came the sounds of furniture being moved.

"They're already moving stuff out, for crying out loud. I hope we can finish before we end up sitting on the floor," Joel said.

The unruffled clerk told him, "Sir, if you'll call me after 1700, I'll come and type your summary. I've got to go report to my new assignment."

Dumbfounded, Joel and the other two men watched as movers emptied the outer office and left it bare.

"OK, let's wrap this up. Here's what I have as our summary; any changes?" Joel said.

Raid Detection [greatly increase]
> RADAR and visual/ships & aircraft offshore
> Shore based RADAR/military and civilian observers

Protection
>Camouflage/false targets
>Blackout rule enforcement

Counter Attack [greatly increased numbers]
>Fighters based near targets
>Regional fighters
>AAA

Overall
>Improved com structure/classification rules
>Well defined rules of engagement
>More weapons, equipment and people

"Naw, you can only polish a rock so much before all you have is gravel, Joel; let's call it quits and go find something useful to do," Bev quipped.

"Yeah," said Higgins, "we're about to polish the brass off the bell as it is. This'll probably end up in the 'circular file' anyway, so why not wrap it up. Call the clerk, and we'll go get supper some place."

"That's the best idea anybody's had all day," Joel laughed.

Chapter 65

18 October 1943

Hanger 321, Millville Army Air Field, Millville, New Jersey

0730 Hours

New Role

Lieutenant Colonel Watkins waited for First Sergeant Blaisdel to call the men to attention, and then strode to the podium. There were far too many men to fit in the Base Theater; essentially, all of the men permanently assigned to Millville Army Air Field were in the hanger. Joel had no idea what was up.

Colonel Watkins spoke uncomfortably into the microphone, leaning awkwardly toward it, "At ease, men. Please be seated."

"There have been lots of rumors about our base since the attack on New York City and I want to set you straight." The speakers squealed, and a sergeant quickly moved a speaker away from the colonel's microphone.

"There are some very big changes coming to Millville." The hanger was silent. Many men were leaning toward him.

"As you know, the 361st Fighter Squadron left for Europe after the attack, and the next scheduled squadron to train hasn't come in. Here's why: Millville has a new mission. We are no longer a gunnery training base. The original slogan for Millville was 'America's First Defense Airport'; well, we're returning to our roots. As of 0600 hours this morning, we are all now members of the brand new 160th Coastal Defense Wing, as part of Coastal Defense Area Two. Our new mission is to defend America's shores.

"In keeping with our more important role, a new commander has been assigned; taking my place will be Brigadier General Adrian White. I will point out that ordinarily, a change of command demands a parade and formal ceremony. In view of this on-going rainy weather, and the critical war situation, General White decided to forgo the formalities, and meet with you immediately. General White, sir." Watkins stepped aside and a distinguished looking gray-headed single star general stepped to the microphone.

"Thank you, Colonel Watkins. Good morning. I am privileged to be here. Gentlemen, make no mistake, your mission at Millville has been important. This new one will be even more so.

"The new 160th will be comprised of three squadrons, later to be four if I have my way. The 160th Detection and Patrol Squadron will be tentatively comprised of sixteen B-23s, with supporting maintenance and supply personnel. The B-23s, as you know, are RADAR equipped.

"The 160th Coastal Defense Fighter Group will be made up of older B and C model P-47s, at first. There will be about a hundred airplanes, divided into several squadrons and flights later on. As quickly as possible, they will be modified with long range fuel tanks. The strategy is the B-23s find the Germans, and the P-47s shoot them down. I hope to get new P-47s off the production line in a couple of months."

There were shouts and applause, the men clearly liked the idea they would be striking back. The General smiled in spite of himself; he liked the idea of taking it to the Germans himself.

"A third squadron, the 160th Search and Rescue Squadron, will rescue offshore survivors from both sides. They will probably have lifeboat-capable C-47s, although that hasn't been firmed up. We may use some war weary B-17s. Looks like about twenty aircraft.

"All of these missions will be done in cooperation with our Navy counterparts at Pawtuxent and Lakehurst, as well as other bases. They will probably use PBY Catalina's and other flying boats, and F6F Hellcats and F4U Corsairs. We will share patrol missions as well as attack; we'll work up the protocols and command structures in the coming weeks. Men, get used to the idea of seeing many more Navy and Marine uniforms. You enlisted men should bone up on Navy uniforms, so you know what to salute.

"There will be a Defense Central Command Center established somewhere nearby, probably in Philadelphia; that name is tentative. Their job is to coordinate ships, patrol planes, and fighters in the district from south of New York City to north of Hampton Roads, Virginia; those boundaries may change a bit as we work things out. Our district is charged with defending our nation's capitol." The last comment resulted in a marked reaction of determination on the faces of the men, Joel noted.

"Now, beginning Monday, the Corps of Engineers will descend upon us like a biblical plague. The Military Police will be stretched pretty thin controlling traffic and corralling the civilian contractors. We have help coming, but they're coming from Kansas by rail, so it'll be a few days.

"The Corps is going to expand transient parking and lengthen both runways. We'll get miles of new taxiway and revetments. They'll build a new tower. There'll be additional barracks and BOQs, a consolidated mess hall, two new hangers, a bigger paint shop, a bigger prop shop, and the engine shop will double in size. It's probable we'll see large numbers of both Army and Navy heavy bombers and patrol aircraft."

He looked over the top of his reading glasses. "Not that I believe them, but the Corps says they'll have the runways done by the end of November, and the rest finished before March. In any case, you all will have heavy workloads for the foreseeable future. Our existing personnel structures will be melded into the new squadrons. First Sergeants will be getting additional administrative support right away. Our pay will still come out of Philadelphia.

"As to unit commanders, Lieutenant Colonel Joel Knight will command the 160th Coastal Defense Fighter Group; his deputy will be named later. The 160th Search and Rescue squadron will be commanded by Major Delbert Moore, with First Lieutenant Tom Cook as deputy. Finally, the 160th Detection and Patrol squadron will be commanded by Captain William Fillbert with Captain John Wooten as his deputy. All will report to me. We'll sort out support organizations later.

"I mentioned a forth squadron. I've petitioned Air Corps Headquarters for a full squadron of the new Northrop P-61 night fighters. Those ships have the speed, firepower, and endurance to allow us to defend our shores at night."

He looked even more serious, "Nobody said the Germans couldn't bomb us at night. Remains to be seen if the Pentagon will go along with it, but I've talked to a couple of pretty powerful Senators who think it's a very good idea.

"I've also petitioned Headquarters for antiaircraft installations on base. The artillery battalion will report to me through a separate line from the aviation units."

He looked at the assembled men, "I'm looking forward to working with you to meet these new challenges. An important aspect of all this is our relationship with our civilian neighbors. Millville Army Air Field has excellent relations with Millville; I insist that we do whatever is needed to maintain that. Those civilians are very much a part of what we do, especially these days. We must maintain and even improve the way we get along with our civilian hosts.

"And lest I forget, Colonel Watkins has a new, secret assignment at the Pentagon along with a promotion. He'll be as successful there as he was here. A round of applause for Colonel Watkins." The applause was loud and long; Watkins was well thought of.

Joel listened carefully to everything General White said, and especially to what he *didn't* say. He wasn't surprised, but it looked as if the Joint Chiefs had ignored his group's recommendations for improved coastal defense.

Well, he thought, *old habits die hard in the military, and none of the Chiefs are used to taking the "advice" of a bunch of lowly O-5s. I just hope their staffs read our report, and convince them, or the country will pay the price.* He shook his head; he'd done all he could.

Complications

General White asked for questions.

A slender, brown haired man stood. "Sir, I'm Captain Edwin Ross; may I change the subject somewhat?"

"Yes, Captain, what is it?"

"General, before I was assigned to Millville, I was operations officer for a B-23 squadron in Cuba. Sir, I think we'll have a problem using them to find German bombers."

"Why is that, Captain?"

"Sir, the RADARs on the B-23s are British ASV Mark Is, which are specifically designed to find submarines. They have a useful range of about three and a half miles from 200 feet, when conditions are right.

"Without getting technical, General, B-23 RADARs can't discriminate well enough to detect aircraft at a distance where they couldn't already be seen with the Mark I eyeball.

"Sir, they're designed to see submarines on the surface." He gestured with his hands, "Their antennas point down. To point them upward, or make them able to point up would require serious engineering work. It might be necessary to change the shape of the antenna cover on the nose as well. One last thing, sir; that airplane is out of production, and all of them are about worn out. We've been flying the wings off of them. Sorry to be the bearer of bad news, sir." He didn't mention that getting any of the sub-hunters away from the squadrons using them would be next to impossible.

Captain William Fillbert raised his hand. The General nodded toward him. "General, after I was told I'd be the CO of the Detection and Patrol squadron, I spent some time investigating B-23s. I can confirm what the Captain said. They fly low and slow, sir, not what we need, I think."

For a moment, White appeared deflated, then he straightened. "Well, Captains, that does put a different blush on the rose, doesn't it? What other aircraft are possible candidates?"

After a brief silence, Joel interjected, "General White, sir, there are some ex-Lend-Lease Douglas B-70s we might be able to get. They're converted from A-20 Havocs. They have AI RADARs." AI was the designation for Airborne Interception. "They don't have P-61 performance, of course, but they may be available and could do a reasonable job temporarily."

The General's face brightened, "Check into that for me, Colonel, and report back as soon as you know anything."

Two days later

Joel stood as General White walked out of his office, "Good morning, sir. I have the story on the P-70s, if you have a moment."

White glanced at his watch, "I have about seven minutes, Colonel; can you brief me quickly?"

"Yes, sir, I believe so." They moved into White's office.

"Sir, the short answer is the airplanes aren't available. As you know, the British sent them back to us. Before the Army could reassign them, State Department got involved."

"State Department? What did they want with them?"

"Sir, somebody at State got the cock-a-mamie idea that those ships should go to Russia under Lend-Lease. The War Department and the Army are totally against it, of course, but State won't budge. It may go to the President before it's all over, but that doesn't help our problem, I'm afraid."

"Dear God, those idiots at State would actually give the Russians some of our best RADARs? No wonder the War Department and the Army are against it. Does General Marshall know?"

"Not officially, that I'm aware of, sir. General Arnold has been briefed."

"Well. Now I guess it's time for me to light a fire under the Secretary of War for those P-61s you wanted. Hap Arnold has already bought off on the plan, if you're not aware of that, Colonel."

"That's great, sir; always good to have the Chief of the Army Air Forces behind your request."

"That can smooth out a few bumps along the way," White said dryly, by way of dismissal.

Chapter 66

20 October 1943

Office of the Commanding General,
Millville Army Air Field, Millville, New Jersey

1330 Hours

Analysis

General White sat with his officers and senior NCOs, preparing for yet another Pentagon meeting.

"I want your opinions, gentlemen: why did the Germans attack us and what did they think they'd gain? What possible tactical and strategic reasons are behind the Germans making such a huge expenditure of time, money, and resources for so little obvious gain. If we understand the why of what they did, perhaps we can defend against it better."

Major Moore cleared his throat, "Sir, I believe it was psychological, to frighten Americans, undermining our sense of security and determination to fight. The propaganda that Goebbels has been putting out sure sounds like that."

"That may well have been part of it, Major, but it doesn't seem like reason enough by itself. Anyone else?"

Joel interjected, "Sir, Major Moore may be correct but I believe there may have been a strategic rationale as well. If they attack us, our response would be to defend our coast with more troops, aircraft, and ships. That means fewer troops, aircraft and ships to fight in Europe."

White was thoughtful for a moment, "To hold us hostage, Colonel, wouldn't they have to strike us repeatedly? Will they attack us again?"

"Well, sir," Joel answered carefully, "using the aircraft they hit New York City with, no. Those ships were cobbled together for that mission, I think; the fact they were unarmed says they depended on surprise. If they try that again, we'll kill 'em."

"What do you mean 'cobbled together'?"

"General, when I flew next to the Germans that day, I saw covers riveted over gun turret openings; it's in the photos. There were marks on the undersides where something dropped off. They all had an angled pipe coming forward from the left leading edge – that sort of thing hasn't been seen before. If you look at the photographs, sir, there were a couple of planes that had torn up landing gear doors. One had no wheel in the wheel well. The paint schemes sure weren't standard Luftwaffe. If I may be so bold, sir, I respectfully submit that those aircraft were not standard production Gotha's; I think they were specially modified just for this mission."

White turned to his new G-2 colonel, "What about that, George? Any idea what a standard production Gotha looks like?"

The man hedged his answer, "Sir, while I agree with Colonel Knight that the features he mentioned are not what you'd expect to find on ordinary production ships, at this time, I don't think we can say what is standard and what isn't. They've only been encountered a few times in Europe."

"Hmm. Next question: why weren't they armed?"

A young looking Captain spoke, "General, my guess is that they were restricted in the weight they could carry and still get back, so they risked not being armed in the hope they'd surprise us."

"That's certainly reasonable, sir," Joel said. In this case, his engineering background gave him an edge over the other pilots.

"For the size of the aircraft, the bomb loads they carried seemed small – mostly incendiaries, which are pretty light."

Another man commented and there was conversation about it. Joel sat, deep in thought. When the opportunity arose, he interjected,

"General White, sir, could the Germans know where I am stationed?"

"Why do you ask, Colonel?" White said, a puzzled look on his face.

"Not to sound self-centered, sir, but in 1936, von Schroeder vowed to come to America and kill me. He has repeated that threat several times since. I didn't pay much attention to it until now. Since he commanded the New York raid, it's reasonable to assume he'd be part of any additional attacks. If he still has those feelings, and he finds out I'm here at Millville, sir – well, that could increase the possibility of an attack on this base."

The G-2 Colonel cleared his throat, glancing at the major beside him, "General White, it's likely the Germans know that Colonel Knight is stationed here. Personnel lists for about a dozen bases, including Millville, were recently stolen. The thief contacted a known spy in New York City. The documents have already been passed on, probably through Canada. The FBI is involved as well as Army Intelligence. If you would like, sir, I can check into what the Bureau knows."

"Yes, George, do that. Let me and Colonel Knight know what you find." He made some notes.

25 October 1943

Staff Meeting

"General White, regarding the FBI investigation into the thefts of base personnel lists, I spoke with the Special Agent in Charge. He told me the thief rented a boat, and sailed out of New York Harbor a couple of days afterward. The Coast Guard found it adrift; we think he was met by a submarine. The trail of the Canadian spy has also gone cold. My opinion is you should assume the Germans have our personnel list, and that they know about Colonel Knight."

"Thank you, George. If you hear any news about this, let me know."

He turned to Joel. "I'm not sure what to do about this, Colonel, beyond staying alert for attacks. It amazes me that this von Schroeder duck was allowed to lay on a bombing mission for personal vindictiveness, but stranger things have happened with the Third Reich."

Chapter 67

9 November 1943

Colonel Joel Knight's Office

0810 Hours

Unexpected Confession

"Colonel," Bill Madsen said, "personal call on line one."

"Thanks, Bill," Joel said, picking up the receiver, "this is Lieutenant Colonel Knight."

"Hello Joel, this is Susan." The normal lilt in her voice was missing.

"Sorry to bother you at work, so I'll be quick. Can you meet me tonight at the Second Street diner? I really need to speak to you."

Slightly taken aback, Joel said, "Well, hi yourself! Can't you just tell me what's on your mind right now?"

"No," she demurred, sounding a little distant, "we need to talk face to face." They agreed on a time, chatted just a bit, and then said goodbye.

This feels ominous, Joel thought. *Has she found somebody else?* The question unsettled him. The day seemed to drag from then on.

Just before 6:00 p.m., Joel parked the Packard near the diner, and saw that Susan had borrowed Mildred's dark blue '37 Ford sedan. Steeling himself for the worst, he went inside.

Susan saw him from the corner booth, and smiled what she hoped was brightly. She stood, and kissed him on the cheek. Inside, she was clenching her stomach, worried how he would take what she had to say. He kissed her back, a bit distantly, and sat, a worried look on his face.

The poor guy has no idea why I had asked him here, Susan thought.

"Thanks for coming," she said, screwing up her courage, "I know this isn't real convenient for you. I really—." A waitress interrupted her. Joel ordered coffee and a slice of pie.

He's distracted, she thought, *he didn't notice that I ordered a meal.*

They sat mostly silent until her meal was served, while her tension rose. Then, steeling herself, she looked him earnestly in the eye.

"What I must tell you, Joel, is that I haven't been fully honest with you about myself." Joel got a worried look on his face and sat very still.

Carefully, she said, "Do you remember wondering how I got in to see you when you were in the hospital after our accident in the plane?"

"Yes," he said, slowly.

"Well, I got on base and into the hospital because I have an ID card that's a pass."

"What? What ID card?" He was frowning, and looked confused.

"This one," she handed it to him, her heart beating a little faster. On it was an unflattering photograph of her. At the top it said OFFICIAL; on the line below it read:

CIVILIAN EMPLOYEE
WAR DEPARTMENT

Where a military ID card listed rank, it read GS-11. A bottom line said:

CLEARANCE TOP SECRET
Special Access

He looked up at her, his eyes slightly narrowed. "Civilian employee? GS-11? What the Dickens is this all about?"

She took the card, slipped it into her purse, and swallowed.

"It means that I work for the War Department on a contract basis. Mostly with Army G-2. Not many people have the education I have, Joel, and they hired me some time ago. What I told you about teaching and getting a masters degree is what they call a 'cover story.' In fact, I already have my doctorate."

His look was blank, uncomprehending.

She took a breath, and pressed on.

"For the Army, I have been looking at reports on certain high ranking officials and serving officers, to determine whether they are trustworthy, or whether they could be at risk for emotional breakdown under the extreme pressures of combat."

"Have you been investigating me?" he said, a shocked look on his face.

"Oh, no! No, not at all!"

She hadn't anticipated the question. She put her hand reassuringly on his.

"Not you. I just wasn't allowed to tell you until now. I hate that I had to lie to you; please forgive me? With your promotion and new responsibilities, they decided I should fill you in about my work, in case you need my help sometime. That, and then I wouldn't have to make up excuses for why I'm always going to Washington. They may ask me to come to Washington full-time soon."

Joel sat back and blew out a breath she didn't know he'd been holding.

"That's a relief; I thought—I was afraid you were going to say goodbye."

It was Susan's turn to be surprised, as a pain leapt up inside her.

"I don't want to say goodbye to you, Joel," she said softly, "is that what you want?" Her voice sounded somehow small to her.

His blue eyes were intense. "Susan, I love you; that's the last thing I want. And of course I forgive you." He held both of her hands, and she relaxed. "So, tell me, what do they have you doing?"

She noted that he didn't ask for names. "The public doesn't know—," she looked around to see how near the other diners were, and continued quietly.

"The public doesn't know there have been several cases where men in combat 'snapped' – I hate that term, it doesn't explain it at all – with some pretty serious consequences. For example, a Marine Captain on Guadalcanal, who'd never been in combat before suddenly went wild and began shouting senseless orders; several of his men died. His Lieutenant relieved him, but the man has never been the same, and should never have been put in that position. That's just one example; in another situation, a man just froze, and did nothing. There are others in Europe, including a very high ranking officer who was relieved for reasons I can't go into. And, they've had me analyzing the behavior of several senior Nazis, to see if we can predict what their reactions to certain situations might be. I've had some success at it, but not as much as I want or that we need. They're asking me to concentrate on the Nazis."

She squared her shoulders and looked him in the eye. "Joel, I've been ordered to interview you about von Schroeder. They want me to work up some ideas on him, and you are one of the very few who have ever spent any time with him. Your experience is unique."

She cleared her throat and spoke more firmly than before.

"You are to clear your calendar next Thursday, and spend the day with me discussing this man, on the record. Your office is acceptable if we can arrange to not be disturbed; otherwise, it will have to be away from the Headquarters building somewhere." Her chin was stuck out resolutely. "I'm sorry to say it this way, but those are orders from the Air Corps General Staff."

Chapter 68

11 November 1943

Building 21, Military Police Headquarters

Millville Army Air Field

1000 Hours

Interview

Joel decided against his office; they would be constantly interrupted. He explained to Chappy he'd be unavailable except for emergencies, and left him in charge.

He drove through crunchy snow to the Military Police building and parked. He still had mixed feelings about what she'd told him. He was a little miffed on one hand that she hadn't told him, and proud of her on the other for doing such an important job. And he was worried that he wouldn't be able to concentrate; she had a way of very pleasantly distracting him. That thought made him smile.

All day, together!

He found the office, and walked in to discover Susan speaking to a short, spare looking WAC [Women's Army Corps] Technical Sergeant. The contrast between the two women could not have been starker. Susan was wonderfully female in a way that even the plainest clothing couldn't hide; the other woman was slender to the point of being skinny, with all the shape of a flag pole. Her face was drawn up in a tight scowl, accentuated by heavy, wireless glasses. Her dark hair was straight and cut severely.

"Good morning, sir. Are you Colonel Knight?" her voice was thin and reed-like, her gray eyes probing.

"Yes," Joel replied, "good morning, Sergeant. And good morning to you, Susan."

"We'll be a bit more formal today, *Colonel* Knight," Susan said, emphasizing his rank. "This is Technical Sergeant Lucile Morgan. She's a psychologist, and will be assisting me today as we learn what you know about Oberst Freiherr Gerhard von und zu Schroeder."

His visions of being alone with Susan all day vanished as he followed the women into a second room. It contained a large wooden table, on one side of which was a single chair. On the other side there were two chairs. A reel to reel tape recorder sat on the table. A microphone sat in front of the single chair. Against the wall was a smaller table holding a coffee service and three cups.

This must be where they conduct interrogations, he thought grimly. *"Ve have ways of making you talk." No torture instruments visible, at least.*

"Help yourself to coffee, Colonel, if you'd like, and we'll begin," Susan said, sounding very businesslike. Joel filled a cup, and sat.

"State for the record, please, your name, rank, and serial number."

"I am Lieutenant Colonel Joel T. Knight, United States Army Air Forces, serial number O-1772330."

"Thank you, Colonel. You don't have to lean toward the microphone. It will record you where you sit," Sergeant Morgan said primly.

Susan began, "Very well. Where and on what date did you first meet the German officer named Gerhard von und zu Schroeder?"

Joel cleared his throat. "It was on the thirteenth of June, 1936, at the German air base at Hannover, Germany."

"Why were you at that place at that time?"

Joel explained about the flight demonstration assignment and the tour through Europe.

"So tell us, Colonel, what was your first impression of Gerhard von und zu Schroeder?"

"He was a walking caricature of a uniformed German 'aristocrat'. About all he needed to complete the picture was a monocle. He quickly made sure I knew he was a 'Baron,' and it rattled him when I wasn't impressed. There was a sense of arrogance about him, but—," he hesitated.

"Go on, sir," said Technical Sergeant Lucile Morgan, watching carefully.

"Well, it was as if he was acting, or pretending, and that he knew I knew he was lying. And that he expected me to call him on it. Seems silly."

"How did that make you feel?" Morgan asked in her shrill voice.

"Feel?" He laughed, "I was a cocky young pursuit pilot. I thought he was a buffoon. Then, I remembered he outranked me as a Captain. I had to show him respect because of that. And, I was in his country as a guest. Remember, we weren't at war then. If I insulted him, it could have been an international incident; any friction between us could have been a barrier to selling the aircraft I was demonstrating."

Susan interjected, "Please tell us how he came to challenge you to a 'dog fight'." She emphasized both words equally, making the term sound contrived, as if they were little boys at play on a schoolyard.

Joel shrugged. "He said something to the effect that my airplane's performance impressed him, and would I like to fly against him in his new Messerschmitt. My answer was 'of course.' The ME-109 was brand new then – hadn't even been selected for production yet. Nobody had any real idea of how good it was. His offer was a golden opportunity for me and for the Army."

"So you flew your airplane and pretended to fight against his, is that what happened?" Morgan asked.

It's obvious her ideas of dog fighting come from movies, Joel thought.

He chuckled, "No, even that would have been unbelievable. What really happened was—." He spent fifteen minutes detailing the mechanical problems with his own airplane, and his attempts at goading the German into letting him fly an ME-109.

"Did you think it was unusual that von Schroeder and his superiors agreed to this contest?"

"Oh, I'll say! It was nuts! In my wildest dreams I wouldn't have thought that they'd go for it. My suspicion is that somehow, von Schroeder and his boss thought they were upholding the 'Honor of Germany,' something like that. I mean, I was manipulating Schroeder like everything, and they just went along."

"Did you think that 'honor' was a motivating factor then?"

"I don't care what their motivation was as long as I got to fly the ME-109. My boss and the Ambassador thought it was a trick. They – the Germans, that is – were taking quite a risk. After all, I could have crashed one of their two prototypes. I could have been killed, and that would have created a big international incident. I doubt that they considered I would beat von Schroeder. The whole thing was so – un-German, going forward on the spur of the moment with an outrageous plan without the approval of Göring or Hitler. In retrospect, I suspect they were hoping I'd be so impressed with their plane that I'd tell the Army they were invincible, something like that."

He looked steadily at the two women,

"And we were taking a big risk, too. The Germans had no idea I was anything but just another low ranking U.S. Army pilot. We kept the information about my being an aeronautical engineer very close to our vests. In truth, I collected a lot of very important information about that airplane, information that a pilot not trained as an engineer would have missed. I have no doubt that they would have called me a spy if they had known. It was actually quite a coup for our side."

"If we may, let's get into the actual 'dog fights.' What was it, do you remember, that made it possible for you to defeat him?" Susan said.

"Oh, I remember, OK. It was – it's just that—well, he just had no imagination, no creativity."

Both women looked at him blankly.

"See, a dog fight pits one pilot against another on a real basic level involving a lot of skill and finesse. It also requires gut level intuition, how to anticipate your opponent's next move, how to take advantage of what he just did, that sort of thing. To do it well, you must also be master of your aircraft. In some ways, it's like sword fighting, with parry and thrust, move, countermove. And just like sword fighting, if you're predictable, you're dead. If that fight had been for real, von Schroeder would have been dead after our first encounter."

Susan said, "You say that he was predictable; in what way?" She was making notes while the tape recorder whirled.

Joel said, "He always feigned twice one way, then turned the other. And on initial break, he always broke left."

"Initial break? Please explain." asked Morgan, also taking notes on an Army issue tablet.

"See, when two fighter planes come at each other head-on, they have to 'break,' or turn, to join the fight." He demonstrated with his hands.

"In our four dog fights, von Schroeder broke left – turned to his left – all four times. In real combat, it would have been the kiss of death."

Morgan accepted what he said, but he could tell she didn't really comprehend.

"What else do you remember about how he fought?" Susan said.

"Well, he was very mechanical, as if he'd only read about how to do it in a book. He just performed the basic maneuvers, with no variation. All of his maneuvers were graceful, gentle. He didn't seem to understand that an Immelmann or a split-S or whatever was supposed to give him an advantage over me. His worst sin, as a fighter pilot – a fatal sin – was that he didn't think in three dimensions. He wanted to fight on a horizontal plane. He forgot about the vertical dimension."

He paused; the women didn't interrupt.

"He was supposedly a champion; or so he claimed. I don't see how, unless they let him win for some reason. And why would they do that?" Neither woman responded, but both wrote on their pads.

"Now, tell us, after you defeated him –four times, wasn't it? How did he react?" Susan said, "Was he angry, for example?"

"Oh, yeah! 'Angry' doesn't begin to cover it," Joel said, smiling.

"He was furious. I mean, I've never before or since seen someone so mad. He was apoplectic – red in the face, his neck veins standing out, eyes bugging out. It was kind of scary, actually."

Joel hesitated for a moment, then leaned toward the two women, "Then, he threatened me, threw down his glove, as if challenging me to a duel! And honestly, I think from his viewpoint, he was. He swore he would kill me if he had to come here, to the U.S. If his Colonel hadn't intervened, he might have tried to kill me on the spot."

"Did you believe him?"

"No. I was young and stupid. Then, when I heard he was still saying the same thing years later, I was concerned. When I saw his airplane during the attack on New York, I knew it couldn't be coincidence. I think the word is vendetta."

There was a moment's pause when no one spoke.

Then Joel said, "It's as if he blames me, personally, for all the bad things that happen to him. That he was an orphan."

"Let us draw the conclusions, please," the sergeant said a bit primly.

"Wait," Susan said sharply, "he was an orphan? Why do you think that?"

Joel shrugged, "When Colonel Bigsby and I saw him, Ambassador Dodd's master sergeant briefed us on von Schroeder's dossier. His old man was killed during the Great War, and then his mother, brothers and sister were all killed were moving to Berlin or somewhere."

"I'm unaware of this dossier; do you know of it, Doctor Johansseson?"

"No, I don't," Susan said. "Do you remember this master sergeant's name, Colonel?"

"No—," he hesitated, "it was something common, like Smith or Jones, but I'm sure you could find it fairly easily. He was assigned to the Military Attaché's office. When they closed the embassy, they brought out all that stuff. It's probably in the State Department's archives."

Sergeant Morgan turned toward Susan and said, "This could be the break through we've been wanting."

"Yes," Susan agreed, "this could help us explain a great deal."

1944

Chapter 69

Monday, 10 April, 1944

Millville Army Air Field

Joel's Office

0630 Hours

Attack On Millville

Joel and his deputy were going through pilot personnel records, deciding who they wanted, where each would be assigned, trying to balance experience with skill, bravado with reasoned caution. The idea was to separate them into piles of similar qualities. It sounded great, but it just wasn't working. When they gave the personnel files a close look, they saw that other commands had sent them their "problem children," as Joel had put it.

Captain Derek Chapman shook his head, "Look at this, would ya; just *look* at this!" He snapped the folder with his index finger.

"This guy busted two check rides in a row, then gets a 'superior' a week later, just before he's shipped to us – are we supposed to be so stupid we don't notice that?"

He snapped another, "And this guy can't stay out of a bottle. A lush: just what we need. And here! 'An officer and a gentleman' who thinks it's funny to buzz the parade for a new commanding officer! What're we gonna do with these misfits, Joel?"

"Ah, the challenges of leadership, Chappie. And ain't it fun? I keep telling myself that somewhere there must be a couple of guys who could actually lead a flight. I'm beginning to wonder."

"Say, I'll give you my take on it, boss: they're a bunch of yo-yos! We'll have to come down on these guys like a ton of bricks, give 'em a lot of discipline, try to get them on the straight and narrow, 'cause they're all we've got to work with."

"I agree, and—" Joel began, when the red scramble phone on his desk suddenly rang loudly. As he reached for it, they heard heavy explosions from the south-east portion of the base. Both realized they were not ordinary bomb range sounds.

"ACP-2, Colonel Knight speaking," Joel said briskly.

"This is Central Command: RADAR and visual sightings confirm attack imminent, your base. Scramble alert aircraft, I say again, scramble your alert aircraft."

Joel slapped the button that started the Air Raid siren before dialing the alert shack. As the phone rang, he heard the throaty, window rattling roar of a pair of P-47s taking off. They were immediately followed by two others.

Chappie peered out the window, "Alert birds are off."

Joel hung up and dialed the ready room. "Colonel Knight here; what's the status of our aircraft?"

"Sir," came the laconic reply, "there are seven birds down for maintenance, and nine available for flight."

"We are under attack: get all available birds armed and pre-flighted ASAP. Tell the OD [Officer of the Day] to call every pilot on the roster until he gets those planes manned and airborne."

He dialed Master Sergeant Hillborne at the maintenance shop.

"Hill, Colonel Knight. Is the P-61 fueled? Can you arm it? Good. Get it preflighted and started ASAP. Get Johnson there, too; we'll need the RADAR. Do you feel up to running the guns?" He paused. "Good, I'll be there in ten."

He grimly turned to Chappie, and said with frustration, "I *knew* they'd hit us again before we could stand up! Keep after the OD to get those birds airborne; I'm taking up the Black Widow." Inside, his gut was a tight knot.

Another explosion, much closer, shook the windows, followed by several more.

"Get to the bomb shelter! Take the office crew with you," Joel shouted over his shoulder as he raced out of the office.

Several more explosions, very close, were smaller, but sharper in sound.

Those aren't bombs, he decided, *are they rocket shells?*

Joel looked up as he ran, and saw white, smoky streaks race down from the sky. They slammed into buildings and destroyed several trucks. Then, to his horror, red-orange explosions burst above the aircraft revetments, and his heart sank. Those air-burst shells were filled with shrapnel, to destroy or damage parked airplanes. None of his planes had even moved yet.

The staff car's tires squealed as he screeched to a stop, and raced to the Black Widow. Its props were spinning slowly. Hillborne had just finished the pre-flight.

"We're ready, Colonel. Pre-flight's done. Johnson is warming up his set."

Joel glanced to the west, in the direction that the now vanished German formation had flown through the scattered clouds.

"They're going for Philadelphia! Let's go!"

He ducked under the nose gear door, and quickly climbed up into the cockpit. Hillborne was right behind him, and squeezed past to take his place in the gunner's seat just behind and above Joel's. Johnson, with his own access at the rear, was behind them both, getting the RADAR calibrated.

Joel glanced at the engine instruments and ran the control wheel through its range of motion. Ready! He signaled the ground crew to remove the wheel chocks. He called for taxi clearance; in minutes, they were climbing hard, turning westward in the direction of the vanished German formation.

"Got 'em on the scope yet, Johnson?" he shouted over the roaring engines.

"We're at extreme range, Colonel, but it looks like there's a bunch of them," the Marine said. "There are smaller targets around them – probably our Thunderbolts."

"OK. Give me a heading." Joel quickly turned to the heading and glanced again at the instruments. Everything was in the green. Good. He set the radio frequency, and snatched up the mic.

"Central Command, ACP 2 [Airborne Control Point] airborne at 4-7 after the hour, west bound and climbing through 1-7 thousand feet. Armed and up. Over." The last comment informed the controllers his RADAR was working; they didn't want to reveal their capabilities before they became obvious.

Central Command acknowledged his call.

"CC, ACP 2; what fighters are airborne? Over."

"ACP 2, CC. We have four P-47s, plus six P-40s from Washington. New York has P-400s standing by; Navy has F6Fs at Lakehurst and Pawtuxent standing by. Over."

That's only ten fighters airborne, Joel thought, and keyed his mic.

"CC, ACP 2. Recommend scramble New York and Pawtuxent at this time. Call Wildweed NAS and Ocean City NAS to see if they can help. Call when on station. Over."

"CC, roger. Out," came the reply. The Naval air stations at Wildweed on Cape May and Ocean City had similar missions to Millville's old one.

They were too late; the Germans had already dropped their bombs. Now, the formation was wheeling left, headed south along the Delaware River. Hundreds of deceptively puffy clouds of black smoke dotted the sky. Philly's antiaircraft guns were hammering away, but Joel knew he was in as much danger from them as the Germans. He saw heavy smoke and explosions roiling out of the big DuPont munitions plant.

There was fire and smoke all along the riverfront, too, as ships and warehouses burned. He saw two of his P-47s weaving back and forth but strangely not closing in for the kill. Before he could radio them, white rocket gun streaks from two of the bombers converged on one of the P-47s. To Joel's shock, it exploded in a brilliant flash, and fell in thousands of glittering pieces toward the river below. One of his men had just died. His stomach turned sour.

A P-40 shot in from the other side of the formation, its guns blazing. It too exploded and fell away broken. The P-40's wingman pulled up, aborting his attack.

With sudden, bitter realization, Joel understood: the rocket guns had a much longer range than the 0.50 caliber guns on the Thunderbolts and P-40s; they couldn't get close enough to shoot without being shot themselves.

"CC, ACP 2. Advise all fighters the Germans have the range on us. Their rocket guns go out a thousand yards at least. Scramble, I say again, scramble the P-400s. Advise them to use only use their cannons. Over."

The P-400s were an older version of the mid-engine Bell P-39 without engine superchargers. Great Britain had turned them down for poor performance. Each had a huge 37 mm cannon that fired through the propeller hub.

"Hill, did you arm the 30mms too?" He knew that the four 30mm cannons buried in the sides of the P-61's fuselage had a little longer range than the 0.50 caliber machine guns.

"Roger, Colonel, but only about two dozen rounds each – all we had time for," came the reply. Normally there would be 200 rounds each.

"Well, boys, until the P-400s get here, it's up to us."

He turned toward the formation and grimly chose his target.

Chapter 70

10 April 1944

Near the South East Delaware Coast

0711 Hours

First Encounter

As they rapidly closed in from above the bomber formation, Joel suddenly realized he was seeing six propellers on each plane, not four.

"Hill, do you see six props on those Krauts?"

"Yeah, I sure do, boss; all of 'em have six! And they're a lot bigger than I thought. Ya know, sir, I don't think these ships are the same as what you saw over New York City."

"You're right, these *are* bigger. Don't look cobbled together, either. I think we have a whole new problem to solve," he added needlessly.

A P-47 slashed across in front of them, firing its eight machine guns at the trailing German bomber. White rocket shells reached out, and the P-47's right wing disintegrated in a brilliant flash. Joel watched open mouthed as the fighter snap-rolled viscously onto its back. Then to his intense relief, the pilot left the stricken plane. In a few seconds, a parachute opened. Joel silently thanked God for sparing the pilot.

The P-400s won't be here for ten minutes or more. I've got no choice; I've got to attack the Germans because nobody else can.

The German formation was stringing out, the lead plane miles ahead.

"CC, ACP 2. Taking direct action. Advise when P-400s available. Over." That meant he was attacking the Germans himself.

He wasn't exactly sure what his aim point should be on the big flying wings.

When you attack an ordinary bomber, you aim for the wing root, or the engines. This thing is all wing, and the engines are buried! Now what?

Deciding, he armed the cannons, and selected "single round"; that way he'd fire only one shot at a time, and maybe make better use of the few rounds he had. He gripped the control wheel hard, and slammed the throttles into Military Power.

When he liked the sight picture, he squeezed the trigger. The big guns were mounted just below his seat, and the noise and vibration was terrific. He was concentrating so hard, he scarcely heard them. The 30mm rounds were loaded one-in-five with tracers. He walked the tracer streaks across the center of the Gotha's wing, toward the cabin. White rockets screamed past them, their roar terrifying audible.

How did they miss? They dove below the smoking enemy.

Joel turned left tightly, pulling a lot of G's. Hillborne grunted into his oxygen mask. Johnson held the papers on his desk, and fiddled with the RADAR.

As they climbed back toward the formation, Joel saw the plane he'd shot was trailing thin white smoke. One of the propellers was feathered.

"Central Command, ACP 2," he called tardily, "targets on heading 0-9-6, one trailing smoke. Over."

This time, he attacked the Gotha from below, stitching the big rounds ahead of one of the props still turning. More white rocket rounds screamed at them. The smoke was heavier, and flashes of fire leapt through jagged holes.

He rolled to the right, almost inverted, and dove away. White rockets chased them, he saw in the mirror above his seat. They were near the shore line.

Where are those Marine F6F's? And as he thought it, a swarm of the dark blue fighters whipped through the light cloud layer directly toward the invaders.

In anguish, Joel realized the Marine pilots were oblivious to the long reach of the German rocket guns as they raced to attack. First one, then another, then a third of the F6F's were shattered as the rockets found their targets. The broken aircraft tumbled from the sky trailing smoke and fire. Joel didn't see any parachutes. Other F6Fs dove on the German formation from above.

He quickly dialed the Navy frequency from memory, "Pawtuxent flight, APC 2. Hold your attack, I say again, hold your attack. The German rockets out range us. Stand down. ACP 2 out."

Another F6F shot through the formation, already on the attack when Joel radioed. It was chased by a half dozen white smoke trails, but somehow wasn't struck.

The Marine's attack had not been in vain, Joel realized. One of the Gotha's faltered, and nosed straight up. Almost instantly, it nosed down again, trailing an impossibly large smoke plume. Orange-red fire engulfed the entire center of the aircraft as it began to gyrate violently. The big airplane suddenly flew apart in a fiery rain of parts big and small, and smashed into the sea.

"Central Control, ACP 2. Marines scratched one bogey, loss of three friendlies. Out." His own voice sounded shaky.

Maneuvering into position on the smoking Gotha he'd first attacked, Joel aimed for the upper rocket gun turret. In seconds the rocket gun was smashed, the gunner dead. The doughty Marines harried the German plane, drawing off its fire.

That's a good tactic; gotta remember that.

"Now I've got you!" he shouted, as if the faltering bomber could hear him. He walked the 30 mm rounds across the center of the wing, from one inner engine cover to the other. Other aircraft in the formation fired at them, the smoky trails going wide.

"Good hits! Good hits!" Hillborne shouted excitedly, as he fired the four 0.50 caliber machineguns in their turret. Pieces of the Gotha flew off and nearly struck them. Joel glanced at the cannon round counter: empty.

Joel dove away to the left. Above them, the Gotha shuddered and skidded drunkenly. Sooty, black smoke poured from three of its engines.

Suddenly, there was a brilliant flash, a huge fireball, and a heavy detonation they heard over their own engines. The big aircraft folded, wing tips all but touching. It gyrated crazily, in what was not quite a spin. A shower of parts flew off in all directions. A man was flung from the dying aircraft, his body silhouetted against the sky. He was followed by another, and then two men together. The wreck fell very fast, spinning as it went in a long, violent, twisting arc toward the ocean below. The smoke column was etched inky black against the grayness of the ocean.

Joel dove to follow and confirm its crash. Far below, the German airplane was suddenly swallowed up by the sea in a mighty splash. The smaller pieces spattered the sea's surface like metallic rain. The smoke column hung over the spot like a towering tombstone.

Joel leveled off, looking for the crew.

There! Drifting towards land.

"Central Control, ACP 2, second bogey down. Three, correction, four parachutes visible, drifting to the northwest about ten miles off Rocky Point. Notify the 160th Search and Rescue. Enemy A/C is scratch. ACP 2 out." "Scratch" meant the downed aircraft was not recoverable. The Joint Chiefs really wanted to get their hands on an intact example of this menacing weapon.

He advanced the throttles once again, turned, and began to climb after the disappearing formation. In moments, they caught a straggler. Roaring in from underneath the German, Joel gave Hillborne a target. He didn't disappoint; the four .50 cal machine guns tore into the Gotha's underside. The Gotha's rocket turret turned toward them, but the aircraft suddenly rolled onto its back and dove toward the sea.

"ACP 2, CC. The P-400s should be there momentarily, call sign 'Black Horse.' Over."

Joel switched radio frequency.

"Black Horse lead, ACP 2. Do you read? Over."

The response was noisy, but discernable. "ACP 2, Black Horse lead, how do you read? Over."

"Black Horse lead, I read you 4x4. Be advised, you are to use cannons only, I say again cannons only – the German rocket guns have a long reach. Be careful. Do you understand? Over."

"Roger, ACP 2. We're going in now. Black Horse lead out."

Joel watched the olive drab aircraft move in on the Germans by two's and saw the smoke from their cannons. Sparks flew up from the bomber they were attacking, but it continued on as if nothing had happened. The second pair of P-400s dove on the formation with similar results.

Suddenly, it hit him. Joel radioed, "Black Horse lead, ACP 2. What ammo are you loaded with? Over."

"ACP 2, Black Horse lead. It's AP, sir. Over."

Joel shook his head. AP was armor piercing, designed to take out tanks. The thin aluminum skin of the Gothas didn't even trigger the explosive on the 37mm rounds, they just punched holes.

"Black Horse flight, ACP 2 recommends you concentrate on the engines; shoot forward of the propellers. ACP 2 out."

The P-400s circled for a few moments; only the lead aircraft could receive Joel's commands. They moved away from the German formation, then dove in for the attack in groups of four aircraft.

White rocket trails flew at the attackers, but somehow the first batch of P-400s made it through unscathed. Not so with the bombers as one of the giants slowed and began descending toward the sea below. Immediately, a second set of P-400s fell upon the hapless aircraft and it was a ball of flames as it crashed into the sea. The last aircraft in the formation was the target of the next attack by the P-400s, and it too suffered a fiery fate.

"ACP-2, Black Horse lead. We've reached our service ceiling, and we're low on fuel. Request permission to withdraw."

"Black Horse lead, ACP-2. Permission granted. Good shooting. ACP 2 out."

The P-400s formed up and turned toward shore. Joel turned with them and watched as they disappeared. Two of the enemies were trailing smoke. Now it was all up to him.

When he brought the P-61 around again, the formation was well ahead of them, still climbing.

"Johnson, can you get a count of how many are left?"

"Only if you hold the nose steady, sir!" the young man countered, not meaning disrespect as he intensely concentrated.

"OK, how's this?" Joel said, carefully holding the nose in the direction of the Germans.

"Come right about twelve degrees or so... hold it, there they are. I count... let's see, twenty-seven fairly distinct returns. Many others are indistinct. May be more than twenty-seven. Can you get us closer, Colonel? I'm showing about ten miles range – that's about max for this RADAR, and it's tough to distinguish clearly They just don't show up very well."

Joel again advanced the throttles to the "Military Power" setting. With the two-stage engine superchargers in the "high" setting, they leapt upward, climbing steeply as the engines roared lustily. Within minutes they were five miles from their enemy, and closing.

"Come left three degrees, pilot. Good. Good. Hold it there as steady as you can; I'm going to high magnification." With the RADAR screen set at its highest magnification, the slightest movement of the aircraft was amplified, making Johnson's job all but impossible.

"OK – OK. I now count fifty-six targets. They are very smooth at 223 knots, heading112 degrees, altitude is … 26, 500 feet."

Joel glanced at the instrument panel. Fuel was getting low and they had to be 200 miles off the coast.

"Good, Johnson, very good. We're gonna go out in front of them, and do a head-on attack, then we'll head for the ranch." He climbed through the thin cloud layer and raced out ahead of the formation.

❖ ❖ ❖

They were a mile ahead and 5,000 or 6,000 feet above the Germans as Joel rolled into a dive toward the front aircraft in the German formation.

"This'll be all you, Hill," Joel said over the intercom. "I emptied the canons."

"Roger, sir."

They were closing fast, and Hillborne broke in anxiously, "My trigger's dead! The fuse must have blown! Take it, Colonel!" Joel quickly switched his "fire selector" switch to "pilot," and flipped on the "pilot's gun sight rheostat," and prayed that the blown fuse didn't affect his trigger.

It didn't. At Joel's touch, the four 0.50 calibre machineguns thundered, smashing the Gotha's cockpit glass. Joel held the trigger down as long as he dared, then rolled sharply to the left, to avoid a collision.

Terrifyingly, a white rocket reached out for them, and slammed into their right wing. Bang! The aircraft jolted, and twisted, the noise very loud. Joel glanced to his right and thought he could see damage to their wing tip. His heart leapt into his throat, and beat even faster.

Behind them, the stricken Gotha turned uncontrollably to its left, and collided heavily with the airplane flying beside it. In an instant, they locked together and began a grotesque, twirling dance of death to the sea below.

"They collided! Two Germans collided, and they're gonna crash!" shouted Johnson.

"Watch them hit, or we'll have to call them 'probables,'" Joel told him. He was busy switching fuel tanks.

"I can't see 'em any more! The clouds got in the way!" Johnson shouted.

The aircraft was shaking as Joel established their course toward Millville.

"Central Command, ACP 2 inbound. Confirm five, repeat, five enemy A/C scratch. Two probables. Unknown total friendly losses. Last known heading of formation...," he repeated what his RADAR operator had told him. "ACP 2 inbound to Millville with moderate damage. ACP 2 out."

The aircraft continued to shake and was getting worse. He felt a definite pull to the right as well. He ran his seat up, his head pushed against the canopy, and peered down the top of the right wing. A piece of the wing tip seemed to be fluttering in the slipstream. He couldn't tell how bad the damage was, but it just didn't feel right.

"Boys, I'm going to slow us down. We got hit on the right wingtip and I can feel it banging around out there. Let's see if 200 might be little smoother." The aircraft slowed, and the vibration lessened.

"Colonel, we took shrapnel in the left wing leading edge outboard of the engine. Are we leaking gas?" Hillborne asked him, concern in his voice.

Joel scanned the instrument panel – "Everything looks fine, Hill. Keep an eye on it. Let me know if you see anything leaking. Johnson, take a look at the underside of the wings and the tail booms, especially the right side – see any damage?"

Johnson responded immediately, "Ah, yeah, sir, there's something screwy with the right wingtip, alright. Big chunk hanging and flapping around. It's more than just the wingtip. It's a good four to five feet inboard from the tip. It's a pretty ragged hole. I can see structure, so we're missing skin—"

Bang! They all felt it as much as heard it. Johnson shouted, his voice suddenly high pitched, "Wow! We lost the whole wingtip! It's just gone! And the pieces are really flapping around now!"

Joel didn't need to be told. The airplane jerked and bumped in several different directions at once. The aircraft wallowed first to one side, then jerked back, like a fast train on very bad track.

He reduced the throttles and keyed his mic.

"Millville Control, ACP 2 is declaring 'emergency.' I say again, ACP 2 declares emergency. We have significant damage to our right wing. Request straight in approach with crash trucks standing by. Over."

"Roger, ACP 2, understand you are declaring 'emergency,' what's your ETA?" [Estimated Time of Arrival] Over.

"ACP 2 estimates fifteen minutes. Be advised, we may have to slow to just above stall because of the damage. Over."

"Roger, APC 2. Keep us informed; advise when you make landfall. Do you want an alternative field? There are three fighters inbound to Millville also in emergency status; be prepared to divert as necessary. Over."

"Negative on the alternative, Control; we'll go for Millville. ACP 2 out."

The aircraft's shaking got worse. The control wheel felt like a wild animal in his hands. Joel slowed down even more, praying as he did so, keeping a close eye on the airspeed indicator; the last thing he needed was a stall. At their airspeed and weight, he mentally estimated the stall speed with full flaps as about eighty-five miles per hour. He kept them just above ninety. Carefully, he lowered the flaps part way. "Johnson, do the flaps look OK? Do you see any vibration in the right one?"

"Looks pretty normal, Colonel. 'Course, with the flaps down, I can't see the wing."

This was a case where being an engineer meant he knew more than he really wanted to. The slipstream was tearing away the broken aluminum skin and it would continue to tear away as long as they were flying. He'd seen wings with most of the skin torn off because of the slipstream: on the wrecks of crashed airplanes.

I could probably go slower with full flaps, and drop the landing gear for more drag, if I have to. The engines are unhurt, so I could throttle up to overcome the drag and still not go too fast. The thoughts raced through his mind. *Sure sounds good! Yeah. Oh, Lord, please have mercy on us all!*

He keyed the intercom again, "Listen up, you two. I want you to tighten up your parachutes and be ready to jump if I tell you. Johnson, you remember how to open the escape hatch?"

"Yessir." Johnson's voice was thin, nervous.

They crossed over the coast at last, and Joel told Millville Approach their condition had worsened.

"Millville acknowledges, ACP 2. Two of the P-400s are on the ground, the other bailed out. Runway 1-4-0 is clear, winds out of the southeast at1-6. Recommend approach from northwest. Crash trucks are standing by. Millville out."

Holding his breath, Joel lowered the landing gear, and dropped the flaps to full down. The Black Widow was still wallowing, but more slowly. The nose came up a little, and he bumped the throttles to compensate. Airspeed was steady at ninety. His controls felt a little better. They were descending, passing through 10,000 feet.

"OK, boys, your call. I think I can put this busted eagle on the ground, but you can jump if you want to. Need a decision *now*."

"I'm staying." Hillborne said firmly, immediately.

"Uh, me, too," Johnson added, less forcefully.

"OK, here we go."

Their flight path took them north-east of Millville; in case they had to abandon the ship, he didn't want it coming down in town. They saw smoke rising from the base, and from the nearby town as well. Random craters in the farmland showed that some of the German bombs overshot their targets. More smoke columns caught his eye, and Joel suddenly realized they were from Stanton Township. The errant bombs had struck the town where Susan lived! Suddenly, he was very attentive, hardly daring to breathe. Alexander Hamilton Junior High School came into view. To his shock, it was a smoking ruin. His anguish poured out.

"Oh, Dear God! Don't let it be Susan! Oh, Lord, don't let her be hurt!"

0827 Hours

Safe on the Ground

Joel concentrated fiercely, making his approach as perfect as possible. There was just no way to know if this damaged bird could stand the stresses of going around for a second try if he messed up the landing, and a hard landing could break up the airplane. Carefully, he flared, reaching, reaching, for the runway surface, as if the airplane was an extension of his body. To his relief, the main gear tires gently touched down almost at the same time. Carefully, he lowered the nose until the nose tire chirped. Tentative braking brought no sudden surprises, so he took the first runway turn off they came to and brought them to a halt.

"End of the line, boys. Get out, *now.*"

They stood to the side, pale, shaking with adrenaline, thinking of what might have been. The emergency crews checked the aircraft over; with no fire or leaking fuel, the danger seemed to be over. Joel walked a bit unsteadily towards the right wing tip, unzipping his brown leather A-2 jacket.

The damage the single rocket shell had caused was amazing and terrifying at the same time. At least four feet of the wing was missing, not just the wingtip. As Johnson had said, there was structure exposed on the underside of the wing, the bright yellow-green of the zinc chromate anti-corrosion paint starkly contrasting with the olive drab exterior. An anti-collision light bulb from the missing wing tip swung forlornly at the end of a long frayed wire. The aluminum on the wing's lower surface was curled back like a banana peel. He saw rivets popped loose all over the bottom of the wing.

This was a very close thing, he decided, his knees feeling weak. *Thank you, Lord.*

Hillborne walked up, an unlit cigar clamped in his mouth. "That was a close call, Colonel," he said as he surveyed the damage, "I can fix her up," he said with forced bravado.

A crew arrived with a tug and tow bar, and hauled the battered P-61 toward a hanger. As its shaken crew watched, a canvas-topped Dodge weapons carrier rolled up, and they climbed in. Seeing their ashen faces, the driver drove wordlessly to the debriefing room. Before they walked into the building, Joel hurried off to the side and noisily lost his breakfast. It didn't make him feel any better.

Johnson looks like he might lose his as well, he thought, wiping his mouth. Even the doughty Hillborne was pale as the adrenaline began to wear off.

As Joel was answering the de-briefer's questions, a runner came in and handed him a note. Fearing the worst, he opened it.

"Colonel, Miss Johansseson called to say she is OK, and is staying with her friend Mildred. Would you please call her when you can."

A phone number was written below the message, above Bill's signature. Joel felt a flood of relief.

Thank you, Lord, he breathed.

Suddenly, a frightened young soldier slammed open the door, his voice cracking, "There's another attack! They're hitting Baltimore!"

Joel leapt from his chair and raced to the situation room.

Chapter 71

10 April 1944

The Outskirts of Baltimore, Onboard Gotha Go 460 Serial Number 303173

0903 Hours

Baltimore Afflicted

Oberleutnant Johan Braun gripped the control wheel of his Gotha so hard his knuckles turned white. His heart pounded, his mouth was dry, as it always was going into combat. Despite the naps he'd taken on the long transatlantic trip, fatigue hung on him like a heavy blanket. He'd have to be especially alert as they approached the target. He wished, belatedly, that he had taken a Benzedrine tablet.

The flak was heavy, but not very accurate. Several shells had gone off nearby, but his plane was unaffected. They were only two minutes from their targets in the harbor. The cloudy air at 14,000 feet was bumpy, and he was having a little difficulty maintaining his spot in the formation.

"Fighters dead ahead!" yelled his top gunner, and the flying wing vibrated as he fired the rocket gun. Braun saw them now, one coming straight at him at terrific speed.

"Thunderbolt P-47," an analytic part of his mind cataloged. He remembered all too well how hard these barrel-chested American fighters could hit; he'd been on the receiving end of their tender attentions before, in a Heinkel HE-111 over England. He'd barely been able to limp home.

The enemy aircraft loomed huge in his windshield, unaffected by his gunner's firing. Deadly, bright flashes winked along the American's wings. Suddenly, Braun was slammed hard back into his seat as the instrument panel exploded in a shower of sparks and smoke. Huge hammer blows hit his chest, he felt incredible pain. His world went black.

Baltimore Police Patrolman John Kryszka strained his neck upward, watching in horrified fascination as the huge German bombers wheeled overhead. The throbbing, beating of their engines combined with the wailing air raid sirens to make a terrifying din. He'd been hurrying several civilians towards the bomb shelter when the airplanes thundered into sight. They had an eerie, unworldly aspect as they roared along, occasionally hidden by the clouds. Only blocks away, anti-aircraft guns pounded away with a terrifying racket. He gasped as American fighter planes flew right into the formation from the front; he winced, hoping they wouldn't collide.

Even this far below, he could hear machine guns hammering away, accompanied long seconds later by a disconcerting clatter of spent cartridge cases rattling down on the street. The big planes were turning south, toward the harbor. All but one; one of the bat-winged bombers continued westward, toward the farm country. It left a shimmering trail as the sun reflected off the fuel cascading from ruptured tanks. The fighters were oblivious to the lone breakaway bomber as they continued to savage the formation. Kryszka was puzzled; *there's nothing in that direction worth bombing, that I know of.*

Shrugging, Kryszka ran for the nearest police call phone, mounted in a silver box on a telephone pole. He had to report this. His was one of dozens of reports on the errant German, but for now, the focus of Baltimore's defenders had to be on trying to stop the rest of the formation.

Leutnant Arnt Schmidt, Braun's co-pilot, had been struck simultaneously with Braun. His left arm was nearly severed, he was bleeding profusely. Through intense pain, he felt his life ebbing away. Struggling, he keyed the intercom.

"Crew! Abandon the aircraft! Bailout! Bailout!"

The last word was whispered as he died. The two gunners, radio operator and navigator wasted no time; within seconds, they scrambled out of their assigned hatches, and fell on parachutes toward the scattered houses on the western outskirts of the city. The abandoned Gotha shuddered slightly as the open escape hatches added more drag to that caused by the shattered pilot's compartment. In moments, it settled into a slightly nose down attitude, and continued westward over the Maryland countryside.

Chapter 72

10 April 1944

Rural Frederick County, Maryland

1011 Hours

Surprise Visitor

John Garfield got up before dawn, of course, like farmers since time immemorial. His crops were in the ground, and the hard work was over for a time until they came up. He was headed down toward the river where trees were sprouting along the edges of his fields by the hundreds, limiting what he could plow. He pulled a low trailer behind his green John Deere tractor as he bumped around the perimeter of the big field; he'd cut down the saplings and haul them to the dump. He'd sharpened a heavy hoe to a razor-like edge; the less he had to bend over, the better. If he had to, well, there was the saw.

He heard the beating drone of the engines, then muffled backfires. Puzzled, he stopped and craned his neck trying to see.

The nearest road's a couple of miles away, and besides, nobody around here has anything that makes sounds like that.

He nearly fell off his tractor seat in shock as the noise swelled, and a huge gray-green aircraft suddenly burst through the top of the trees and flew nearly over him. Before he could react, the monster backfired again and settled onto his freshly planted field with loud, hollow, metallic noises and a billowing cloud of dust.

"Dear God in Heaven, have mercy!"

In an instant, Garfield was running toward the smoking aircraft, fearful it might burst into flames or explode. A vague question stirred as he ran – *where's the body and tail of this strange airplane?*

As he got close, he heard the ticking of the hot engines as they cooled, and a gurgling, liquid sound somewhere, but no cries for help. The airplane was much bigger than it seemed when it flew over him.

I can't believe something so big can get off the ground. He was puffing with the exertion of running across the soft field. The sight of the propellers, now bent and distorted, confused him.

*Never heard of an airplane with propellers on the **back** of the wing.* He ran around the left wing tip toward what he could now see was a crew compartment.

Like all farmers, Garfield had slaughtered his share of animals and the sight of blood didn't particularly bother him, but that didn't prepare him for the carnage he saw through the shattered, blood spattered cockpit glazing. The man in the left seat had been all but cut in half, his torso leaning at a crazy angle from his legs. Blood was splashed all around on the cockpit walls. The other man seemed to be untouched as he lay on his left side, then Garfield saw the dark pool of blood at his feet.

He bled to death, Garfield thought in shock. He'd never seen humans dead from violence. It wasn't until he saw the strange lettering in the cockpit that it suddenly hit him.

This is a German airplane! That realization shocked him to the soles of his feet; *my farm is at least forty miles from the Chesapeake, and close to seventy-five from the Atlantic. How'd this thing get here?*

Just as shocking was the sudden thought*; if there are survivors, I'm liable to get shot!* His gun was back in the barn, and the hoe he'd been using was still on the trailer. Quickly, he hid under the wing and waited, listening, his heart pounding. The aircraft was silent and he finally got up the courage to check it out some more.

Within minutes, Garfield determined that the two dead men in the front of the airplane were the only occupants. He ran to the tractor, disconnected the trailer, and drove as fast as it would go toward his house.

I'll get Millie, and we'll drive the Buick over to Barn's Grocery & Supply for a phone, 'cause the Army has gotta be very interested in that plane in my field.

Chapter 73

11 April 1944

Bachelor Officers Quarters

Millville Army Air Field

0432 Hours

Moment of Truth

Joel had not slept well. Every time he closed his eyes, he saw the Gotha exploding and falling into the sea.

I don't how many men are in a German crew, but I killed them all. Search and Rescue didn't find any of the men we saw parachuting. I killed at least five men on that plane, men like me, men just doing their duty. The same for the other three bombers that crashed; that means I'm responsible for the deaths of close to twenty men.

He sat on the edge of his bed, his mind reeling. All his adult life, he'd gloried in being a pilot, and he especially loved the glamour of being a fighter pilot. The looks of admiration for his uniform and its silver wings, especially from women made it worthwhile. The idea of being a dashing warrior of the skies had charmed him since he was a kid.

Now, though; this wasn't at all what he had expected. He'd tried repeatedly in the past to get transferred overseas, thinking he'd become a true hero in aerial combat. He'd seen the far-away, blank look on the faces of bond tour Aces, but had dismissed it as fatigue. The feeling in the pit of his stomach wouldn't go away any more than the images. He'd tried to pray, but couldn't find the words. More than ever, he felt the gulf between himself and God. He felt dirty, despoiled, unworthy.

When the clock finally, mercifully, read 0630, he went to the Day Room and called Susan's boarding house. He put on his most professional voice when the landlady answered.

"Good morning Mrs. Morris, this is Colonel Knight at Millville Army Air Field. I need to speak with Miss Johansseson immediately, if you please, on official business." She fussed at him about the early hour, but seemed to hear the urgency in his voice. Without much argument, she fetched Susan.

"What is it, Joel?" Susan's voice was concerned.

"I—," His voice cracked, despite himself. "I need to see you, right away, about yesterday. Can we meet for breakfast, or can I pick you or—" His voice trailed off with an almost plaintive tone, he noticed with annoyance.

"Of course," she said quickly. "I won't have classes for a few days until they decide what to do about the school. Why don't you pick up me up and we'll go to the diner?" There was warmth, concern in her voice; it comforted him that she cared.

Thirty-five minutes later, they sat in the little diner, steaming cups of coffee in front of them, waiting for their breakfasts. He'd hardly said a word. Susan sensed she shouldn't ask what the problem was; he'd tell her soon enough.

He looked at her, with a haunted look in sleep-deprived eyes. He was pale, she saw, which made the scars on his face stand out more than she'd ever seen before.

"Susan, I killed twenty men yesterday," he blurted out in anguish. "At least twenty. They never had a chance. One airplane just blew up, and—." He stopped, a look of shame on his face.

Susan blinked her eyes in surprise. *I thought this might happen some day; he's "play-acted" the valiant aerial defender for too long*, she thought.

"Joel," she said firmly, but softly, "get control of yourself. You are in a public place, in uniform."

He looked up at her in surprise, eyes widening; she'd never spoken to him with such firmness before. Before he could say anything, she steeled herself and went on.

"Joel, all of your life you have trained for this; you are a warrior. You haven't committed a crime, you haven't violated any of God's commandments. You acted in defense of your country, literally. You shouldn't feel ashamed, you should be proud that you faced an enemy for the first time, and acquitted yourself well."

His face was still contorted with anguish, "But those men—"

"Those men were trying to kill your countrymen; you stopped them. It's too bad that they had to die, but it was them or you, or some fellow citizen." She surprised herself at what she was saying. She regarded him in silence for a moment to let her words sink in. He seemed to be responding; his head came up and he looked at her. She pressed on.

"I'm not saying you should relish the death of your enemies, but you mustn't unduly mourn them either. You'll have to do this again, you know, and send your men to do the same or die themselves. Reconcile yourself to what you've done, and go on.

"If you think you must, pray and repent; present it to God, and let Him be the judge. I think you are judging yourself too harshly."

He sat motionless, staring past her, even when the aging waitress brought their breakfast plates. Susan waited, then said, "Joel, it's all right. You're going to be fine. Do you hear me?"

"Yes," he said, his voice a little less flat and emotionless now.

She'd been tough, now it was time for softness. She put her hand on his cheek.

"Joel Knight, you're a good man, and you did your duty. I'm so thankful you are safe."

He blinked in surprise; "You were worried about me?"

"Of course, you silly flyboy!"

She smiled in the way that brought out her dimples; he was a sucker for that.

"What do you think a girl's going to do when her man's out running around chasing the nasty Germans?"

He smiled faintly, and she knew things were better. He confirmed it when he picked up his fork and began attacking his breakfast.

Chapter 74

12 April 1944

Joel's House, Millville, New Jersey

0330 Hours

Repentance and Reconciliation

Joel sat at the kitchen table in the small house he'd rented in Millville after General White insisted he move out of the BOQ following his promotion.

"You're part of senior command now, Joel," he'd told him. "You need to keep yourself more aloof from your men. You are no longer one of them, you are their leader. Too close a relationship with those men can taint your ability to command."

Joel knew it was true, but that didn't make it any easier. Some of the guys were old friends, long time flying buddies. The forced separation contributed to the sense of isolation that he felt in this house by himself. And, he couldn't sleep. The words that Charles had said to him that night at the restaurant still nagged his conscience. Charles had been right; he was a backslider in every way.

Without really thinking about it, he found and opened his Bible, worn from his travels all around the world. It still felt like a dear old friend, though it had been months since he'd actually spent time in it. Randomly, he opened to Luke and began to read. When he got to Chapter 15, the Parable of the Prodigal Son leapt off the page and grabbed his heart.

That's me, Lord, he thought. *I've taken you for granted all these years. I've squandered the riches you gave me.*

It had been a long time since Joel had gone before the throne of God seeking forgiveness. He thought of his father's words from years past.

He had been eleven or twelve, and his dad had caught him; the exact transgression was lost in the passage of time. He stood, rubbing his backside, having received what would be his last spanking.

"You haven't just sinned against me, son; you've sinned against God as well. I've already forgiven you." His dad was serious but loving. "Now, you've got to make things right with Him."

"How can I do that," Joel had asked miserably, "I don't even know how."

"Let me teach you, then," his father had said. "There's no fixed, absolute way to do this – we aren't bound by ritual. But there is a thoughtful approach, an attitude that you should take whenever you pray, whether for forgiveness or anything else. Remember, Psalms 100 says, 'Enter into His gates with thanksgiving and into His courts with praise; be thankful unto Him and bless His name.' That's a good way to begin: thank God for what He has done, and praise him for His mighty attributes. That establishes who God is, what your relationship with God is.

"Then, remind God that you accepted his salvation; He knows that, of course, but again, that puts you in proper relationship to Him. That means you are no stranger to him, you are part of his family. His heart is predisposed to you."

His dad had turned Joel's thin shoulders towards him, and looked him straight in the eye.

"Now's the hard part, Joel, confess to Him exactly what you have done; be a man, son, don't try to pass off some generality as a confession. Don't think you can say 'I was bad and I'm sorry.' Nope, that won't do. You tell Him 'I confess that I did thus and so, and I beg your forgiveness.' Don't use fancy words, and don't act like you're a lawyer – you have no excuse. Just tell Him what's come between Him and you; you must be honest, because remember, He already knows.

"You've already reminded Him that you're saved; now's the time, after you have humbly confessed your sin, to plead the blood of Jesus. Remember what it says in 1 John 1:9, 'If we confess our sins, He is faithful and just to forgive us our sins and cleanse us from all unrighteousness.' Then, ask Him for forgiveness. Straight up. When you finish you thank Him for his forgiving grace. Can you do that?"

"Yes, sir." Joel remembered feeling clean afterward; that was what he needed now.

He hesitated, part of him fighting against what his dad had told him.

It isn't like what you've done is so bad; you haven't gambled away your paycheck like some of those guys; you didn't chase off to the whorehouses like those other guys in the Philippines, you've never smoked; you don't drink a drop. You've never cheated on expense reports or smuggled stuff past customs. You're a straight arrow, Joel! You don't need to confess anything.

He thought for a moment, then realized what he'd just played in his mind was self-justification, fancy excuses. There was only one reason for the sense of spiritual isolation he felt: he'd let sin come between himself and God. Joel got off the chair and kneeled on the floor in front of it and began to pray.

"Dear God, thank you for that quality of mercy that is your very essence. Thank you for how longsuffering, patient, and loving you are toward your own, and toward me especially. Most of all, I thank you for your perfect salvation through Jesus Christ, my Lord. I praise you, God, for your greatness, for your mighty acts of love. You are deserving of all the praise that man can give and far more.

"You know I accepted Jesus as my Lord and Savior those many years ago, as a boy. My belief was genuine and that salvation was real, and I count myself as one of your own, a Child of God."

He swallowed hard, knowing what was next.

"I confess to you, Lord, that I willfully turned away from you, and put my own interests, especially flying, ahead of you for all these years. Contrary to what it says in Proverbs, I did walk in my own understanding. You've kept me safe in all the situations I've been in despite the fact I turned my back on you. I failed to recognize your hand of mercy on me, and acted as if I was the reason I am alive. I have neglected to give you the praise and thanksgiving you deserve, and avoided worshiping with your people, all the while claiming to be Christian whenever it seemed to be to my advantage. I am ashamed of that. Worst of all, I've acted as if I don't need you in my life. Now, I am alone and lost, and feel a desperate need to be back in communion with you, to reestablish the loving relationship we had before.

"Please, Dear God, in the Name of Jesus, whose shed blood I plead, forgive these sins, and restore me back to my right place with you. Thank you for your Grace, which flows so freely. In the holy and righteous name of Jesus I pray, Amen."

He got up, and wiped away the tears he hadn't even felt run down his cheeks. He knew without question that he had been heard. Inside him, there was a feeling of being clean, being set right.

Chapter 75
Saturday, 15 April 1944
Central Command, Philadelphia, Pennsylvania
Main Conference Room
0800 Hours Eastern Time
Post Mortem

Major General White and several other field grade officers sat at the conference table speaking in low tones. Beside Joel in the audience was the silver-haired Army Reserve Lieutenant Colonel who commanded the P-400 detachment in New York. Lieutenant Commander John Bell Higgins and Marine Captain Mark Best from Pawtuxent Naval Air Station, representing the Marine Corps F6Fs were in the next row. Everyone was waiting for the commander of the P-47 squadron based at Bolling Field, Washington, D.C. Various staff members, aids and senior enlisted made up the audience.

All the "guilty parties," Joel thought sardonically. *It's like waiting for the other shoe to fall, or worse, the axe.*

A low, subdued murmur of conversation buzzed among the men. Everyone knew this session would be rough; no one in the military was happy with the responses made to these last two attacks, to say nothing of the civilian "movers and shakers." If General White decided to find a scapegoat, many could suffer severe consequences. Losses had been high, and the enemy had bombed their intended targets, even if they had also suffered losses.

The conference room door opened; conversation halted and every head turned, expecting the missing squadron commander. Instead, a Navy yeoman in sharply creased whites took a message form to General White.

The silver-haired man read it, cleared his throat, and said to the silent group,

"Well, now, men, here's a bit of good news. The Maryland State Police report that a large aircraft with German markings crash landed in western Maryland. The pilot and co-pilot are dead."

He looked up. Joel, like everyone, was hanging on his words.

"Must be the plane those captured crewmen jumped from. Here's the best part: the plane is essentially intact. We'll finally get a good look at one of these behemoths!"

The mood in the room brightened immediately.

Now, Joel thought, *maybe we come up with a way to counter those rocket guns.*

Long minutes passed. A harried-looking Army Major entered, "General White, Major Thorton, James L., reporting as ordered. My apologies for being late, sir, and respects from General Arnold. He asked me to brief him before I flew up here. We ran a little long."

"Apology accepted, Major. I can't fault you for speaking to Hap first, if he asked you to. Please take a seat, and we'll begin."

"To review, fires are still burning along the Baltimore waterfront. Civilian losses are being tallied, but they will probably be over 300. Military losses –, we don't have a final number yet either, but they will be painfully high.

"What we'll do next – well, it's a lot like going over your game plan after you've been whipped playing football, men," he said. "No, it's an awful lot worse than that, but take the analogy. Command knows most of you have barely been stood up, and we haven't provided operational protocols or even well defined chains of command. Given all that, and more, you responded resolutely and bravely. My heart-felt consolations on your losses." he said with empathy.

"Now," he went on, his voice determined and strict. "Here's what we're going to do. Each commander will write on this blackboard what went wrong in his district. When he's done, we'll add in anything anyone else wants to add, have it recorded by this yeoman, and go on to the next man. I'm not interested in inter-service rivalries, but if a sister service let you down, get the facts out without finger pointing. Are we agreed on this point, gentlemen?"

He looked pointedly at a scowling Rear Admiral and a stony-faced one-star Marine.

"Yes, sir," the men chorused, with seeming reluctance.

Joel become increasingly nervous as they waited; as the sergeants often said, he had "screwed up by the numbers," and this was his day of reckoning. It came as a shock when he was called on first. Somewhat shakily, he went to the blackboard and wrote:

<u>What Went Wrong at Philadelphia:</u>

Warning too late

Under strength/Too few alert aircraft /Too few aircraft flyable

Poor tactics [attacked from rear of formation]

Inadequate weapons

Incorrect ammunition (P-400s)

Inadequate fuel (P-400s)

Too few backup aircraft called in /too late

No backup for ACP aircraft

Communications poor

Training inadequate, top to bottom

He turned to the men at the table, his hands wet with sweat.

"General White, sirs, I am Lieutenant Colonel Knight, Joel T. I command the 160th Coastal Defense Fighter Group at Millville Army Air Field, New Jersey. On the morning of the attack, I was flying a P-61 as commander, Aerial Command Post, Region 2, call sign ACP 2."

Feeling steadier, he said, "To begin, the first problem was that we were only warned about the attack as bombs were falling. The question must arise as to why the coastal observers didn't notify us sooner.

"My group is under strength; we only had four aircraft on alert. They launched immediately, but were too little, too late. Our flight-ready aircraft were nearly all were destroyed in the attack, even though they were in revetments. When the alert planes caught the enemy, they attacked from the rear, and were beaten up pretty badly.

"We almost immediately discovered that the German rocket guns have much greater range than our 0.50 calibre machine guns. It was suicidal to fly into range for the 0.50s. Worst of all, the German rocket guns were deadly; in several cases, a single rocket downed a fighter."

He looked General White in the eye, with bravado he didn't feel.

"As Commander, ACP 2, I waited too long to call in reserves, and failed to account for their flight time; I refer to the New York Air National Guard P-400s. To their credit, they launched promptly when I called. When the P-400s arrived, the enemy was already over the Atlantic. Again, we faced a stern-chase situation. Then we discovered the P-400 cannons were armed with AP rounds, which initially proved ineffective. When they got hits, the rounds just punched through the Gotha's skin, and failed to detonate. They attacked again, concentrating on the engines, and consequently got two kills. They ran low on fuel and had to recover; they were not equipped with drop tanks. Also, the enemy was steadily climbing, and the P-400s had reached their service ceiling.

"The Marine Corps response from Pawtuxent Naval Air Station was timely, and in reasonable numbers, but like the other fighters, their guns were too short on range to get inside the perimeter the

Germans could protect with their rocket guns. They, too, were generally in a stern-chase situation."

He paused, swallowing his pride.

"I erred in using the P-61 I was flying to attack the formation; I should have preserved it as the sole ACP 2 flying command post. Not having a replacement aircraft or crew contributed to the losses over Baltimore in the subsequent attack.

"Finally, the level of training and readiness was inadequate from top to bottom in my command; we had not so much as practiced an interception scramble, or the tasks necessary to coordinate a counterattack."

He stood silently, waiting for the response, his heart pounding in his chest.

General White looked up from the notes he was making.

"Good brief, Colonel Knight. In addition to no advance warning, there's another fundamental problem; the bases under your command were not notified of the attack; that could have reduced response times for both the P-400s and the F6Fs. Further, I observed that the anti-aircraft batteries at Millville Air Field and elsewhere were ineffective and inaccurate. I will address that issue with the artillery commanders later.

"Your mea culpa regarding the use of your P-61 is noted, Colonel, though one can hardly fault your courage or perseverance in pursuing the enemy. One also notes that four enemy aircraft were downed by you and your crew. In case you were unaware, the ship *MV Conrad Conyers* saw the two Gothas crash, and subsequently picked up four bodies and some important wreckage. She'll dock in Philadelphia tomorrow, and we'll see what they have. Some of it is documents of some sort.

"Command let you down by not providing a back-up ACP 2 aircraft; we should have foreseen that combat damage or even ordinary maintenance could have caused the same situation. As to training, your statements are true for every element of this organization; none of us had properly prepared. That must and shall be addressed immediately. You may be seated, Colonel."

Joel walked toward his chair in surprised relief.

General White turned to the New York Air National Guard Lieutenant Colonel, "Colonel Graham, would you care to comment?"

"Yes, sir. Sirs, I am Lieutenant Colonel Graham, Toland L., U.S. Army Air Corps Reserve. I command the New York State Air National Guard. Our unit flies the Bell P-400s Colonel Knight mentioned. One of my soldiers was monitoring the Central Command radio frequency when the Millville attack began. He immediately notified his superior, and we were ready when Colonel Knight called. Had that advance notice not been received, we could have been ten or fifteen minutes later in responding.

"As to the AP rounds in the P-400 cannons, we had prepared for live fire training against simulated armored vehicles, at the Millville Air Field range. There simply wasn't time to have the aircraft rearmed even if we had been so advised.

"In defense of my pilots, sirs, they are not trained for air-to-air combat. Instead, they provide close support to infantry and artillery troops on the ground. If we are to use them against enemy bombers, may I suggest, sirs, that we be provided HE cannon rounds with proximity fuses. My unit has not been issued external fuel tanks. In addition, I must say that Colonel Knight is correct; our P-400s are altitude restricted to about 20,000 feet."

General White said, "Your request is noted, and agreed with, Colonel Graham. Your men responded admirably. We'll get the communication situation taken care of as soon as possible. As part of that fix, I will direct all units in District 2 to monitor Central Command radio around the clock. We'll also train your men in aerial combat. You'll have drop tanks within a day or so. As an aside, Colonel, I'll also look into reequipping your unit with fighters capable of supporting your new responsibilities. Please convey my congratulations to your unit; they responded most professionally. You may be seated, Colonel."

White turned to a Brigadier General sitting at the front table with him.

"General Furston, I understand that the defense against the attack on Baltimore was controlled by you here at Central Command, in the absence of Colonel Knight's ACP 2 function."

"That is correct, General White," the crag faced man replied in a deep voice. He reminded Joel of the actor Victor Jory. He stood to address the panel.

"Even if Colonel Knight's ACP 2 aircraft hadn't been damaged, it would've needed refueling and rearming before going aloft again. Given the timing of the raid on Baltimore relative to the one on Millville and Philadelphia, it was all but inevitable that his P-61 would be caught on the ground. I tip my hat to Major Thorton from Bolling Air Field. He launched his P-47s on his own recognizance, and I have to say, they saved the day. Without them, it would have been much, much worse; well done, Major."

General Furston walked to the blackboard, which had been copied. Standing ram-rod straight, he said, "I'll only expand on what is different from Colonel Knight's brief,"

<u>What Went Wrong at Baltimore:</u>

Poor anti-aircraft gunnery & too few guns

No fighter aircraft reserves

No plan for dealing with POWs

ACP function poorly handled; never asked for help from the Navy/Marines – why?

No prior coordination between flights from different locales and services (who's in charge, what are the combined tactics?)

Joel was surprised; general officers rarely, if ever, took the blame for a foul up, and especially not in public.

This General Furston shows a lot of courage.

Furston turned to the men in front, his voice a low growl, eyes nearly shut with the intensity of his message.

"Sirs, like Colonel Knight, we were notified of this attack as it began. To my embarrassment, I discovered later that a priority message detailing the enemy formation had been sent to us fifteen minutes before the attack by the Ground Observer Corps [GOC] in Delaware. Since it came from a civilian source, it was handled as an ordinary message. It reached the staff hours after the raid. It could have given Colonel Knight a few precious moments more to respond. This was a failure in procedure that has already been corrected."

His face hardened and his voice rumbled even lower.

"Because of the earlier raid on Millville and Philadelphia, the available fighter force was significantly depleted. Surviving aircraft were being serviced and rearmed as the Baltimore raid began, but on a peace-time basis – slowly, no sense of urgency. There were no reserve aircraft; none. We re-launched only seven aircraft, and they went aloft when the raid was nearly over. Without Major Thorton's fighters, the Germans would have been unopposed."

He rapped on the blackboard, "In common with Millville and Philadelphia, the anti-aircraft gunnery in and around Baltimore was grossly ineffective; more damage was caused by dropping shells than to the Germans. The gunners seemed to be firing blindly.

"While Colonel Graham's P-400s were not involved, it is my contention that we also were fighting with the wrong ammunition, or better said, the wrong weapons. These two raids have demonstrated clearly that our 0.50 cals are no match for the rocket guns. Somebody had better come up with a solution to this, and soon, or we'll continue to take it on the chin. Make no mistake, gentlemen, the Germans will only improve this weapon. If we don't counter it quickly, we could end up essentially defenseless."

Several heads nodded in agreement at the front table.

Joel thought, *I sure like his candor. He's got real moxie.*

Furston manfully stuck out his chin; "I am embarrassed to tell this panel that I had made no provisions for dealing with enemy prisoners. The need to deal with them took us – more correctly, me – by surprise. The four men who bailed out of the Gotha were captured and arrested by the Baltimore police. The prisoners will be taken to Fort George Mead, Maryland for interrogations and assignment to a POW facility."

He smacked his hand with a fist, "We must establish a policy for handling prisoners including, I recommend, mobile teams of Military Police who can quickly take them into custody in accordance with the Articles of War."

Furston glanced down at the notes in his hand, then at the officers in front of him. "The ACP function in particular in this attack was handled poorly; I accept responsibility for that. I had not prepared a backup in the event Colonel Knight's aircraft was incapacitated. I didn't ask for help from either the Navy or Marine Corps, even though they were within range of the attacking aircraft. I put this down to my faulty thinking; I acted as if only Army assets were available to me. I didn't request aid from Colonel Graham's P-400s either.

"Finally," the general said grimly, "the proper, prior coordination among all the elements that could and should have taken part in this defense had not taken place; that includes every Army, Navy, Marine Corps, Coast Guard, and National Guard unit capable of contributing. I haven't confirmed it, but I am sure the same is true of every other city and military facility within District 2. In short, sirs, we were caught with our drawers down again, and the fact that we had been in existence only a few weeks is no excuse. I accept personal responsibility for all those shortcomings."

Joel was amazed; *This brave man is airing all his dirty laundry. That's a calculated risk that could really backfire if this inter-service cooperation isn't real; he could get fired.* He thought for another moment; *knowing the Army, he could get fired anyway.*

General White said grimly, "There are shortcomings aplenty to go around, General Furston, and by no means do they all fall upon you. This command did not provide you or any other commander with the protocols and policies necessary. Even more shameful, we did not provide you the means to execute your orders. Are there any other comments?" The room was silent. Joel let out a little breath; General White seemed disinclined to leap on the man's confessions.

"Very well. Thank you, General. Commander Higgins, if you please."

Higgins strode to the front of the room as the yeoman finished copying the blackboard and then erased it. He said,

"Sirs, I am Navy Commander John Bell Higgins, assigned to Pawtuxent Naval Air Station. I command the fighter training squadrons there.

"Sirs, as you are all aware, the Marine Corps falls under the Department of the Navy, so I was detailed to brief you. Marine Corps Captain Mark Best, who commanded the aircraft that responded to Colonel Knight's request is with me."

He turned to the blackboard and wrote:

<u>Navy/Marine Corps Shortcomings in Response to the Philadelphia Raid:</u>

Force levels not determined in advance

Tactics not in place/no training

Radio protocols not in place: open vs. coded messages

Reserve forces not defined or in place

No priorities for refueling/ rearming

Commander Higgins said, "Sirs, unlike our Army counterparts, the Navy and Marine Corps had a sizable force of aircraft on alert and standby. This resulted primarily from my combat experience in the South Pacific, and was not Navy direction." The Rear Admiral at the front table winced, and scowled at Higgins.

Joel smiled and thought, *well, my already high opinion of Higgins just went up another notch.*

Higgins said, "The pilots had not been trained regarding, or even been made familiar with, the most basic aspects of the Gotha bombers. The existence of the rocket guns was unknown to us, and we suffered several losses as a result."

He set his chin firmly. "Colonel Knight's urgent attempts to warn my pilots were too late, through no fault of his own. That we were so uninformed is a major lapse on the part of senior command." Joel saw the Rear Admiral's scowl turn into a red hot glare.

Now he's in for it.

The Rear Admiral leaned forward, pointed his finger, and growled, "Commander, be warned, you are treading on dangerous ground here."

General White interrupted immediately, sternly. "Not so, Admiral; these men were directly ordered by me to tell us exactly what they experienced, no matter whose shoes are stepped on. Please continue, Commander."

Higgins said, "Thank you, sir. I beg your pardon, Admiral. Radio protocols had not been established; only because Colonel Knight and I know each other were we aware what frequency to tune to. In addition, no direction was given concerning what could be broadcast in the clear, and what had to be obscured by codes.

"My command was not directed to establish a reserve force. Finally, there was no provision for rearming or refueling the aircraft, had General Furston so requested."

General White looked sharply at the Rear Admiral, who understood the implied warning.

"Any comments?" White asked.

"Sir, Captain Best, Mark T., United States Marine Corps. I commanded the F6Fs that attacked the Germans. I'd like to suggest, sir, that assuming adequate warning, a way to overcome the tactical advantage the Germans have with their rockets guns is high speed attacks. Their rocket guns are hand laid, just like the MGs on our own bombers. That means that they'd have a hard time tracking a fast fighter, even inside the effective range of their rocket guns. This would be especially true if there were multiple high speed gun runs from different aspects. Ships like Mustangs or Lightings could fill the bill, in addition to F6Fs. Attacking the standard way is ineffective because we can't get inside the effective range of the rocket guns.

"Sirs, to address the short range of the 0.50 caliber guns, couldn't we take a page from the German's own book? How about using the 5" HVARs [High Velocity Aircraft Rocket] our Marines use on F4Us in the Pacific? They're cheap, plentiful, and easily adapted to any aircraft. Best of all, their range is about 2 ½ miles, so we'd put the Germans at a disadvantage. They're not terribly accurate, but Gothas are pretty big targets. They'd need proximity fuses; they already have HE warheads from 5" anti-aircraft shells."

General White sat upright. "Excellent suggestion, Captain! Are HVARs also referred to as 'Holy Moses?'"

Captain Best nodded with a grin, "Yes, sir. They're called 'high velocity' because they go over 900 miles per hour, *and* they don't smoke like the German rockets."

General White turned to his adjutant, "Make sure Aberdeen Proving Grounds follows up with the Navy on that, ASAP. I want a memo on my desk in a week. Copy the Admiral as well." His adjutant wrote furiously.

"Now then, Major Thorton, we'd like to hear your comments."

"Thank you, General. Sirs, I am Major Thorton, James L., the temporary commander of the 4743rd Provisional Fighter Group forming up at Bolling Army Air Field in the District As you know, sirs, we had just begun transferring from Maxwell Army Air Field Alabama a few days ago. That transfer is still incomplete. At this point, I am the ranking officer. We are to learn who will be taking command sometime this week.

"Now, about the Baltimore attack; one of my men was also listening to the Central Command frequency as the attack began. It was obvious that General Furston's forces were being overwhelmed. On my own authority, I launched a dozen aircraft, and put them at General Furston's disposal. I am gratified we were able to contribute."

The look on the young man's face was earnest and sincere.

"If I may be so bold, General, with respect, I'd like to emphasize strongly that as the district defending the nation's capital, we *must* have an organized communications setup, sir. Before I was wounded and sent home, I fought with the 8th Air Force; we had an excellent radio network we could depend on. Many missions were too complex to work otherwise. I believe we need that same kind of support and control here. We're simply too short on planes and pilots to risk not supporting each other. Thank you, sir."

Summation

General White finished his notes, "Thank you, Major. I commend your initiative. We need the benefit of combat veterans like yourself. I will personally direct such a radio net be created immediately.

"Now. I will summarize these comments, and review them with the other senior officers present. Soon, I will address the Joint Chiefs about Central Command's organization and these attacks."

He nodded toward Major Thorton. "I intend to request – no, demand – that our District be provided new, first line fighters in large numbers, along with top quality pilots to fly them ASAP." He glanced briefly at Joel; he and Chappie had told the General about the substandard pilots they'd been assigned.

"On Wednesday next, I am to testify to a congressional subcommittee in a closed door session; the following day, the Senate has asked for my presence. It is possible both may be political scapegoat hunts; I intend to do all in my power to turn those politicians into advocates and supporters of Coastal Defense.

"If Almighty God is gracious, winter on the Atlantic will give us two or three months to get reorganized before any German spring offensive against the ZI [Zone of the Interior – the contiguous forty-eight states]. Let us pray we will be more prepared to defend our homeland than during these last two attacks. If there is nothing else, gentlemen, you are dismissed."

Chapter 76

25 May 1944

Office of Base Commander, General Adrian White

0930 Hours

Gotha Exposed

"Joel, it's especially important that we get your assessment of this," General White said urgently, handing him a thick document. It was Foreign Service Division's report on the Gotha. The German bomber had been carefully disassembled in John Garfield's cornfield, and trucked to Wright Patterson Field.

Opening the TOP SECRET cover, Joel glanced at the executive summary: *conventional aluminum construction, no unusual instruments or controls. Engines are double supercharged, that's something*, he thought as he read. *What's this? A new bombsight? I wonder if it's the one John Bell Higgins told Admiral Stuart about? What's the low power radio for? There are sleeping facilities on board; that helps explain things. The crew was provided anti-fatigue drugs. The autopilot is a new design as well. Humm; they didn't stint on anything, did they?*

"Wow. Listen to this, sir: 'the tubular structure protruding forward of the left leading edge is connected via piping and valves directly to the aircraft main fuel tanks. It is assumed that the structure is used to fuel the aircraft in flight.' They're gassing up in the air, sir! That's how they get so much range, or at least part of it."

General White nodded, "I saw that. Surely that isn't the only thing they are doing to extend their range; the fuel tanks just aren't large enough, even if they do refuel in the air. Those big engines must use a lot of gas. And where do they refuel? Somewhere over the ocean? That seems improbable; how would they ever find each other? What if it's at night? And why do the wingtips have those strange stabilizers? The preliminary aeronautical analysis says the airplane is stable without them."

"Yes, sir, that's a mystery, alright. I have no idea what they're for. We can bet that they're on there for a specific purpose, though, because this airplane is well thought out. They wouldn't add that extra weight if it didn't help," Joel replied.

"Now, this's unexpected – the aircraft has a manufacturing joint running down the center line – that's common, of course, but it's not bolted, it's held together with 'clips'. There are eight clips top and bottom. Say, I wonder – could that account for the way we've seen several of these ships fail in the air? They just fold up like a butterfly, with the wingtips touching. If some of the clips failed due to combat damage, the aerodynamic forces would cause the rest to fail as well, and there she goes!"

Joel thumbed through the document a few pages, "General, could I borrow this for a couple of days, sir? I'd really like to study it carefully."

"Yes, yes, certainly; that's why I had a copy sent here, for you to review." He handed Joel an envelope for the document.

"Remember this is Top Secret; you can review it with Chappie, but that's all, OK?"

"Now, then, have you heard about the the HVAR rockets? I'll be briefing all the commanders tomorrow."

He smiled under his white mustache, "It's going swimmingly. Got approved wing mounts for P-47s and P-51s, and the Navy F6Fs now, too, in addition to the F4Us. Navy's new twin engine Grumman F7Fs will be equipped on the production line. The P-38s should be through testing and approval in a couple of weeks. And, a new more powerful rocket motor is being developed. They're building two munitions plants in Indiana just for HVARs."

Joel brightened, "Say, that's good news, sir. Here's a thought; has anybody looked at putting them on the P-61s? That'd be a big help, it seems to me."

General White smiled broadly under his handsome, white mustache.

"The fellows at Northrop are a step ahead of you, Colonel. They're testing that modification in the California desert. Now, keep this under your hat: Browning Arms has a working duplicate of the German rocket gun. They're working with the boys at Aberdeen Proving Grounds; they think it can be made more accurate with a smaller round, which means a possible rapid fire version. They think they can increase the velocity at least 20 percent. Northrop is also looking at how to replace the turret on the P-61 with one that uses rocket guns. Wouldn't that be something?"

"Yes, sir!" Joel replied enthusiastically. "We'd be taking it to them with their own idea, but with greater firepower, a longer range, and more accuracy. Any idea when we might see some rocket gun equipped P-61s, sir?"

The gray headed man shook his head, "Congress turned up the heat about as high as it can go, Colonel. I'd guess an optimistic estimate might be six or eight months, at the minimum."

Chapter 77

12 November 1944

Colonel Joel Knight's Office

1730 Hours

Invitation

Mrs. Agatha Morris, Susan's landlady, gave her a frowned warning and reluctantly handed her the telephone.

Joel said, "Hello there, young lady! How's my favorite teacher this evening?"

"Hi, Joel," Susan responded, her voice smiling, "I'm doing fine, if you can be 'fine' grading papers and pulling out your hair!"

Joel laughed, "Oh, don't pull out your hair; I love it! It'd drive me nuts, doing what you do. Listen, I won't keep you long; I know that down deep, you really want to get back to those papers." She snorted derisively.

"If you don't have plans for Thanksgiving, how'd you like to go to a dinner dance at the O Club? There will be plenty of good food, a pretty good band, and all sorts of brass to rub elbows with."

"You had me convinced until you started talking about the brass, fella!" She laughed back. "I'd love to go; what time will you pick me up?"

"Let's see, it starts at 1700 – let's say 1600, and we won't have to hurry. How's that sound?"

"It's a date, flyboy! See you then."

"Say, boss, two more of the new P-61s just landed. That's six; only twenty-four to go" Chappie announced.

"Good. Have to keep our fingers crossed they keep coming, 'cause everybody else wants 'em too!" Joel replied.

Chapter 78

18 November 1944

Joel's House, Millville, New Jersey

0710 Hours

Travel Plans

Joel hadn't spoken to Susan since they'd made Thanksgiving plans; she'd been busy with some special project, so he was pleased when she called him.

"Say, listen, Joel, I've got a little favor to ask. Could you drive me over to Philadelphia on Monday the 20th? I've got to deliver something I can't talk about, and they don't want me to take the train."

"Official business, right?"

"Oh, yes, of course, I wouldn't ask otherwise."

"OK, sure. The Packard needs to be serviced anyway, so I'll get that scheduled. We can have lunch somewhere, and drive home by dark. Pick you up at 0800?" There was no Packard dealer in Millville, and Joel just couldn't bring himself to let any of the local mechanics touch the nearly new car.

Monday Morning, 20 November 1944

The sky was gray and threatening as they drove out of Millville.

Joel asked, "So, can you can tell me about this, or do you have to keep it to yourself?"

"Well, I don't know much about why I was asked to do this." She frowned, wrinkling her forehead. "They asked me to look at several foreign-born scientists, to decide if they are trustworthy. Say, have you ever heard of a Dr. Niels Bohr?"

Joel was surprised, "Niels Bohr? Oh, of course; he's the Danish physicist who won the Nobel Prize in Physics a while back. Cracking the atom, or something, I think."

Susan was very serious, "Well, there are three others. There's Leo Szilard, a fellow named Eugene Wigner, and Edward Teller. They are all physics PhDs; all three are Hungarian, two are Jewish. What could the government want with them, Joel?"

"Don't know; it's not like we don't have a lot of physicists ourselves. They must know something the government wants, something like that."

Susan set her chin; "Well, it must be important, because they really made me hurry. Funny that they all fled the Nazis, though. I really do wonder what they're up to."

"Well, maybe some time when the war's over, we'll find out. Probably nothing."

So far, everything has gone swimmingly, Joel thought. *The Packard dealer got the tune up done just in time. We found a nice café and had a pleasant lunch.*

A glance at his watch showed it was only 1400; they had plenty of time. Maybe on the trip back they could talk some more, and not about "business."

They paid the nickel toll to cross the Delaware River bridge to Camden, New Jersey, and turned southeast on Highway 41. In a few miles, they'd be on Highway 47, directly into Millville. The road was smooth, the company delightful as they chatted. Joel hardly noticed the first snowflakes.

A powerful gust of wind shook the Packard, forcing Joel to take notice of the increasing snowfall.

"Say, what's with the snow? It's not supposed to be here until tomorrow."

"Apparently, somebody didn't tell the weather," she laughed.

"Man, it's really coming down. Look, it's even starting to stick to the highway."

"Are your tires good, Joel? We sure don't want to get stuck out here." Susan worried. "Do you think we should stop at Clayton?"

"Let's decide when we get there. I really need to be home tomorrow morning."

When they reached Clayton, the road was snow covered, but the pavement was visible in the tracks of cars ahead of them. Joel pulled into a gas station.

"Philly Radio station says it's only gonna be flurries, Colonel," the man told him, "'course, it already looks like more'n that here. I talked with a fella who drove in from Vineland about an hour ago. Said it was slushy, that's all. I think you and your lady will be just fine."

Dubious but somewhat reassured, they gassed up, thanked the man, and started towards Millville.

Two Hours Later

"I hate to criticize that gas station man, but I think we're beyond 'slushy,' don't you?"

Joel was bobbing his head to see through the snow the wipers were leaving behind. The heater was roaring; he switched it from heat to defrost every few minutes.

"Do you think we should turn back?"

"I'm not sure I could turn around without getting stuck. Let's see, we went through Malaga back there, so it's only about ten more miles. Let's press on, and watch for a farm house where we can stay overnight, and go in to Millville come morning."

"Mmmm." She sounded dubious. "I wish we'd already stopped. If we see any civilization at all, we need to stop."

"I agree. Keep your eyes peeled."

From growing up in Colorado, Joel knew it was a full-on blizzard. The wind was blowing hard and wet snow was packing under the wipers. He had to reach around through the open window with his hand to try and clear the blade. They jounced over a hidden bump, and the wind caught the car, turning it a little sideways. Joel fought the skid, turning the big ivory steering wheel rapidly only to have the vicious wind again push the car. This time, both right wheels fell off the pavement. The piled up snow pulled them part way into the ditch. Before he could correct, they lurched to a halt.

They looked wordlessly at each other as he attempted to move the car. Even rocking it forward and back, shifting between reverse and low, did little to free them. He got out and attempted to dig the car out with his hands, but quickly realized it was futile.

Joel shook off as much snow as he could and got back in the car, "Well, that decision's made for us. Looks like we're here until the storm lets up."

Susan looked scared, "Joel, we'll freeze! And we don't dare walk somewhere. What will we do?"

Joel made his voice sound confident, "Not to worry, my dear! I'll not let you freeze. Let me get my 'winter kit'."

Before she could ask, Joel got out, opened the trunk and brought a sturdy box back into the car. Shaking the wet snow off his head, he opened it.

"My dad and granddad never drive in the winter time without a winter kit. Look at this."

Inside were smaller boxes. "This one has candles – you'd be surprised how much heat they put off." He held up another, "Waterproofed matches. Two warm blankets, some candy bars – not very fresh!– and a flashlight. Here's a nice chain, to pull us out of the ditch. And some road flares so folks won't drive into us. Even a pair of wool mittens to keep those beautiful hands all toasty!"

He could see Susan was by turns amazed and pleased that he had foreseen this situation.

"Do we dare burn the candles? Won't the bad air kill us?"

Joel smiled, "It might, if we don't crack open the wing window and let in a bit of fresh air. Now, here's the plan. We'll wrap up in these blankets, and I'll run the engine 'til the heater takes the chill off. Then we'll light a candle and see if it's warm enough; if not, we can light a couple more. If we don't run the motor too much, we'll have enough gas to keep mostly warm 'til morning."

Joel remembered the time when he was fifteen, and had gotten his dad's pickup stuck miles from the ranch house. There'd been a winter kit stuffed behind the seat. He'd been colder than he'd ever been before or since, and had just avoided frostbite on his toes, but he survived. He mentally kicked himself for failing to include a shovel in this winter kit.

He had no idea how cold it was, but it felt very cold. He was fiercely determined that Susan would come out of this experience with nothing but funny stories to tell, no matter what he had to do.

At first, they wrapped up in the blankets individually, but were soon cold again even running the heater. Outside, the storm raged on, and darkness fell.

With a lecherous grin, he told her, "Too bad, young lady! Looks like you're going to have to snuggle with me if you want to survive. Heh, heh, heh!" He mimicked twisting a mustache like a vaudeville villain.

She giggled, and moved over next to him. He was secretly delighted that she wasn't put off by the idea; having two blankets over them, and sharing body warmth really did help. Susan pulled her feet up on the broad seat, and lay her head on his lap.

They began to talk. Joel discovered that Susan loved baseball, even if she did follow the Minneapolis Twins; Joel was a big Yankees fan, probably because his granddad was. Susan loved F. Scott Fitzgerald, especially *The Great Gatsby*. Joel mentioned he liked Booth Tarkington's *Penrod* and the second book, *Penrod and Sam*.

"Those are boys' books," Susan said.

"Well, yeah, I was a boy when I read them; I don't have a lot of time for novels these days, ya know!"

She laughed, and said she loved Will Rogers. Joel enthusiastically agreed.

"It's so sad he died, right at the top of his popularity," Susan lamented.

"Yes, and it was terrible to lose Wily Post too, 'cause he was doing such important aviation research."

"Now, I'm not much for movies, but I did like *Stage Coach* and *Gone With the Wind*; what about you?"

"Oh, Clark Gable was so dashing in *Gone With the Wind*, don't you think?"

"Don't know; I was too busy watching Vivian Leigh to notice!" She poked him with her elbow.

By the time the luminous hands on his watch read 10:15, they'd covered music as well. Joel loved that they had so much in common. He just felt, well, comfortable with her.

They fell quiet, and Susan fell asleep, breathing softly. He put his face down in her hair; it smelled wonderful.

He dozed off, waking up stiff and cold. It was almost midnight, and snow was still falling. He started the engine, and ran the heater. Susan stirred, but slept through it. Twice more through the night, he awoke and ran the engine and heater. The candles were down to stubs, and the gas gauge was reading below ¼ full. He prayed that help would come with the morning.

The rap on the window was loud, "You folks alright in there?"

Joel was jolted awake. He sat up, and rolled down the window. The sun was very bright against deep snow. He blinked, and squinted up at the face of a worried looking New Jersey State Trooper. Susan sat up, looking disoriented.

"Yes, sir, we're just fine. Do you think you can pull us out of the ditch?"

As he nodded yes, the trooper noticed Joel's uniform, "Say, are you Colonel Joel Knight? The Army's got us looking for you. I need you to come to the patrol car and call in and tell 'em you're OK."

Immensely relieved, Joel gave Susan a quick kiss and a wink, and disappeared toward the officer's cruiser.

Chapter 79

23 November 1944

Millville Army Air Field Officers Club

1630 Hours

Thanksgiving Dinner

Joel and Susan sat waiting for their friends. The tables were covered with starched white tablecloths, and set with fine china and glassware. White napkins were neatly rolled in silver MAAF monogram rings. The centerpieces were bisque china Pilgrim figures, the man in his buckled hat, holding a turkey by its feet, the woman in a gray floor length dress, carrying a pie.

Major Chappie Chapman and his wife Regina joined them. Regina was radiantly expecting her first child in two months, and the two women immediately began discussing the upcoming event.

"Would you ladies care for a hot roll?" Joel offered, trying to get the women to join the conversation he and Chappie were having.

"Oh, yes, please," Regina said, "I'm just so hungry all the time. Eating for two, you know." She looked happily smug.

They were served lettuce with a green, vaguely opaque molded gelatin tower in the center. A small bowl of mayonnaise sat at the side. The two men eyed it suspiciously.

"Even *that* looks good," Regina exclaimed, to everyone's laughter.

Chappie, like Joel, was wearing his green dress blouse [jacket] over "pink" trousers. Other officers were wearing all green uniforms, some with brown blouses, others with green. The ladies, by delightful contrast, had managed to conjure up the current fashions; that they had managed it with the diminished availability of cloth and sewing needles amazed Joel.

Susan's outfit must be fashionable, Joel wryly decided, *judging by the attention she is receiving from the other women, and not a few of the men.* He knew nothing of women's fashions, all he knew was that she looked great.

Of course, he admitted to himself, *I'm just a bit prejudiced! I think she always looks great.*

In the background, the seven-man Millville Army Air Field band played light classical music. By mutual, if unspoken agreement, no one discussed the war; this was a time to celebrate with friends, and to pretend that it was just another Thanksgiving.

❖ ❖ ❖

Susan noticed a change in Joel. He was more at peace with himself. The sense of heaviness was gone.

Did he repent? she thought, *I surely hope so. I'll ask him next time we're alone.*

❖ ❖ ❖

The dinner's main course was served, and the meal was wonderful.

"Oh, my! This turkey is so good," Regina said around a mouthful, "how do they do that?"

"I don't know, but these Southern style sweet potatoes with pecans are nothing short of delicious," Chappie said.

To Joel's delight, dessert was cherry pie a la' mode.

"Well, what do you think, Joel?" Susan asked him.

"Say, you can't beat this," he said, a big smile on his face.

"Men," said Regina said with mock disgust, "a little good cooking, and they're satisfied."

"Guilty as charged, ma'am," Joel smiled, as a waiter refilled his coffee cup.

Susan made a mental note: *cherry pie*; *that just might come in handy some day.*

Chappie and his wife excused themselves before the dance began.

"My doctor would have a fit if he found out I was dancing, but I sure wish I could. I haven't danced hardly at all since—." She looked at Chappie, who smiled at her warmly.

"Not to worry, my pet, you'll be dancing again soon enough."

Susan thought she looked tired, and went with her to collect her coat.

The band played a variety of popular music, and Joel and Susan tried them all.

The music seems to have been written just for us, Susan thought dreamily.

She laid her head on Joel's shoulder as they danced to an instrumental version of Lena Horne's hit, *Stormy Weather*. Later, she held him tightly as they danced to a very credible version of Benny Goodman's *Taking a Chance on Love*.

The drive home found her again resting her head on his shoulder as he drove; she could hear him softly humming. It somehow made her feel safe and secure. The smell of his wool Army overcoat had begun to be very familiar.

Joel walked her to the boarding house door, their breath a frosty cloud around them. At the door, Susan turned to him. Joel took his cap off with his left hand and tenderly kissed her. It seemed to last forever, then she stepped back. "Good night, my love," she said softly, and was gone through the door.

Chapter 80

15 December 1944

Millville Army Air Field, Base Theater Building

0800 Hours

Reorganization

Joel watched First Sergeant Bill Madsen, waiting for the signal. Madsen nodded, and Joel strode onto the stage of the Base Theater as Madsen shouted, "Room, Attention!"

Joel looked at the men standing rigidly in front of him for just a moment.

Either I'm getting old, or they're really sending me kids these days, he thought.

"At ease, be seated. I am Lieutenant Colonel Joel Knight, Group Commander of the 160th Coastal Fighter Group. I want to welcome you as the first members of the 162nd Coastal Defense Fighter Squadron which will be exclusively P-61s. Your sister squadron is the 161st, flying P-47s. My deputy, Major Chappie Chapman, will be acting squadron commander for the 161st, and I will be acting squadron commander of the 162nd until we assign permanent squadron commanders.

"Some of you may be disappointed at not being posted to the European or Pacific theaters, but I think you'll find we'll have some excitement for you here. We will be using the P-61 differently than they do overseas, but then we have a different kind of war to fight here.

"In the weeks and months ahead, you'll help us develop the unique character our mission requires. One thing I'll not do is break up your crews; you've all trained together too long and hard on this complex piece of equipment for me to throw away that teamwork." He saw several men relax a bit; Bill had been right, some were worried about that.

"We will be dividing you up into flights, with groups of flights assigned similar search areas off the coast, both day and night. What we're going to take advantage of, men, is your ability to 'see' the enemy when they're far away. Unlike our counterparts in Europe, where Black Widow crews seldom encounter more than one enemy aircraft at a time, you'll be intercepting formations numbering from fifty to a hundred or more bombers. We need your ability to give us advance warning, so we can scramble lots of fighters, both P-47s and P-61s to help you out.

"Once we've seen how you work, six crews will be chosen for special training as ACP – that's Airborne Command Post – duties. We have a very long coastline to defend – from south of New York City, to north of Hampton Roads, Virginia. That means we defend our nation's Capitol. ACP directs fighters from more than a dozen bases, from all branches of the armed services. ACP controls these fighters to bring the most firepower against the German formations." Joel could tell from their expressions that these men had no idea they would be defending the Capitol.

"Training begins tomorrow. I'm thankful that you've been trained to fly in bad weather; I can promise you, we have plenty of that to share with you." There were a few chuckles in the audience.

Joel cleared his throat, "I'll have gatherings like this at least a monthly. If you – any of you – think there's a need for a meeting, let Bill – First Sergeant Bill Madsen – know, and we'll pull one together. I try to have an open door policy. If you need to see me, get an appointment with Bill, or if my door is open, knock, and we'll talk."

1945

Chapter 81

4 January 1945

Millville Army Air Field

0800 Hours

More Changes

Chappie Chapman wrinkled his forehead in concentration, "Now, let me get this straight: General Furston has been sacked, General White has taken his slot, Colonel Randolph gets a star and takes over for General White, and you are now bird Colonel Knight doing Randolph's job?"

"You're almost right, *Lieutenant Colonel* Chapman!" Joel said with a big smile.

"And now you're going to take over my job! And you better get this place shaped up, if you know what's good for you!" He handed the surprised man a set of his own silver oak leaves.

Chappie sat down. "Wow, that's a lot to digest, sir. Are you sure I'm ready to take over, sir? I've only been your deputy for about seven months."

"To be honest, Chappie, nobody's sure that any of us are ready, but 'exigencies of war' and all that. You'll do OK, my friend. Look how well you've done all the times I've been away."

"Yeah, well, Joel, it's one thing to 'act instead of' and quite another to actually be the guy in charge—"

"If you need me, Chappie, I'm a phone call away, but I don't expect I'll be receiving any calls."

Chappie looked thoughtful, then said, "Say, what about General Furston? They're not going to drum him out of the Army are they?"

"No, they just had to show Congress that somebody high up took the fall. He's too competent a man to just send out to pasture. Actually, he's taking leave, then going to Kentucky to take charge of the new B-29 plant. That will be the fifth plant; two in Washington State, one in Nebraska, one in Georgia, and now Franklin, Kentucky. When it's up and running, I'll bet among the five factories, we'll be making fifty a day," Joel told him. He was wrong, but not by much, and on the low side.

"Now, I'm taking Bill with me, so your first two decisions are who's your deputy, and who's your First Sergeant. Good luck with those."

"Believe it or not, sir, I've actually thought about that. What would you think of—."

Chapter 82

24 January 1945

Joint Chiefs of Staff Conference Room, The Pentagon

0910 Hours

B-29 Decision

The morning briefings for the Joint Chiefs were over; they shooed their staff out so they could have a private conference.

"Let's get down to brass tacks on the B-29 issue," Admiral Bill Leahy, Chairman of the Joint Chiefs said, refilling his coffee cup.

"You know LeMay will have a fit if FDR does this," Admiral Ernest King said to General Henry "Hap" Arnold.

Arnold put down his coffee cup, and said evenly, "Ernie, Curt LeMay doesn't run the Army Air Forces, despite what he thinks. And he doesn't own the B-29s, either. I have no intention of discussing this beyond telling him he'll have 100 less Superfortresses than he expected. After the fact."

"Besides," he added, "that new factory in Kentucky's coming on line soon, we'll be able to make up the differences quickly."

Bill Leahy shook the ash off his morning cigar, "What about the camera planes – what are they – F-13s, Hap? Can we take what we need without putting Curt in a bind?"

"Yes, a photo recon B-29 is an F-13, and they are in short supply, Bill. It's the cameras, not the planes, that's delayed us. There's only one plant in the whole country making those big lenses," Arnold replied.

"But I think Curt can get along with what he has for awhile. Don't forget he's got a few photo

B-24s, too – called F-7s. The reason we need those F-13s in Europe is that we're basically blind along the French/Spanish border. The Germans throw up lots of jets to intercept every single-seat photo bird sent along that route. Even Mosquitoes don't have the range or speed to do it."

General George Marshall asked, "You're trying to fly the entire length of the Spanish/ French border, is that it? Why?"

"Yes, that's it, George. Intelligence believes the Germans built their batwing plant somewhere along the border. But we've had no luck finding it. Not even De Gaulle's partisans have turned up much. Seriously, I'm worried they put it underground, like the Messerschmitt plants. If they did, we'll have a hard time finding it; you know how good they are at camouflage. I reluctantly asked Mr. Roosevelt for General Donovan's help; he sent a team into France a couple of weeks ago. Seems like a long shot."

"An F-13 can fly non-stop from Iceland to North Africa right down the border, and can take a phenomenal number of photographs."

"But aren't they as vulnerable as the Mosquitoes to those German jets?"

"Probably, on an ordinary run; German RADAR sees everything that takes off in England. The thing is, they'd have no idea where our birds are going when they take off in Iceland, even if they knew about them. If the weather's good, we can send an F-13 in at 35,000 feet, at a ground speed of over 400; that's a tough intercept, even for jets. They probably won't even spot it until the ship is over France, since they'll be coming in over the Bay of Biscay. I think the odds are pretty good, at least at first. The Germans will be looking in the wrong place, or so we hope."

George Marshall said, "Speaking of Iceland, how soon will the runways and hangers be completed?"

"That's a good question; how soon can your SeaBee's pull this off, Ernie?" asked Arnold.

Admiral Ernest King tugged at his right ear and said, "Well, it'll be another six weeks of preparations before they can start the runways, then maybe a month for the concrete, weather permitting. That could be a problem. Hangers go up pretty quickly, even in those Arctic storms, but there's good news in that: we keep building during all but the worst weather, but that same bad weather keeps the Germans in Norway grounded. They'll discover us eventually, but hopefully not until after we've made several photo raids with the F-13s. I'll base additional fighters there to fend off the Germans once we start flying bombing missions. You're all aware that we're preparing for the contingency of pulling back most or all of our heavy bombers to Iceland if the attacks from the Gothas can't be stopped?"

There were nods around the room; that was a contingency none of them wanted to face.

Leahy was silent for a moment, "Once you find the batwing plant, you'll use the entire B-29 force against it?"

"Yes, sir, that's the plan," Arnold replied. "I suspect that it'll only take a couple of raids to keep their heads down, once we locate them. It's possible we could launch out of North Africa, too, depending on where the plant is. I plan on hitting it regularly until it's shut down."

They all knew that bombing a German aircraft plant didn't mean that production stopped; the enemy was just too adaptable. The best they could hope for was a sharp curtailment in production.

"What about the 'special squadron'?" Leahy asked softly, reluctantly bringing up the subject.

Arnold had a look of distaste, "Sir, they have separate facilities on Iceland, at an auxiliary field, just like the 509th in the Pacific.

You know they trained with Tibbett's group, right? And their airplanes are modified just like his?"

"Yes. I'm aware of that. Are we agreed, then gentlemen, that we'll go to the President with a recommendation for 100 B-29's, plus at least 6 F-13s, to be based in Iceland? The special squadron will also be provided for, if the President so decides."

"I'll go on record again," Arnold said firmly, "I'm absolutely against using the special squadrons in Europe."

"So noted, Hap."

Chapter 83

9 February 1945

Joel's Office

1000 Hours

Mid-morning Challenge

First Sergeant Bill Madsen looked in on his boss, who was slumped in his chair, distractedly staring out his window. Madsen shook his head.

That poor guy doesn't know which end is up, he thought wryly. *Well, now or never, here goes.*

"Got a moment for somethin' personal, sir?" he asked.

Joel's head popped around in surprise.

He didn't even know I was here.

"Oh, yeah, sure, Bill. Come on in. What's your problem," Joel said, turning, and sitting up in his chair.

Here's hoping, Bill thought, closing the door behind him.

"Actually, sir, it's you."

Joel's eyes widened a bit. "Oh?" he said.

Madsen put his hands on his hips, and spoke like a father, "Ya know, sir, I've been in this man's Army for more than twenty-five years and I gotta say, I've seen what you've got in every form it can take. Sometimes it ends pretty, and sometimes not, but take the advice of an older guy who's been there and back, Colonel, and ask that girl to marry you. Until you do, you're not gonna resolve this confusion in your head, and we can't have you mopin' around much longer."

Gad, I've got a lot of cheek, he thought worriedly, *will he hand me my head?*

"What are you talking about, Bill?" Joel asked cautiously, with a faint look of disbelief on his face.

Bill looked around again to be sure the door was closed. Gently, he said, "Sir, we all know you're crazy in love with Susan; don't you think it's 'bout time you admitted it, and did something about it? Really, sir, it's startin' to interfere with your work."

"Interfering with my work? How?"

Ha! He didn't deny it! OK, in for a penny, in for a pound, Bill thought.

"Forgive me, sir, but like just now: you were lookin' out the window instead of concentrating on that report; that's not like you. And last week, after staff meeting, General Randolph asked me if you was sick, 'cause you sat so quiet during his meeting. Now tell me, honestly, you were thinkin' about her just now, weren't you?" He smiled, crossed his arms, and waited.

"How'd you know?" There was a trace of a smile.

"Well, it might have something to with the sighs you can hear clear out in the hall, for one thing, sir!"

"So you're saying I'm acting like a love-sick kid, are you?"

Bill laughed, "Those're your words, sir, but if the shoe fits—."

Monday 12 February

Joel walked up and down High Street, wracked with indecision.

What if she tells me to go jump in the lake. I couldn't stand that. But I've just got to know. I've got to ask her. If she finds somebody else because I'm too scared to ask her, it'd be my own fault. I've never felt like this about anyone else. I can't stop thinking about her. She's all I can think about. Bill's right, I'm letting my duties slip because of her. If she says no, I think I'll die. Now I do sound like a love-sick kid. Oh, Susan, you've just got to say yes.

Finding his resolve, he squared his shoulders, and went into Robert H. Harding Jewelers, to the tinkling of a little bell.

The old clerk in the store clearly had seen this before, and kindly guided Joel as he made his selection. In the end, it was a ½ carat clear white diamond solitaire in a starkly plain setting of gold that he chose. The old gentleman quietly assured him that the establishment would change the setting for a modest fee, if she didn't care for it. Lighter of wallet, but soaring in spirit, Joel left the store.

Chapter 84

14 February 1945

Union Lake

Late afternoon

Proposal

Joel picked up Susan at the temporary building being used for Alexander Hamilton Junior High School, and drove to their picnic spot at Union Lake. Here and there, patches of snow from the last storm still clung to shady spots. The lake was mostly frozen, with dark water showing in areas. The trees hadn't begun to bud. Still, there was a calm, quiet beauty to the location; they were far enough from the airfield that even engine noises didn't interfere.

"This is where we got caught by that storm last summer, remember?" he said, smiling.

"Oh, yes. Say, isn't that the tree that was struck by lightning? That was scary!" she said pointing.

"Maybe it is. Let's walk down there and see."

The air was cool, but not as cold as it would be when the sun set. They strolled hand in hand to the tree, and saw blackened marks on the tree's trunk. Joel turned to her, still holding her hand. Her wonderfully blue eyes were wide with anticipation. He swallowed hard.

"Susan Johansseson, ever since I first saw you that day at Alexander Hamilton, I've been totally enchanted by you. Never in my life have I met such an intelligent woman. We've been through so much together since then. I dream about you at night, and think about you all day. You've totally taken over my conscience and sub-conscience, my days and nights. I have fallen completely, totally, head-over-heels in love with you. I can't stand to be apart from you. I love everything about you. The hours crawl for me until we can be together again. I desperately want you to be my wife. Susan, will you marry me?"

He pulled the little white box from his pocket, and snapped it open. His heart was pounding wildly, and his mouth was dry.

Her eyes filled with tears, and she gasped, "Oh, Joel, yes, yes, a thousand times, yes! I thought you would never ask! Yes, I'll marry you!" She held him so tightly it almost hurt. Almost. Joel's heart sang.

The next few weeks were a whirlwind. Susan proudly showed all her friends the diamond. Her girl friends and fellow teachers were all a twitter.

"Susan, how wonderful for you!"

"So he finally came around! Good for you!"

"I'm so happy for you, Susan."

"Oh, he's so handsome! What a beautiful couple you make."

Millie hugged her. "Isn't it wonderful? Both of us get to marry such wonderful men. I'm so excited for you. Wait 'till I tell Charles!"

Even Awful Agatha, her landlady, smiled kindly. "I thought he was coming around to see you a lot, dear. I hope you'll both be very happy. He's a fine looking young man."

"There is no way you're taking this ring back now, buster!" Susan laughingly informed Joel when he mentioned that she could change the setting if she wanted. "I like this just fine, thank you. You're on the hook, and I'm not letting you off!" She pulled him close and held him, laughing.

At the air field, Joel's back was pounded in congratulations. Even General Randolph joined in, "You've chosen a great beauty, Joel, and she's a fine person too. Congratulations to both of you."

First Sergeant Bill smiled in satisfaction as he said gruffly, "Maybe now we can get some work done around here, sir!"

Chapter 85

26 February 1945

Joel's House in Millville

1930 Hours

Plans

"Joel, I've spoken with my folks again, and they just can't come for the wedding. Dad can't get off work, and train tickets cost so much, even if they could get them. Going to a wedding doesn't rate a very high priority, I'm afraid."

"Yeah, I was afraid of that," Joel grimaced. "My mom still wants us to come to Colorado for the wedding, but we'd have the same problems getting tickets, and we'd still have to get your folks there too. I hate to say it, but I think we'll just have to get married here in Millville, and go see our folks later when we can. Unless, of course, you just want to call the whole thing off!" He laughed at her reaction.

She put her hand on her hip, and waggled a finger at him, "Oh, no you don't, flyboy! You're committed now. No use trying to wiggle out of it, either! I'm going to marry you if we have to stand in front of a Justice of the Peace!" She playfully pounded on his chest, then hugged him.

"OK, OK, can't you take a joke? It's not like I can't get a refund for the ring!"

"Oh, you're just horrible to say such a thing! That ring is never going to leave my finger. You know that, don't you?"

He was serious now, "Yes, I feel the same way. Let's what we can arrange at Millie's church; Stanton Township First Baptist, isn't it? Would you like that?" He cupped her face in his hands, and kissed her.

A visit with the pastor brought his blessing and congratulations. He checked the church calendar.

"Well, you young folks are in luck. The church is available the afternoon of the June 10th. I'll just write it in; 2:30 p.m., you say? Good. Now, have you gotten a license and your blood tests yet? I must have those a few days before the ceremony, you know. Don't wait; it may be February, but June will be here before you know it."

He smiled warmly at Susan, "If you're like every other bride-to-be my dear, you'll find there's barely enough time to get everything ready. Stay in touch with me, will you, or the church secretary, especially as the time gets closer. June is the favorite time of year to get married, and I'm sure somebody'll want the date you've chosen if you have to change. Be sure to let us know if you want the Congregational Room for a reception; it's in pretty high demand, too. We can seat about 250 or so in that room. Do you think you will have a band?"

Susan glanced quickly at Joel, "We haven't decided that yet, Pastor." In truth, it hadn't crossed either of their minds.

Joel made a note on his ever present pocket tablet about the license and blood tests. In the swirl of excitement around their engagement, he mustn't let such details get lost.

Chapter 86

12 April 1945

Off the East Coast of Iceland

0313 Hours; Sunrise

Secret Hideaway

U-56 rocked uneasily in the rolling, gray-green waters, her engines at full stop. She hovered at periscope depth while Kapitanleutnant Herbert "Bo" Schuster surveyed the waters around them. In truth, the seas weren't all that bad, it was just that the round bottomed submarine wasn't designed for surface roughness no matter how gentle. Alone among the crew, Schuster felt the slight twisting in the roll his old ship experienced with each wave. Her hull had been badly damaged in that British depth charge attack in 1939, and they'd never gotten it exactly right.

Schuster was only thirty-seven, but his hard eyes looked twice that age. His reddish blond beard was showing the gray that had already begun to fleck his head. Worry lines around his blue eyes were deeply etched in his pale submariner's face.

U-56 was an early Type IIC, built in the late1930s; most of her contemporaries had long since been sunk or salvaged. Indeed, the first reaction of the yardmaster when she limped back into port was to scrap her. Somebody somewhere decided to retrofit her as a one of a kind covert supply boat. It had taken two years; she'd been gutted, her hull lengthened, and compartments for cargo, both human and materiel, built in. She had limited armaments, only four torpedoes forward and none aft, and a couple of deck guns, but that kind of war wasn't her purpose anymore. With modern batteries and the latest in powerful, silent motors, she served her new function well.

Schuster spotted the signal light on shore, and checked the horizons again; British ships rarely sailed in these mostly uncontested waters, and American ships never, but he simply couldn't take the chance.

Nothing, empty seas; good. He elevated the periscope, and made a quick survey of the sky. *Again, nothing.*

Grunting with satisfaction, he triggered the periscope signal light in acknowledgement to the men ashore, and lowered the instrument. This date had been carefully chosen; tonight there would be a full moon. If there was some unexpected delay, they could work into the night with at least some visibility.

"Shore party, prepare to disembark," he said softly, as if someone might overhear him. The coxswain repeated the command over the boat's intercom.

"Take him to the surface," Schuster told the helmsman.

Schuster's crewmen were well trained, and within twenty minutes, two heavily laden boats struck out for the rocky coast. There was a narrow "beach" they could ground on, more coarse rocks than sand, but it had sufficed before. As he watched the progress of the boats from U-56's sail, a third boat was preparing to launch, this one carrying the replacement personnel for the covert weather station. He always sent his Exec on the personnel boat, reluctant to leave his sub at such a vulnerable time.

When the personnel boat was a hundred yards away, he submerged to periscope depth. No sense giving the Brits a fat target, should they wander this way. An hour later, the sub resurfaced and the empty boats were taken aboard. A signal from shore told him the boat with the returning personnel had launched.

With the confidence of experience, the boat crew retrieved the thrown line, and the boat was pulled securely against the looming submarine. A slight, bespectacled man in his late twenties looked up at Schuster from the boat and nodded. Schuster turned and immediately went down into the submarine, awaiting his passenger.

"Hello, Bo," the serious man greeted him with a solid handshake.

"Good to see you again, Wilhelm," Schuster replied. Both were patriotic Germans, but neither was a Nazi Party member; by unspoken agreement, they never used Nazi greetings.

"We must speak in your cabin at once," Wilhelm Miller said, intently.

Schuster pulled the cloth drape across the entrance to his tiny compartment.

"As you can see, I am not well equipped for private conversations," he told his visitor dryly.

"This will do, Bo. I must tell you so that you can send immediately the message to Berlin; I do not trust the weather message encryption device," he said almost as an aside.

"What's so important, coming from this God forsaken ice-encrusted rock?" Herbert crossed his arms; he knew this serious meteorologist wasn't the sort to jump at phantoms or waste his time.

"Just this, Herr Kaptain: we are not alone on this end of the 'ice-encrusted rock'."

The submariner's face contorted as he tried to make sense of the statement.

"What? You don't mean the Icelanders—."

"No, sir, I mean **Americans**. They are building what may be a new air base no more that fifteen kilometers from here. One of my men was taking early morning temperature readings, and saw the earth moving tractors. He foolishly crept up and observed them, and somehow got away."

He held up a heavy, waterproof envelope. "I have photographs of them, with clear American Navy markings."

Schuster was amazed, "When was that, Wilhelm?"

"About ten days ago; since then they have made amazing progress. Bo, there are men and equipment swarming all over the place. My guess is that the runway, if that's what it is, will be about two and a half kilometers [8,000 feet] long, perhaps longer yet. It would seem that they are expecting some very large aircraft. Don't you agree we must radio this immediately?"

"Of course, but first answer this: you are *sure* that neither you nor your men have been spotted? Did you inform Klein? We must not reveal this location."

"Yes, I informed him. I suspect he will be told to curtail his work once Berlin finds out. I hope so. I also suspect that you'll return here sooner than you planned; they'll want to bring in spies, or so, to see what the Americans are up to."

"And I suspect you are correct on both counts." The captain reached for the bulkhead microphone, "Radioman to the Kapitan's cabin."

The radioman appeared while Schuster was still writing.

"Send this highest priority, using a one-time pad," he told the young fellow. "We will stand by for instructions, to be sent to us at –," he looked at the chronometer on his wall. "At 0900 Greenwich."

Again, he took the microphone, "XO, advise the Kapitan when you are secure for diving."

"Aye, aye, sir; no more than two minutes," came the tinny voice over the ship's intercom.

They dived and waited silently, every man watching the hands of his watch. As 0900 Greenwich approached, Schuster said, "Take him up to periscope depth."

Again carefully surveying the surrounding seas and skies, Schuster satisfied himself that they were alone.

"Run up the radio mast."

Exactly on time, the radioman began receiving the encoded message, his hand flying as he wrote it. In moments, he handed the decoded message to his captain. Schuster read it, as Wilhelm read over his shoulder.

"It would seem that Berlin both believes us and takes us seriously, Wilhelm. I must send a man ashore with these new orders."

❖ ❖ ❖

Gustavus Klein shook his head as the sound of the rubber boat's muffled motor faded as it headed back to the submarine. This was his third tour at the hidden weather station, but they'd never before sent a man ashore with a message. He turned, and walked into the entrance of the warm cave they lived and worked in. It was one of the thousands of geothermal vents on the volcanically active island. It maintained an even seventy degrees, no matter the arctic cold only feet away.

He sat at his desk, and opened the envelope. In seconds, he leapt from his chair, and called for his men.

"We have new orders. From the highest levels," the men all knew who that meant. "The authorities have ordered us to stop all weather observations, and to remain inside the cave. All outside instruments must be retrieved immediately. We are to immediately dismantle the radio tower, and bring it inside. We will return home within thirty days and be replaced with SS intelligence specialists and special soldiers."

He again shook his head in disbelief, "We are prohibited even from cooking sausages or sauerkraut, because of the smell! It seems this new American air base is more important to the Reich than our mere weather reports," he finished with a note of bitterness.

Chapter 87
29 April 1945
Coastal Defense Command Headquarters
Philadelphia, Pennsylvania
General White's Office
0800 Hours
Report

Admiral Thomas Flanagan and Navy Captain Gerald Whitman joined General White and Joel in General White's office for a debriefing on the attack on Hampton Roads.

Before the men seated themselves, General White said, "Admiral Flanagan, Captain Whitman, please meet Colonel Joel Knight. Joel is my ACP for Region 2. Joel, Captain Whitmore is your ACP 3 counterpart."

The pleasantries completed, White turned to Whitman. "May we have your report, Captain?"

"Of course, sir. The first warning came from a PBY on patrol at about 0640 hours. Central Command was immediately notified, and by 0700, we had fighters airborne. Coastal artillery from both Fort Monroe and Fort Story fired AAA, but to little effect." He continued for fifteen minutes, carefully recounting the battle, answering questions as he went.

"Now, preliminary statistics look like this: despite fighter pilot reports that seventy-five plus bombers were shot down, we believe the accurate number is thirty to thirty-five. Photographs indicate 200 to 210 aircraft, so their losses were between 15 and 20 percent. Our trailing aircraft reported three more bombers crashed during the two hours it followed the Germans, so they took awful heavy losses."

He sighed, "For ourselves, sir, it's been more difficult. Several fighter units not on my roster joined the fight and we haven't identified them all yet. What we do have isn't pretty: forty Navy F6Fs were officially involved; six were lost and seven damaged. There were about a dozen more F6Fs from an unidentified unit; we have no notion of their losses. The Marine F4U unit had eighteen fighters, and lost three. There were twenty-four Army P-38s, and they lost five.

"There was a small group of old F4Fs, going to gunnery practice; we're not sure how many were involved, but they lost five or six. Those pilots showed exceptional bravery, by the way, sir. Those old planes only have 0.30 calibre guns, but they pressed in and finished off several stragglers.

"So, using the official numbers, we lost fourteen aircraft out of eighty-two, a loss rate of almost 17 percent. It is possible – I'm hopeful – that this number could be revised downward later, but for now, that's it. In addition, about eighteen aircraft were damaged and may have to be written off. Not a good day.

"On the ground, the damage was also severe. An ammunition ship, the *USS Baxter James*, took a direct hit, and blew up; at least seventy-five dead. Fortunately, it was isolated, or the causalities might have been higher. Seventeen or eighteen other ships were damaged, several of them badly. Hundreds of buildings were damaged or destroyed by severe fires; incendiaries again."

He continued with a look of distaste on his face, "Considerable damage was caused by our own AAA shot dropping on military and civilians alike. There are reports of damage caused by German rocket fire, but they're unconfirmed. I'd be surprised if at least a few of our losses in the air didn't result from friendly fire. I have no figures for casualties on the ground, military or civilian."

General White looked grim. "Why did we get hit so hard in the air, Jerry?"

"Sir, it's early to draw conclusions, but my opinion, for what it's worth, is that our guys pressed in too close; given the range of our new rockets, they could have stood off farther, and still been effective. Our guys aren't using the rockets effectively yet, and the Germans are devastating with their defensive fire."

The senior officer digested what he had just been told.

Whitman cleared his throat, "Sir, there is better news as well."

White motioned him to go on.

"Sir, the PB4Y trailing the German formation was never spotted, so far as we know. He watched for more than two hours, and recorded a heading change they made. They originally were on 090 degrees, which would have meant landfall on the Continent near Gibraltar. They turned north, to about 070 degrees, which results in landfall on the Spanish coast west of Seville. Here's the best part, sir, a British flying boat sighted the formation, and confirms it flew into Spanish territory."

"That's stunning!" White exclaimed, "Has Washington been informed?"

"Yes, sir, right away. There's another detail of interest, sir. The PB4Y reported that when the Germans were at 18,000 feet, before the heading change, all of the airplanes – every single one – feathered the two outboard engines. We took some telephoto pictures, and you can see the stopped props."

Joel sat up and exclaimed, "Sir, that's it! That's the missing piece! That's how they are able to fly so far – they shut down some of the engines, and fly on the remainder. That would really cut fuel consumption. Wow, that's clever."

Admiral Flanagan frowned, "How can they fly long distances with engines off? Wouldn't they just use more fuel on the other engines?"

"Actually, no sir. They can fly on a lot less power once they've dropped the bombs and used up most of their fuel. They'd probably slow down seventy-five or a hundred miles per hour, but that gives them the range they need."

General White said, "Colonel Knight is an aeronautical engineer besides being a crackerjack pilot. He's been trying to figure out how the Germans are able to fly back and forth across the Atlantic."

He looked thoughtful. "Joel, do you think they do that on the way here as well? Wouldn't they be very vulnerable to attack?"

Joel nodded; "Yes, sir, they probably do. Now, their speed would be higher because of the weight of the bombs and fuel, but yes, I think they do. In fact, as I think about it, they must do that. That accounts for how they got all the way to the sub yards in Maine a couple of months ago, and why they dropped so few bombs. If we could find them, yes, I'd say they would be sitting ducks."

"Now," he mused to himself, "we need to discover where they're fueling in flight, 'cause we could really nab them then."

"By the way, gentlemen, in his enthusiasm, Colonel Knight just revealed a classified fact: the Germans are fueling their aircraft in flight. You will not repeat this.

"Is your report complete, Captain Whitman?"

"No, sir, not quite," Whitman replied. "We captured around 100 German crewmen, many injured. If our estimate of thirty-five Gothas downed is right, at six men per crew, about 210 Germans fell on our soil. Not all survived, of course, but we assume about 100 more Germans are unaccounted for. We've contacted the civilian police authorities, including the Virginia State Police, telling them that their officers and troopers should approach crash sites carefully, and to contact the SP [Shore Patrol – the Navy police] or the Army MPs before getting too close."

"Are there facilities for so many POWs?" General White asked.

"Yes, sir, at Naval Operating Base Norfolk there's a facility that can handle 300 POWs for two or three weeks. They even set up a field hospital for the less seriously wounded.

"The Red Cross has been notified, and has representatives on the scene. Everyone has been thoroughly briefed on the proper treatment of POWs; as soon as they're processed, the plan is to ship them out to the POW camp in Colorado."

General White grunted in agreement. Sending German prisoners 1200 miles into the country's hinterlands diminished the likelihood of a successful escape to near zero. It was a good solution.

Chapter 88

10 May 1945

Iceland Weather Station

0610 Hours

Replacements

The weathermen were evacuated on the 28th day. In their place was a team of ten combat-hardened soldiers, all experienced in clandestine military work. Once again, no Allied ships or aircraft were nearby as the men and dozens of heavy crates were brought ashore.

Inside the cave, SS Major Georg Bergerman spoke to his troops in unnecessarily hushed tones. "I tell you again that our work here is most important. Our first goal is to remain unobserved. This we must do at all costs. Your time in Russia toughened you; you can do this."

He looked at the solemn faced men. "I expect and demand the most careful attention to maintaining the secrecy of our location when we venture outside; that means strict efforts toward hiding completely tracks or any other evidence. Don't fall into the trap of thinking that these Americans are less attentive than the Russians. If they only *suspect* we are here, they will be relentless in finding us."

He looked at his watch, "In approximately two hours, the Luftwaffe will drop bombs on Reykjavik. Their real purpose is to photograph the new base. We will receive photographs within forty-eight hours."

"Now," he looked at a toughened unteroffizier [sergeant]. "Hugo, take two men, and go photograph this facility. The new gear is far superior to what we had last year; the camouflage is especially effective. Schmitt – raise your hand – is our supply sergeant; see him for supplies as well as tent halves to hide under. Take also weapons, but use them in the most dangerous situations only, understood? If you must kill someone, bury his body well." The man nodded. "Go. Be back before midnight, yes?"

As the men left, Bergerman said, "Unteroffizer [Sergeant] Hansson and Gefreiter [Corporal] Unser are in charge of our new photograph laboratory.

"Their special radio equipment is the most advanced and secret in the Reich. I tell you this because we are few in number and living in such a small space. This secret machine sends photographs using radio waves to Berlin in seconds. Ask no questions of the men operating it."

He continued, "The Americans will eventually discover our messages, and then look for where they were sent from. To make their task more difficult, you will practice how to assemble, erect, lower, and disassemble the new radio tower quickly. It will be erected only for actual transmission, yes? We want nothing that American RADAR, or a sharp-eyed soldier can see.

"Fortunately, we will be warm here. Our scientists provided means for us to create electricity from the hot water underground. We will have a life of ease, compared to the steppes of Russia!"

Right on time, the JU-88 twin engine bomber roared over Reykjavik harbor. The few bombs did little damage beyond angering those on the ground. Two pilots at the nearby airbase ran to a pair of tired P-40Cs and taxied for takeoff. The JU-88 pilot put on a spurt of power, and "escaped" toward the northeast, which "accidentally" took him over the new base.

Photographs taken, the pilot triggered the recently added nitrous oxide system which fed the oxygen-rich gas directly into the cylinders. Instantly, the engines roared loudly as their output nearly doubled. The aircraft rocketed upward, leaving the P-40s hopelessly behind.

The camouflaged schnellboot, an older, larger version of the American PT boats, risked heavy seas for hours coming from Norway's western coast. No submarine was available so the small, fast boat was thrown into service on short notice.

The young, sunburned captain turned to port, and slowed as they approached the Icelandic shoreline. He had only the barest information on his rendezvous point.

"Don't worry, Herr Kapitan! They will find *you*!" his commander had assured him.

They cruised southward along Iceland's eastern shoreline for twenty-five kilometers, then a bright flash from the rocky coast caught his eye. It repeated, sending the expected signal. "Steer toward that signal light," he ordered.

SS Major Georg Bergerman took the water-proof package of photographs, and dismissed the teenaged Kapitan.

The weatherman was correct; there is a major airbase being built, all but under our noses, mused Bergerman as he pored over the glossy prints. *Why such a long, broad runway?*

His orders were to watch and wait. What were the Americans doing? If he was careful, the Reich would have advanced warning about whatever it was, if only they weren't discovered too soon. He had no illusions about this cave remaining secret long once they began sending reports and photographs. The Americans weren't the stupid brutes that Goebbels pretended they were. He intended to go down fighting.

Chapter 89

17 May 1945

Reykjavik – East U.S. Army Air Field

1137 Hours

First Landing

The SeaBee's paused to watch the largest airplane they had ever seen gently land on the virgin runway with a puff of smoke and a rubbery squawk from the dual main gear tires.

As a Jeep with a jury-rigged flag guided the aircraft to the hangers, a second landed. Within an hour, there were thirteen others, each with a distinctive purple trapezoid painted on its tail; the first B-29s of the 513th Bomb Group had arrived in Iceland.

The B-29 engines had hardly cooled before the carefully camouflaged SS men crept to 100 yards of the aircraft.

"Americans are so arrogant!" one whispered to the other, "Look, no fences or guards!"

His unteroffizier [sergeant] corrected him, "It's not arrogance, Luther, it's complacency. But either way, we get our photos, yes? And think how easy to destroy them!"

Eight Days later

The order to destroy the B-29s wasn't given to the unteroffizer [sergeant] and his men, for that would reveal their existence, something neither had considered.

Berlin was shocked, "I cannot believe the Americans are bringing these huge Boeings against us," said a senior Luftwaffe Oberst, shaking his head in disbelief. The head of the service agreed. "A bad omen," he said darkly

"Can they reach us from Iceland, sir? It seems so far," asked a younger man.

"They must believe so, Leutnant, or else why build an airbase? Still, I agree; intelligence doesn't think they have the range. We must take the offensive and attack at once. Notify Luftflotte 5 in Norway."

Stavanger, Norway

Oberst Karl Liebermann inherited Luftflotte 5's strange mix of aircraft only weeks before. Now, he had to decide how to carry out his orders. *A mixed force would be more likely to succeed and would be harder for the enemy to fight*, he thought.

Liebermann signed his name reluctantly, and said to his adjutant, "Well, here we are, Conrad. Prepare for launch as quickly as possible. How many of the Greifs [Griffons] can we get airworthy in time?"

He referred to the Heinkel HE-177, the once promising but now discredited "super-bomber." With an unusual arrangement of two engines driving a single propeller on each wing, the aircraft was at best temperamental, and at worst, deadly; massive engine fires were common. Its major attribute, when it operated properly, was the big bomb load; it could carry twice what the JU-88s could. The rest of the Luftwaffe had replaced the Heinkel's with the far superior Gotha GO-447. Luftflotte 5 had the unenviable luck to be the last to operate them.

"Sir, we can probably launch twenty-three of the twenty-five Greifs; this weather gave us a week to work on them, and most are operating as well as they ever do. As to the JU-88s, I can promise you sixty aircraft, no later than tomorrow evening."

"Hmm," the older man replied, "we shall see."

25 May 1944

0225 Hours

After several more days of bad weather, the clouds and winds abated. In the predawn darkness, engines echoed across the base.

At 0300 exactly, the control tower signaled "takeoff." The JU-88s were first, taking off in pairs and forming into groups of five. They immediately headed for their targets. Next, the He-177s, faster and capable of higher altitude, took off singly. Lieberman's adjutant was proved wrong almost immediately; one caught fire as it took off, and two others turned back with severe overheating. Still, a formidable force of sixty-two JU-88s and twenty-one He-177s thrust toward Iceland.

Corporal Andrew J. Harder, U.S. Army, field stripped his illegal cigarette out of sight of the guard shack. He adjusted the Caliber 0.30 Carbine on his shoulder as he walked down the line of B-29 tails toward the warm shack. It was the third time he'd spent boring hours guarding the big airplanes from – what? He shook his head in disgust.

What griped him most was that he, *a Corporal*, had to walk guard duty. It didn't help his chagrin to know that until more troops arrived, everybody Buck Sergeant and below was taking their turn.

Those new guys can't get here soon enough, he groused to himself. *What's the use of being an NCO if ya still have ta pull guard duty?*

As he mused over his horrible fate, a beating, ominous rumble interfered with his thoughts. He glanced wildly around.

Airplanes, but not ours!

He glanced to the east; low flying planes headed straight towards the parked B-29s! High above were more aircraft. Training took over: he grabbed the whistle around his neck, and blew it hard.

The guard sergeant burst out of the shack like he was on a spring, "What's up, Harder?" he yelled.

"Germans, Sarge, coming right at us!"

The NCO gaped at the aircraft only a couple of miles away. He dashed into the shack and grabbed the telephone.

"Air attack! Air attack! Aircraft inbound from the east!" he shouted into the instrument.

Harder unslung his weapon, and jacked a round into the chamber.

"Oh, God! Oh, God, have mercy," he prayed, and shot at the rushing airplanes as they thundered over his head. The bombs fell toward him like a dream; they hung in the air for an eternity, then suddenly were on him and his world dissolved in a paroxysm of fire, noise and pain.

Chapter 90
2 June 1945
Joel's Office
1117 Hours
Bad News

"Bad news, Colonel," First Sergeant Bill Madsen said solemnly.

"What is it, Bill?"

"The Germans bombed the new base in Iceland, sir, and destroyed most of the B-29s. We lost a lot of people, too."

"What?" Joel said in astonishment, "How did they know we were there? Where'd they come from?"

He paused, "What planes did they use?"

The sergeant shook his head, "They were JU-88s and those crazy HE-177s. They must have come from Norway, but I didn't think JU-88s had the range. Do they, sir?"

"Well, that's farther than you'd expect JU-88s to fly, but I suppose with extra fuel and a light bomb load, yeah, they could probably do it."

He shrugged, "They obviously did. Thinking about it, they've hit Reykjavik now and then. It's easily within range of the HE-177s. What a shock."

"Did we at least shoot down a few?"

Bill showed grim satisfaction on his face, "Oh, yeah, we sure did, sir. Those P-38s hit 'em hard. They're claiming fourteen Ju-88s, and six or seven Heinkle's. The report doesn't say anything about German rocket guns; guess the northern outposts haven't been reequipped yet, thank goodness."

Chapter 91

10 June 1945

Stanton Township First Baptist Church

0230 Hours

Wedding

Weeks Before

It seemed to Joel that certain dates hurled themselves at him; first, when he was eighteen and was preparing to say goodbye to his mom and dad and brother and sister before boarding the train for the lonely cross-country trip to West Point. Then, at the Point, as the *final* final exams pressed in on him, and he faced graduation and commissioning. And now, his wedding.

There was so much to do: he had to host a rehearsal dinner, choose a best man and groomsmen, help with invitations, buy a ring, plan for the honeymoon, and get a week's leave. And he knew that Susan's tasks were even more formidable.

"Here're my choices, Susan: Chappie for best man – if there was any way to get my brother here, it would have been him, but that's just not to be. As groomsmen, Commander John Bell Higgins, Lt. Colonel Carl Tucker, and Captain William Rich. How's that sound? OK?"

"Yes, they're OK; I'm anxious to meet John Higgins, you've spoken about him so often. Have they all agreed, then?"

"Well, all but Chappie; he still has to get a 'kitchen pass' from Regina!" Joel chucked. He knew that Susan had already asked her to be one of the bridesmaids.

"Now, you've asked Mildred Angleton to be your Maid of Honor, right? Who else will be bridesmaids besides Regina?"

"A teacher from school you don't know, Joyce Witherspoon, and Tech Sergeant Lucy Morgan."

"You're asking Lucy Morgan? Why?" Joel could see the plain, skinny sergeant in his mind's eye.

"Joel, she's a very nice girl, and don't forget, she's a colleague. She's really a big help." She cocked her head, "You don't know her, Joel; away from the job, she's a very warm, loving person."

Joel put up his hands in surrender, "OK, OK, your choice. Now, I need to know: do you want to honeymoon at that hotel in Philly, or at a shore-side cottage at Atlantic City?"

"That's easy; I want to get you as far from the Army as I can. It's the cottage, no question about it!" She ran her finger softly across his cheek, and smiled a special smile he was soon to love. "I want you all to myself, flyboy!"

Now, it was upon him. The cake and flowers had been ordered and delivered, a really huge number of invitations mailed out [or so it seemed to Joel], the rehearsal and dinner had gone well, and suddenly he was standing at the front of the church with Chappie at his side.

So far, so good, he thought as the organ played. His hands were sweaty, and his necktie was suddenly tight. He glanced around the congregation; most of his squadron was there, including Generals Randolph and White. John Bell Higgins was beside him wearing brilliant Navy dress whites, in stark contrast to the green Army uniforms of Joel, Carl Tucker and Bill Rich. In the congregation he saw Sergeants Hillborne and Ledbetter. The bride's side of the church was nearly full too, with friends of Susan's.

The music stopped abruptly and there was a long second of silence, then Susan stepped out into the aisle on Mr. Kneebone's arm, her long white bridal gown rustling. The congregation rose with gasps and murmurs of appreciation. Joel noted absently that somebody had gotten Mr. Kneebone an up-to-date suit.

The Wedding March began and they started down the aisle. Joel stopped breathing; she was more beautiful than he imagined. Through her veil, she was looking at him with wide, expectant blue eyes.

*Oh, God, how do I ever deserve **her**?* he thought in awe. Chappie touched his arm and whispered, "Steady there, ace!"

She shifted her bouquet, and took his arm. She hadn't looked away from him yet.

"Who gives this woman in marriage?" the pastor asked.

"I do," said Mr. Kneebone clearly, "in substitution for her mother and father who couldn't be here."

The ceremony raced forward: "—for better and for worse, until death do you part." and before he knew it, Joel said "I do" in a distant voice.

Susan said "I do" clearly, sweetly, never taking her eyes off of him. They exchanged rings and solemn vows: "With this ring, I thee wed and all my worldly goods to thee I do endow."

"By the authority vested in me by the State of New Jersey and the Baptist Church, I now pronounce you man and wife. You may kiss the bride," the pastor said, as if it was just an ordinary thing to say.

A teary-eyed Millie reached over, pulled up Susan's veil, and took her flowers. Susan turned up her face, and closed her eyes. It was the sweetest, warmest kiss Joel had ever experienced.

The pastor gently turned Joel around by his elbow, and pronounced, "Ladies and gentlemen, I present to you Colonel and Mrs. Joel T. Knight."

The walk down the aisle was dreamlike. *She actually did it! She married me! I can't believe it.* Susan pulled him close. He smelled her perfume and the strange, wonderful crispness of her gown. *She really is my wife!*

The reception was a blur, all handshakes and congratulations. There was a small mountain of gifts, many from Wisconsin and Colorado. They cut the beautiful cake, and fed each other bites of the sweet goodness as they laughed. Susan disappeared, and then was back, in a smart looking travel outfit. Joel would travel in uniform.

They made their way out to the waiting Packard through handfuls of thrown rice. The car had a big "just married" sign on the rear bumper. They climbed in, and Susan kissed him again. He almost missed the first shift as they drove away.

Chapter 92

22 June 1945

Reykjavik – East Army Air Field, Iceland

0230 Hours

Reconnaissance

First Lieutenant Thomas "Tom" Bellingham took off in his F-13 and began a climbing turn toward Norway. He patted the pocket of his A-2 jacket; the sun would be up soon, and he wanted the sunglasses ready.

Unlike the shiny natural aluminum finish on the B-29's, Bellingham's photo version was a dull gray-white. Under the cockpit window, a buck-toothed cartoon man peered into a crooked telescope at an ugly caricature of Adolf Hitler, above the name "Peeping Tom."

His radio man turned toward the cockpit as he leaned back in his seat. "Pilot, we got a weather update. We'll fly out of these clouds in about fifteen minutes or so, and have clear skies all the way."

"Sounds good. Pilot out."

Bellingham's flight was the third in three days sent to find which German base in Norway the JU-88s and He-177s had come from. Two days earlier, Bellingham's roommate, Lt. Timothy "Tiny Tim" Scarlatti, had flown over the sprawling German Navy base at Trodheim, but most of the aircraft were Kreigsmarine seaplanes. Yesterday, the squadron's "old man," thirty-two-year-old Captain William "Wild Bill" Brown had flown north, but the German base at Bodö had almost no activity.

Bellingham's crew had gotten the toughest target – the German base at Stavanger. The base was the south-most, and had hosted Heinkel HE-111s early in the war. It seemed logical that the longer range JU-88s and He-177s would be based there, on a Westward bulge in the Norwegian coastline that minimized the distance to Great Britain or Iceland.

The Norwegian resistance repeatedly warned the Allies that the base was heavily protected by anti-aircraft guns and a mixed staffel of long-winged ME-109s and a handful of older FW-190s. A small number of ME-109Es rounded out the defensive force.

Just what we need – "special models" of the 109, and they're just waiting just for us, groused Bellingham to himself. That the long wing '109's were old models, originally intended for the still-born Nazi aircraft carrier didn't lessen their danger, at least in his mind. His mood was morose on this his first real combat mission. He hadn't slept well.

As promised, they flew out of the clouds into brilliant sunshine. His navigator quickly spotted the tiny, unnamed island used as an intermediate checkpoint, and had Bellingham adjust his course a bit.

"This far north, you just don't dare to trust magnetic compasses," the man drawled in his Tennessee accent.

Bellingham leveled out at 30,000 feet, and settled in; they had close to two hours to go.

A smudge on the horizon signaled they were getting close. Bellingham spoke into the mic, "OK, crew, listen up. As briefed, we're coming in straight over the base, heading about 0-1-5 degrees. If 'Shutters' gets what we need, we'll high tail it home. Otherwise, we'll swing north, and make a pass heading due south. If that doesn't work, we go home anyway; no sense in pushing our luck."

Nineteen-year-old Second Lieutenant Lyle "Shutters" Ryan grinned at the nickname. He loved working with the big cameras on this airplane more than anything he'd ever done. He was anxious to show the pilot what he could do. Even though he had checked them several times, he carefully went through the checklists for each camera, making sure that the heaters were on, the fuses weren't blown and the lens covers were off. His hands were sweaty from nervousness inside his leather gloves.

Bellingham surveyed the base with powerful binoculars, *looks like normal activity.*

Then he spotted several JU-88s being prepped for flight. He hoped the enemy observers on duty were all looking to the south-west, the direction the British attacked from. Bellingham had carefully verified his aircraft wasn't leaving a revealing vapor trail. The Norwegians had assured them the German base wasn't equipped with RADAR; Bellingham sure hoped so. His aircraft would be invisible and silent to those on the ground. Or so they had been assured.

Below him in the nose of the plane, Shutters bent over his task, with intense concentration. All of his cameras were working just fine. The scene below was perfectly lit; the young man hummed a nameless tune as he worked.

Moments later, Bellingham heard his intercom, "Pilot, this is the Camera Operator. We got some swell exposures of the entire facility. I believe we can go home, sir."

"Good work, Shutters. We're heading home, guys." Bellingham wheeled the big airplane around, and set a reciprocal course.

Five hours later

"Excellent photographs, Bellingham. Thank your camera operator. We'll visit our new friends as soon as possible," said the now affable colonel. He patted Bellingham on the shoulder, "Good work, son."

Chapter 93

26 June 1945

Iceland

1500 Hours

Strike Back

Late the next afternoon, as thirty B-29s took off and formed up, camouflaged Germans photographed them. The Germans were astonished at how quickly the Americans replaced the destroyed bombers. It bespoke a production capability far beyond their own. They raced back to the cave; Berlin would want to see these photos.

"The timing," the briefer had told the B-29 crews, "is intended to put you inbound into Stavanger just as the sun is setting, to put the sun in the eyes of any snoopy Germans."

Major William "Billy" Johnson was commanding the attack with great anticipation. A twelve mission B-24 pilot with the 13th Air Force in the Pacific, he'd been thrilled with the transfer to B-29's.

He'd discussed this attack long and hard with the mission planners and the Colonel as they poured over the aerial photographs, and he'd convinced them at last to let him attack at 20,000 feet instead of 10,000 feet higher.

Lower is more accurate, he kept reminding them, and in the end, won them over.

Truth is, I'd rather go in at 15,000 – even more accurate, but those German 88 anti-aircraft guns in the photos changed my mind.

"Look! We caught 'em with their pants down!" his co-pilot shouted. They could see more than a dozen JU-88s lined up to take off as they swept over the airfield. Other German aircraft were waiting nearby with engines running.

"Bombs away," intoned their bombardier. Twenty-nine other B-29s followed his example.

"Tail end Charlie, report bomb strikes," Johnson yelled into his mike as if shouting would help the radio operator on the last airplane in the formation hear better.

With bombers on the runway, maybe they can't launch fighters, he said to himself, hopefully.

"Lead, tail end Charlie; we got good strikes right across the planes waiting to take off, lots of secondary's, and it looks like we hit the runway pretty good too. Wait – aw, crap! They're launching '109's and Focke Wulfs downwind from the other end of the runway. We're gonna have company soon, and how!"

"How many bogies, Charlie? What're we up against?"

"Flack, too, Lead, and lots of it. We better scram now! Uh oh, it looks like three '109's got off, looks like maybe five or six more may join in. Can't see any more. Charlie out."

"Lead, Yellow four. There are about eight Focke Wulfs taking off from an auxiliary field."

On Johnson's urgent command, the formation began a graceful, if ponderous, turn to the left, back toward Iceland. He didn't need to tell the pilots to go to full throttle.

"Oh, man, here they come, and they're madder'n hornets! Blue Two, on your port side! Look out!"

"Yellow 5, on your tail!"

"Get him! Get Him! Good shooting!"

"Gotcha, you dirty Nazi SOB!"

"To your left! To your left!"

The radio chatter flew as the angry Messerschmitts darted in and out of the formation. The Focke Wulfs joined moments later. Johnson felt the guns on his own ship pounding away. A gray-green blur flashed past the cockpit, then another, and in an instant, both were gone.

Without warning, a B-29 rolled onto its back and in a huge ball of bright red fire, dove straight down.

"Bailout! Bailout!" someone shouted, but the stricken craft smashed into the icy sea with no parachutes. A German fighter cartwheeled across the sky, leaving a crazy corkscrew trail of smoke and sparks; a second turned back toward land, trailing a thin line of smoke. As suddenly as the battle began, it was over.

"Close up the formation. Tail gunners, keep a sharp eye for long range fighters; we're still in range for ME-410's. Aircraft commanders, give me casualty and damage reports," Johnson commanded.

They had drawn blood, but not without cost, Johnson knew. There had been eleven men on that B-29, and he had known most of them. Three other bombers were damaged, and might fall short on the return trip. He clenched his jaw as they flew west through darkening skies; he had some very difficult letters to write.

Chapter 94

26 June 1945

Luftwaffe Headquarters, Berlin

Generalleutnant Wever's office

1830 Hours

New Assignment

A staff Colonel waved a dispatch as he walked briskly into Generalleutnant Wever's office "Have you seen this—this outrage, General?" His face was red with anger.

"No, Horst, I haven't, you haven't let me see it yet," Wever replied evenly.

"The Americans attacked Stavanger-Sola with those B-29 Boeings, and destroyed most of I/JG 77s Messerschmitts, and at least twenty of KG 30s JU-88s! Can you imagine it? And JG 77 lost several FW-190s as well."

Wever tapped the ash from his cigarette, "Did you think, Horst, that Norway is our private playground? If the British attack us there, why not the Americans? Let me see that."

Wever shrugged; he'd been expecting retaliation for the destruction of the big new American planes. He'd already decided what units to take planes from to restore Stavanger. He initialed that he had read the dispatch, and wordlessly passed it back to the outraged Colonel. The man took it from him a bit briskly, and stamped self-importantly out. Wever put the event out of his mind; he had more important issues to resolve.

To his astonishment, the General Staff was far more disturbed by his Colonel's report than he was. Even more amazing, he was ordered to attack Iceland with heavy bombers as soon as could be arranged.

He sat at his desk rubbing his forehead, pondering, then suddenly knew exactly who should be given the task: von Schroeder! Schroeder had accomplished little since the first American raid; Wever had forbidden him to fly any more of the transatlantic attacks. The man needed an assignment, so he wouldn't grow stale. The more he thought about it, the more attractive the idea became. He reached for the telephone.

Von Schroeder leapt to his feet holding the telephone, "Jawohl, General Wever! It shall be my honor, sir!" Already, his mind was racing, choosing mentally the pilots he would lead, because of course, with such an important mission, who else would lead it?

Before he could complete the thought, Wever said, "You are not to lead this attack, Gerhard; you are too valuable. Plan and execute this carefully, and I assure you, there will more missions in your future."

Von Schroeder immediately began assembling a Besondere Aufgae Gruppe [special task group] for the attack, bringing together the best of his experienced pilots from the American raid, over the outrage of their current commanders.

"So, you would like to discuss this *personnel* issue with Generalleutnant Wever himself?" he asked an irate Oberstleutnant squadron commander mildly. The man sputtered, and hung up. Von Schroeder smiled, and placed another tick mark on his list.

Schroeder stayed up all night, planning, thinking, playing issues one against the other. By dawn, he had made his decision and drawn up his orders: sixty of the six-engine GO-460s of I/KS 17 would be dispatched to Norway; on 12 July, a counter raid would be launched against Reykjavik-East U.S. Army Air Base. He smiled in grim anticipation. He'd be there to watch them launch and return. Wever might forbid him to fly combat missions, but he could be there to cheer on his crews. They would bring him victory yet again.

At Reykjavik – East Army Airfield, the 513th Bomb wing had been reinforced with two full squadrons of new rocket-equipped Lockheed P-38s.

Chapter 95

12 July 1944

Stavanger-Sola, Norway

Early Morning

Retaliation

Von Schroeder stood wrapped in his leather overcoat, his arms folded, watching in pride as his Gothas taxied to takeoff. The crews he'd brought back together had quickly gelled into a tight, well disciplined unit, as he'd known they would. Many had become friends preparing for the America raid, and had worked together well then. There was no reason to think they wouldn't this time.

With a great roar, the lead Gotha raced down the runway, and lifted gracefully into the air. Its landing gear had hardly retracted as a second bomber lifted off behind it. A continuous roar echoed off the mountains as all sixty took to the air. They were formed up nicely as they flew out of sight, von Schroeder noted with satisfaction.

"Let's see now how they like a taste of my Gothas," he gloated as the thunder of 360 engines faded.

Reykjavik – East Army Airfield

The RADAR operator jerked upright in his chair.

"Air raid! Air Raid! Bogies inbound at 3-2 thousand feet, heading 3-4-5 degrees at 2-7-5 knots. Estimate forty plus aircraft; returns indicate Gotha bat planes. Estimate in bombing range in seven minutes."

The duty officer slammed his hand on the alert Klaxon button; a second button started the air raid sirens wailing. He reached for his phone.

At the alert area, thirteen pilots raced toward their P-38s, behind the crew chiefs and other crewmen. Across the airfield, anti-aircraft crews ran toward their guns.

First Lieutenant John "Jonnie" Johnson swung his P-38L into position, and roared down the runway. On the nose of his plane, his caricature grinned over the name "Jonnie Boy." As he lifted off, he radioed, "Norse Green flight, form up on me." Second Lieutenant Mike Phillips, his wingman, was on his left wing.

As Johnson's flight climbed toward the attackers, a second group of P-38s raced skyward; Norse Yellow flight would "tag team" with the first flight. The Gothas were in for a rough reception, if these pilots had anything to say about it.

Jonnie Johnson saw the stark white contrails being traced across the pure blue sky; the German bombers were leaving arrow straight lines.

There sure are a lot of them; I'm not sure we can get there soon enough to prevent the attack.

He took his flight above the Germans, and rolled into the attack.

"Norse Green flight, watch out for rocket guns. Don't get too close – remember our rockets are longer range than theirs. Follow me down."

Sure enough, the Gothas are firing rockets at us, he thought as he dove through the formation, his engines a thundering roar in his ears. *Let's see how they like **our** rockets!*

With grim satisfaction, he watched his rockets blow chunks off the left side of a Gotha. He saw Phillips firing out of the corner of his eye, also to good effect.

As Johnson pulled up to attack again, a broken P-38 plunged past, rolling wildly out of control as angry flames streamed from the right engine. There was no right wing. A stick figure man separated from the stricken craft, and a parachute opened. The aircraft dove straight down and slammed into the glacier in a spray of ice he could see from altitude.

The previously perfect sky was marred with twisting, swirling vapor trails as fighters from both Norse flights hammered the attackers. An ugly black smoke trail marked a dying Gotha as it fell nearly straight down to the pristine snow below. Another of the huge flying wings blew apart in the air, filling the sky with shiny, flashing shards. A third suddenly folded in the middle, its wingtips touching. It flopped awkwardly through the sky to smash into the ice below.

"They're turning!"Johnson shouted. Resolutely, the German bombers were tracking for the American base and the defenseless B-29s. Before Johnson could get in range, bombs begin to fall.

The sight enraged him, and he shoved both throttles into War Emergency setting. He raced the sleek Lighting through the German formation from rear to front, firing at every bomber he could. Only a couple of German gunners dared to fire at him; they risked hitting their own planes. Grimly, he dove away to the right, twisting to throw off the gunners, coming back for another pass. His wingman was nowhere to be seen.

Climbing again to get above the Germans, Johnson saw the formation turning, heading to Norway. A glance revealed that Phillips had somehow found him again; the kid gave him a thumbs-up sign. Johnson pointed down, and they attacked the invaders again.

Post Attack Debrief

"Here's what it looks like, sir," Johnson grimly told his wing commander. His forehead still wore the red marks from his flying cap. "Green flight lost three – Arnold, Kingsborough, and Magee. Elliot and Fitzpatrick are wounded, but got back OK. Graysen is missing; somebody said they saw him belly in on the glacier, but we haven't found him. I claim one bomber and Timmons another. Several were damaged, but I don't know of any probables."

"What about Yellow flight, Lieutenant?" asked the Lieutenant Colonel quietly.

"Sir, I lost four pilots – Greenberg, Anderson, Montgomery Jr. and Landers. Montgomery Jr. and Landers collided." He stopped and swallowed, blinking back tears. "There are two of my flight missing – Potter and Evens. Neither was seen bailing out, but we haven't finished searching. We got one Gotha – not sure who should claim it yet, and I agree with Lieutenant Johnson, we damaged a lot of them."

"Not our best day, gentlemen: seven KIA, three MIA, two wounded, for three Germans destroyed and several damaged. We're going to have to work up better tactics before we take these Jerrys on again."

Aboard Retaliation Flight

200 Miles from Norway

"Tell me our losses, Berger," Oberstleutnant Walter Pieper, the senior pilot said to his radio man.

"Three lost over the target, sir, and another dropped out of formation about twenty miles back. He may not make it back. Seventeen of our aircraft have damage, three severe, with possibly thirty-five wounded. At this point, the three severely damaged

Gothas all believe that they can make it to Stavanger, sir, but may have to crash land."

Pieper sighed, "These are not such horrible losses, but I fear we inflicted far too little damage for our trouble. Von Schroeder is not likely to be pleased."

Chapter 96

17 July 1945

Millville Army Air Field Building 1, Colonel Joel Knight's Office

1530 Hours

Discovery

"Well, I'll be! Say, Joel, look! They found the German bat wing plant! You'll never believe where!" Lieutenant Colonel "Chappie" Chapman was reading a classified intelligence dispatch from the secure teletype.

"Where, Chappie? What is this, 'Twenty Questions?'" Joel teased.

"No, it's in Spain! Spain, of all places! Fer crying out loud, no wonder they couldn't find 'em; they were lookin' in France."

"Spain? Really! Who would have thought of that? Boy, I wonder if we'll declare war on Spain – that's a violation of the Neutrality Act. That'd be another front if they do. Man, oh man! Where in Spain?"

Chappie said, "Near the town of "Boltana". Where's that?"

"No idea whatsoever. I'll have Bill get us a map."

In forty minutes First Sergeant Bill Madsen not only found a map of Spain, but neatly highlighted the little town. The map was shaded to show terrain. Boltana was in the Western foothills of the Pyrenees Mountains. Madsen stood silently as the two officers poured over the map.

"Doesn't make sense, Chappie. Why build an airplane plant in the mountains? How do you fly them out once you built them?" Joel wondered out loud.

"Sir, pardon me, I think you'll find a plateau there between two of the ridges. Looks like plenty of room for a plant and a runway," Bill interjected.

Lieutenant Colonel Chappie Chapman said, "Say, those Jerrys are too clever by half. Even if we'd flown right over the border, this place is behind the ridges and we probably would never have seen the plant, even if we looked in its direction. How'd they ever find it?"

"I heard some scuttlebutt at the NCO club, Colonel," Bill said offhandedly, as he inspected his fingernails.

"And just what was that, pray tell, First Sergeant?" Chappie said, cocking his head skeptically. In truth, he knew that Army Master Sergeants, like Navy Chiefs, had a grapevine that somehow distributed even the most secret information hours before official channels got it; he knew not to question the "how" of Bill's information.

"Sir, the story is that a teenaged German soldier at the Spanish base went AWOL, got to France, and was caught by General Donovan's guys. The kid was a guard at the plant, and he sang like a canary. He just wanted to surrender, because he thought they'd let him go home." He shook his head at the naiveté.

"Interesting scuttlebutt, Bill," Joel told him, "any confirmation of that cock and bull story?"

Bill smiled inscrutably. "The next dispatch will confirm it, sir," he said with confidence. It did.

Chapter 97

19 July 1945

Andrews Army Air Field

0710 Hours

Conference

The big, four-engine Douglas C-54 transport dropped out of the misty overcast and landed smoothly. Such landings were common, but the attention paid to this arrival was far from normal. Within minutes, a triple-tailed Lockheed C-69 military passenger plane landed; as it taxied in, a Consolidated Aircraft C-87, the passenger version of the B-24, also landed.

A line of Packard and Lincoln limousines, and formal Cadillac sedans waited for the passengers to disembark. The left side propellers had hardly stopped turning on the Douglas as Army enlisted men pushed wheeled stairs into position. At the foot of the stairs, a two star general and his full colonel aide waited. The aircraft door was opened and latched into place. Several senior officers began their decent.

The general and his aide came to attention and presented parade ground perfect salutes, "Good morning, General Eisenhower. Welcome to Andrews Army Air Field. I hope you had a pleasant trip, sir."

Eisenhower returned the salutes wordlessly, his face solemn. He and his entourage entered two of the cars and were whisked away. Behind them, other senior U.S., British, and French officers were escorted to the waiting cars and followed Eisenhower. The last aircraft began disembarking passengers as well; the general couldn't remember when he'd seen so much brass all arriving at the same time; something big was up.

The Pentagon

The room was tension-filled as everyone awaited the cars from Andrews. The protocol officer was working overtime setting up the polished oak table. He had to contend with the President, the Secretary of War, the Joint Chiefs, and senior British officers. And the French – he rolled his eyes; they were especially difficult.

It still wasn't clear who all had come from Europe, but the sweating Lieutenant Colonel knew that at least General Eisenhower, General "Tooey" Spaatz, General Patton, and Field Marshall Montgomery were confirmed. One of French General Charles de Gaulle's senior colonels was rumored to be on the last plane. The Colonel was working out the relative dates of rank and position in the Allied command structure so none of the delicate personalities would be offended.

"Sirs, may I have your attention, please? General Eisenhower and company are in the building."

Harry Truman watched Eisenhower closely; it was the first time he'd seen him since the invasion.

He's a good man, he thought, *but the strain is showing.*

The greeting civilities over, a grim faced Dwight Eisenhower began his briefing. His aide had set up an easel with large maps.

"Mr. President, Mr. Secretary of War, gentlemen of the Joint Chiefs, Field Marshall Montgomery, General Sir Burns, Colonel Piccard. Good morning. With your kind permission, Mr. President, I'd like to begin with an overview before getting into specifics."

Harry Truman gave a curt nod, his sharp eyes shining behind his glasses, "That's fine, General Eisenhower."

Ike just plain looks tired, Truman thought; *have to see if I can get him some rest.*

Ike turned to the maps, his flat Midwest accent clear and careful, "In the thirteen months since D-Day, our initial progress has slowed to the point of stagnation. The Allies currently hold some 30,000 square miles of territory in north western France. Let me put that in perspective: that is less than 15 percent of French territory. Our moves to the south and especially to the east have slowed to the point of stalemate. As we all feared, the Germans moved large numbers of reinforcements to the West following the Russian capitulation, and continue to do so. Paulus has moved a significant number of his 4th Panzer Army under Hoth to block our progress here and here." The long wooden pointer tapped the screen.

"General von Bock has similarly sent at least five – I think closer to ten – divisions of his former Army Group Center to reinforce the large Panzer army Rommel aggregated. Movement of these so-called 'mobile forces' when they get to the front has been minimal on both sides; in many cases, it has become little more than a huge artillery duel. It is reminiscent of what happened in the last war.

"A major disappointment has been our inability to maintain air superiority for any protracted period. General Spaatz will address that later. Our British, Canadian and French Allies continue to fight bravely by our sides, but for them as well, true progress is an infrequent thing.

"General Patton will brief the armor situation later. Overall, I can report that Allied troops are well supplied, and morale is good. We've begun a rotation process for troops who have been under fire for long periods, relieving them with rested, seasoned troops. Casualty rates are always too high, but remain somewhat below projections.

"What you will hear from the men following me will be variations on the same theme. To anticipate your questions, our prospects of altering this situation are slim unless we can make some major changes in our situation or the enemy's."

Truman interjected, "I don't need to hear the same thing six ways from Sunday, Ike. If time permits, we'll listen to General Patton and Field Marshall Montgomery. I want to know from General Spaatz – why do we have such a devil of a time gaining air superiority?"

General Spaatz stood, taken off guard at being called upon so soon. His aide scrambled to bring maps and photographs to the easels at the front of the room.

"Mr. President, the Germans have been throwing some remarkable new aircraft at us in the last year. Simultaneously, they are withdrawing several types; our pilots seldom report ME-109s or short-nose FW-190s. The long-nose FW-190D-9, or more properly, TA-152, is everywhere; it's a match for our Spitfires and Mustangs. They have a follow-on to the Messerschmitt ME-262, the Me-610, shown here, in production. Initially, poor engines hampered them operationally, but this aircraft is virtually invincible in combat. We believe they have produced 150-200 of them.

"Dornier's two-engine push-pull DO-335 fighter, shown here, is an effective night fighter. Now, it has a jet engine in the rear. The performance improvement is stunning and it's been deadly to those who have encountered it. It is in volume production.

"Gotha is producing improved versions of the six-engine flying wing bombers at high rates. A little-known German manufacturer, Blohm & Voss, mostly known for flying boats, is building the powerful, destructive three engine ground attack aircraft you see here; sorry for the poor quality. It is designated BV-271. It's been encountered in small numbers so far, but it is very effective.

"Our British cousins rushed their jet powered Gloster Meteors into production, but they are having problems, mainly short range and random flame-outs – that means the flame in the engine goes out, and it's hard to restart. By late November, we hope to have some Lockheed P-80 jets available. They also have problems, including similar engine problems as the Meteors, and compressor stalls, at high angles of attack. Now, Republic Aircraft's XP-84 looks very promising; it has a different jet engine which is not so sensitive to high angles of attack, but it is still several months off."

Truman's confusion at the last statement showed on his face. Spaatz quickly added, "Sir, compressor stalls happen when the engine can't get enough air when the nose is too high. Until those airplanes are sorted out and available in numbers, we're going to have a hard time countering the German jets, sir."

Truman thought, *I appreciate the information, but I still didn't understand the why.*

"General, remember that I was an artillery officer, not an aviator. Explain to me why our Mustangs and Spitfires can't stop the German jets."

Spaatz spread his hands, "Simply put, sir, the German jets are 100 to 150 miles per hour faster; some are nearly 200 miles per hour faster. They attack our fastest fighters, then zoom away and we can't catch 'em. Gunners on Allied bombers can't traverse their guns fast enough to shoot them. They have large numbers of them, and are fighting over their own territory. Nearly all are equipped with the rocket guns, too."

Truman nodded. *These Krauts are tough nuts to crack,* he thought, *how do they keep coming up with new weapons?*

"When it comes to piston powered aircraft, even their big bat-wing Gothas are difficult to knock down. And I must say with grudging admiration, they've been using their bombers brilliantly. That attack on Plymouth and Portsmouth in May was amazing – they used their long range to fly out over the Atlantic to the northwest, then turned and came in from a direction no one was expecting. Caught us by surprise, and did a lot of damage.

"That attack is just one example of new tactics they're using: they also do multiple attacks simultaneously. Must take incredible coordination. Last week, they hit Bristol, Coventry, Liverpool, several airfields in East Anglia, and Birmingham within thirty minutes of each other, all different raids. They used hundreds of

Gothas, escorted by swarms of fighters which they brought into the fight in relays.

"As General Eaker will tell you, even though we have thousands of fighters at our disposal, these multiple attacks are very difficult to defend against, since the first attack draws off the majority of our fighters. They've become adept at hitting us just as our planes land, too. I'm told the Gothas have some sort of anti-RADAR device which makes a hash of our RADAR screens, and they're hard enough to see on RADAR as it is.

"Lest I give you only bad news, Mr. President, there are several bright spots. B-29s are moving to Europe in numbers now; the 513th heavy bomb group has set up shop on Iceland. There will be nearly 300 B-29s available by next week, double that in six weeks. While we were in the air this morning, the 513th hit the German airfield at Stavanger Norway with about 200 airplanes – what was the result, Colonel Gregory?"

A slight, bespectacled man stood, "Sir, the raid was a success. Every building was damaged or destroyed, and the aircraft destroyed. They also clobbered the runways, sir. Best of all, Norwegian resistance moved in afterward and destroyed what was left, and took a lot of prisoners. You can scratch that base, sir."

A slight smile crossed Truman's face; *Small potatoes,* he thought, *but I'll take good news where I can get it.*

"OK, that's all for now, General Spaatz. What I'd like to hear next is G-2. Can we do that?" Army G-2 was the division that collected and analyzed intelligence.

The President always set the agenda, and always had the prerogative to change it. A rustling of papers and men began before General George C. Marshall could respond.

"Yes sir, Mr. President, it'll be one moment while we gather the materials." He addressed the crowded room, "Gentlemen, the following material is classified 'Top Secret'; all of you with lower levels of clearance will leave the room now."

A sallow-faced, pot-bellied Brigadier General waddled self-importantly to the front of the room. "Good morning, Mr. President. I am Brigadier General Angel McGuire, G-2 Division First Deputy Chief of Staff." He raised his nose imperiously, "If the security chief will inform us when the room is secure—."

"Ah, very well; may I begin, sir?" His voice was high and scratchy, and the smirk on his face was smarmy and insincere as he rubbed his hands together like a used car salesman closing a deal.

This pompous little man is already getting under my skin, Truman thought, then reined himself in. *Don't shoot the messenger, Harry, at least not yet.* Chuckling at his own little joke, he waved the man to begin.

"As you are no doubt aware, Mr. President, we have had multiple peace negotiation contacts from the Germans recently, mostly through the Swiss. The most recent from SS Führer Heinrich Himmler himself. It's all nonsense, of course—"

"What did he say?" Truman asked, irritation creeping into his voice.

"Oh," the man said dismissively, "he proposes a cease fire, a return to pre-war German borders and all is forgiven, with himself in charge, of course. It's just self-aggrandizement on a grand scale. He's not sincere."

Truman's famous temper got the best of him, "General, you will kindly leave such assessments to your superiors. Has there been any thing we can take seriously?"

Shaken at the reprimand, the general continued. "Sir, we have been piecing together what appears to be a serious attempt by the German 'troika,' probably without Himmler, to remake their government into a form we might like better. For example, we obtained a draft memo directing all government agencies to remove the swastika from buildings, letterheads, uniforms, battle standards, and the like. To use the Russian term, there seems be the beginnings of a 'purge' of Nazis from senior government positions."

Truman looked sharply at the man's superior, Major General Clayton Bissell; "Is this true, Bissell? Why haven't I been informed?"

"General McGuire, why wasn't the President informed? I directed that he be given everything on this as quickly as possible." The voice was cold and menacing.

McGuire's pig-like eyes sweep to and fro, "Uh, sir, I felt we needed a more complete story, and confirmation before—"

"You are dismissed, McGuire; I will see you in my office later." The man reddened, then paled as the implications sank in. He left the room to silence.

"Mr. President, I apologize. You should have been informed days ago. I was lead to believe you had been. Here's the situation as we know it. Himmler has been arrested, and possibly executed. Many high ranking Nazi Party officials are under arrest and in custody. Our sources tell us that 'Gestapo' Müller has taken Himmler's place; he's well known to be apolitical – he's no Nazi – but he's still a tough customer. He is quite skilled at intelligence as well.

"Now, Albert Speer is a long time party member, but because he's a pragmatist more than a true believer. And frankly, they can't run the country without 'im. So, looks as if he's staying. Most of the senior Abwehr are not party members; that's true of Field Marshall Fedor von Bock, the third member of the troika, or 'dreifach,' as they call it. Some communiqué's have proposed a truce in place, to negotiate a peace."

"Never! We shall only accept an unconditional surrender!" burst out General Patton.

"I'll keep negotiations as an option, George, if you don't mind," Truman said, raising his voice only slightly. "How many of you knew about this arrest of Nazis? What about the truce request?"

Only a small handful of the men in the room raised their hands; all were G-2.

General Bissell cleared his throat, and said with a concerned look on his face, "Mr. President, there's another issue: are you aware of the contact we've had with the Russians?"

"If it's been in the last six weeks, no. What have they to say?"

"Quite a lot, sir. Again, my apologies. You recall that Marshall Stalin was badly wounded during his escape from Moscow. Whether due to his injuries or just the Russian penchant for conspiracy and intrigue, he was removed from office three days ago."

"What! My God, man, why wasn't I told? If McGuire is responsible for this, I'll fire his a--!" the President roared, slamming his fist on the table. "Not only that, I'll throw him in jail!"

"I'll find who is responsible and take the appropriate action, sir," Bissell replied through clenched teeth, very angry that his orders had been ignored a second time.

Composing himself, Bissell went on, "Do you recall the name Lavrenti Beria, sir? He was head of the Russian secret police, the NKVD. He's a ruthless, vindictive man, a Georgian like Stalin. He's responsible for the deaths of thousands of Russians. He has taken power in what amounts to a coup, and is marshalling his forces.

"According to a Russian diplomat, he has General Zukov heading up a 'Central Soviet General Army' that supposedly numbers in the hundreds of thousands, perhaps nearly a million men. He claims he'll have 10,000 heavy tanks, 20,000 aircraft, and 100,000 artillery tubes available to move westward in two months or so. We view these numbers as highly suspect; however, if they should prove to be even partially true, it would reopen the

Eastern front for the Germans, and leave them very vulnerable to us. We are attempting to confirm his claims."

"What about Marshall Stalin, then?"

"If Beria is true to form, sir, I would not be surprised if Joseph Stalin is already dead."

Truman sat back in his chair, stunned at the duplicity of a high ranking general, and the momentous news he'd just heard. He struggled to organize his thoughts while the room was silent.

"What about the German position, General Bissell? Could they withstand a Russian attack? Are we in position to take advantage of it, should it happen?"

"As to the German position, sir, they are vulnerable even without the Russians attacking. Their forces are thin almost everywhere, notwithstanding the reinforcements recently moved in. We have made the front very, very wide, and hope to make it wider yet. We believe that even without full-time air superiority, we have hurt them badly. We think they are near the end of their rope when it comes to production, especially submarines and aircraft.

"We are relentlessly pursuing the locations of munitions plants, and following up with heavy bombing when we find them. They can only do so much in caves. They are especially vulnerable when it comes to transportation: highways and railroads can't be hidden, and Allied flyers hit 'em frequently. I must defer to my combat brothers-in-arms as to our ability to take advantage of their situation."

General Ira Eaker, head of U.S. air forces in England and Iceland addressed the President, "Mr. President, in short, we are ready to hit them very hard. We and the RAF are preparing for a massive multi-city raid using more than 1500 heavy bombers and twice that many mediums. For the first time, we will include large numbers of B-29s, which carry enormous bomb loads, as you know. Weather permitting, we'll be ready within a week."

"How soon can you hit them again after that?" the President asked.

Eaker smiled, a snake's smile, the sort of smile that would have made the enemy's blood run cold, had he seen it. "Sir, it's our plan to smack them with nearly continuous raids for about a week, day and night. The idea is to spread out their fighter forces, exhaust them, and kill them, while at the same time —," He glanced at Eisenhower and Bradley sitting stoically. Patton had the look of a hungry wolf. "—At the same time, my colleagues in Infantry, Artillery and Armor are about to embark on a push of their own. If it works out as planned, the Germans will be pushed much closer to capitulation."

"And if not?"

"Then, sir, we'll have to come up with another plan." The Joint Chiefs exchanged glances; no, now was not the time.

Chapter 98

3 August 1945

The Outskirts of Berlin, Underground Operation Center

0800 Hours

Operation Intrepid, Day Two

Generalmajor von Schroeder stood stoically, arms crossed, as he watched General der Luftwaffe Galland direct fighter forces against another Allied raid. This one was headed directly at Berlin. Galland was as cool and calculating as if he were playing chess. Von Schroder had to admit that the man knew how to use his fighters; the Allies had taken heavy losses the day before.

"Ah, von Schroeder, we have a new situation here! My pilots report that this raid is made up of the new B-29 Boeings. You have had some experience with these, yes?"

"Yes, sir, and they proved to be tough nuts to crack, much harder to shoot down than the older bombers."

"We shall see; for now, prepare your Gothas; I want to hit the English Midlands again, as soon as possible."

Von Schroeder left the room immediately, and immersed himself in the planning for the raid. Two hours later, as he and his team were finishing up, a weary looking Major entered the room.

"General von Schroeder, you are requested to attend a briefing in General der Luftwaffe Galland's office immediately." A cold surge of fear coursed through von Schroeder's body.

Galland stood at the front of the room, rubbing his eyes, his usual upbeat demeanor not evident.

"Ah, von Schroeder, you are the last. Sit. Sit. Gentlemen, we have taken heavy losses this day, in the air and on the ground. You were right, von Schroeder, those B-29 Boeings are very difficult. They got through our defenses, and did significant damage to Central Berlin, including Luftwaffe Headquarters. We brought fresh forces against them as they retreated, and dropped a number of them, but too late, they had already done their jobs."

He had a deeply weary, grim look, "They hit Luftwaffe Headquarters; the building complex was destroyed, and the wreckage fell into the basements. Many, many lives were lost, including senior staff."

Von Schroeder felt his blood run cold – *Dear God, General Wever was on duty today – is he—*

He forced his mouth to say, "What of General Wever and his staff?"

Galland's normally smiling face was somber, "The General would not evacuate to the shelters; he and his staff are dead."

Von Schroeder's ears rang with shock; he felt intense sorrow at the loss of his mentor and friend, to the point of physical pain in his chest. He stifled a great sob only with great effort. Then, the anger, fierce, bitter, inconsolable anger burned like an unquenchable fire. He raced from the room, and violently threw up in the men's room. The bile burned his throat. His face, when he washed, was hard, as if carved from flint.

The Americans, again! Always, the Americans! Once again, they have destroyed everything I value! I will kill them! I will kill them! And that miserable upstart, Joel Knight, if it's the last thing I do!

Chapter 99
15 August 1945
The White House Briefing Room
1730 Hours
Mixed Report

All of the Joint Chiefs looked fatigued, weary, as men bearing heavy news.

"Mr. President," began General George Marshall his voice strained, "Things haven't exactly gone our way the last ten days, to understate it. The air raids, code named Intrepid, did not accomplish our goals. We bombed targets around the clock all over Germany, often simultaneously. Yet, the Luftwaffe is more resilient than we expected, and even hit us back.

"We believe that German losses have been high, but so have ours. We and the British lost more than 300 bombers between us, and close to 400 fighters. In terms of men, that's over 2800 men. Many, of course, bailed out and were captured. Probably a third or more of that number are dead.

"As to German losses – well, it's likely they are at least as large as our own, but actual numbers are hard to establish. Our best guess is 200-300 of their fighters were shot down.

"Our ground forces met with terrific resistance, and made only scattered breakthroughs; overall, we advanced only a few dozen miles. In the final analysis, despite tremendous efforts by everyone, on the ground and in the air, we failed to make the progress we hoped for."

Truman sat with his elbows on the tabletop, his chin propped on his clenched fists, saying nothing. He was steeling himself for what he was sure was coming.

"Well, boys, where do we go from here?" he said finally.

Marshall glanced at Admiral William Leahy, Chairman of the Joint Chiefs.

"Sir," Leahy said heavily, "we have decided to ask your permission to use the bomb."

Truman's jaw set, and Leahy was sure he'd decide to turn them down.

Truman sat back in his chair, suddenly looking smaller, somehow; "Boys, this is hard for me to tell you. Looks like you've been feed some bum dope on the bomb. The test was a fizzle, didn't work worth a damn. Oppenheimer says they can fix it, but it could take awhile. I don't know whether we can believe them, or not."

Leahy felt like he'd been hit in the gut; he'd counted on being able to pull the atomic bunny out of his hat. His stomach hurt.

How can we get out of this mess, he asked himself. *We can't depend on the Russians.*

"How long until we'll have a useable bomb?" he asked, grasping at straws.

Truman answered, "They say about six weeks. 'Course, they'll have to test again. How do you propose to use it?"

Leahy licked his dry lips; "We're divided on that, sir." He glanced at Hap Arnold; he knew Hap was against using the powerful weapon on European cities –"on fellow Christians," as he put it.

"Two of us want to hit Berlin first; the others want to do a demonstration, maybe against an uninhabited Baltic island." He'd promised Hap not to reveal his feelings to the President.

I hate that we're not united on this.

The President screwed up his face in thought, "Hmmm. Can't see the sense in wasting an expensive bomb on a demonstration.

Let's just kill 'em. We'll go for Berlin soon's they have a reliable one to offer us. Is the Atomic Squadron in Iceland ready?"

"Yes, sir, they're well trained and practiced. All they need is a bomb."

"OK," Truman said, "we'll keep up the pressure, and use the bomb when it's ready. What else?"

Again, Leahy felt his gut tighten. *I'm getting too old for this*, he thought, not for the first time.

"Well, Mr. President, a strange situation. Our troops – some of the few actually moving forward – were closing in on a small Belgian town on the German border, with every expectation of crossing over and actually being on German soil." Admiral Leahy said. "As we began our artillery barrage, a German officer suddenly appeared, waving a white flag, asking for a brief truce and a parley."

"A parley? They wanted to surrender? Why are you telling me?"

Leahy continued, looking grim, "No, sir, not a surrender. The German, a young Lieutenant, said it was vitally important to both sides that the most senior American officer present come at once under flag of truce to speak with his colonel. The senior man was an infantry captain, but just as he was leaving with the German, a halftrack drove up with a colonel in it. His name is Tobias Bromley—"

"I know 'Cough' Bromley, sir," said George Marshall, "he served on my staff back in '38 or '39. Good man, very good man. He'll have a star before this is all over."

"Cough?" asked Truman.

Marshall smiled, "Army humor, Mr. President – Tobias Bromley – TB – cough?"

The President shook his head and smiled slightly, "Go on, please!"

"Yes, sir. Well, Colonel Bromley immediately ordered a cease fire, and went with the German. They took him to a building destroyed in the Great War, and then rebuilt on the same foundation. The Germans were using it as a local headquarters, and moved to a basement as our forces moved in. That's when they discovered about thirty tons of phosgene gas shells."

Truman's head jerked, and he gasped, turning pale; he'd never been gassed, but he'd seen plenty who had been. "Phosgene – that's a slow, horrible way to die, and no honor in the bargain," he said slowly. The men with him nodded silently.

"What do the Germans want?" he asked, his voice shaken. "Those shells were supposed to have been destroyed after 1918."

"Apparently, they were overlooked because the building had been destroyed. Bromley says the German colonel was very upset. He was afraid that we'd think they were going to use the shells. The fact that he had no artillery tubes backs up his story. That and the fact that the shells are dated around 1917. He proposes a local cease fire while his troops aid Allied troops in moving the gas out.

"Sir, here's the thing: they're not far from the Demer River. The Demer connects to the Rupel, then the Schelde, and finally comes out to sea at Antwerp. We could truck the shells to the river, load them on barges, and haul them out to sea. We need your OK. The Department of State told us just before this meeting that they received notice from the German government through the Swiss Embassy confirming this story. This could be a breakthrough, Mr. President; they're trying to show us that they can be reasonable and are willing to cooperate."

Truman said intensely, "Do you know how dangerous those old shells are? And getting them to the river and out to sea – all it would take is one hot shot fighter pilot, one rifleman on either side with a lucky shot, and we'd have a first class disaster on our hands. Do we have any atropine on hand as antidote? Do the Germans?"

"There is no antidote, sir. None. If it's liquid, it can be neutralized somewhat with sodium bicarbonate. If it's gas, ammonia can be used, but that's dangerous by itself."

"My God, what a mess," Truman said.

As Truman contemplated, a messenger knocked discreetly, and entered. Truman sat back as he read. He blew out his breath.

"Boys, the German government has officially proposed a twenty-four hour truce all across Europe while we work together to move those gas shells out. Guess they realize how touchy those shells are, too. Department of State is clamoring to see me; I suppose they'll want me to surrender first!" Truman had little respect for what he termed the "striped pants boys."

George Marshall said urgently, "Sir, if we handle this right, we might be able to extend the truce indefinitely. Sir, this could be the first step to peace, and we wouldn't have to use the bomb."

"Yes, George, it could be; it could indeed. Let's see how to cover ourselves and our troops and still get those shells removed. And make sure this isn't some elaborate hoax. Have the Brits and French been informed? Where do they stand on a truce? Get some answers pronto."

Generalmajor Freiherr Gerhard von und zu Schroeder flew to his headquarters immediately after hearing that Wever died. His staff had never seen him so distraught; he paced back and forth in his office, muttering and swearing under his breath, then slamming his fist on his desk. Through the office windows, they could see him waving his arms wildly, his muffled shouts a mixture of curses and prayers. He sat quietly and wept. Then he got up abruptly, and went to the cabinet where the Order of Battle tables were kept.

He was rifling through the documents when his worried adjutant knocked on the door and entered the room discretely, "Sir, may I bring you anything?"

"What?" von Schroeder roared, spinning around, then softening when he saw who it was. "I am in need of nothing, thank you Anton. You and the staff may leave for the day."

"Of course, sir. Until morning, then." He backed out the door.

Leutnant Anton Kriebs entered Bomber Command headquarters the following morning at 0600 hours; his boss was an early riser. He brought the first cup of coffee and gasped slightly when he saw Generalmajor von Schroeder still pacing, in need of a shave, talking out loud, his uniform disheveled. His bloodshot eyes looked out over heavy, dark bags. He had obviously worked through the night.

"Yes, Anton? Ah, my morning coffee, on time as always!" Schroeder took the steaming cup with a sudden, grateful smile. He glanced at his watch.

"Assemble the senior staff at 0800 hours, for mission planning. Thank you." He lifted the cup in salute, sipped the strong brew, and sat it on the cluttered table.

As he left, Anton Kriebs thought, *last night he was wild eyed, a crazy man; I thought he would hurt himself. Today, his old intensity is back; what does he have in mind?*

In his office, von Schroeder told himself, *I always do best when I have firmly decided upon a course of action. Now I know what to do.*

Before his men assembled, von Schroeder shaved, put on a clean shirt and tidied up his office.

"Have you heard, Herr General? The government announced a twenty-four hour truce while the Whermacht and the Allies clear out some old gas shells from the Great War?"

Von Schroeder's eyes were still bloodshot; he never could sleep when he was upset. He waved away the man's question.

"Yes, yes, that won't affect us. Now," he said fiercely, slamming the table with his fist, his voice rising with every word, "we shall strike back as never before. So far, the American capitol, Washington D.C., has been struck glancing blows only. We will hit them so hard they will be 100 years rebuilding! We shall use every available Gotha, overwhelm their defenses, and drive them down as Germany has been driven down!" He slammed his fist on the table again and looked sharply at his men. There was surprise on several faces, but to his satisfaction, more than a few were nodding in agreement with him.

Unbidden, a sinister look came on his face, "There will be also a mission within a mission; I require six crews and aircraft – volunteers."

He looked at each man harshly. "This will be a one way mission, for the Glory of Germany; there will not be fuel enough to return. I do not ask for suicide, but I require a willingness to surrender afterward. This is not to be spoken of, except to the crews you recruit. You must allow them to decline, yes? It must be truly voluntary."

To his gratification, the men looked eager to learn more. *I knew these men were not cowards*, he thought proudly.

"What is the target, sir?" an eager major asked.

"You must all swear to secrecy, yes?" Again, he looked at each man, and each looked steadily back.

"I have learned the Americans are developing a new type of super bomb, that somehow uses the energy within the atoms of the mineral uranium." He shrugged to show that he had no understanding of how that could be.

"They have a massive facility near the town of Oak Ridge, in their state of Tennessee, to purify this mineral, to build this bomb. If we don't try to return, we can reach this easily. We must, we must destroy it before they can use it at against the Fatherland. Who will volunteer?" To his immense relief, every man quickly raised his hand. It filled him with pride that such fine warriors would be so willing to follow him.

Chapter 100

10 August 1945

Oval Office

1330 Hours

Teleconference

Harry Truman said loudly, "Mr. Prime Minister, we heard that the Luftwaffe Chief, Generalleutnant Wever, was killed in Berlin. Has there been any confirmation? If so, who will replace him? My Air Corps men are very anxious to know who they're up against."

Through the noise and static, Churchill said firmly, "Mr. President, his death has been confirmed within the hour. We believe Generaloberst Adolf Galland, the former head of the German Fighters, will take Wever's place. We are not quite sure who will take over for Galland. In the meantime, a familiar name, Generalmajor von und zu Schroeder, is taking over Bomber Command. You surely recall him, Mr. President; he's the chap who led the first raid on New York City."

"Only too well, Mr. Prime Minister. He and his dammed flying wings have become a major distraction."

"A distraction, Mr. President? One would have thought they were pummeling your cities to rubble." Churchill's dry tone held little pity; he believed the American raids were only nuisance level compared to those against Britain.

"How capable is this new man?" Truman ignored the jibe, even as it galled him.

"He is capable enough, but prone to mercurial mood changes, and precipitate action from time to time. He is Wever's chosen successor, however."

"Very well. Now, what about this twenty-four hour truce? Are you and Parliament ready to go for it? We believe it could be a door to possible peace talks, but we're wary as to their ulterior motives."

"Yes, yes, quite so," Churchill replied. "We, too, are chary as to possible skullduggery on the part of the Bosch. Parliament have given me discretion to make the decision. It is quite the conundrum. However, one of my chaps did a keen bit of research, and discovered in the records of the Armistice Commission a notation regarding a gas shell depository in the town where the shells were discovered. There is no disposal record, so the German story holds water. As the saying goes, 'the devil's in the details'; how do we notify every Tommy and GI to hold fire? For that matter, how will the Jerrys tell their troops? The whole thing could dissolve into disaster in a heartbeat."

"I agree, Mr. Prime Minister, yet this could be a momentous opportunity; we mustn't let it pass us by."

"What I have to propose to you. Mr. President, is—"

Chapter 101

29 August 1945

At Home

1930 Hours

Warnings

"Joel, we need to talk."

Joel was still very much an "apprentice" husband, but he'd learned what those words meant; something was really bothering her and he needed to help her work it out, *now*.

I wonder what's worrying her?

Susan went into the living room and turned on the second hand Zenith floor console radio. It hummed for a moment as the tubes warmed up, then an announcer was reading the news. Susan tuned to music, and turned it up louder than it had been. She sat across from him, a worried look drawing her face.

*"*Are you afraid someone will hear us?" Joel teased.

"Yes," she said flatly, and motioned him to sit on the couch.

No, she's not just worried, she's afraid.

She sat in the overstuffed chair and leaned toward him. "I shouldn't be telling you this," she said softly, "And you must say nothing about it, but von Schroeder's planning more raids. Big raids."

Joel tried again to lighten the mood, "Aren't you obsessing about him, just a little?"

"Not when he's obsessed with killing my husband," she said seriously.

"How do you know that?" he asked.

"I can't tell you, Joel; don't even ask."

She stood and paced back and forth across the room, then said softly, "Joel, we know that von Schroeder's mentor and father figure, General Wever, was killed by the B-29 raid on Berlin. This has me very worried; General Wever was the only 'family' von Schroeder had. He exerted an awful lot of influence over him.

"In the past, von Schroeder has struck out viciously whenever he's been hurt emotionally. Remember how he wanted you to duel? Wever's death has hurt him greatly. He will again feel alone and helpless, as he did years ago when he lost his mother and siblings. Now, I think he'll strike out at something, someone. We know he sees you as the cause of his troubles. You – we – could be in a lot of danger here at Millville."

As Joel mentally sorted it out, she continued, "And here's another thing: remember how you told me that he feints one way before striking another? Well, have you noticed that Washington, D.C. hasn't been struck, yet cities on both sides have been? Von Schroeder could strike Millville to get you, and Washington as the root of all American power."

She looked at him with those clear, ice blue eyes, "If he does, it won't be patty-cake, either; their bomber forces are bigger than ever. I think he would go all out. He's taken over for Wever, you know."

She stopped, then asked, "Joel, do you know the German term 'Gotterdammerung'?"

Joel was taken by surprise, "It's an opera – one of Wagner's, I think.

"No, not exactly." *Where is she going with this?*

"It doesn't translate exactly into English, but conveys the idea that 'if I can't win, I'll die and destroy everything around me in the process'."

"Sort of like Samson in the Bible, when he destroyed the temple of Dagon?"

"Um, yes, sort of, but without the nobility or the forgiveness. This is willful, spiteful destruction of all things good, for no justifiable reason; it's a dark view into the black depths of the German soul. Von Schroeder seems to have adopted it since Wever died."

Joel looked at her, thinking hard. His conclusion left his stomach in a knot, "Do'ya think he'll try to destroy us then, even if he dies in the attempt? Like bomb the White House, or Pentagon, something like that?"

Susan stood, crossed her arms and said firmly, "I think it certainly is possible, even probable, that he is suicidal, considering his situation. I think we'd better call General White right away, and have him warn everybody. Maybe they should persuade the President to leave town for a while."

Chapter 102

3 September 1945

Generalmajor von Schroeder's Office

0700 Hours

More plans

"Sir, that Order of Battle is out of date. I have corrections, if you wish."

"Yes, Colonel, please correct these figures; I must know exactly where we stand before we go any farther," said von Schroeder. "I must know about heavy bombers, yes? We shall discuss medium bombers later. Continue." He sat back with a placid look on his face, even though his mind was leaping from idea to idea.

"Certainly, sir," the man said, shuffling his papers. "Ah, here we are. Now, of the four-engine GO-447 aircraft, we have 397 aircraft, of which probably 75 percent could be used. By the way, of those 397, thirty-five are veterans of your first raid on New York City."

Von Schroeder smiled; *it is good to know that those sturdy airplanes are soldiering on; they served me well.*

"Of the newer, and more capable six engine GO-460s, we have 390, of which nearly all could be available. And production is robust – we are taking delivery of ten new aircraft weekly."

Von Schroeder frowned, "I'll need all the GO-460s for my America raid, but 300 GO-447s are too few to satisfy what Generaloberst Galland desires."

"Sir, if I may submit?" a Hauptman [captain] interjected. "We have not included the HE-177Greifs [Griffons]."

"No, they are far too dangerous to the crews and too few," von Schroeder growled dismissively.

"Forgive me, sir, I misspoke: I meant to say Über Greif [Super Griffon], the HE-277. I don't have the most current figures, sir, but, about 250 of the old He-177s have been modified with four engines. They could be a formidable force, I believe."

Von Schroeder sat forward, "Yes, if I could send 500 heavy bombers to England, even if some are Greifs, that would satisfy General Galland, at least as to numbers. How have these HE-277s been working out, do you know Hauptman?"

"I can speak to that, Herr General," said a major, "the modified aircraft are performing well. With two good, reliable BMW engines on each wing, it gives more than adequate service. They carry an impressive load, as well."

Von Schroeder made some notes.

"Sir, not to leap ahead, but an important component of the America raid is the number of JU-290s available to fuel them; have we enough aircraft and crews?"

"What do you think, Albert? Can we fuel 400 or so GO-460s?"

The graying Oberstleutnant bit his lip, "This would require at least 225 JU-290s, but I suspect that crews might be the bottleneck."

"So, then, we are able to refuel two GO-460s with each JU-290?" von Schroeder asked.

"Yes, sir, but not simultaneously. The addition of jet engines to the JU-290s lets them take off with such a load. They always had the capacity to hold enough fuel, just the inability to take off with it."

Just like the New York raid, von Schroeder thought, *once again, the equipment is ahead of the crews. Well, I know how to resolve that: hard work!*

Chapter 103

5 September 1945

Generalmajor von Schroeder's office

0700 Hours

Diversion

Generalmajor von Schroeder listened carefully to General der Luftwaffe Galland on the telephone.

"Von Schroeder, the government has informed me that a cease fire will go into effect for twenty-four hours beginning noon day after tomorrow, Berlin time. Can you execute the raid on the English Midlands before then? I want to make a power statement before we stop shooting."

"Jawohl, Herr General, that is possible. I have only just completed coordination with Fighter Command for escort and defense aircraft. We can launch in approximately twelve hours."

"Excellent!" Galland said, "how large a force can you field?"

"I don't have precise numbers, Herr General, but it will be in excess of 500 heavy bombers, and at least 700 medium bombers. Fighter Command has promised every available fighter, perhaps as many as 1500, about half of which will be the jets. We'll strike a heavy blow, sir!"

"Well, Mr. President, any thoughts that we face a beaten foe have been rudely dashed. The Bosch put up a huge force of bombers, the most ever seen. Birmingham and Coventry have been struck staggering blows; war production in both has ceased. The human losses are simply appalling. Dear God, how do they do it? Our forces are great, but they somehow always find a way to rally. I did not conceive that such a strike was still possible for them."

"My deepest condolences, Mr. Prime Minister," Truman said with conviction. "Your people have suffered greatly through this whole war. My information is that they used every bomber they had. I have no reports of bombing anywhere else in Europe the day before. Seems like they wanted a show of strength before the cease fire. Did we at least inflict heavy losses on them?"

"Bah!" Churchill said with disgust deep in his voice, "We threw every fighter we had at them, American and British alike, but they had swarms of escorts, many of them jets. We may have taken down fifty or seventy of their bombers, perhaps a few more, but the majority were older, two-motor planes that are more vulnerable. We lost hundreds of fighters to those damnable rocket guns. And worse, they caught several hundred of our heavy bombers on the ground. It was a bad day. A bad day."

"We shall see how the cease fires and the unofficial peace talks go, Mr. Churchill; they may have their own 'bad day' if things don't go well."

Chapter 104

6 September 1945

Luftwaffe Headquarters

1730 Hours

Insubordination

General der Luftwaffe Galland walked wearily into his office, and removed his uniform blouse. He sat heavily and thought about the meeting he'd just come from. His fatigue was profound, from emotional and mental stress; he'd been fatigued as a fighter pilot, flying four or more missions a day, but this was worse.

Minister Speer said it forthrightly, for which Galland was glad; the Nazis always twisted reality into something it wasn't, or worse, denied it.

"We must be honest with ourselves, gentlemen," Speer had somberly told the gathering of the most senior Germans, "This war is lost. Our soldiers are brave, and will attempt anything they are ordered, but there comes a time, yes? A time when hard facts must be faced.

"Logistically, our production peaked months ago. Our future is to slowly starve our forces of everything they need, and no remedy. Already, it takes more effort to manufacture spare parts for artillery pieces, tanks and airplanes than it used to take to build them."

He sighed, "The Allies control of the air, as sporadic as it is, is destroying nearly 80 percent of what we manage to manufacture while it's in transit, on the railroads and highways. This I cannot overcome. We must seek out what terms the Allies will give us."

Field Marshall Fedor von Bock somberly followed the high ranking civilian, "Speaking for the uniformed services, I must tell you that our situation is, at best, precarious. All forces redeployed from Russia have been dispersed throughout the Western front, and still we are being slowly, steadily pushed back. There is a feeling of inevitable defeat seeping into every man, a hopelessness that, unfortunately, is all too real. Given what Minister Speer has told us, I estimate that we can realistically continue to resist no more than three or four months.

"And I would remind you of what Galland's photo-planes revealed: the Russians are quickly gathering great forces, and will fall on us in two months, three on the outside. I strongly urge we negotiate as good a peace with the Americans and British as we can before we have Bolshevik hoards breathing down our necks. We must take advantage of this cease fire, and do all we can to extend it into a permanent peace."

Everyone turned to look at the third member of the Dreifach [triple], Minister of Internal Security Heinrich Müller. The youngest of the three men wielding power in post-Nazi Germany, as they liked to term it, was equally bleak.

"Gentlemen, we are barely holding down the Nazi diehards who desperately want to regain their lost power. The country, I needn't tell you, is this far from civil war." He held his fingers a scant ¼ inch apart.

"As for the general population, they are profoundly weary of this war, and desperate for it to end. If we do not soon end the war ourselves, we shall have as much to fear from an internal revolt as from the Russians."

He took a swallow from a glass in front of him, "The country is rife with spies, many of which are Russian or Russian sympathizers. My policemen cannot follow up on every suspect, so many are there. My power is being eroded rapidly, and soon, I will be unable to guarantee the safety of this government. These are harsh words, but they are true. I agree; we must move immediately to negotiate peace with the Allies. Far better that than 'negotiating' with a Russian bayonet at our necks."

Albert Speer nodded, "So, we are agreed. We will contact the Allies immediately, through the Swiss, asking for terms. I will send our best negotiators, with full authority from this group to begin discussions. The first order of business will be to extend the cease fire indefinitely, yes?"

And so the first serious German attempt at ending the war was put into motion before Galland had even left Speer's luxurious office.

An irritating thought crossed Galland's mind; all his senior staff had been there, except for the Chief of Bomber Command, von Schroeder. Galland had intended to congratulate Schroeder publically, in front of the assembled Dreifach, but the man had never arrived.

He pushed the intercom switch, "Have von Schroeder come to my office immediately."

Galland sat mulling over what his fate might be when peace came.

I never joined the Nazi party, that might be in my favor. I always went out of my way to make sure captured Allied pilots and crew members were properly treated. I have severely punished anyone in my command who violated the rules of civility in war: I court-martialed and shot those two fools who killed that British pilot and stole his watch. I've always fought hard, but fairly; that has to work in my favor.

His thoughts were interrupted by a sharp knock.

"Sir, I am Leutnant Johan Bachman, on Generalmajor von Schroeder's staff. How may I be of help, sir?"

Galland returned the young man's salute, "Why are you here, Leutnant? I wish to speak with Generalmajor von Schroeder."

"Sir, I beg your pardon, I am senior man on duty. Major Schultz went off duty about two hours ago, after a twelve hour shift. I can have him wakened if you wish, sir."

"Where is von Schroeder?"

The young man looked puzzled, "Sir, with respect, Generalmajor von Schroeder and his crews are about fourteen hours into their mission. We expect them back late tomorrow."

Galland's heart leapt as he leaned forward.

"What mission? What are you talking about?" *Mein Gott, what has Schroeder done now?*

The young man looked startled, and a little afraid, "Why, sir, the Final Revenge mission, to attack the American capital."

"What?" Galland roared, leaping to his feet, "The American capital? This is impossible; I gave no permission for an attack! Quickly, when will they arrive? I must stop him!"

Bachman shrank back in fear, nervously looking at his watch, "Sir, they should attack the Americans in less than three hours."

"Oh, Mein Gott! This is disaster! How many aircraft did he take? Are they all bound for Washington?"

"General, sir, there were 410 bombers. Yes, sir, that is the only target."

"That large a force – how will we turn it around? You! Get out of here! Get that major – what's his name? – Schultz, in here immediately, and round up any other officers of von Schroeder's over the rank of major and bring them too. Go! Hurry!"

Galland's head was spinning; *that fool! That egotistical fool! His bombs will be dropping just as our envoy sits to negotiate! How? How we can contact them?*

His heart pounded in his chest as he called Field Marshall von Bock.

438

"Jawohl, Herr Field Marshall, I knew nothing of it. He has taken every available GO-460. Yes, the target *is* the American capital; we have two hours or less to stop them." He listened to the older man's excited rant, then heard him bring himself under control.

"Listen to me, Galland: contact him somehow and order him to turn around, immediately, do you hear?"

Galland swallowed hard, "Sir, Luftwaffe transmitters don't have the power or range; I must have permission from Müller to use the propaganda radios."

"Yes, of course; contact him immediately, with my authority. Call me if he is reluctant."

Chapter 105

6 September 1945

Office of the Minister, State Security

1748 Hours

Recall

Minister of State Security Heinrich Müller prided himself on the quickness of his decision making, when the chips were down.

This is such a time, if ever there was one, he decided. *This is total disaster; the whole house of cards could come down around our necks.*

"Yes, of course, General Galland. I will preempt all programming. Come to the studio at once – you know where, yes? I will meet you there."

He hung up, then immediately redialed, calling the main Berlin studio for the powerful State Radio.

What did they tell me? It has 200,000 watts of power? I hope this is enough to reach them. Along with the Gestapo, he had inherited the Bundepost, the post office, and all of its far reaching radio transmitters.

He left immediately for the studio.

Müller felt the sweat in his armpits; this was going to be close. He shut off the propaganda program in mid-sentence, and handed Galland the microphone as the technician reset the frequency.

Now to see if Galland is up to the challenge.

Without hesitation, Galland spoke, "Final Revenge flight, this is General der Luftwaffe Adolf Galland, my authentication code is

—" He read one of the most secret codes in Germany, over an open microphone.

That will curl some Allied hair, I wager, Müller thought ruefully.

"Final Revenge flight, this attack is unauthorized! You are *ordered* to immediately turn and fly to the nearest German airfield. You will begin the turn *now*. You are *ordered* to drop your ordnance over the ocean, away from ships. Every aircraft commander *will* radio his obedience to these commands every hour on the hour until he has received acknowledgement. Your government is negotiating a peace for us all; do not continue this attack, for the sake of the Fatherland, for the sake of your families, return home. Galland out."

The sweating man handed Müller the mic, "There, that will do it, I hope. It must."

"This is what we shall do, Herr General: your message was recorded and we shall rebroadcast it every twenty minutes until we receive acknowledgement from the aircraft, yes?"

Galland looked thoughtful; *what is he thinking,* Müller worried.

Galland said earnestly, "Minister Müller, our aircraft radios have a range of perhaps 300 miles maximum, even at high altitude. This means we won't hear from them for another six to eight hours, unless – do you not have some sensitive receivers in Western Spain that could listen for their replies? We must know immediately that they have turned around."

Müller regarded him suspiciously for an instant; those receivers were among his most secret. *Ah, well, it matters little now*, he thought, mentally shrugging.

"Jawohl, Herr General; I will order them to begin listening at once, at this frequency. When we hear from them, I should contact – whom?"

Galland looked a little relieved; "Me first, Herr Minister, then Field Marshall von Bock, and then Minister Speer. I only hope we can recall them in time. It would be a disaster if—" his voice trailed off.

"Yes, it would," Müller agreed softly.

Minister of Production and de facto head of the German government Albert Speer allowed himself the smallest hope, the tiniest glimmer of encouragement. Talks with the Allies through the Swiss government had gone well; Speer's secret fear was that the American and British envoys would refuse negotiations. He knew there was strong opposition within both governments and their militaries to anything less than "unconditional surrender."

At least some of them are facing reality, Speer thought; *they can't beat us before the Russians get involved, and the last thing they want is to have to treat them as equals.*

That fool, that bomber man – what did von Bock call him? Ah, yes, von Schroeder. How stupid can a man be? Can he not see we are beaten? And how does a military man do this, attacking without permission? He will be shot if a single bomb falls on Washington. What a bleak future we shall have if he succeeds. Müller, at least, understands; God help us if his transmitters don't reach them.

A ripple of excitement raced through the formation as the powerful Gestapo transmitters blasted Galland's message. To everyone's astonishment, it was General der Luftwaffe Galland himself, and the broadcast wasn't even in code! Immediately, requests to turn around flooded into von Schroeder's airplane over the low power radios.

"No! No! I forbid it! This man is an imposter! He is lying! We must continue; we must destroy America!" von Schroeder radioed back. "It is a plot! It is an anti-German plot, to make us the coward, to turn with our tails between our legs, like a dog. Galland is a true hero of the German people; he would never order such a cowardly thing."

Von Schroeder watched with increasing rage as entire squadrons of GO-460s begin to turn.

"No! No! I forbid it, I tell you! I will have you shot! You must continue!" His voice was high pitched and desperate. "Please, my fellow Germans! I beg you! Do not abandon me now! We are so close to victory! I plead with you, stay the course!"

Even as he made his desperate pleas, von Schroeder saw more and more of his bomber strength turning away; soon, there were only the volunteers. Then, to his bitter dismay, they too, began turning back toward Spain.

Chapter 106

6 September 1945

ACP 2 Headquarters, Millville Army Air Field

1444 Hours

Attack Revealed

"As the first word about a proposed truce extension arrived in Washington, D.C., ladies and gentlemen, this reporter felt a sense of exultation, almost euphoria, sweeping the capital – could this war in Europe finally be nearing its end? Then, cruelly, those high hopes seemed dashed as a huge, unauthorized attack upon Washington, D.C. was revealed. A very large force of fighter airplanes, hundreds of them, we are told – from all over the East Coast have roared off to meet them, to engage in mortal combat."

The slick haired radio announcer leaned into the microphone he was uncharacteristically gripping, and took a deep breath, "Then, astonishingly, ladies and gentlemen, the new, anti-Nazi German government itself has ordered the attack recalled, lest it cause the peace talks to falter. As I speak, the peace initiative hangs precariously in the balance, as Washington and the nation, holds their collective breath. Will the bombers turn back? Will they attack despite the recall? Surely, if Washington is attacked, the peace talks will immediately fail, and the war may go on indefinitely. We will broadcast more news regarding these momentous events as soon as we are informed. This is your reporter, John Tully Sullivan, speaking to you on the World Wide Network. Good Day."

Joel Knight listened to the civilian radio broadcast in the ready room at Millville Army Air Field while he also monitored the radio chatter between the P-61 flying as ACP-2 and the hundreds of fighters racing toward the German bombers.

Abruptly, General White's distinctive voice came over the speaker, "ACP-2, Central Command. The President has ordered all fighters in your district to hold their fire, I say again, *hold their fire*. You will *not fire*, repeat, *not fire* upon German bombers that have turned away. Fighters are to escort the Germans until their fuel requires them to return to base. Acknowledge. White out."

A moment passed, then, "ACP-2 to Central Command; we acknowledge; we have relayed the message, over." There was a brief pause.

"Fire! Uh, ACP-2 is declaring emergency, repeat, we are declaring an emergency! We have an engine fire! Pull the fire bottle again! We have to abandon the aircraft! Oh, it's bad! It's bad! Bail out! Bail out! Get out now—" the transmission ended abruptly.

Joel jerked; he knew Major Bruce Myers, the ACP-2 pilot well. Immediately, the radio was filled with calls:

"Parachutes! I see three parachutes – they got out OK! Call for SAR [search and rescue]. Somebody stay and circle 'em!"

The red phone from Central Command rang. The duty officer quickly answered it, and turned to Joel, "Sir, it's for you, General White."

"This is Colonel Knight, sir."

"Colonel, get your backup ACP bird airborne ASAP. Meyers is down, with an engine fire. Go circle the capital, and wait further instructions. White out."

"Yes, sir," Joel said to dead line.

Joel raced to the flight line, wondering which airplane they'd have for him. He hadn't paid attention to the ready room status board. As he jumped out of the car, a smile crossed his face. There sat his familiar old P-61, ready to go; across its rounded nose was the yellow script *Scintillating Sue.* It made him feel good, just to see her name.

Two crewmen hurried out, their seat pack parachutes smacking them in the backsides as they climbed into the big fighter.

"Get her started, Joe," Joel told the crew chief, "I'll grab a 'chute and be right back."

Gall rose in von Schroeder's throat as he cursed those who had abandoned him. It never occurred to him that the crew of his own aircraft might be similarly minded.

Americans, the fools! They expected me to attack Washington directly. Now, they think we have all turned tail. Never will they suspect what my real target is! He chuckled humorlessly to himself.

The Delaware coastline was just visible through the ever present haze, ten or twelve miles ahead. Smoothly, firmly, von Schroeder banked to the left, toward the massive U.S. Navy complex at Hampton Roads, Virginia. As the James River came into in view, he banked right. His strategy was to fly south of the American capital, and avoid the flak and home defense fighters based there. Staying north of Hampton Roads lessened the likelihood they'd be spotted.

They will not expect me here, and I can bypass Washington, and fly unmolested to Tennessee. A cruel smile flitted across his face. *Yes, I will take them entirely by surprise, and their super bomb will never touch Germany!*

He advanced the throttles, and began to climb. *At 11,000 meters [35,000 feet], no one will see us from the ground. We will arrive undetected!*

Unfortunately, the atmospheric conditions worked against him; as the Gotha climbed through 30,000 feet and crossed majestic Chesapeake Bay, long lines of white condensation from the engine exhausts formed in the sky. They pointed to his aircraft like a giant arrow in the sky.

Chapter 107

6 September 1945

Over Washington, D.C.

1527 Hours

On Patrol

"Central Command, ACP-2, on station at 2-7 minutes after the hour. What's the situation, over."

"Roger, ACP-2, Central Command. The Germans turned back. You are ordered to circle the city and standby. Central Command, out."

Joel relaxed a bit as he keyed the intercom, "Well, boys, that's really good news. Maybe we won't have any work today after all; let's pray that's so. This is a chance for you to do some sight-seeing."

"Say, sounds good, Colonel," said the RADAR operator cheerfully, "let's also pray that the Ack-Ack boys know we're friendly!"

It was the first time Joel had seen the Pentagon up close from the air.

Guess I know why I got lost in there a couple of times, he chuckled to himself, *that place is **really** big.*

They made a second circuit around the city, with the gunner and RADAR operator exclaiming enthusiastically about the famous monuments and public buildings they could see.

Abruptly, the radio sprang to life, "ACP-2, Central Command. Come to heading 1-9-5 degrees, and commence immediate climb to 3-0 thousand feet. Over."

What in the world? Joel wondered as he turned toward the new heading. He put on his "war face."

"Roger, Central Command, ACP-2 turning to 1-9-5 degrees, and starting climb. What are we looking for? Over." The engines roared as he advanced the throttles.

"ACP-2, Navy at Norfolk reports a single aircraft at high altitude heading in the direction of Charlottesville, Virginia. It's leaving a con trail, that's how Navy spotted it. They think it's German. Over."

"Central Command, ACP-2, climbing through 2-0 thousand feet, on course. What're they up to? There's nothing in Virginia, or even West Virginia to bomb. Doesn't make sense. Over"

"We agree, ACP-2; that's why you need to catch them. We may have a 'Flying Dutchman' situation here. Advise when you're close enough to observe. Central Command out."

Twelve Minutes Later

Joel leveled out at 30,000 feet, and was carefully hand flying while the RADAR operator scanned at the equipment's highest magnification.

"Colonel, something's just starting to show up. We're still maybe twelve miles or so behind them," the RADAR operator told him. "We're at the limits of my range, sir, so that's mostly an educated guess."

"OK, Phil," Joel said, "keep working. Gunner, you've got younger eyes; can you see a con trail?"

"Ah, no, sorry, sir, we're too far off to spot that yet. I'll tell you soon's I see somethin', sir."

"Roger," Joel said, looking at the airspeed indicator.

Let's see, 410 indicated. If we're twelve miles out, that'll take— He shook his head; that was a bit too difficult to do in his head.

He reached for his knee pad, and did the calculation. *OK, just a tad more than another minute! I shouldn't be so anxious.*

"Sir, I've got contact, at seven miles. Come right five degrees, sir, and we'll be directly astern of them," the RADAR man said.

"I've got 'em in the bi-nocs, sir – it's a Gotha, for sure. Leaving a pretty strong con trail, too. Permission to charge my guns?"

"Do it, Guns. Here's the plan; I'll climb above them, and make a fast pass in front of the cockpit. Guns, watch for internal movement."

Joel saw the bomber was maintaining altitude and a speed of about 250 knots. Long white condensation trails followed it. The P-61 climbed another 5,000 feet, and overtook the camouflaged German. Just as Joel was about to dive across in front of the Gotha, the gunner yelled, "Top turret traversing! They see us! They're firing!"

Chapter 108

6 September 1945

Over West Virginia

1603 Hours

Pursuit

"Wow, that scared the crap out of me – sorry, sir. I saw two guys jump like crazy, then the gun turret fired. It's no Flying Dutchman, it's got a crew," said a rattled Sergeant Rex "Guns" Argon.

"Yeah, I saw 'em too, Guns. Good job! Keep a close eye on that turret. We'll make another pass."

Joel swung the fighter around, nearly level with the Gotha. "There! The red baronial seal! It's von Schroeder!" he shouted, even as the Gotha's top turret fired at them. Joel jinked hard, and the rockets missed. He moved out of range, and keyed his mic.

"Central Command, ACP-2, do you read, over."

We're pretty far from Philly, Joel worried, *hope they can hear us.*

To his relief, they responded immediately, if a bit faintly. "ACP-2, Central Command, we read you weakly, over."

"Roger, Central Command, be advised that we confirm, repeat, confirm, a Gotha. Also, be advised, aircraft carries the personal markings of General von Schroeder. We are receiving fire, and are about to return it. ACP-2, out."

"ACP-2, stand by – standby – someone needs to speak with you, over."

There were some clicks and pops as the microphone was passed.

"Joel, this is Susan, at Central Command. You *must* shoot that airplane down!" The urgency in her voice sent a surge of fear through him. The radio signal began to heterodyne as a competing signal interfered. Susan's voice was fading, dropping out, and changing tone.

"– target – secret plant – Oak Ridge, Tennessee. – devastating – country if they succeed. Do you understand? This is – suicide – we talked about. Von Schroeder – knows about – plant and will die – destroy it. Over"

"Susan! What? Are you sure? I'm having trouble understanding you. Over."

"No, listen to me: – target *is* Oak Ridge; – had confirmation – Europe – last hour; that's – target. Please, Joel, he – not be allowed to do this. It's – important – he not –. You have to stop him!" Her voice was pleading.

"Roger, ACP-2 understands, WILCO. ACP-2 out."

"Well, that changes things, boys," Joel said grimly. "I'll gain altitude, go in front of them and we'll do a diving, angled pass across 'em front to rear. That'll force them to try to traverse their guns fast enough to hit us. I'll hit 'em with rockets and save the 30mm's for later if we need 'em. Guns, wait 'till we're in range, then do your deed. Don't rotate your turret."

Early P-61s like *Scintillating Sue* suffered severe buffeting when the gun turret was rotated, so the guns had to be fired from a fixed, straight ahead position.

"Phil, find any military radio in the vicinity. We won't be able to get through to Philly again. Fill 'em in on what's up, and make 'em stay on with you; if we force von Schroeder down, I want all the help we can get, OK?"

Chapter 109

6 September 1945

Over Eastern Tennessee

1641 Hours

Final Encounter

They flew a long arc, climbing above and ahead of the Gotha, which had not changed course.

"Here we go!" The fighter's engines roared as it dove steeply toward the German. Joel armed the rockets hanging under the wings. They closed very quickly, their combined speeds over 600 miles per hour.

"Now!" Joel shouted, and squeezed the trigger. A pair of rockets, one from each wing, shot toward the Bomber. Above him, the four 0.50 calibre machine guns thundered. In an instant, they flashed past the Gotha. Unexpectedly, Joel saw gun flashes in return.

*Uh, oh – now they have guns **and** rockets,* he thought.

"I hit him! I got good hits!" yelled the gunner as Joel used their momentum to climb above the Gotha again. "I think I did, too," Joel said.

Von Schroeder was ignoring the American fighter as he concentrated on maintaining his course.

We are only minutes away! I must destroy it, for the glory of Germany! I must not fail!

For an instant, the screams of his mortally wounded top gunner intruded, but von Schroeder remorselessly shut the sound out.

"They are coming around again, General! On the port side!"

Von Schroeder did not look away, but leaned forward, urging his bomber on, his lips moving in silent supplication. His knuckles were white as he gripped the wheel. A thunder of jarring impacts accompanied the roar of the American plane as it raced over the stricken flying wing. The Gotha shook and shuddered from the impact of the American rockets and machine gun fire. The lower gunner was hammering away with his machine gun; sparks flew from the underside of the fighters' left wing.

"Fire! Number One, Number Two engines on fire! Pulling the fire bottle handles! One went out, but I'll have to feather number Two. We've got bad fuel leaks, General!" The co-pilot was scrambling to save the airplane.

Again, the huge fighter swung around, and approached, this time from the right. In horror, the crewmen felt the flying wing shudder and shake as they were hit again and again. Now, there were fires on the right side as well. Von Schroeder did not divert his eyes.

"General! General! The fires, they are out of control! We must abandon the aircraft!" the co-pilot shouted, but von Schroeder's gaze was fixed.

Quickly assessing the situation, the co-pilot shouted over the intercom, "This is the co-pilot – Bail out, Bail out! Abandon the aircraft!" He moved quickly toward the escape hatch as the others copied him. With a glance at the still fixated General, he leapt from the faltering plane.

Chapter 110

6 September 1945

The Horse Farm

1659 Hours

Down and Out

"They're bailing out! We got 'em, boys!" Joe shouted.

"Only five chutes, Colonel. Somebody's still on board."

"Yeah, you're right, Guns. I doubt von Schroeder would miss the chance to go down with his ship. Let's see."

He started to turn toward the bomber, then thought better of it, Joel kept an eye on the smoking Gotha, and keyed his mic.

"Central Command, ACP-2. The Gotha is going down, we've spotted five chutes. The aircraft appears to still be under control, so we'll hit it again. ACP-2 out." There was no response.

"Colonel, we were hit on that last pass. We're leaking fuel pretty bad from the lower left wing. It's away from the exhaust, I think," Phil told Joel.

Von Schroeder jerked like a sleeper rudely awakened; they had all left him! He was abandoned *again*! The anguish, the unbearable pain of abandonment, which he thought he'd buried in his childhood, rose up in his chest and he thought he would die. He squeezed his eyes shut so hard they watered.

All the warning lights were flashing, the emergency bells ringing. A glance at the altimeter: *This is hard to control, I'm too low to jump; I'll have to ride it in.*

A surge of fear hit him as he remembered: *the bombs; I haven't dropped the bombs!* They'd blow him to Valhalla if he didn't dump them. He pulled the Bomb Jettison handle. The aircraft leapt up a little as the weight dropped away.

Now, find a place to crash land, and quickly!

"He's dumped the bombs! He's going to do a forced landing. Phil, have you raised anybody on the radio yet?"

"Roger, Colonel, I've reached an Army Reserve infantry detachment on maneuvers; they're west of La Follette, West Virginia. They can get to civilian telephones, otherwise, they only have a twenty mile range."

"OK, quick as you can, tell 'em to relay what you've told them to Philly, to District Two Central Command. Tell 'em to call collect, the Army will pay for it; just keep 'em on the radio as long as you can. Where ever Schroeder goes down, we'll need help."

Who knows where he'll go down? The way that thing is burning, it could come apart any second – why doesn't he get out?

A trail of black smoke and sparks was following the stricken German. Von Schroeder was turning to the right, in a North-Westerly direction.

What's he up to now? – Oh, I see.

"Boys, von Schroeder has spotted a pasture up ahead; I think he's trying for that."

Von Schroeder had seen the green grassland contrasting with the surprisingly dense forest. It was taking all the considerable skill he had to keep the flaming, lurching Gotha headed in the right direction. The three remaining engines were at full throttle, screaming their mechanical lives away, and still he was sinking.

A jolt of terror coursed through him – *the aircraft isn't responding – is it going to crash?*

Then, he discovered an only slightly comforting fact – the aircraft sluggishly responded if he moved the wheel to absurd positions.

This means the control cables are heated and stretching, from the fire. I don't have much longer before they break or burn through, then—.

He was sweating hard, deeply afraid. He moved the landing gear lever to the down position –nothing .

So, the hydraulics are gone, this means the flaps are not operational. I don't know how long this meadow is. I must land as short as I can.

As he straightened out to align with the meadow, he felt the airplane faltering – the engines were dying, and airspeed was falling off.

To stall is instant death! Without a thought, he lowered the nose, in a desperate attempt to keep his airspeed up. The trees ahead were rising in the windshield – *not good; I will zoom over them, so—*

The small branches at the tops of the 300-year-old oaks snapped off and flew in every direction as the Gotha rammed through them to the clear air over the meadow.

Chapter 111

6 September 1945

Horse Farm

1711 Hours

Confrontation and Capture

Some analytical part of von Schroeder's mind noted the orderly white fence surrounding the meadow, and that he was well to the left of the center. More suddenly than he expected, the Gotha just stopped flying, and dropped the last thirty feet with a sickening lurch.

The impact was incredible. Von Schroeder slammed into his flying harness so hard it knocked his breath out. The dying airplane caromed along the grassy surface, and began to porpoise, smashing the nose down, then pitching it back up, only to repeat. The noise was incredible. White fence poles and boards scattered as the left wing shattered them. Von Schroeder was slammed around in the cockpit like a rag doll. The back of his head smacked the seat support, hard.

The right wing tip caught the grass, and spun the slowing aircraft to the right. A slight rise in the ground pitched the nose up again. When it slammed down, the crew compartment, which stuck out like a man's nose ahead of the wing, nearly snapped off. The still burning wreckage skidded, bouncing, to a halt. Von Schroeder hung in his harness, unconscious.

Joel gasped as the staggering Gotha flew through the tree tops; he was above and behind it, and couldn't tell how low it was. Then, suddenly, the Gotha slammed to earth with a huge spray of grass and dirt. He didn't breathe until the wreckage spun almost to a halt, then they flew over it. Making a climbing turn to the left, Joel spotted a wide dirt road alongside the meadow.

"Boys, I'm putting her down on that road. Phil, tell' em what we're doing, and to get somebody up here on the double-quick."

The left aileron must have been hit, too. This thing's getting squirrely, Joel thought.

He searched the road side for power lines or phone poles; not even a P-61 could win that fight. It looked clear, so he began to throttle back, and lowered the landing gear.

The road seemed to be just wide enough, then he abruptly realized the trees all along the right side were too close. Reacting as quickly as the increasingly sluggish airplane would let him, he "S" turned to the left, and lined up with the pasture.

Hope I can squeak past Schroeder's plane. He flared, then the tires settled solidly onto the grass and they were down. When they were nearly stopped, he used the left wheel brake, turning the aircraft around to face the wreckage of von Schroeder's plane.

"Phil, you still got that infantry outfit on the radio? Good. Make sure they understand the urgency of the situation. Guns, rotate the turret if you have to and keep me covered, but be careful! I don't want to get shot in the back! I'm going to see if he survived."

Joel stepped out warily with his Army issue M1917 Smith and Wesson revolver firmly gripped in his right hand. The standard Army pistol for flyers was the Colt M1911A1 .45 automatic, but his long familiarity with revolvers made him more comfortable with the S&W. He began to advance carefully across the meadow.

Gerhard von Schroeder shook his head, gathering his wits. His head throbbed . The world was at a crazy tilt. He finally realized the shattered crew compartment was lying partly on its side. He hadn't lowered the landing gear – couldn't, in fact. That meant the emergency exit, through the Plexiglas over his head. One panel was held in place with fasteners that looked like hinges.

Instead of hinge pins, it used lengths of steel cable attached to big red handles. His injured back screamed as he reached over his head and pulled the cables. The panel fell free, clattering to the ground. A movement caught his eye, and he saw the fighter land on the meadow. With great effort and much pain, accompanied with not a few curses, von Schroeder pulled himself through the hatch, and slid to the ground. The heat of the fires seared his face. He moved quickly away from the aircraft, toward the woods on the other side of the broken white fence.

In the P-61's gunner's seat, "Guns" watched intensely as his pilot moved towards the wreck of the German plane.

Joel was halfway when von Schroeder limped away from the far side of the crumpled nose.

"Halt! Drop your weapon! You are my prisoner!" Joel shouted.

In the upper seat of the P-61, "Guns" moved the turret back and forth, as he leaned to one side, then the other, trying to find a clear bead on the German.

Colonel Knight is too close to the guy! I'll hit him sure as Jesus if I shoot. He forced his hand away from the trigger, grinding his teeth in frustration.

Von Schroeder had unsnapped his holster as soon as he'd hit the ground. Now, he held the walnut grips of his Walther P 38 pistol firmly in his right hand. When Joel shouted, he spun around and fired twice, rapidly.

To Joel, the first round sounded like a big, very angry bee. The second round kicked up the dirt at his feet. Von Schroeder fired again and ran for the woods just beyond the broken fence.

Stepping behind a too-small tree, he leaned against it heavily, and fired.

Something slapped Joel's left arm just above the elbow. It felt like he'd been smacked with a baseball bat. He staggered a bit to the side, then fired his revolver. A puff of dirt proved he'd missed. He shot again – wide.

Von Schroeder moved from behind the little tree, dropped to one knee and took careful aim. Joel remembered the two-handed stance he'd been taught at the Academy. Bracing his right hand with his left, he fired twice, rapidly. His left arm screamed in agony. Von Schroeder fired, missed, just as Joel fired, and then was thrown back as Joel's second shot hit him on the right chest. He fell heavily to the ground, and lie still.

Chapter 112

6 September 1945

Horse Farm

1729 Hours

Owner

Sergeant Phillip Lloyd, the RADAR operator/radio man, stood on the road warily watching, his .45 in his hand. He turned at the sound of a car. A tall, slender, white haired man stepped out of a beautiful Maroon 1936 Ford station wagon. On the front door a sign on the gleaming wood read "Colton Sutter Farms ," under which was "Champion Tennessee Walking Horses."

"Boy," the old man said. "Ya'll are going to have to move that machine off my property. Ya'll are trespassin'." He gestured toward the P-61 with a beautifully polished wooden cane.

For the first time, he saw the crashed airplane and the huge, still burning fire. One wingtip was skewed toward them, with a clearly visible white cross outlined in black.

"Oh, my lands! It's a Nazi plane! How'd it ever get here? Who's shooting?"

"Sir," Phil said, "you'd better take cover."

Joel was alert, eyes intently focused on the inert form as he crept warily up to where von Schroeder was lying. A few feet away, he spotted the barrel of von Schroeder's P 38 pistol, and relaxed a bit. A muffled groan revealed that his long-time adversary was alive, at least for the moment.

Joel kicked the gun out of reach, and bent down carefully. Von Schroeder was on his back, his chin tilted up. An ominous red stain was spreading on the right breast pocket of his uniform blouse. A faint gurgling accompanied his labored breathing. Joel unceremoniously yanked the man's dagger from its sheath; *no sense in taking chances*, he thought.

He yelled to Phil, "Bring the first aid kit, quick!"

Phil handed him the first aid kit, and said, "Colonel, I got in contact with an L-5B operating with that infantry company. The pilot relayed what I told him, and he's on his way. I gave him basic directions, but the guy's familiar with the area 'cause he's from around here. Anyhow, I figured you'd want to take this character to the nearest hospital, if he's still alive."

The Stinson L-5B was a light aircraft that performed scouting duties for the Army; the –B version was equipped to fly a litter.

"You're right, Sergeant. Now let's do what we can to keep him alive 'till that bird gets here."

Chapter 113

6 September 1945

At the Edge of the Woods

1743 Hours

Forgiveness and Salvation

Von Schroeder blinked his eyes, and shook his head a little, as if to clear it. He struggled to focus on Joel, and a grimace formed on his face.

"You. I thought you had killed me. Why didn't you?"

"I don't want to kill you, Gerhard, just make you stop shooting at me."

"Bah! You hate me; are you too much the coward to finish it?"

Joel's voice softened just a bit, "I've never hated you Gerhard. We're adversaries, that's all."

"But I have hated you, for years! I have wanted to kill you! Do you not understand this?"

Joel smiled from the side of his mouth, "That's OK, Gerhard, I forgive you. Now, how do you feel?"

"I think I will not live much longer. The pain is great." His breath came out as a gurgling sigh as he put his hand over the already blood soaked dressing on his chest. "I can barely breathe. How can you forgive me?"

"The same way I am forgiven, Gerhard, by the Grace of Jesus Christ. Have you accepted Him as your personal Lord and Savior?"

"What? I do not understand."

The pain from his shattered arm suddenly swept over him, and Joel staggered.

"I,-uh," Joel stammered.

Joel felt a hand on his shoulder. It was the white haired owner of the farm, Colton Sutter. "I was a Deacon for years at Wartburg Baptist Church, son. Let me help you here. Ya'll sit down; help is on the way."

The old man leaned on his cane, and spoke to the wounded man.

"Son, there comes a time in every man's life when he must make the most important decision there is: where you do stand regarding Jesus?"

Von Schroeder looked puzzled, "I know of him. He is the Christ of God. I was often in church as a boy."

Sutter smiled wanly, "The Scripture says that the very demons in Hell know Christ, and shudder in fear; just knowin' *about* him is not near enough."

"But I have gone often to church—"

"Being accepted by Christ as one of his own isn't like joinin' a club, son. You don't just show up at the meetin's and get into heaven. You – you personally – have to ask Him into your heart, have you done that?"

Von Schroeder didn't answer.

Joel said gently, "Gerhard, I think you are right; you won't live much longer. You must make this decision now, while there's still time. Will you accept the forgiveness of Christ?"

"How can He forgive me? I have done much bad, and too little good." There was self-pity in his voice.

"Nope, you've got that wrong too, son," Sutter said in his confident way. "See here now, ya'll can't earn your way into eternal life – there's just no way you could *ever* do enough 'good' to justify God overlooking your sins. Why, the only way is to accept the sacrifice that Jesus already made for you, because his blood will wash your sins away and make you white as snow."

Schroeder coughed soggily, bloody foam now on his lips. Sutter bent down stiffly and gently wiped it away.

"Here's the thing, son. Christ died as a substitute for you – he died in your place, and because He did, if you accept His sacrifice, and believe, God Almighty will see only Christ's blood, not your sins. Then and only then will God accept you."

"How can I do this? I do not deserve forgiveness."

"Not a man that's ever been born does. But Jesus made a way, he gave us all a gift. All you have to do is accept that gift, and it's done."

"Truly? How do I accept this gift?"

Sutter knelt down beside the stricken man, his joints popping.

"You just need to pray a simple prayer and believe. Just follow after me, all right?"

"Yes, say it."

"Say this: Dear Lord Jesus – repeat after me."

"Dear Lord Jesus," Schroeder croaked.

"I confess to you that I am a sinner."

Schroeder repeated the phrase, watching the old man's face intently.

"I confess that I believe that you died to save me from my sins, were raised again on the third day, and now sit at the Father's right hand."

Again, Schroeder repeated Sutter.

"I humbly ask forgiveness for all my sins, and that you will wash them away with your blood."

He had to stop to cough, but Schroeder repeated the words.

"Nearly finished. Now say, I believe that your sacrifice has saved me, and that I will be raised up with the saints on the last day. In Jesus' name, Amen."

Von Schroeder finished the prayer as tears cascaded down his cheeks.

"I have been saved? My sins are forgiven of me, yes?" he asked urgently.

"Yes," chorused Joel and Sutter together.

"Then I can die in peace," Schroeder said, and visibly relaxed.

Joel thought he had died, then the irregular breathing began again.

"There's a plane coming to take him to a hospital, sir," Joel said as Mr. Sutter got back to his feet. "And thank you; I would not have done so well."

"Don't sell yourself short, Colonel. You say the words, the Holy Spirit does the work; you need to remember that."

Chapter 114

6 September 1945

Sutter's Farm

1813 Hours

Evacuation

Much to Colton Sutter's consternation at the continuing invasion of his farm, the camouflaged Stinson L-5B landed lightly in his pasture, and taxied to where Sergeant Lloyd was gesturing. The pilot jumped out and ran to Joel.

"Sir, I'm Lieutenant Brian Carter. Is this man to be evacuated?"

Joel nodded his head, "We've done all we can for him, Lieutenant. Now it's between him and God. Get him aboard. Where will you take him?"

The man gestured over his shoulder, "To Knoxville, sir, if that's OK. It's about thirty miles or so." There was an unmistakable Tennessee twang in the man's speech as he pronounced the city's name "Knoxvull."

"OK, Lieutenant, where will you land? Where's the airport relative to the hospital?"

The man grinned proudly, "I'll land on the street right in front of the hospital, sir! I'm from Knoxville, and I've done it before. I'll radio ahead and get my Uncle Max to stop traffic – my uncle is Chief of Police there, sir – and the hospital staff will meet us."

He stopped and looked thoughtful, "Say, sir, since this guy is a POW, do we need a guard for him? Do ya'll want me to do it until we can get some MPs there?"

"Good thought, Lieutenant. Yes, guard him. Have you a weapon? Good. Maybe your uncle would loan us some officers until the Army can relieve them. Ask him, please, and let me know. Don't forget to check in with your commander; we don't want him worrying about you."

"Yes, sir, I'll do that. And I'll be right back for you, Colonel. You need to get that wound looked at right away, sir."

Joel closed his eyes against the pain, "Yes, you do that Lieutenant." Blood was dripping from his fingers. He sat heavily on the grass.

Joel opened his eyes; time had passed, but he had no idea how much.

"He's awake, sir," somebody said.

An Army Major bent over him. "I'm Major Timmons, sir, with the reserve unit your radio man called. I got here as fast as I could. My medic gave you some plasma, and put a splint on your arm. Lieutenant Carter is ready to fly you to Knoxville, sir, but we gotta hurry, 'cause we're losing daylight."

Joel licked his dry lips, "Good, Major, my thanks. I want – you need to put a guard around the wreckage. Don't let your troops take any souvenirs, either. Umm, have my radio man call for mechanics, will you? My plane is shot up and can't fly out." He paused, "Did you give me something?"

"Yes, sir, a shot of morphine. You rest easy, now."

Chapter 115

5 December 1945

Oval Office, The White House

1030 Hours

Recognition and Reward

"Ladies, Gentlemen, if you will follow me? This way." They were led into the Oval Office, where President Harry Truman was waiting.

"Hello, hello, welcome to the Peoples' House," he said, smiling broadly as he came around the big mahogany desk. Turning to Joel, he said, "Colonel Knight, kindly introduce me to your wife."

Flustered at being in the president's presence and being acknowledged by name, Joel introduced them. Joel's injured left arm was still in a cast, and supported with an Olive Drab sling. Truman moved down the line to Staff Sergeant Phillip Lloyd and his wife Dianne, ending with Sergeant Rex Argon, and his fiancée, Miss Imogene Alexander.

Having completed the introductions, Truman moved aside, and General Henry "Hap" Arnold, Chief of Staff, U.S. Army Air Forces, stepped forward. Joel had been so focused on seeing the President, he hadn't even noticed the white haired general. The three men snapped to attention.

The smiling general said, "Attention to Orders: we are gathered here today to award some of our nation's highest honors to three brave men. Colonel Knight, step forward."

Joel moved one step forward, his eyes locked on a seam in the wallpaper across from him. A photographer's flash barely registered.

"Colonel Joel Thomas Knight, it is my privilege to award you the Silver Star for Gallantry in Action Against an Enemy of the

United States. The citation follows: On or about 1700 hours on the afternoon of 6 September 1945, Colonel Knight and the crew of his P-61fighter aircraft engaged in single aerial combat with a deeply penetrating enemy bomber over the state of Tennessee. During the course of said combat, Colonel Knight's aircraft was fired upon repeatedly by the hostile invader and was damaged. Despite the damage, Colonel Knight distinguished himself by exemplary airmanship and courage in pursuing the attack and shooting down the enemy in disregard of the risk to his own life. Colonel Knight's aircraft was the only U.S. aircraft in close enough vicinity to engage the enemy, whose target was a highly secret U.S. Government facility, the loss of which would have had extremely deleterious effects on the nation's defense. After forcing the enemy aircraft to crash land, Colonel Knight landed his own aircraft nearby, and engaged its pilot using his handgun. Colonel Knight was wounded in the exchange of gunfire. Despite his wounds, Colonel Knight boldly persevered with his own attack, wounding the enemy, and taking him prisoner. Colonel Knight's expert airmanship and bravery on the ground prevented a disastrous event from occurring, and resulted in the capture of a high ranking enemy officer. It must be further noted that with the downing of this aircraft, Colonel Knight became only the third ace among the pilots defending America's Eastern seaboard. This fact by its self would have merited this award, so it is doubly deserved. In addition, I award you the Purple Heart in the name of the President of the United States for wounds suffered while serving in the Army of the United States in armed conflict with an enemy of this nation. It is also my pleasure to award to Colonel Knight and his crew the newly authorized Coastal Defense Medal." The purple, yellow, green and white ribbon seemed garish to Joel.

General Arnold turned to Susan, "Mrs. Knight, would you assist me, please?" Susan wiped the tears streaming down her face, and took the star-shaped Silver Star with its red, white and blue ribbon, and helped General Arnold pin it to Joel's chest. The heart-shaped Purple Heart medal with the image of George Washington hanging from a purple ribbon was pinned just below it. Lastly, the Coastal Defense Medal, a gold disc with the image of a Revolutionary War Minuteman was hung beside the Purple Heart. The photographers' flashes went off several times.

"I'm very proud of you, Colonel. Good job, you made us all look good." Joel saluted and stepped back into line, his head whirling.

While Joel remained at attention, General Arnold awarded Staff Sergeant Phillip Lloyd and Sergeant Rex Argon each a Distinguished Flying Cross and a Coastal Defense Medal. Their citations weren't as flowery as Joel's but nonetheless acknowledged their significant contributions to the event.

I sure couldn't have done it without them, Joel thought with gratitude. Each man was photographed separately, with his wife/ fiancée, and then the three men were photographed together.

President Truman shook their hands for more photographs. He congratulated them warmly, and invited everyone to join him in the Rose Garden where they would meet the press and answer questions.

In the Rose Garden

To Joel's dismay, the Rose Garden was full of reporters and photographers, and they all wanted to talk to him.

An eager young reporter thrust a microphone at him: "Colonel Knight, how does it feel to have earned a Silver Star, the nation's third highest medal?"

"You never 'earn' a medal, young man, it is *awarded* to you. A medal awarded for valor isn't like the prize in a box of Cracker Jack; no sane man ever seeks it. To answer your *intended* question, I am humbled that I have been deemed eligible for this high honor." The man looked shocked at the rebuke.

Another reporter asked, "Colonel Knight, now that the war in Europe is over, will you be going to the Pacific?"

Joel smiled, "That's up to the Army. Once this arm is healed, I'll go where I'm ordered."

An older man, with a radio network logo on his microphone asked, "Sir, are you aware that your German opponent, General von Schroeder, passed away at the hospital in Knoxville?"

"Yes, I was told that he had died. I regret he didn't survive; there was much we would have liked to have learned from him."

"Isn't it true that you and he had a long-time grudge against each other?"

"No; I did not hold a grudge against General von Schroeder; it appears that he held a rather strong one against me, however."

"Colonel, I understand that you shot him down once before, in the '30s; is that true?"

Joel chuckled, "No, no, I certainly didn't shoot him down; we engaged in a series of mock dogfights, which I won. He took that outcome rather badly, I'm afraid."

The man swiveled and turned to Susan, all but pouncing on her, "Mrs. Knight – Dr. Knight, I am told that as a psychologist working for the government, you had determined that von Schroeder was insane and would attack America, and—"

Joel stepped in forcefully, "I'm sorry, my wife has no comment." The look on his face intimidated the man, and he stepped away. The look on Susan's face would have curdled milk; her relationship with the government was Top Secret.

A glance around the Rose Garden revealed that both his crewmen were also facing the gauntlet of reporters.

A grizzled reporter stepped up to Joel, "Neil Ferguson, *New York Times*, sir. We have heard reports that the Russians are quite upset at being left out of the peace accords that ended the war in Europe, and that they are building up forces and may invade Germany from the east. Can you speak to that?"

Joel shrugged, "The Russians made their own peace deal, and weren't involved in the war the last year or so, so I don't think they can squawk too much. As to the possibility of an invasion, I simply have no idea. You're asking the wrong fellow."

The grilling went on and on, with only an occasional question that had anything to do with shooting down the Gotha.

Most of these questions are just inane, Joel thought, and it was beginning to irritate him. His arm was aching, and he really needed to rest. He looked around for the Press Aide.

Susan beat him to it. She came across the lawn, with the man in tow.

"OK, folks, that's all for today, thanks for coming," the man announced, waving his arms in a herding motion.

"Thanks," Joel told him as the reporters and camera men retreated, "I could sure use a break. That was more tiring than I expected. Some of those guys are just plain rude, you know? A few others are stupid, from their questions."

"I know only too well, Colonel," the man said as he escorted them all back into the White House.

EPILOGUE

17 January 1946

Joel and Susan's Home, Millville, New Jersey

1730 Hours

Epilogue and Beginning

Susan heard Joel on the porch before he bounded into the house and announced, "Hey Susan, I have two pieces of news, and they're both great!"

"What?" Susan responded, looking up from the typewriter where she was writing her mother a letter, "Tell me, don't make me guess!"

"OK! First," he held up his left arm, "look, I got my cast off. Boy, does it feel good. Look how skinny my arm is!" He pulled up his sleeve to show her.

She clucked and agreed with him, rubbing her hand on his arm, looking at the hollow depression that was all that remained of his wound.

That makes me hurt to look at it, she thought. "Now, what's the other news?"

He grabbed her shoulders excitedly and looked deep into her eyes, "We've got orders, beautiful lady; we're going to sunny California! I'm going to be wing commander for a brand new night fighter unit at March Field."

"Where's that?" she asked, a feeling of dread rising up; *all my friends here—*

"It's near a pretty little town called Riverside, northeast of LA. Say, isn't this great?"

"Oh, it sounds nice," Susan said without a great deal of conviction. "But what about my work with —." She never used the name "OSS" in their house.

His enthusiasm hadn't abated, "That's the sweet part, darling! I have it on the very best authority that you'll continue your work on the West coast. In fact, they want you to start looking at the top players in the Soviet Union!"

"Oh," she said, "what was it Churchill said about the Russians? That they're a 'Riddle wrapped in a mystery inside an enigma?' They're such a fascinating people—."

She saw him sober up; "We'd better hope we don't have to fight them, 'cause they're incredibly tough."

He brightened again as he told her, "Say, here's the best part – I've forty-five days leave coming, and they'll give us two weeks to get to California. Since I'm a Colonel, they'll not only ship our household goods, they'll ship a car, too. So—I'm thinking, why don't we let them ship the Packard, and take the train to Wisconsin to see your folks, then to Colorado to see mine? What'd ya think, kiddo?"

"Oh, Joel, that sounds just wonderful! When will we leave? Oh, I just have a mountain of things to do first. I've never been out West, you know."

"I promise, you'll love it. California is about the prettiest place I've been, except Hawaii, and it's almost always warm, and the sun shines a lot, and the beaches are so much better than here." He rambled on, but Susan didn't care. The dread she'd felt at first had given way to growing excitement; this would be their first assignment together. What awaited them in California?

ABOUT THE AUTHOR

Jeff Kildow was born in Iowa and grew up in Colorado Springs, Colorado. He is an Air Force veteran and graduated from Northrop University where he received his engineering diploma from aviation and flying wing pioneer John K. Northrop. He received his MBA from the University of Northern Colorado. He was employed by Martin Marietta/Lockheed Martin for more than thirty years as a Systems Engineer.

A thirty-three-year resident of Littleton, Colorado, he is a life-long vintage car and aircraft enthusiast. He has an extensive library of books on WWII aircraft, and owns a 1937 Chevrolet.

He has been married to his wife Janell for forty-four years.

Intermedia Publishing Group

Publishing That Works For You

Do you need a speaker?

Do you want Jeff Kildow to speak to your group or event? Then contact Larry Davis at: (623) 337-8710 or email: ldavis@intermediapr.com or use the contact form at: www.intermediapr.com.

Whether you want to purchase bulk copies of *America Under Attack* or buy another book for a friend, get it now at: www.imprbooks.com.

If you have a book that you would like to publish, contact Terry Whalin, Publisher, at Intermedia Publishing Group, (623) 337-8710 or email: twhalin@intermediapub.com or use the contact form at: www.intermediapub.com.